CAPTAIN
OF
STORMS

THE IRONFIRE LEGACY
BOOK THREE

JANEEN IPPOLITO

This is a work of fiction. Names, characters, businesses, places, events, and incidents are either the products of the author's imagination or used in a fictitious manner. Any resemblance to actual persons, living or dead, or actual events is purely coincidental.

Line and copyediting by Sarah McConahy
Formatting by Sarah Delena White

Cover Design by Christian Bentulan

For Sarah Delena White
Because ya gotta
(even when it hurts)

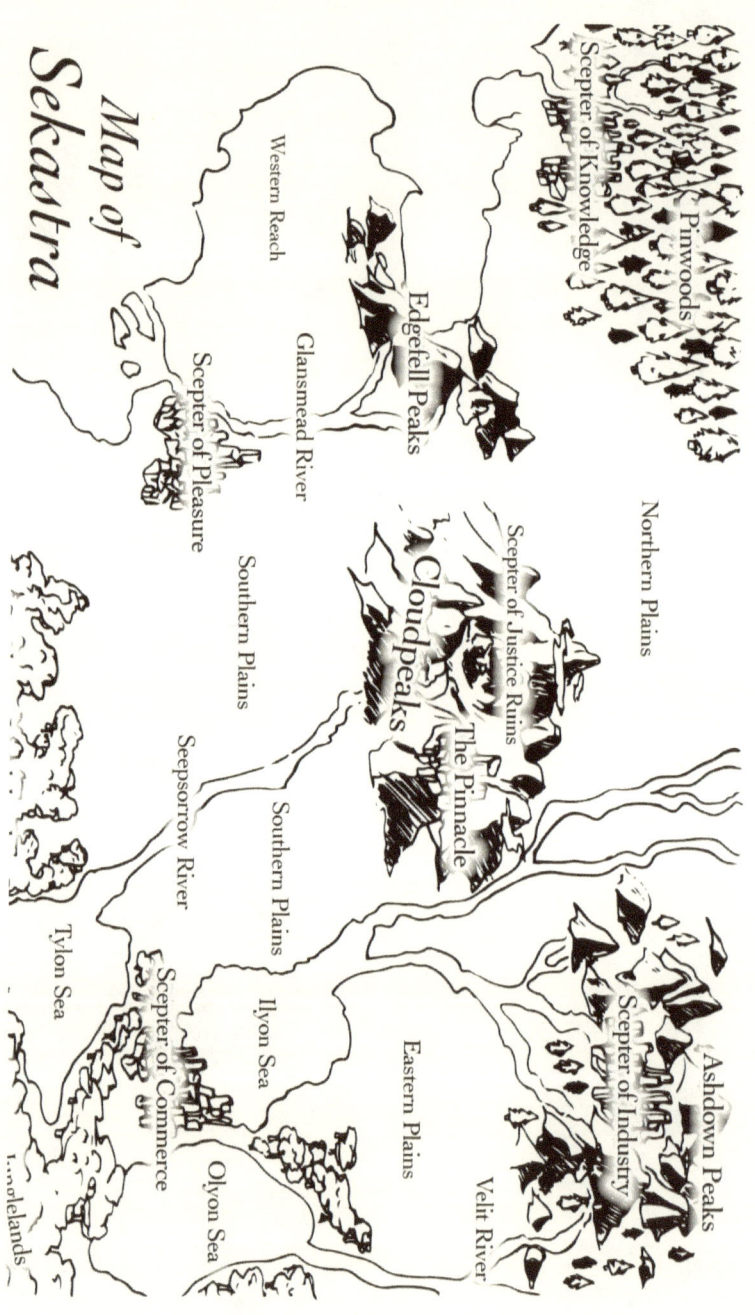

Map of Sekastra

CHAPTER ONE

Officially, the Scepter of Knowledge had never formally entered the dragon-human war. After twenty years, the decision remained mired in the debate courts with no resolution in sight.

Unofficially, three dragons and an airship were attempting to blow *The Silver Streak* to smithereens, and it was taking everything Captain Shance Windkeeper had to keep the enemy at bay. Another blast of cannon fire laced with Talent-cancelling green smoke barreled at him from the other vessel.

He gritted his teeth from his position floating above the airship, still within earshot of his first officer, but able to focus better in the breezes. He wasn't about to let the Curious Intrigue take out his crew or their Talents with the noxious smoke. He summoned a powerful gust of wind and turned to Commander Tegan.

"Brace yourselves!"

The middle-aged woman nodded and repeated his warning over the voice-horn to the rest of the airship. A second later, the ship wheeled sharply around, ducking the enemy ship's attack. He released the wind into a targeted wave that blew the green smoke back onto the enemy. At the same time, his own cannoneers fired into the evening sky. The metal and wood mast of the enemy ship exploded in flames and gray smoke, and another gaping hole appeared in its side, right in the engine room.

The turbines on either side of the airship sputtered, trying to ignite. But the ship had already begun to fall toward the Northern Plains below. The emergency balloon inflated, yet with the main mast down, Shance could see the soldiers struggling to tie it effectively to the rest of the ship. Parachute boats were already launching, but many wouldn't make it.

Relief mingled with frustration in Shance's heart. Any loss of life in this stupid sham war gave him no comfort. Even if their enemies on the other vessel believed in the Curious Intrigue's values, they had no idea how much they were being deceived. They had no idea that they fought for mad scholars and scientists bent on progress at any cost, allied with criminal masterminds who only cared about their own power.

Still, better the other ship go down than any of his crew.

Flames narrowing in on his bow distracted him from further thought. Shance called up another gale and thrust his ship out of the way. Even so, a section of the railing was set ablaze, despite the new metal shielding layered overtop of the wood.

"Tegan! Get Fitch on that!" The sergeant had a Talent for water manipulation.

"Already done, sir!"

Good woman, Tegan. Even if she was a bit dull. Shance turned his attention back to the fight, aiming a tight missile of air at a yellow dragon, knocking it off course. It roared and spun around midair, opening its massive jaws for another round of flames. Although with that maw, the beast could just as easily chomp out half his ship.

Damn it! Kesia and Zephryn were supposed to be handling

them. To be fair, there were three dragon foes and only two on the side of the Lawless in this battle. He glanced around. Fitch was still busy putting out the flames. Tegan was nowhere near the voice-horn. Shance used the wind to amplify his next words. "Ready the starboard cannons!"

The bronze guns swung into place. "Aye!"

"Aim!"

The dragon inhaled and flew at them.

"Fire!"

The cannons blasted at the beast. It ducked and wove around the cannonballs, screeching as one hit its mark, ripping away part of its tail. Suddenly, another dragon with greenish-red scales flew directly into the yellow dragon's path, blowing out flame and smoke. Good. Kesia had shown up to the fight.

The yellow dragon pulled up with a furious rumble that shook *The Silver Streak*. Kesia responded with a piercing shriek and whipped around the larger dragon with her slender, swift body, slicing her claws through its stomach and sinking her sharp teeth into its neck.

The yellow dragon gave a strangled roar, flailing around in mid-air, trying to knock her off. Shance's gut twisted in fear. But Kesia hung on, flames and smoke pouring from her mouth. Some of the smoke almost seemed to be tinged with green.

That couldn't be. Thanks to her uncle's experimentation, the dragon could eliminate the green smoke. But she couldn't create it.

With a sickening groan, Kesia bit through the last of the yellow dragon's neck. It fell to the ground in pieces, still bleeding and spewing guts. She spat out detritus from her mouth, careful to avoid splattering the ship. Another dragon, midnight blue and larger with ridges on its back, materialized out of thin air and flew next to her.

Zephryn Nightstalker, using his invisibility Talent. Blood and gore coated his scales. The two dragons studied each other in a moment of silent communication. Another roar filled the air. Kesia shifted into sun-dove form and flew toward *The Silver Streak* while Zephryn whirled around to face the attacker.

"Unlock the turbines!" As much as Shance hated using the foul, fuel-guzzling things, he needed to be out of the air and in his cabin getting the updates from Kesia. With a flick of his wrist, he landed on the deck. "Tegan, take command."

She nodded. "Aye, sir!"

He ran across the deck, down a few stairs, and threw open the door to his cabin. Kesia flew in, shifting into skin form and grabbing the tunic and trousers he kept laid out for her.

Who would have thought five weeks ago that Shance would be setting out clothing for dragonshifters instead of trying to blow them out of the sky? Not him. But after Zephryn and Kesia had arrived in the Scepter of Commerce, fleeing their imprisonment by the totalitarian Pinnacle, everything had changed. Because of Zephryn, Kesia, and the Lawless, High Command had turned against the war, and the Scepter of Commerce had withdrawn from the conflict in favor of the Lawless. Now the Lawless wanted to influence the Scepter of Knowledge to join their side as well. All four Scepters needed to be aligned in order for the fifth, the Scepter of Justice, to be restored.

Meanwhile, the war raged on and more people died.

"Numbers?" he demanded.

Kesia shoved her brown hair out of her sweaty face. "One dragon left. Zephryn's going to take her out now, but this one has a Talent for increasing the density in different parts of her body."

"Wouldn't that make her heavier?"

Kesia grabbed a canteen of water and guzzled some down. "Yes. But she's clever about it. Only uses it when she's about to strike. I know Zephryn can take her, but you should be around, just in case." The dragon resonance of her voice lightened in pitch. "Then we need to get back to the Scepter of Knowledge. Our next meeting with the Lawless allies is happening this evening."

Shance frowned, leaning on the table. "The big one? That's only forty-five minutes away."

The dragon choked on her next swallow. "Forty-five minutes? You jest."

"Eight o'clock, right?"

"Yes." The word came out as a hiss.

He gestured to a timepiece bolted to the wall. "Only forty minutes now."

"Fewmets! We're still fifteen minutes outside of the city! It's not enough time, especially with—" Kesia broke off, and her amber eyes turned to slits. She started yanking off clothes.

"Whoa!" Shance averted his eyes. "I control the winds, remember? You'll get there."

She breathed out smoke. "We don't just have to *get* there, we have to get changed and presentable. And there will be so many people! Too many people! If we're late—"

"You'll survive—Kesia!"

"We don't have time!"

The dragon had already shifted into her sun-dove form. Shance reached out and grabbed her, holding her tight before he could think better of it. She was a dangerous dragon, after all. A natural predator, top of the food chain, even though by their old code dragonshifters didn't eat other sentient creatures.

But he had a ship that needed repairs. A soldier going off into battle flustered and angry wasn't a good idea, even if she was technically able to kill him without a thought. And even though she was the dragon crown princess, through her embermate bond with Zephryn.

"Listen. I know you can hear me." Shance kept his voice level, never mind that she was pecking at his fingers and drawing blood. "If Zephryn needs help, he can tell you, and we'll give it to him. But nothing horrible is going to happen if you're a few minutes behind schedule. Besides, I could really use your help on my ship. I can hear that some of the mechanisms are out of line, and Virna likes to work with you the best. So please calm down."

He released her and grabbed the discarded tunic and trousers. She shifted back, and he tossed the clothes at her. A growl escaped her, belying her light voice. "Never do that again."

"I can't promise that. Friends don't let friends fly off half-cocked." He grabbed at a spare stocking and pressed it into his fingertips to staunch the tiny punctures she'd made as a sun-dove.

Kesia grabbed his arm and glared at him, her pale face hard with anger and rippled with greenish-red scales. Her grip, each finger tipped with sharp claws, reminded him just how easily she could rip him into pieces with her dragon strength. "And friends don't entrap convicted felons who've spent far too long in prison already."

"You're not a convict anymore. The Lawless dropped those charges. You're free."

"The people I'm speaking with tonight still need to be convinced. Along with so many others." She sighed out a stream of smoke, her gaze turning inward. Then she nodded. "But Zephryn says he has the last dragon handled. I'll see to your engines."

"Thank you." Shance paused. "I'm sorry, Kesia. I didn't mean to bring up the past."

She gave him a wan smile, letting her scales and claws vanish until she appeared entirely human. "No one does. But it still happens. It always will."

As the dragon left the room, Shance's heart sank. She still saw herself as a criminal, no matter what she did. Always the outcast experiment of her uncle, Garishton Razorclaw, the dragon dictator, head of the Pinnacle and representative of the Curious Intrigue.

And the worst part was, he couldn't tell her she wasn't a danger, or at least in danger. Not when the smoke still hanging in the room was tinted green. What was happening to her?

Something he might ask Zephryn later, if Kesia's embermate was in a less-stoic mood. A few drinks should help the dragon man loosen up. Shance discarded the stocking and wrapped a longer strip of cloth around his punctured hand.

In the meantime, Shance had an airship to repair and a crew to lead, after winning another battle he didn't want to fight. After leaving High Command, he'd thought he might be done with war. But even after joining the Lawless, it seemed like bloodshed was all he was good for. Unlike his dragon friends, he had no appetite for it. If only these situations could be resolved by talking over a few pints. He enjoyed talking.

But that role didn't exist. Not even for him.

At least his life wasn't boring.

CHAPTER TWO

Kesia paced the floor in the small anteroom outside the meeting hall. Like the rest of the building, the chamber was made of red brick paneled over with creamy white pinwood. She paused and stared at the brick for a moment, reaching out and touching an exposed area.

The brick was almost the same shade her scales had been before she unleashed her power over the green smoke. Before her freedom. Her fingertip traced a pattern in the mortar, and she let her scales show through her skin.

Greenish, with red around the edges. Definitely more green than red now. Green like the smoke, only a darker shade. She swallowed hard and yanked her hand away, allowing the scales to disappear once more.

She clutched the cloud lily pendant that dangled from a chain around her neck. The Scepter of Knowledge used tepstone infrequently and dragon resonance wasn't noticed as much, since dragons weren't technicaly forbidden from the city. There wasn't a real need for the pendant here. But the present from Zephryn reminded her that no matter what, he'd be there for her.

Though right now he was taking far too much time to arrive.

Even with taking down the last dragon.

Kesia had landed as soon as she could in order to prepare, a process partly composed of changing into appropriate clothing for the Scepter of Knowledge, and mostly composed of pacing and waiting while members of the Lawless and others filed into the confines of the rented meeting hall. Unlike their previous meetings with only the inner circle of the Lawless, this one was open to the public, as allowed by the Scepter of Knowledge since they had not entered the war. Tonight's meeting was a chance to gain new followers and strength in the city where public vote held the greatest sway.

And Zephryn, the crown prince, was running late. As usual.

She resumed her pacing, her heeled boots clicking on the stone floor. Absurd inventions, heels. One of the many ridiculous aspects of human fashion favored in this city.

<Are you almost here?>

<I am one moment closer than the last time you asked me.> He sent teasing warmth through their embermate bond. <For a dragon who jumps into new and dangerous situations so heedlessly, you are curiously afraid of time, Rose-Wing.>

She frowned. <The earlier you are, the less likely you are to receive punishment.>

<You aren't in a cell anymore. No one is going to punish you.>

<You don't know that for certain. It could happen. I remember the lashings.> Of course, as a royal detainee, Zephryn had been exempt from the various torments afforded to prisoners of the Pinnacle. He'd once said that he purposely arrived late to show the Pinnacle that they had no power over him. The habit had remained even after his escape.

She could appreciate the sentiment of rebellion. But her body still remembered the barbed whips, the hours spent in frozen water, naked and shivering. Almost entering the Cold Sleep coma that dragons never woke from.

Her limbs trembled in memory, and she shoved her thoughts away. As Zephryn said, the torture was over. It shouldn't affect her now. There was no need to be irrational. Kesia pressed her sweating palms into her rough ankle-length skirt. A despicable tube of fabric.

Assurance filled her embermate's mental voice. <You know I'd never allow any torture to happen. Nor would you. We are free.>

<Tell that to this costume.> She plucked at her blouse, which wrapped her neck nearly to her chin in stifling white linen. White cuffs clamped tightly around her wrists, and a stiff corset finished the attire. Barbaric fashions that never allowed the skin to breathe. She missed the Scepter of Commerce clothing with its lower necklines and loose pants.

<At least you don't have to wear a hat.> Kesia could picture his rueful expression. <After this is done, we can relieve each other of these trappings entirely.>

Ah yes. Sex. What did humans call it? Lovemaking, bedding, tumbling, and too many other terms. She had been trying to learn their euphemisms to navigate conversation better. Regardless of what it was called, it was a good incentive.

She smiled, her throat heating. <We certainly shall. Hurry up and get here so we can get this entire speech over with.>

<I come with all speed necessary.>

She groaned, her pulse racing. With the emotion, her scales surfaced again in all their hideous array. Kesia sighed deeply and focused, pressing them down once more. <I can't reveal my scales tonight. Not yet.>

Curiosity mingled with irritation came from Zephryn. <Why not? We've spent the last three weeks studying the public speaking customs here and gathering information. We've had opportunities to practice on the designated street corners—and you fared better than I at extemporaneous speaking! You can do this, Rose-Wing.>

<No, I can't. It's one thing to speak when people think you're human. And speaking in general isn't so difficult when you know what you're doing.> She'd certainly had enough practice facing the Pinnacle as a prisoner. <But as dragons?>

<Our resonance already gives us away.>

<Yes, but not as conclusively as scales.>

At her words, Zephryn strode into the anteroom. As usual, he wore black. Black suit with trim breeches and stockings, an old fashion the Scepter of Knowledge clung to ardently. Black shoes, black waistcoat, dark gray shirt, and a black top hat that he immediately cast aside with a sneer. The only mark of color was a dark blue cravat that matched his eyes.

It would add a little additional fun to undressing him later. Kesia smiled. His lips twitched in response, but then he continued their argument.

<You don't need to fear anyone at this event. These are allies and sympathizers of the Lawless.>

<And whoever else wants to stop by.>

<Yes, but dragons are not banned from this Scepter.>

She shook her head. <But revealing scales that match the green smoke? That is another matter entirely. We want them to be thinking of how to assist the plight of the dragons, not distracted wondering what kind of disease I might have.>

Zephryn sighed and stepped toward her. <You don't have a disease—>

<But I was experimented on.> She pressed her hand to his chest, her palm warming at the nearness to his heartflame. The one they shared through their bond, their hearts beating as one. <There are many rumors circulating about me. Not even the dragon council trusts me.>

His expression darkened. <Yes, they do. You are the crown princess—>

<By embermate bond to the crown prince. They respect you. We're traveling together to create support for restoring the Scepter of Justice, but without you...> Kesia shook her head. <You are the focus tonight, Zephryn. Not me.>

Her embermate rested his hands on her shoulders. <Are you sure? The longer you delay, Rose-Wing, the more difficult it will be. These are our allies and future allies. Our people. They need to know the truth about their leaders.>

<*You're* their leader.>

"We are both their leaders." Zephryn's deep voice was firm. "We will rule as a team, as the dragon royal family has always done. You have just as much to offer as I do, if not more."

"Yes, but my uncle betrayed that royal family and overturned the old kingdom. That doesn't endear anyone to me." She sighed. "We don't have time to argue this. I'm not showing my scales. Not yet. Tonight we can open the speech together, then I'll stand to the side and monitor the crowd. You take the bulk of the speech and reveal your scales."

"I would much rather monitor the crowd," he grumbled, fiddling with his cravat. "You engage others far more easily than I and adapt to the unexpected questions."

"You can command a crowd. Especially with that royal face." She traced the edge of his bronze, angular jaw.

He caught her hand and held it, his eyes serious. "Yes, but you charm them."

She shrugged. "I'm not sure how. I just … pick up on things and ask questions and learn. Lately, it's been even easier."

Zephryn smiled. "Perhaps you are beginning to realize you're no longer a prisoner."

"Perhaps. And…"

And sometimes she just knew. Sometimes Kesia felt things, on her skin or in her heart or mind. How people would respond, what mood they were in. The intuition had only emerged in the last two weeks. It could be a natural part of her, although it didn't seem to be connected with either of her Talents.

It had to be natural. She didn't need another reason to be an outcast.

Zephryn continued to stare at her intently, as if she were an oddity he was trying to comprehend. <We'll learn what's happening to you. We'll figure out what your uncle did. But I won't complain about your additional insights.>

<Says the man who doesn't have them.>

"No, I simply have to make most of a presentation by myself." He gave an exaggerated sigh.

Kesia chuckled and stood on her tiptoes to reach his ear. "I'll make it worth your while later."

"As will I."

His lips found hers in a brief, intense kiss. For a moment, all was lost to his taste of peak pine and hot coals, his fire in her mouth, suffusing her body.

Maybe they didn't always understand each other, but Zephryn was hers. And when she had him, she was safe. She always had been, ever since he found her in the depths of prison when they were still children. Kesia might be bold at times, but in the end, it was better to hide in her embermate's protective shadow.

He pulled away with a small grin and an exhale of smoke. "And now, to get this over with. I have books to read, after all."

"Yes, can't let anything get between you and those books." She rolled her eyes and took his arm.

Together they walked onto the stage, a wide platform that spanned one end of the hall, and came to a stop in front of the large audiceptor fastened to a thick stalk of wires and gears. Before them, illuminated by chandeliers with gas lights, sat a mostly filled audience. Loud conversation echoed through the high ceilings of the hall. The citizens of the Scepter of Knowledge were all used to their voices being heard and having influence.

Kesia took a deep breath and exhaled. Thankfully, no green-tinged smoke appeared this time. All she had to do was speak. Her pulse raced with fear and a surprisingly pleasant excitement as the crowd died down and focused on her and Zephryn.

She had a voice. It mattered when she spoke. No one would hurt her, especially with her scales hidden. And maybe, just maybe, her voice could stop the horrors for others as much as her fighting did.

As one, they stepped up to the audiceptor. Zephryn gave a slight nod. <As rehearsed. You first, Rose-Wing.>

Kesia smiled as she surveyed the crowd. "Greetings and thank you for attending our meeting held on this night of..."

The customary words of opening address slipped easily from her mouth. Swiftly the room quieted, listening to every word she spoke. Watching every careful hand gesture she made, practiced in front of a mirror and in front of Shance, who was a far tougher audience than Zephryn. The words of introduction, explaining the perspective of the Lawless and the points of discussion for the evening, flowed effortlessly out of her.

"As you will soon learn from Zephryn Nightstalker, the Scepter of Knowledge needs to decisively move in favor of the Lawless."

Kesia paused. It was an intentional choice for effect. But this time, something dark and eerie crawled along her skin. She searched the crowd, trying to find the source among the general goodwill, skepticism, and curiosity that emanated from them.

This was different. Watchful and menacing.

Her breath caught.

Zephryn mentally nudged her. <I think the pause is long enough.>

<Ah! Yes. Agreed.>

"Please allow me to cede the platform to Zephryn Nightstalker, senior elocution acolyte, and far more, as you will soon learn."

Applause rattled through the building as Kesia stepped into an unlit recess on the side of the stage. Thus concealed, she allowed herself to frown as she stared into the audience. The menacing sensation remained, but scattered and indistinct. It didn't seem to be near the stage.

That was some small comfort.

Still, she heard little of Zephryn's presentation, even though she was meant to critique him afterward, as he did her. The only time he had her attention was during his revelation as the crown prince of dragons. His cobalt scales gleamed against his bronze skin. Kesia grinned appreciatively. As for the audience, the ripples of confusion, understanding, and excitement lasted for the remainder of her embermate's speech.

At the end, he fielded a few questions, and then bowed off. This was a declared presentational speech, designed to whet the appetite of the public. From the roar of conversation, it had certainly done that.

Hopefully, it would catch the attention of those in power, allowing Zephryn and Kesia to ascend the city-wide campaigns that reached the courts and general assemblies. This had the potential to cause real change in the Scepter.

All of this would have happened faster if Cadence Folham, their Lawless agent in the city, had been able to help them. But after making surprising statements against the Lawless, he had vanished. Despite their best efforts to locate him, he remained missing.

Their agent a turncoat, then missing. A battle today near the Scepter of Knowledge. The menacing feeling during their speech that night.

She shared as much with Zephryn as they returned to the safe house in the library district. They had chosen to walk instead of chancing one of the electro-carriages the city favored. The vehicles ran on the electricity that pulsed through the city on cables and was caught by lightning rods on their roofs. For some odd reason, this made Zephryn nervous.

<So you think everything is connected somehow?> He raised his eyebrows. <Don't you always?>

She stepped around a deep puddle on the street. <Yes, because it is. Well, it often is, when it makes sense. And in this case ... I'm not sure. Someone is aware of us. Someone terrible.>

He nodded with a wry smile. <I think many people are aware of us. That is one point of our being here. Despite my desire to remain holed up in a library.>

<We do that too much already.> She swatted at him.

<Pardon me for enjoying books.>

Kesia huffed. <You love them. I enjoy them. But then, I enjoy

doing things with the information. Using it somehow.>

<As do I.> He guided them through a patch of darkness. Tonight they remained within his Cloak, due to her misgivings. <And I do believe you, Kesia. I just wish we knew more. Had more information than—>

<My unorthodox sensing. I know.>

She fell silent as they turned the corner down the last street to the safe house. As usual, she was helpful, but it wasn't enough. It was never enough. It could never justify the weight of her existence. <I'll try harder.>

Zephryn stopped and turned her to face him. His expression was firm. <You always do. But you don't need to explain that to me. You are my embermate. Whatever was done to you, know that I love you. You are worth more than you know, and I will always keep you safe.>

His words stilled her fear, replacing it with relief and warmth. Kesia smiled up at him. <You did well tonight. It was the best speech I've ever heard from you.>

<Good.> He sighed and tilted his forehead down to lean it against hers. <I would appreciate a more thorough evaluation later, but for now...>

Zephryn pulled her closer, pressing her against his chest, desire in his eyes and a half-smile twitching his lips. His hands cupped her chin, tilting it up, even as she grabbed at his coat.

"What? Can't finish the sentence?" she whispered against his lips. "So much for your eloquent words earlier—"

He silenced her with a deep kiss that she returned fiercely, forgetting all else but his heat flowing through her. His strong arms lifted her up and carried her the short distance to the safe house door, even as he nuzzled her cheek and her fingers tangled in his cropped black hair.

Yes. In this moment, in all the uncertainties.

They still had each other.

<And we always will.> His voice assured her, sensing the turn of her thoughts.

And within the confines of the underground safe house, they freed each other of the despicable clothing. The need to hold him close and forget everything else overcame Kesia. To soar with him, to be united with him in every way.

Thankfully, their room had a cavernous ceiling. Not as freeing as the sky, but high and broad enough to breathe more easily. Although right now, breathing was an afterthought, a brief necessity while tasting his mouth, his neck, so many other wonderful parts. As Kesia clutched his body close to hers, she felt the satisfying shift that let her wings emerge, even in skin form. She knew that Zephryn, at least, would not judge her for their greenish-red hue.

His approval, his desire, flooded hot through her, pushing out all thought. And together they rose into the air.

Unbreakable.

Chapter Three

Kesia was incredible. Just because she didn't believe it didn't negate the truth. Eventually, she would come to understand. And he would help her as much as he could.

At that moment, entwined with her in their bed formed of generous layers of mattress and cushions on the floor after the dragon fashion, all Zephryn wanted to do was kill the insistent chirping of their wireless commers.

Waking next to him, Kesia groaned and buried her face in his shoulder. Her face was shadowed in the dim gaslights anchored in the walls. <Make it go away. Burn it with fire.> Suddenly, she seized, ready to leap out of bed. <Unless we're in trouble?>

<We aren't in trouble. Even if we were, we could handle it.> Zephryn sighed, kissing the top of her head where greenish strands of hair mingled among the brown. He would personally like to eviscerate the Pinnacle soldiers who had inflicted such torture on Kesia, making her so fearful.

Regret squeezed his heart. He hadn't been there for her then. He hadn't protected her or rescued her. With what he'd known at the time, he had made the best long-term decision for their eventual escape from the Pinnacle, the totalitarian dragon regime allied with the Curious Intrigue. He'd chosen to stay, to wait out the imprisonment with her until the opportune moment arrived. But Kesia endured the consequences of his decision daily, no matter what he tried to do. She had been the one suffering in her cell, alone.

He couldn't think of how to mend that damage.

And the damn chirping wasn't helping matters. Zephryn's pulse raced with the urgency to answer it.

Kesia traced his chest, drawing his attention back to her. <I can sense you thinking about the Pinnacle.>

<I didn't say anything.>

<I know that regret well. You did the best you could, Midnight. And now we have the future. Which includes whatever that call is.> Her muscles relaxed, and her anxiety faded enough to show irritation. <Where are the horrid things?>

<Wherever our clothing ended up.>

<I should create something to turn them off from a distance. They're already remote communicators. A remote shut-off device should be able to work on the same system.>

<So clever.> Zephryn grinned. <But right now, we might as well be about the business that brought us here.>

He felt her silent agreement. Fluidly he sat up, and she eased off him. They stood and made their way across the smooth stone floor, checking through their various articles of clothing for the commers. Humans really wore far too much clothing, even in the damp, cold climate of the Scepter of Knowledge. Why not just make their existing fabric warmer?

At last, they found the small, square devices, which easily fit into the palm of a hand. Zephryn toggled at one gear to answer. He cleared his throat. "Who is this?"

The answering voice was bright, with a dry edge. "Maira Ukerys.

The death unicorn queen."

Zephryn's mind raced as he exchanged a look with Kesia. Maira and Lirome Ukerys, the unicorn siblings who had traveled to the Scepter of Knowledge to assist them. The mysterious pair had yielded precious little information to the Lawless, and their official file had been redacted. Yet they had helped Nula and Tiers with their potentially life-threatening embermate bond.

Lirome had insisted on speaking with them in person, but hadn't specified when or where, simply telling them to be ready when the moment came. Zephryn glanced at the timepiece on the wall.

"You want to meet at 1 o'clock in the morning? Why?"

"I see Tiers Sunscaler didn't exaggerate about your lack of tact. This is the ideal time to meet for a private conversation. Meet us at the Niversill Falls on the edge of the Cresida Inlet within an hour. On the platform at the bottom of the stairs."

The wireless commer gave an end-of-call chirp. Kesia sighed. "Back into the uncomfortable clothing again."

Zephryn caught her arm. "Not necessarily."

"Oh?" She raised her eyebrows.

"I'll use my Cloak the entire way. Wear whatever you choose."

Kesia grinned, her face lighting up. "I'm very glad you have that Talent."

"As am I."

And not only because he could make her smile for a moment. His Cloak was only the surface level of his Talent. It was the most obvious use of his ability to perceive and alter the elements that bound the world together, elements that allowed dragons to shift their forms to and from the Nether. But he'd never been trained—his family had disappeared before they could teach him. Regardless, being invisible was the most useful aspect of his Talent at present. Particularly since he could avoid the bothersome stockings and shoes for trousers, boots, and a plain shirt. And a literal cloak that would help to stave off the damp air.

Kesia opted for even less. She wore boots, trousers, and a wide band of cloth wrapped many times around her breasts and torso and fastened with a pin. She pulled on one of his coats and sighed in satisfaction. "Much better. I do not understand why humans make corsets so stifling."

"One of their many confusing facets. Shall we go?"

She nodded, her amber eyes glinting with excitement. A new adventure was enough to perk up his embermate. Zephryn enjoyed the rush of her enthusiasm through their bond. It balanced out his own wish for a book and quiet time alone to think.

They silently exited the safe house. Once on the street, they ran quickly through the narrow alleys and around the tall brick, stone, and pinwood buildings that filled the Scepter of Knowledge in neat blocks and squares. Mist from the inlet drifted through the air, combining with smoke from chimneys and steam from the factories on the edge of the city.

Zephryn loathed the claustrophobic atmosphere and cloying smoke, but it allowed his Talent to shield them more easily. At this time of night, there were only post-carousal drunks, city watch, and the odd homeless beggar on the streets. There might not even be a need for his Cloaking Talent, but he wasn't going to take any chances. Silence, speed, and stealth were their greatest allies.

At last, they reached the southern edge of the Scepter of Knowledge. Without speaking, he and Kesia slowed to a swift stroll as they stepped onto the stone walkway near the Niversill Falls. The three waterfalls spilled over massive boulders and were considered appealing to many, judging by the well-worn pathways, the coin-driven sight-scopes, and the food wrappers that littered the ground around stone benches.

He didn't share the humans' love of this place. Water was water, and it was only useful when bathing in skin form or slaking thirst. Zephryn glanced at Kesia, expecting to see similar trepidation on her face. But instead of the distaste familiar to dragons, she studied the cascading water with fascination and took a step closer to the iron railing around the walkway.

<Are you all right, Rose-Wing?>

Kesia's lips parted in awe, her amber eyes wide. She leaned over the railing, her hands reaching toward the cascades.

Alarm surged through him.

<Kesia!> He touched her shoulder.

She jumped, clutching the railing. "What? Oh. I'm sorry."

<What happened? You seemed transfixed.>

<I didn't mean to be.> She swallowed and pushed loose strands of hair behind her ear. <I've never noticed how beautiful water is until recently. Can't you see it?>

<It splashes down rocks, obeying the laws of gravity. I suppose I should be grateful it isn't flowing upward. Although that would be unique.>

Her shoulders shook in suppressed laughter, and tiny trickles of greenish smoke left her mouth. <Wouldn't it? Then we could touch the streams easily.>

Kesia's wonder suffused their bond, causing confusion in Zephryn's mind. He remembered her dislike of boat travel from their journey to the Scepter of Commerce. She had even grown ill. Yet now, she was enraptured.

Perhaps it was the late hour? Neither of them had slept much, and she often became silly when fatigued. Then again, he had urged her to cast off her fear. Maybe she had just chosen an inconvenient time to do so.

<Midnight? What's wrong?> Concern dampened her thrill, and her face became reserved. <I'm too distracted. I'm sorry. We should go closer to the falls.>

Before he could say anything, she whirled around and started down the slick stone steps. Zephryn followed her, regret gnawing at his stomach. Should he apologize? He had done nothing wrong, only shown honest worry. First Kesia's scales and hair had started turning green, instead of the red she had been born with. Then her smoke had begun to look green, and she'd started sensing things. And now, the water.

Kesia was becoming something because of the experiments of Garishton Razorclaw. And Zephryn had no idea how to handle it.

Both the unicorns were healers. Tiers had spoken highly of their abilities. Maira had a strong healing Talent, and Lirome was apparently an unparalleled physician. If they proved trustworthy, perhaps one of them could assist him in discovering what was happening to his embermate.

Meanwhile, he had silenced the joy of someone who still considered herself a mistake.

Kesia stood quietly at the bottom of the steps, studying the moonlight as it shimmered through the mist and pools of water. The joy was still there, but it was now tainted by sadness. Zephryn sought for words.

"It's all right." Her voice could barely be heard above the crashing water. "I didn't mean to disturb you. You were only trying to care."

With her words, Kesia buried the sadness, her lips twitching into a smile that didn't quite reach her eyes. Fewmets. Before he could respond, she turned and glanced behind them, looking up at the stairs.

The unicorns?

Zephryn followed her gaze. <The stairs appear empty, Rose-Wing.>

<I know. And yet...> She frowned, flicking at some of the water. <Maybe I am going mad.>

Suddenly, a voice spoke out of the shadows on the opposite edge of the platform. "I've never known a dragon to willingly touch moving water. Outside of bathing, of course."

"I love water," Kesia blurted out.

A figure emerged from the shadows of the platform, throwing back its hood to reveal a wide face with high cheekbones narrowing to a firm jaw. Black hair framed his face and fell down his shoulders and back. "So I see. Interesting. Why is that?"

She froze, then shrugged with a little smile. "I suppose I'm all right with anything or anyone who isn't trying to kill me. Or put me into prison. Or hurt others. Well, hurt innocent people. Not that anyone is entirely innocent..."

Kesia trailed off, and the strange man chuckled. "I understand completely."

She sighed, and an odd relief filtered through the embermate bond. Zephryn frowned. The two were connected already, yet it wasn't like anything Zephryn had ever felt from her. It was a contentment that settled in deeper than the Cloudpeaks yet was lighter than a single dragon scale.

True and strong.

Another figure emerged from the shadows, unhooded. This one was far smaller, her face framed by long black hair. She had delicate features and a pointed chin. Her violet eyes were lined with black and her lips were painted entirely black as well. <Are we ready to talk, or are you going to goggle at your new friend all day?>

The man snorted. <Considering how many close *friends* you have, sister, I would think you'd be more patient.>

<After I get my chief mate back, you're welcome to spend all day explaining the situation to your new friend and her ember-mate.>

Zephryn's head snapped up. <What situation? Who are you?>

The female paused. <My apologies. Maira Ukerys. Unicorn queen, here to speak with the crown prince of dragons, Zephryn Nightstalker, and the crown princess of dragons, Kesia Ironfire.>

<Pleased to meet you,> Kesia said automatically. She moved closer to Zephryn, her eyes never leaving the male.

Maira continued, gesturing to figure standing next to her. <And this is my rather presumptuous twin brother, Lirome Ukerys. One of the best physicians of all time, and the best physician among the Lawless, among other specialties,> the unicorn made a little cough, <and apparently a soul-friend of you, Kesia.>

Zephryn frowned. <What is a soul-friend?>

Lirome gave a sheepish smile. <Unicorns have other kinds of deep, often instantaneous connections in our culture, most notably friendships.>

Kesia frowned. <Is it like the fleetwing bonds between those of the same gender?>

He nodded. <Yes. It simply means we find a compatible soul and know, upon first meeting, that a friendship shall occur.> He nodded toward Kesia. Something like disbelief flickered in his eyes, then vanished. <There are no rules governing it, other than the wills of both involved. A soul-friend bond happens frequently

among our herds and builds community between them. The bond can happen with humans as well, but I admit it's never happened with a dragon in recorded memory. Interesting.>

Zephryn reached out for Kesia through their bond. She didn't feel disturbed in the slightest by the connection with the unicorn. If anything, she felt more level and centered. He opened up their private mindspeak link. <What do you think about this?>

After a moment, she gave a mental affirmation. <All that he's said feels accurate. I'm not worried. He's not a threat. Neither of them are, at least not to us. I would question them about others and evaluate their intentions carefully.>

<Agreed.> He touched her hand lightly, then turned to the unicorns. <You wanted to meet with us. Speak your piece.>

Maira took another step forward. <I'm sorry for my impatience, but our time is short, and the journey was far too long. We are here to tell you truths about your situation. Truths that the Lawless authorities have kept from you and from many others.>

Resignation and concern crept through Zephryn. <Go on.>

<History would tell you that unicorns are extinct, and the Lawless would say our emergence was … unexpected.> Maira shook her head. <Long before the war, there was another great conflict in our home country of Elotrin. In that conflict, the unicorns were largely obliterated.> Her mental voice caught for a second, then she continued. <Myself, Lirome, and my husband led the remainder of the unicorns into Sekastra and sought asylum from the dragons in the Scepter of Justice. They gave it to us, and we have dwelled in anonymity in the Lost Refuge ever since. That was about fifty years ago.>

Shock reverberated through Zephryn. <You knew my parents?>

The two unicorns exchanged a look, and Lirome spoke. <Yes,

when they were not yet rulers. And we observed the situation that led to their downfall, at least in part. Much was hidden from us because we were ever the outsiders even in the home we now call our own.>

<How do you look so young?> Kesia asked.

<Humans live at least eighty years. Dragons live at least one hundred. Unicorns live at least two hundred. My sister and I are only eighty-five years old.> Lirome gave her a smile so unlike those that Windkeeper had given to Kesia in the Scepter of Commerce. The unicorn's expression was full of goodwill. A touch of the dangerous, perhaps, but no lust or malice.

Good.

Maira cleared her throat. <We came to the Scepter of Knowledge to assist you in your efforts. We learned that Garishton Ironfire—I mean, Razorclaw—had experimented on you, Kesia, and we wanted to help.>

Hope lighted Kesia's face, although her amber eyes remained guarded. <How can you help?>

Lirome spoke up. <I have my own extensive knowledge of experimentation.>

<How?> Suspicion flared within her, echoed by Zephryn.

The unicorn's expression turned inscrutable. <To answer that would be to take more time than we have at this moment. But I assure you, my knowledge was gained only in assisting others with their consent, never in cruelty.>

Zephryn nodded. <Be prepared for many questions.>

<We are well acquainted with answering them.> Maira continued, <My husband and at least one of my sons are in this Scepter, so I am here to investigate and recover them in addition to helping you.>

Zephryn tilted his head. <Who is your son?>

<Cadence Folham was the name he used.> The unicorn queen's face fell. <My people are gifted soul empaths, and some of us used our gifts in secret among the Lawless. After the persecution we experienced in Elotrin, we are not eager to come out in the open again.>

<I understand,> said Kesia, her expression kind and serious. <And your husband?>

The siblings exchanged another glance. Zephryn felt the background hum of private mindspeak. Maira's face twisted in grief, and her brother squeezed her hand in comfort.

At last, Lirome spoke. <My sister and her husband were abducted ten years ago in the Scepter of Commerce, taken captive by the Curious Intrigue. Maira was put into an electrified coffin-like box to siphon her healing Talent and use it to cure others. As for Tyrius—>

<Shance,> Maira put in abruptly. <Tyrius was his formal name, but he always preferred Shance. Shance Windkeeper, using the name the dragons gave him after our arrival in the Scepter of Justice.>

A jolt of surprise ricocheted through Zephryn. <Shance Windkeeper?> His words were slow, hesitant. <The man who is fond of having sex with women, always seeking his one true love?>

Maira sighed ruefully. <Yes. That would be him. Or it sounds comparable to what Shance was like when I first met him many decades ago. He changed. But the Curious Intrigue has done something to his mind. Brainwashed him to forget himself and his allegiance to us and, it appears, his allegiance to his beliefs. I think they were hoping to turn him and his Talents to their side, but when they couldn't, they created a false identity and drafted him

into the military.>

<Because we all know how much Shance enjoyed being in the military the first time,> Lirome added grimly.

<He does hate it,> Kesia said thoughtfully. <But why keep this from us? From him?>

Maira sighed. <It was a decision made by the Lawless founders and my regents, not by us. I can provide full records at our official meeting in a few days. I had been captured. They feared that Shance had been made into a sleeper agent, that his will was not his own. Which has since been proven false.>

Anger twisted her face, and the faint smell of sulfur filled the air. The scent jogged Zephryn's memory. Nula Thredsing had warned Kesia about sulfur. Sulfur and blood red eyes. Nula had never explained what their purpose was, for she didn't know.

<What of your brother?> Kesia glanced at Lirome.

He pressed his lips together, and his eyes flashed red. Only for an instant. <Leadership in our culture is strictly in the hands of the sovereign and their spouse or spouses. I have no more sway than any other unicorn. And Shance had been thoroughly brainwashed. He didn't recognize me on the street, and although Zilpath has tried to connect with him, he has only resisted her. I knew only Maira could reach him.>

Maira reached up and patted her brother's shoulder, then went on. <So the Lawless simply watched Shance through Zilpath and others. As for telling you, be advised that the Lawless may support you, but they still observe you carefully for any unexpected behaviors that would signal you are not as loyal as you appear. Such is life among spies and rebels. We all have our secrets.> The unicorn queen set her jaw. <Shance is my husband and closest advisor. I will fight for him—and I will win. I need to be able to contact him in

my own way, with as much subtlety as I can.>

<I understand.> With those words, Kesia seemed entirely at ease with both unicorns, even though she had to have seen the eye color shift and smelled the sulfur.

Zephryn was less secure, but he trusted her judgement, at least enough to reserve his own. <And you will assist us as well? You will provide help regarding Kesia's experimentation and our mission to turn this city in favor of the Lawless?>

Lirome nodded. <Yes, we will certainly help Kesia. We are physicians and healers, always. Cadence Folham is a missing Lawless agent and one of Maira's sons. In finding him, we each achieve an objective. In addition, there are hidden forces in the city. A menace in the shadows that neither my sister nor I can fully detect.>

<Granted, I am still recovering from that gods-cursed coffin,> Maira muttered, clearly annoyed at herself. <Give me another week or so, and I'll be ready to deal with whoever they are.>

Zephryn's thoughts churned. He opened the private link again. <A menace in the shadows, Rose-Wing? Similar to what you felt?>

<Yes, but I'm still not sure what it is either. And I'm not a soul empath like the unicorns are. Maybe I'm sensing something different.>

He sent her more reassurance. <Then we will discover the truth about that as well. Do you think we should trust the unicorns?>

<I do. They are hiding things from us—we both know that. We saw their eyes, scented the sulfur.> Zephryn nodded, and Kesia continued. <But their words are true, and they don't recoil from me as the Lawless do. They are meeting out of a desire to inform. Be mindful, but trust them.>

<And if they prove traitorous later, we will deal with that accordingly.>

<Agreed.>

Zephryn turned back to the unicorns. <What would you have us do?>

<Allow me to engage with Shance,> Maira said. <I must be careful, for I do not know all that they did to his mind or what he has been through. As for the rest, allow us to work with you.>

Lirome added, <My sister and I would be glad to examine Kesia and give you insight into her unique physiology due to the experimentation.>

<I'm not sure you'll find anything useful,> Kesia answered, traces of weariness and bitterness in her voice. <The dragon caregivers haven't. Neither have the human doctors. I'm merely a curiosity to be treated with vague fear.>

Lirome moved toward her, his tone gentling. <I haven't had the chance to try. I specialize in treating conditions like yours.>

<Yes, so you've said. You need to explain how and why.>

<I will, in due time.> He glanced at Zephryn, his gaze sincere and respectful. <I would be honored to help you both understand what is happening to her.>

At those words, Zephryn finally felt a certain amount of quietude with the unicorns. He didn't believe for a moment that they were being completely straightforward about their actions or their presence in the Scepter. They were meeting by a large waterfall in the dead of night, for gunshot's sake. But there was a directness to the unicorn that rang true. Right now, he and Kesia needed all the allies they could get.

<All right. We accept your help.>

Kesia smiled. <And appreciate it. Thank you.>

<Our pleasure,> Maira answered. <As Bonilus gives his benevolence, so we extend it to others.> Then she yawned. <If you will

excuse me, I need more sleep to continue recovering from my experience at the hands of the Curious Intrigue.>

<When can we expect to see you next?> Kesia asked.

Lirome and Maira stared at each other for a long moment, seeming to disagree about something. Some rather dramatic hand motions followed, and Lirome stomped his foot. Finally, Maira spoke. <I will be making contact with Shance within the next day or two. I'd rather speak with him privately before our official meeting.>

<I will be gathering supplies to set up a decent medical facility at the central safe house,> Lirome said. <After that, I will speak with both of you.>

<Good. Until then.>

Something should be done to reinforce this agreement. But what?

Ah, yes.

Zephryn stepped toward the male unicorn and offered his hand in a firm handshake, remembering at the last second to hold back some of his strength. Lirome shook back easily and confidently. Then Zephryn moved on to Maira. Kesia followed his lead with the hand shaking tradition.

There was meant to be some significance to this action, but Zephryn could never understand what. But he did feel reassured about both unicorns. If Lirome was as good of a physician as he claimed, there would be tangible hope for Kesia, not merely the empty words of comfort Zephryn could offer. The relief in her eyes as she exchanged words with him lifted Zephryn's heartflame.

That was worth everything.

Maybe he could even get information about his parents, more than the scant details the Lawless offered.

Perhaps they were finally seeing a shift in the wind currents.

At the very least, seeing the expression on Shance Windkeeper's face when he realized he had a wife would be better than two fat mountain grazers.

Even three mountain grazers.

<A small wager, Rose-Wing,> Zephryn said as they ascended the stairs. <I believe Shance Windkeeper will seek to take Maira Ukerys as a companion when he sees her.>

She wrinkled her nose. <How is that a fair wager? He does take women home. But I'm unsure. Maira seems like the sort to want him to have full knowledge of the situation before such private matters as sex and sleeping together.>

<So you take the wager?>

Kesia glanced at him speculatively. <This isn't kind. He takes his quest for love very seriously. And she claims to be his wife. Her caring appears to be genuine.>

<He doesn't have to know.> He ran a finger along the back of her neck, drawing a prickle of pleasure.

She pursed her lips. <What sort of wager?>

<Oh, it would have to involve a library...>

CHAPTER FOUR

Shance Windkeeper's dragon friends were great for many things, but they were terrible drinking buddies.

They were solid comrades in battle. Unrivalled when it came to blunt, unpleasant truth. Driven, hard-working fellow spies in the quest to stop the war and restore the Scepter of Justice.

Yet tonight confirmed again that they had a hard time loosening up and enjoying a pint. At least Kesia was open to trying new types of beer or ale, even wine. She had a particular palate, however, and usually held back around her embermate. For his part, Zephryn flatly said that drinking anything to impede the senses was foolhardy. Which was completely uncalled for, since Shance didn't intend to get drunk. He only wanted to enjoy the delicious food, good wine, and excellent music at The Greenbow, an upscale tavern in the heart of the Scepter of Knowledge. Perhaps he would even find a female companion for the night.

Or maybe he wouldn't, if Zephryn continued to scowl at everyone who gave them a friendly glance. Shance sighed and flashed the winsome waitress an apologetic look, then glanced at the male dragon.

"Zephryn, not everyone here is out to kill you."

"You don't know that," the dragon responded, pulling at the black cravat cinched around his neck. It matched his waistcoat and made him look like he was on his way to a flame-cursed funeral. "One must always be prepared."

Next to Zephryn in the booth, Kesia gave a shrug and fingered the collar of her high-necked blouse. "You're right, Zephryn, but you could also be paranoid. Just enjoy the food and the music for a little while."

She took another bite of her fish roll, then added more vinegar sauce. She closed her eyes in enjoyment and sighed, nodding her head in time with the strings and pipes playing in the background. Zephryn shook his head. "No human food is that good."

"Or you're just limiting your experiences." Kesia gave him a mischievous look. "Which reminds me," she eyed Shance's glass of wine curiously, "have I tried that flavor yet? I could enjoy it."

"It's ashberry grapes, made from local fruit." He signaled the waitress for another glass. "If you don't, I'll drink the rest."

"Deal."

Zephryn rolled his eyes and gave her a mock-glare, which she only returned with an innocent smile. He responded with a har-rumph. The entire interchange showed the dragons were having a mental conversation, although Kesia was clearly having more fun than Zephryn. Even if she did look a bit frustrated. Still, in most instances the dragons presented a united front, something Shance envied.

At last, he sighed. "All right, you two. There's a third person at the table. And Kesia's wine is here."

"Oh! I'm sorry. Thank you." She blinked, then picked up the glass and tried a sip of the yellow liquid. Delight filled her features. "Ahhh."

Shance raised his eyebrows. "You enjoy it?"

"Almost. Maybe." She took another sip. "I'll need to taste more to make a decision."

Zephryn sighed with a trace of warmth. "I do not understand you. The food here is more edible than most, but there isn't nearly enough of it. We should order more."

Shance sighed. "You two can't been seen eating three plates of food apiece. It'll draw attention."

"I gave a speech to over a thousand people the other night. We're already drawing attention. The stipends Kesia and I receive are more than sufficient to cover the cost. Although we do have a meeting soon."

A mixture of excitement and nerves passed over Kesia's face. Before Shance could ask after her expression, or about the meeting, her expression grew peaceful. She sighed and popped the last bit of food into her mouth. "True. We can eat more later. Still, right now, I could eat two mountain grazers easily."

"Yes," Zephryn agreed. "Especially if hibernation season were near, and they were covered with fat and muscle."

Shance's stomach lurched. He *had* been enjoying the sautéed nughra fish and scallops, caught fresh from the nearby Cresida Inlet. Now the thought of food repulsed him, and he pushed his plate aside. "All right, that particular conversation you two need to have up here." He tapped his forehead. "And leave me to enjoy the music."

"If you can," Zephryn muttered.

"Quiet, grazer-breath."

"I'm with Shance on this one." Kesia chuckled and hummed along with the tune. "This would be good music to dance to. If I had someone to dance with."

"I wonder who that someone would be."

Shance turned away from the dragons' bickering to survey the rest of the room. The walls were paneled with warm brown shades of carved pinwood, and the floor featured polished brown planks. Considering how the Scepter of Knowledge was located on the southern edge of the Pinwood Forest, it was obvious where the decorations, the upholstered chairs, and the square tables had come from. One match would set the entire Greenbow Tavern on fire— if everything weren't coated in protective sealant and the lamps weren't lit with rare, expensive electric light bulbs.

Truly, the place was a marvel. It was always fascinating to see how the different Scepters used technology in their regions. Now, if only he could get a date with someone of the local persuasion. Someone captivating. Remarkable.

Someone who held his soul.

Her.

Shance didn't know what she looked like. He didn't know what she sounded like. Doldrums, he didn't even know what she smelled like. But somehow he knew she existed, and when he found her, everything would make sense. And even if he were to enjoy some pleasure and fall asleep in a bed warmed by a woman, at least he would sleep through the night. Sleeping alone often led to restlessness or battle nightmares, both of which weren't worth a second thought.

Seeking out Bonilus, as Zilpath suggested, wasn't an option. The Four Corners religion wouldn't solve anything. Even if they could, he'd already burned that bridge with his own actions.

Metaphysics were cumbersome anyway. He shoved away the thoughts and continued studying the room.

Sleek black hair outlining a delicate profile caught his attention.

Shance leaned forward, trying to get a clearer glimpse of the woman's face. Viorstan, she was short! It was easier to see the man who sat across from her. Perhaps her brother or a coworker. Shance's hand tightened around his glass of whiskey. As long as the man wasn't her husband. No matter how uncomfortable it made him, Shance would get that cleared up as soon as he walked over and met the woman.

Attempting to seduce Kesia had been embarrassing enough. Never mind that she hadn't realized she was married because the dragon Pinnacle had done their best to erase the custom of marriage. It still burned Shance that he had attempted to seduce a married woman. He wasn't going to let that happen again. His own life might be a wreck. He wouldn't ruin anyone else's.

Shance gave the black-haired woman another glance, hoping to catch a clearer sight of her. Part of him was oddly certain she and her companion were not romantically involved. They would sooner have swallowed fire and brimstone. They weren't even the same race.

Confusion swept through him. How would he know that?

"Shance? Shance!"

"Yes?" He turned to see both dragons staring at him. Kesia wore a look of humorous annoyance, and Zephryn looked oddly pleased with himself. "What were you saying?"

Zephryn's cobalt eyes glinted. "Ask him, Rose-Wing."

"Very well." Kesia sighed. "Do you intend to proposition that woman now?"

Shance blinked. "If you mean introduce myself as a polite gentleman to an intriguing lady across the room, then yes."

Kesia turned to her partner. "I don't think that should count, Midnight."

"We both know where his introductions lead, Rose-Wing. So I win."

"You win what?" Shance raised his eyebrows.

Kesia groaned. "We'll be spending all of tomorrow in the library." She glared at Shance.

"You could have waited five minutes. We were about to leave."

Shock stabbed him. "Were you two betting on my romantic exploits?"

Kesia shrugged, guilt flickering in her amber eyes. "It was his idea."

"An idea that you went along with."

"What can I say? I was lured in by the promise of a flight along the northern coastlands or a visit to the unusual mechanics shops or, well, anywhere else in this Scepter except for a library."

Zephryn tweaked her hair. "You enjoy libraries. And reading."

"Yes, I do. But after two weeks of research trying to discover who could be turning the tide against the Lawless, it gets … tiresome." She sighed. "Ah well. This corset and other restrictive clothing are also tiresome. And we have a meeting. Good night, Shance. Remember, you don't have to take anyone to your airship tonight."

Shance huffed. "Why, have you set a bet on that as well?"

She grimaced as she stood, catching his jab more easily than Zephryn ever would. If Zephryn ever managed to at all. "No. I'm sorry if that hurt your emotions. Feelings. Whichever of those is correct. But in this case, I think asking questions first is a good idea."

Zephryn nodded. "Consider that you're human, not a dragon. We have embermates, whereas you have to be careful and discern. Don't be stupid like most humans."

Kesia shoved her embermate with a look that would have

pierced slatesheen. The words were the dragon idea of a comforting thought. Or perhaps just Zephryn's idea. Shance had learned from his time among the other dragons in the Lawless that while bluntness was common among dragons, Zephryn's exceptional lack of tact was notable. Other dragons were attempting to work with him on it, considering he was the crown prince of dragons and civility would continue to be required. At least he was guaranteed to have Kesia at his side.

The female dragon gave him a smile. "You could still have a mate of some kind." There was her attempt at encouragement. Shance appreciated the thought. "Even Tiers waited years before meeting Nula. Just remember, if this woman is the one, you'll have to explain all the other women you've ever had sex with—or bedded—to her."

Shance had to give Kesia credit. The dragon really was trying the euphemisms. Even though they sounded less natural coming from her.

"There's no law demanding that." Although Shance knew full well he would be forthright anyway. He sought for another retort, leaning back from the table. "You're assuming she hasn't been bedding others as well. Nula was certainly active."

"True." Kesia bit her lip. "It's all so odd. I couldn't imagine having sex with anyone other than Zephryn. Still, from what I've seen, human females are far less promiscuous than human males. Which makes little sense, when you think about it—"

Others began to turn toward them. Shance winced and held up a hand. "This is not a conversation to have in this kind of establishment. We can chat later about human mating habits."

"Oh, good. I do want to learn more."

He rubbed his forehead. The dragon woman really did. She was trying to understand and empathize, and it almost made up for the flame-cursed speeches that came out of Zephryn's mouth. Shance briefly clenched his hands, then released them. Right now, he just wanted both of them out of the bar so he could forget everything they'd said, good and bad. "I know. Tomorrow. After your important meeting and world-saving stuff. Good night."

"Good night, my friend."

Kesia gave him a smile as she pulled on her coat, then she and Zephryn left for their mysterious meeting, and likely afterwards, the safe house in the library district on the east side of the Scepter. It was a quiet area with a number of abandoned basements ideal for housing resistance members. A good location for dragons to lay low while the three of them investigated the Scepter of Knowledge for Curious Intrigue activity. So far, there had been nothing except the usual petitions in the debate forums for the official recognition of the war, and the conspicuous absence of Lawless agent Cadence Folham.

Twenty years and no decision on the war was ridiculous. That was one thing Shance and Zephryn could agree on. But Zephryn thought answers would be found in old records. Kesia wanted a more active investigation but was still learning to understand human behavior and act accordingly. Not to mention she didn't trust herself with much outside of supporting Zephryn and fixing machinery.

This left Shance to manage *The Silver Streak*, his crew, and glean what he could through casual conversations at bars and other public areas. The role was oddly comfortable, even more so than his military career as an airship captain, but it was equally isolating. In the end, the dragons went home to each other, whereas no matter how many acquaintances Shance struck up, he remained alone.

Leaving him to his usual occupation of seeking companionship. Maybe, love.

A loud crash and a shatter shook him from his thoughts. Shance stood, seeking the location of the sound. It had come from the same direction as the black-haired woman. Was she in trouble? Fear pulsed through him. He slipped through the maze of tables to her booth on the far side of the tavern—just in time to see her dinner companion push a water glass over the edge of the table for some inexplicable reason. The remains of a glass already lay on the ground in fragments, surrounded by a slowly expanding puddle.

With a flick of his wrist, Shance sent a precise stream of wind beneath the second glass and caught it before it had a chance to tip over. Then he gently eased the glass back onto the table. After a brief glance at the mischievous expression on the man's face, he moved the glass closer to the lady. For some reason, he felt certain that the gentleman with the ginger hair and orange waistcoat would just push the glass over again.

Maybe Shance had already had too much to drink.

Shance turned his attention to the lady—and found every word on his tongue had vanished, leaving him to stare mutely at her petite loveliness. The woman had a sharply beautiful, dark olive face lit by twinkling violet eyes lined in black, a pert nose, and expressive lips also painted black. Long black hair was loosely braided down her back. Her delicate frame was encased in a deep scarlet, high-necked blouse and black corset, and her exposed hands revealed black fingernails that he somehow knew weren't painted. For all her dark clothing, she was a vision of vivacity and humor, with a side of frustration aimed squarely at her friend.

Now Shance was sure the two were close friends, but nothing more. Nor could they be anything more. Theirs was a bond of instinct and devotion, not of romance or physical intimacy.

He sighed. The last time he had been sure a bond wasn't romantic, it had only been because the dragons in question had not been aware of their situation. It was best to be cautious, no matter how sure his soul was.

Especially since an odd bit of guilt was flickering through him. As though … somehow, he should have known better.

Maybe Kesia's words were getting to him.

He summoned a charming smile. "I hope there won't be any more disturbances, my dear lady. I would hate for you to come to harm."

"How kind of you, even though I think the floor was in far more in danger than I." Her dry, melodic voice sent a fresh wave of admiration through him. "Still, thank you for rescuing us, my good sir. It seems my counterpart has too much time on his hands and not nearly enough common sense."

"You're one to talk. And uncommon sense is quite acceptable and far more interesting." The man flashed her a sly smile. "It stirs up the most fascinating meetings." He turned to Shance, his green eyes sparkling with satisfaction. "Ademis at your service. You're welcome."

"I'm welcome? For what?"

"Giving you an excuse to come over here. You will thank me far more later. I also accept small rodents and fresh milk. This lady is—"

"Is very thankful as well. I think the waiter needs you to move this way so he can clean up the mess." She beckoned Shance closer with a fingertip and a look of frank approval mixed with a curious nervousness. He resisted the urge to give his own blue waistcoat and dark gray cravat a quick tweak. "So, have you been enjoying the music?"

"Yes, I have. The musicians are gifted, and the atmosphere is pleasant." For some reason, social niceties felt stale on his tongue. Usually Shance enjoyed the give and take of such conversations, but they felt wasted and trivial on this woman. She was worth far more. "Have you been here long?"

She wrinkled her nose. "Long enough to have attracted the attention of two other men with marriage proposals."

A laugh escaped him, along with a twinge of jealousy. But only a twinge, buried beneath a strong security that this woman was ultimately his. As he was irrevocably hers.

That was absurd. They had only just met. Shance wanted true love, but even he could admit that with humans it did take longer.

He cleared his throat. "Really? Is that part of your Talent, or merely a result of your irresistible allure?"

"Oh, I'm very talented, Shance Windkeeper, but in far more... interesting ways."

She spoke his name easily, and how delightfully it issued from her mouth. Then alarm filtered through the haze of conversation. Shance raised his eyebrows. "Pardon me, but I don't believe I told you my name. Nor have you told me yours."

The woman caught her breath, and Shance barely heard a half-dozen muttered oaths that sounded strangely familiar. She always spoke like that when flustered.

Viorstan, how did he know that?

"Oh, did I forget my name?" She blinked. "Silly me. I must have been distracted by your remarkable appearance. Tell me, where did you get that exceptional waistcoat?"

Did she really think she would outwit him with flirting? Maybe that worked for her before, but not this time. Two could play that game, and he dearly enjoyed playing it with her. It had been too long.

And he shouldn't have been flirting with anyone else over the last ten years.

While a part of him struggled to understand these odd musings, the greater portion of his mind focused on the woman. He leaned forward, daring to trace the edge of her pointed chin. "Tell me, where did you get that exceptional tongue, so capable of lying and yet, I believe, even better when telling the truth?"

"I'm not sure." Her lips parted. "Maybe you should investigate further and tell me."

"Oh Elric, if you two are going to kiss right here, I'm knocking another glass off the table. Disgusting habit, kissing. Unsanitary."

The woman glared at him. "Ademis, no one is forcing you to stay here."

"I would never leave my dear young friend alone to fend for herself. Especially when I believe…" The gentleman pulled out a small bronze device with dials that were frantically whirring and grinding. "…ah yes, the good captain's ship is currently under attack, according to the instruments we planted soon after our arrival in this excessively damp city."

Something in Ademis's serious tone jolted Shance. At the same time, his mind accepted the information as absolute truth, the same way he perceived that the woman's attentions meant far more than typical flirting. "What? Who is it?"

"Sadly, the Lawless still haven't developed technology that combines clipse-mirrors with wireless commers, so we'll need to investigate in person." Ademis flung a wad of bills on the table, some of which looked like squares of blank paper with random drawings on them. "There should be enough payment in there. Maira, dear, this is not the time to be coy. Tell the man the truth."

Maira. He searched his mind for the name. Nothing, and yet the word sang within him like the most haunting music.

"Coy? Says the cat-dragon who wakes me up three different ways out of boredom and then denies them all." She had already eased past Shance and slipped on her coat. That was when Shance realized her slender legs were encased in the tight, short pants and stockings worn by men in the Scepter of Knowledge, and instead of low shoes, her calves were enclosed in boots.

Despite himself, he grinned. Not only because the outfit suited her, just as the black make-up did, but because why in all of Sekastra should someone so incredible bother to fit in? Especially when she had already lost so much.

How did he know that? His stomach turned. This was an unpleasant game.

The two strange individuals were already pressing through the tavern. Shance followed them, grabbing his coat on the way out. "Can you at least tell me what's going on?"

She flashed him a tight smile. "All in good time, my song. Right now, saving our ship is more important."

"*Our* ship?"

"Well, yes. All will be explained, hopefully soon." Maira winked as they exited the tavern. "For now, know that I am Maira Ukerys. Ademis and I are with the Lawless. We were supposed to meet with you tomorrow, but curiosity got the better of us. For many reasons, we are dedicated to ensuring your ship and crew remain intact."

Shance grabbed her arm and pulled her to him. He wouldn't let her slip away that easily. "What reasons besides the Lawless?"

Maira looked up into his face, her eyes wide. Her breath caught as she stared into his eyes. "Ah … that is…"

"Always clever words until your heart gets thrown into the mix, Queen Runt," Ademis scoffed. "Enough of this. She's your wife, Windkeeper. She wants to see you safe and in her bed again."

With that, the odd man made a whistling, clicking sound and signaled an electro-carriage, still sparking lightning from where the top rod connected to the main, boxy section. As it pulled up next to them, an explosion rang out from the direction of the shipyard. His stomach clenched. Not again. His ship wasn't getting blown up again!

Shance stared down at Maira, everything rational in him unable to believe what Ademis had said, while everything in his heart cried out that it was true.

And both parts were quite sure he would need the strangers' help to defend *The Silver Streak*.

CHAPTER FIVE

Maira was certain of two things.

One: Shance Windkeeper looked unchanged and particularly appealing after their ten years apart. Although seeing him unclothed in a more secluded environment would be preferred.

Two: she was going to maim and perhaps kill that god-cursed cat-dragon for revealing her relationship with Shance on the way to rescue his ship and crew. Of all the times! And the rotten beast was pleased with himself! If he'd been in his true scale and fur form, he would have been licking his paw smugly. Currently he was seated next to her as the electro-carriage rattled and squealed along the lightning-track. He persisted in tweaking the buttons on his waistcoat and steadfastly ignoring her glare.

She shoved him with an elbow. <Why, you lice-ridden fool? You knew I wasn't ready.>

<My dear, it isn't always about you. He was ready and quite persistent. You may as well grab him up before he ends up in another woman's bed.>

<Silence! His mind was altered. He didn't remember me.>

Sorrow and anger flashed through her, enough that even the cat-dragon gave her an apologetic look.

Maira stole a glance at her husband, impeccable in the Scepter of Knowledge attire, his face filled with sincere concern and frustration. For all that, he was as charming as usual, making him even more irresistible. She needed her chief mate back. Her Tyrius Stormsong, turned Shance Windkeeper with the passage of time. Always hers.

Maira sighed, turning back to Ademis. <We still don't know what happened to him or how much his mind can take. To presume he was ready just because he showed interest in me was dangerous.>

<You were the one who chose that particular tavern in the first place.>

<Yes, because I wanted to observe him undetected and strategize.>

Ademis raised his eyebrows. <So you needed to strategize his posterior and his chest and his—>

"Oh would you just be quiet, you stubborn reptilian feline!"

Across from them, Shance cleared his throat. "Is there a problem? Other than the usual secrecy and rudeness from shifters speaking to each other when humans are in the area."

Shame filled her, and she met his gaze. "I'm sorry. I forgot."

"I've grown accustomed to it. There are more important things to worry about right now." Fresh pain emanated from him. His blue eyes glinted with worry in the moonlight through the electro-carriage's window. His fingers had already undone the cravat around his neck and loosened his collar. Shortly after, he would unbutton his sleeves and roll them up, revealing strong arms and calloused hands.

Just as Maira remembered from their years of marriage. Within the first year of their marriage, she'd started assisting him, pocketing any loose fasteners he'd discarded. "You aren't wearing any cufflinks, are you?"

He blinked. "What?"

Next to her, Ademis gave a rusty chuckle and a mreow. Maira shoved him again, her face heating. "I'm sorry. My mind jumped ahead to other things."

Shance leaned forward. "Like cufflinks?"

She swallowed. All-Maker help her. She might as well finish the train of thought and watch it derail. "Yes, well, you sometimes wore them with your formal suits. You had a collection of them, at least ten pairs I think, although sometimes you would lose one, and you would get upset—"

"And you would tease me and suggest I wear a mismatched pair and start a new fashion trend." Her chief mate's voice was soft and sure. "Then I would suggest that you wear mismatched clothing to coordinate, and then somehow, we would find the missing piece, come up with a solution, or at least, start laughing."

Maira's breath caught. "You ... you remember?"

"Yes. Although, I don't know how." He frowned and inhaled sharply. More pain and increasing guilt flowed from him. "And right now, my ship is in danger, according to you, and I don't even know you. Why do you care?"

"I'm sorry." She reached over and placed her palm lightly on his knee, sending a trickle of empathic comfort into his body along with a prayer to Bonilus. She didn't dare offer anything more when so much was unknown, no matter how much she longed to help. "This is why I didn't want to speak about this now. It's still confusing for me, and my mind wasn't altered, at least not that I'm aware of. Besides, with our ship under attack, this isn't the time."

Gods, she had said "our" again. But she meant it. She would

be at his side no matter what. Even if he had forgotten everything while she had been imprisoned.

Shance rubbed his forehead, but when he looked up, his mouth was set in a firm line. There was the man she knew. The one who could set his passionate feelings aside for the greater good. The man she still loved.

"You're right. This isn't the time. Yet I still want to know." He set his hand over hers and squeezed lightly. "If you know me at all, you know I want the truth from others. Even if it hurts. And something tells me it will."

Her thoughts scattered into a million possibilities. Could he be trusted with the truth when there was still so much unknown? What if Shance's mind was not his own? Could he still be secretly in contact with the enemy? Would he even remember if he were?

<Even if he does remember, will he still want me?>

Ademis made a clicking sound. <Don't be unnecessarily morbid, child. He came over to your table.>

<After you spilled the glass.>

<He was looking earlier.>

<Yes, but so were many others. I was the only woman in the room with black lips. If he desires me now, will he do so when he remembers the truth?>

<The eve of battle is no time to begin questioning your chief mate's motives.>

Maira snorted. <No matter what you think, cat-dragon, there is no proof to your proclamations other than the confidence you speak them with.>

<That is all they need, my unicorn.>

She sighed. Shance didn't even know that she had a chaste but quite unbreakable bond with the cat-dragon simply because Ademis had decided to adopt her. Then there were other complications with her relationships. Sweet Lady Allandra, that would be disastrous to reveal right now.

But it was her life and her role. Shance would learn soon enough. After all, one of Maira's missions in the Scepter of Knowledge was reclaiming the members of her herd. The herd she had once led with her chief mate at her side, supporting, protecting, and guiding their people.

She needed Shance back.

The electro-carriage slammed to a halt, and the driver frantically pounded on the door. "Out! Out, all of you! This is an evil place."

The driver's fear crashed into her like a wave. Maira quickly put up a mental shield against it, even as her mind snapped into focus. She glanced outside at the shipyard. Nothing stirred in the dark that should have evoked the driver's fear so quickly. A quick drop of her mental shields. The fear writhed in, cold and merciless. A deadly force.

Which could only mean one thing. The fear came from other death unicorns.

She glanced over at Shance. His face was set in hard lines, very much aware of the fear but resisting it. Their soul bond had grown thin from years of separation. He would be little help to her in this state. Moreover, he would be vulnerable.

"I feel an extraordinary amount of fear," he said. "Why do I sense that you know why?"

"There are other unicorns outside, manipulating emotions." Maira pursed her lips and studied him intently. "I don't suppose you'd consider staying behind? Or fleeing to another part of the city?"

"Never."

His blue eyes were ardent and focused, in the same open, handsome face that had captivated her from the moment she'd seen him. Even if she hadn't dared to admit it at the time.

Maira exchanged a look with Ademis, who was already pulling out a pistol and a knife from his coat. He gave her a wink as he opened the door. <Enjoy the disgusting mouth ritual.>

<Go choke on a fish.>

The cat-dragon exited the electro-carriage, then the driver poked his head in and scowled at them, his floppy hat drawn low over a prominent nose. "You have one minute before I'm outta here."

She turned to Shance. "Do you trust me?"

"Yes. I don't know why, but I do."

"Fair enough." Maira sighed. "I'm sorry, but I need to jog your memory sooner than is ideal." She leaned forward, taking his hands in hers. "I'm all for pleasant methods of doing so. Including a kiss."

He hesitated, studying her. Trust, guilt, and insecurity radiated from him in equal measures. Her gut twisted, and she looked away. Asking him was a bad idea. It was too soon, and maybe he didn't even want to. After all, she was a death unicorn, not a human. Maybe the connection from their first meeting decades earlier had vanished.

"It's all right. I can just—"

Then Shance's hand gently cupped her face. "I've spent the last ten years kissing near-strangers. The least I can do is kiss my wife, even if I need more explanation from her later."

Her lips parted in shock. Then his lips were on hers, pressing and searching, instinctively offering her all the magic he had. She wrapped her hands around his neck and pulled him closer. Giving him her own magic in return, trying desperately to heal their bond so Shance could face the emotional attack outside.

Abruptly, he pulled away and reached for a weapon in his coat. She could sense the clash of desire, confusion, and anger within him as he fought to process everything he didn't remember and was trying to understand. "That was—is that enough? My ship is under attack. We need to go now."

"Our ship," Maira reminded him. She would remind him, every time, that he wasn't alone. That she would embrace and care about everything he did. That she wouldn't abandon him, no matter what had happened to him or what decisions he had made. The same as Shance had done for her so many years ago. "Yes, I should be fine now. Stay close. Don't tell the dragons yet. This is unicorn business first. The dragons can be told later. Lirome is watching over them now in case they become a target."

"Understood."

Something about the edge in his voice said he truly did understand, even if he wasn't aware of his place in all of this. That would have to do. Before she could say another word, Shance grabbed the door handle and leaped out, the night winds swirling around him. Always so willing to run into danger, even if it could lead to his death.

Maira's heart tightened, and she shoved aside her feelings. They were liabilities right now. This was war. It didn't matter if Shance remembered her fully. She needed a fighter, and the Lawless needed them both, as did their people.

The chill of terror pouring from *The Silver Streak* enveloped her like a thick, poisonous cloud. The thought of the crew members fighting and dying under attack from rogue death unicorns grieved her heart and tightened her resolve into iron.

Maira exited the carriage, fists clenched.

She would remind these careless brutes who was their queen.

CHAPTER SIX

All of this was happening too fast.

Shance's mind spun, trying understand what Maira had told him, while staying alert for the death unicorns attacking his ship. For they were death unicorns, he was certain of that. Maira had avoided the adjective, cautious about his state of mind. But her own face paint gave her away. As their leader, she always wore the memorial of her people's destruction.

How he was certain of these matters was another mystery. It was as foreign as Maira's name had been, yet as familiar as her smile, the taste of her mouth on his.

The kiss was nothing like the intensity of a first time. No, it was a slow burn, practiced and easy, yet filled with complexity. Through it, he recognized her desperation, her willingness to give him everything, and her hesitancy over his reaction, all of it accompanied with the flavor of fresh dew he recognized as a trickle of her magic.

Magic? Magic wasn't real. His mind fought back. Only people from Elotrin said otherwise. Sekastrans were far more advanced. They recognized that Talents were simply innate abilities that no one understood yet, and thought the same of shifter races as a whole.

He scowled into the night. *Such a stupid idea.* Magic could still be called magic even when it was an energy force. Only fools assumed they would understand everything and master it. Fools like the gods of Elotrin he and Maira had destroyed so long ago. He remembered the storm raging around them, ripping apart the great city of Glenalis. A storm they had created, fulfilling Maira's vision from the Skies Above, received in a Four Corners temple.

Wait, I destroyed gods? I did it in honor of the Four Corners religion? What the flame-cursed depths of Ucurit?

Shock washed over Shance, pushing aside the fear he still dimly felt as they ran toward the shipyard. His temples throbbed, and tension turned his shoulders into stone. Whatever these knowings, these memories were, sorting through them was not a priority at the moment. He pushed the onslaught of confusion into a small part of his mind. Whatever else he was, or had been, he was a soldier. A captain.

His ship was in danger. That was his priority.

He ran through the dockyard, keeping his eyes focused upward. The Scepter of Knowledge used an outdoor suspension dock system located on the left side of the city. Airships landed on platforms on either side of large ten-story towers. *The Silver Streak* was tethered and dry-docked on the top platform of one tower, almost impossible to see through the darkness and misty haze that filled the Scepter of Knowledge.

Except tonight, when it was on fire.

Fear and anger shook his hands. The elevators within the tower wouldn't be fast enough. The winds carried more news down to him. Shots rang out, along with the clash of steel, punctuated by screams. He clenched his teeth and came to a stop.

"Fiarston! Can no one leave my ship alone?"

"Our ship." Maira's response was automatic as she paused next to him. He had to hand it to her. She certainly was determined to stick with her story. He couldn't disbelieve her, even though he could barely process everything. "Can you get all three of us up there?"

Shance raised his eyebrows. "We're just going to march in on a firefight and see what happens?"

"Exactly." She grinned dangerously. "You'd be surprised how effective that can be. Especially since they won't expect us together."

"Should that mean something?" His pulse raced, and winds stirred around him. "Why should they be scared of me?"

On the other side of Maira, Ademis rolled his eyes. "You're the incredibly powerful chief mate of the death unicorn queen. The only one she owns as her husband. If those ingrates on board have any sense, they'll flee before they get their tails handed to them."

"The only one she—" Shance groaned. "No, nothing more right now. Running in and shooting at everything it is."

"About time." Ademis's lips twitched. "Try not to ruffle my fur."

Maira smacked him, saving Shance the hassle. "Oh, please do ruffle his fur. It's good for him."

"As my queen requests." The words flew out before he could stop them. Either the lovely death unicorn was telling the truth, or she had a hidden Talent for bespelling people's minds. Everything in Shance pointed to the first option. "Hold on."

He summoned powerful gusts of wind into his hands, positioning them precisely and effortlessly around himself, Maira, and Ademis. Usually, it took a great deal of focus to move others, but his winds seemed to know their shapes and curled around them securely. Shance breathed out slowly and raised his hands as they flew up and over the ship.

Immediately bullets and knives rushed toward them. He ducked as a short blade whizzed past his ear, and nearby, Maira gasped and pressed a hand to her shoulder. It came away red with blood. Anger surged through Shance, and he threw a blast of wind at the ship below, clearing a path between friend and foe before settling the three of them on a far corner of the airship.

"About time, Captain!" He turned to see Commander Tegan at his shoulder, her eyes wild and her fingers clutching a short sword and a pistol. A few strands of ashen hair had escaped from her tight bun. "Can't hardly see anything through the smoke."

"The smoke?"

She coughed. "Yeah, can't you taste it? Burns your lungs."

He stared around. There was no smoke, only writhing shadows. "Tegan, explain."

"The blasted green smoke, taking away everyone's Talents and stealing our strength. And their numbers! There are too many of them."

Too many?

Even with the dim lights of the few lanterns and the glow of fire on his prized ship, he could only see six shadowy figures with red eyes and small silver horns poking out from their foreheads. Six against his short-staffed crew of fifty. Even with the handful who were enjoying a night of furlough, there was no reason for the bodies strewn about the deck, the people trapped in corners, quaking with fear.

Dread shot through Shance, and he turned to Maira for an explanation. Her blood red eyes were filled with fury and grief, her mouth set in a firm line. Suddenly he knew, through another flash of memory, exactly what was happening.

He grabbed Tegan's shoulders. "There is no green smoke. There are only six attackers and a lot of wounded or frightened crew."

"That's impossible! I've seen—I've felt—" She gave another hacking cough. "It's real, Captain."

"An illusion."

Her gray eyes flared with anger. "I know illusions well, Captain. This isn't one of them."

No. It was far more deadly. It was an attack of soul magic, harnessing and twisting the mind to make the body perceive and react to invisible threats—and in doing so, making those threats real, real enough to kill. Shance didn't expect Tegan to understand that. Doldrums, *he* didn't really understand it!

But their conversation was enough of a distraction for Maira to creep up behind Tegan. In her bewilderment, the commander only saw Shance. The death unicorn woman placed her hand on the back of the commander's head and sent a jolt of magic through her veins. Claiming magic, by a unicorn leader into their herd, just enough to allow Maira access to Tegan's soul. Claiming magic wasn't done without express consent. But times were desperate, and Tegan was a good soldier. They needed her sober-minded and focused to help stop the attack, which meant Maira needed to strip the invasive soul magic from her quickly.

His first officer groaned and swayed for a moment, then quickly found her footing. She shook her head. "What in the name of—" Her eyes focused. "Captain, what just happened? Where is the smoke?"

"Gone. An illusion."

"It wasn't—"

"Not now, Tegan." Shance put iron into his voice. "Where is Sergeant Fitch?"

"Below deck. Once I saw the effects of the smoke—or whatever the doldrums is going on out here—I ordered all remaining personnel to stay below deck and out of sight." She glanced at the flames eating away at the main mast and surrounding deck, her mind following his, remembering Fitch's water Talent. "I'll see about getting him on that, sir."

"As long as you can keep him below deck."

Tegan nodded. "I'll figure out something." Her gaze shifted between him, Maira, and her ever-present shadow, Ademis. "With all due respect, Captain, you have a flaming lot of explaining to do when this is over. As you have time. Sir."

"Noted, Commander."

She flipped a quick salute and ran below deck. Good woman, Tegan. Never would have guessed she had recently been shooting at attackers who weren't real—but could have hurt her all the same, because she had believed they could. Shance did owe her an explanation, right after he figured out what the doldrums was going on with this attack. There was no time for that now. There was only instinct, and his told him that, somehow, Maira and Ademis were needed to save his crew.

How far they had fallen. He spotted some crew members hunched behind storage crates while others were locked in battle with the black-clad death unicorns. Shance's stomach knotted. The rest skulked beneath the ship, rendered helpless by the soul magic fear attacks.

The attackers would pay.

Maira touched his arm, He could feel her matching anger and with it, worry. Not just for his crew but for the death unicorns as well. <We clear them out. No killing except if it is absolutely necessary. They are not all that they seem. They are misled.>

She could mindspeak to him now? The thought was both alarming and comforting. Shance had no time for either emotion. Once more he forced the realizations into a corner of his mind.

"I make no promises."

He summoned a gale of wind and aimed it at the shadowy invaders, invoking a prayer to whatever gods existed that his remaining crew would be smart enough to take cover. Ally and foe alike stumbled, although the death unicorns found their feet quickly while the crew stayed on the ground.

Relief filled him. Good. His crew knew what he was about to do.

Shance aimed his wind currents. Another round of targeted gusts, as sharp and piercing as spears, shot through the air and slammed two of the attackers to the ground, where they lay motionless. Two others managed to dodge them, one halting it with a blast of wind of his own. Then they slipped into the shadows. Shance frowned. Another wind Talent? The gift was rare.

Where had the attackers gone?

Shots rang out from behind him, along with a hissing, spitting sound and a small flash of heat. He knew it was Maira and Ademis, dealing with the remaining two assailants. Part of him wanted to turn and help them, but there was no time. That unshakeable gut instinct told him they were used to working together, that the supposed cat-dragon would give every last part of himself to protect Maira. And Shance as well, through association, and because his death would upset Maira.

How courteous of the fellow.

Suddenly wind rushed at him, shaking the still-fiery mast of his ship. Ah, there were the attackers. He blocked the gust with one of his own, created a wall of wind to serve as a force-field, and drew a pistol and a knife. The death unicorns stepped back, although the wind-Talented one persisted in throwing blast after blast. Foolish. Talents exerted energy. Granted, Shance's never took all that much out of him, but he was a Windkeeper. That made him unique.

No. That isn't what makes you unique.

He shoved away the thought.

"You won't last, human," one of them yelled. "You and everything you're doing is an abomination. We won't let you stop the rightful rule of our queen."

Shance scoffed. "Your queen? The rightful death unicorn queen is behind me, taking down the last of you."

"She's an imposter!" the other yelled, firing his weapon. Shance ducked and took refuge behind a stack of supply barrels. "The old queen has been dead for ten years. She was weak, pandering to both dragons and humans. The new queen is powerful and clever, and she will restore our fortunes."

Maira an imposter? Ridiculous. "Well, you hate me, and you hate my wife. You're attacking my airship and my crew. My herd. You haven't given me any good reason to join you." Shance focused his mind, forcing the wind away from the other attacker and into his grasp, storing it and molding it. It wasn't hard. The death unicorn might be wind Talented, but he had no idea how to use it well. "That means you've gotta go."

"I'd like to see you try—"

Shance dropped his weapons and clapped his hands together. The wind he'd collected whipped out, ensnaring his two assailants in a solid wall of air that smashed them into the ground. He stretched his palm out flat, using it to hold them there. All he had to do was press down a little harder and their lives would be over. Despite the destruction to his ship and crew, his heart sank. Fighting in battle was one thing. Killing after capture was closer to murder. He didn't do that.

However, he wouldn't release the pressure. A little pressure made some people talk, and these two had been chatty enough already. Maybe they would let useful information slip out.

He stepped around other prone bodies, praying that his crew was only unconscious and not dead. Upon reaching the pinned attackers, shock froze his heart. One was Cadence Folham, the Lawless agent who had been their strongest supporter in the forum debates. Shance recognized him from the dossier, but up close, there was something even more deeply familiar about his violet eyes and dusky skin.

Violet eyes were rare among death unicorns, Shance was certain. That made Cadence some kind of family to Maira. A nephew? Something about him seemed closer than that.

Also, why had no one in the Lawless told them Cadence Folham was a death unicorn? Why hadn't the Lawless revealed any of this information? Did they know Shance had a wife? Why keep that from him? All he had searched for these past ten years was that special woman—the woman who was now allying with him.

The pile of confusing thoughts on his mind was growing too large for its corner. Still, Shance managed to direct his attention to the other attacker, who fought his bonds with shudders of wind. Vivid blue eyes. Black hair. Olive skin, but a jaw that was identical to the one Shance saw in the mirror while shaving. The silvery horn that emerged from his forehead was two inches shorter than Cadence's. Barely a stub.

As if he wasn't a full-blooded death unicorn at all.

Shance's resolve wavered, and with it, his control over the wind. The black-haired man punched out with rapid blasts of wind until he was free. He lifted himself into the air and flashed Shance a cocky grin that was all too familiar. "Knew you'd crack eventually. Lady Lurien said you were as weak as Mother. At least she had the decency to die instead of abandoning us like you did."

"Abandoning you?" Now Cadence was almost free. Damn it! Shance slammed the wind down in place, knocking the guy out. "Who are you?"

"You're as faithless as everyone said. I can't believe half my blood is yours." The guy—whom Shance now saw as a youth, no older than eighteen—sneered. "Lurien is a fool for wanting you."

"Brennar!" Maira's voice called from behind him, ringing with authority and desperation. "You don't have to do this!"

The young man's mouth dropped open, and his eyes widened. "Mother? You can't be ... she said you were dead."

"She lied." The death unicorn queen stepped closer to Brennar, her face contorted in a mixture of love and fierce determination. "She's lied about everything. Come here and see the truth!"

Agony rippled across Brennar's face. "No. No, she can't lie! You're not real. This is a trick!" A hideous smirk covered his face. "And my lady plays far better tricks, all over this Scepter. You've already lost."

Shance reached out with a blast of wind, hoping to slap the young man to the ground, but he was too late. Brennar had flown off into the night on a swift air current leaving Shance alone with his estranged wife and a gaping hole in his heart.

"Well, looks like he turned into an ass." Ademis clapped Shance on the shoulder. "Chip off the old block, I'd say."

Shance gave a raw chuckle. "Takes one to know one."

"I liked you better before you started remembering things."

"Tyrius." Maira's voice was a plea. Somehow, Shance knew she meant him. Using his old name, the one that caught his attention first, even though he had abandoned it decades earlier. He turned and saw her kneeling by Cadence's side. "Remove the wind shackles. He's hurt." She turned to Ademis. "Go to Lirome. I can't spare the magic to contact him from this distance and heal all of these other hurting people."

Her anguish flowed through him, through the soul bond that was still barely in place. There was no guile, no agenda. Only a deep passion to see every single person restored.

The cat-dragon closed his hands over hers, his expression intense. "You can't heal everyone here regardless, you foolish girl. You'll collapse."

"I know. But between all of us, we can try to save as many as possible. Get Lirome."

He nudged her forehead with his. "Orders, orders. One would think you owned me."

At those words, the cat-dragon shifted into his scale form—or was it fur? No, it was both. He had the orange-furred body of a cat, golden speckles, dragon wings, and a dragon tail. And he flew off into the night with all speed.

Maira turned to Shance and swallowed hard. "You still know healing methods, yes?"

He swallowed. "Only as a field medic."

She nodded, her expression distant, already focused on the emotions of the wounded. "You should know more, but that's something. Please, we don't have much time."

Shance knelt beside her. "As you wish."

In that moment, regardless of the secrets she held and the memories he had yet to unlock, Shance fell hopelessly in love with the death unicorn who grieved over the pains of so many.

If only he could make sense of everything that had happened that night.

Chapter Seven

All Lirome wanted was a good nap. Not the short snatches of rest grabbed here and there as he worked, but a long, restful slumber. One where he would not be involved in one of his sister's ever-present schemes.

He snorted softly as he followed the dragon pair through the dark, narrow streets, the mist illuminated by flickering streetlights. By all accounts, Prince Nightstalker and Princess Ironfire appeared to be a typical couple out for a stroll in the quiet library district. They didn't speak aloud, though he could sense the hum of their private mindspeak and the flow of emotions between them.

The absence of bodyguards was curious, considering Ironfire and Nightstalker were heirs to the dragon throne. Lirome shrugged. Ultimately, what dragons did was their business. At least it made for a quiet evening of stalking them, keeping his empathic disinterest field active so no one paid him any mind, and he could watch out for others.

Eventually, he would reveal himself. When he met with them at the safe house, he would need to be more open. For now, Lirome savored the anonymity. It was lonely, but a familiar loneliness. One he had grown used to over the decades, especially with the absence of his sister. Besides, additional time to observe the two dragons would be useful.

The sound of heavy wings fluttering through the air caught his attention, and he instinctively held out his arms to catch Ademis. The cat-dragon settled in and immediately dug in his claws into Lirome's arms, emphasizing the urgency radiating from him.

Lirome winced. Ademis was not known for his subtlety. <Is there something you want to share with me?>

<Maira needs you. Now. The airship got attacked by death unicorns.>

Concern flared through him, although not overmuch. If Maira had truly been in danger, Lirome would have felt it. He maintained his pace on the dragons.

Ademis dug his claws in deeper. <Did you not hear me? Maira needs you. All those humans need to be patched up. She's resorted to using Shance, and he doesn't even remember who he is!>

Lirome clenched his jaw against the pain radiating from the shallow cuts. <Remove your claws, cat-dragon, or I will break them.>

<So much for the Rule of Harming.>

The beast dared to cite one of his most cherished rules? As if Lirome didn't know that for every harm inflicted, an equal portion must be healed. As if he wasn't still paying for the lives he'd taken for decades as his sister's personal assassin. Taking care of the details when she couldn't even ask. <Oh, I will repair your claws. At my own convenience. Perhaps I shall make them exceedingly blunt, but the Rule of Harming will be kept.>

<You always were a terrible boy.>

<I'm over eighty years old. When will you stop calling me "boy?">

Ademis fluffed his back fur. <When you start respecting your

elders. Now. Maira.>

Lirome stifled a sigh. The cat-dragon had pledged his loyalty to both him and Maira when they were children, but ultimately his devotion lay first with the death unicorn queen. Never mind the countless times Lirome had seen to his injuries. If Maira needed something, the rest of the world had better listen.

Even when there were other matters to worry about, such as the origin of these rogue death unicorns. He glared at the opposite wall. He should have been tracking them. Should have stopped them. But finding Maira had been paramount. Besides, her mate regents minded the death unicorn sanctuary, the little-known area dubbed the Lost Refuge, on the northeast plains near the Velit River. Even if the death unicorn scouts had known to watch for rogues, they never would have thought to venture as far west as the Scepter of Knowledge. Minding such things had been one of his unofficial duties, until Maira had taken precedence. It had been an impossible choice.

As usual, he would live with the consequences.

<Lirome?>

He extracted Ademis's piercing claws from his shirt and flesh. <In a moment. She has Shance to help her. These dragons are also key figures. The rogue death unicorns have already attacked two major leaders. It is a logical possibility that they will attack the dragons next.>

<Not my fault.> Ademis hissed, the sound low and sibilant in the air. Gods, could the cat-dragon not behave for a moment?

Lirome pressed the cat-dragon's mouth shut. <I still have darts tipped with tranquilizer. Either you leave, or I test one on you.>

The cat-dragon grumbled, waves of reluctance and guilt emanating from him. Reluctance because if he returned he would be put to work assisting with the healing, and he never enjoyed that. But if he delayed, Maira would be grieved.

<Well then, if these two dragons must be watched, I will assist you. As you said, she has Windkeeper and is in no more danger.>

<Then carry your own weight.>

Lirome tossed Ademis into the air in the opposite direction of the dragons, timing it with the rattling of an electro-carriage to mask the sound.

Lirome pondered Ademis's warnings about the rogue death unicorns. He knew Nightstalker and Ironfire were capable fighters, but they were in a new city, on unfamiliar territory. Thanks to Maira's wishes for privacy, neither dragon had been told the truth about death unicorns, much less rogues with an unknown endgame. Lirome had planned to reveal some information at their meeting that night to discuss Ironfire's condition.

Ironfire. His supposed soul-friend. Yes, that was the word for it. *How* was another matter. He inhaled slowly, imperceptibly, and allowed any concern over her to dissipate. The worry had no right to exist until he allowed it to.

Lirome reached for one of the pistols at his waist. He spread out his empathic soul senses. He had only been seeking human or dragon foes, not death unicorns, but they shouldn't be able to hide from him.

If they could, everyone was in terrible danger.

He crept closer to the dragons, intensifying his disinterest field. Even so, the female dragon glanced around, frowning, her delicate brows raised. Confusion emanating from her soul. Lirome stepped into the shadows as her gaze fell on him, amber eyes intent. She didn't appear nearly the predator her embermate was, her innocent face and quick smile in stark contrast to the bronze skin and angular features typical of the royal lineage of her partner. No, Ironfire appeared as guileless as death unicorns in the old days, before they were hunted ceaselessly. Before they were forced to turn to violence.

Yet, she sensed him. Felt him. She just didn't know it yet.

Lirome's heart beat faster. Should he reveal himself now? They were on the same side. At the same time, his people prided themselves on secrecy. Secrecy kept them alive. And these dragons were already on edge. He needed to be cautious.

Her unnerving stare seemed to look inside his soul with the curiosity of an explorer and the focus of a hunter. It awoke a younger part of him that had long been buried underneath years of weight and death.

Impossi—Lirome blocked the word. It clearly didn't mean what he thought it did. They could deal with the soul connection later.

At last, Ironfire turned back to her mate. Their private link hummed. Then both turned and began walking faster toward the safe house.

Relief filled Lirome. Yes, the dragons should depart. Quickly. All the more reason for Lirome to step out of the shadows and urge them on. The time for secrecy was past.

A shudder passed over him. Fear, deep and ferocious and carnal. The sort that reminded Lirome his people had been prey before they became predators. The knowledge gripped him like a physical force, sliding over his skin in shivers.

He shrugged it off, reaching into the parts of him that didn't come from natural bloodlines. The parts that came from a choice to survive and do the work no one else wanted.

Ahead of him, the dragons paused. They whirled around toward him, their eyes turned slit-pupiled. Reddish-green scales showed on Ironfire's face while cobalt ones mottled Nightstalker's. They yanked off their gloves and hats as flames began to dance on their scaled palms and claws emerged from their fingertips.

But Lirome knew that for all their fighting skill they would be helpless against the slithering panic surrounding them. Above him, Ademis yowled. <At all sides, boy! I couldn't sense them either—these death unicorns are strong!>

<They must be, if I can't sense them.> Anger ground through Lirome. <Show me.>

The cat-dragon's senses were unique, being attuned to death unicorn soul empathy but remaining outside of it. <Oh, you want my help?>

"Ademis, now!"

The words emerged from his mouth before he could think better of it. The dragons' expressions turned suspicious and hostile. Especially Nightstalker's.

<Explain yourself> he said, his mental voice resonant and commanding. <What are you doing to us?>

<It isn't me. I'm here to help.> Lirome stepped out of the shadows and walked toward the dragons, projecting as much sincerity as he could. He sensed the death unicorns circling the alleyway, wreathed in mist and shadow. Every hair raised on the back of his neck as they moved closer.

The male dragon stepped in front of his embermate, his dark blue eyes sharp. <Why should we trust you?>

The fear beat down heavily on his shoulders, threatening to shake his teeth. There must be at least eight death unicorns for them to project a terror field of this magnitude. That meant only one thing.

They were there to kill.

Lirome fisted his hands and pushed against the fear, creating a small bubble of free space around himself and the two dragons. The cat-dragon would have to fend for himself. From his absence in Lirome's mind, he knew Ademis had made himself scarce. If there was one thing the cat-dragon knew how to do, it was protect himself.

Finally, he focused on the dragons. Both of them were in battle stances, although not quite as tense as they had been earlier. Ironfire studied him. <Where did you come from?>

<You might have seen me around.> His mouth quirked, despite the situation.

<You were spying in the shadows? Why?>

Some odd, gut instinct provoked him to ask, <Why, don't you?>

Her eyes sparked. <I asked first.>

The urge to retort, to discuss, stirred within him. Why? How would it be useful? Lirome shook his head. <Right now, there are more important matters. We are surrounded by a terror field projected by rogue death unicorns.>

Nightstalker's eyes narrowed. <Death unicorns? You neglected to mention the "death" part earlier in the week.>

<An intentional omission. One I regret now.> Lirome breathed in quickly and pushed ahead before they could ask further questions. <Unicorns are pacifists. Soul empaths. Healers. When threatened with annihilation, we weaponized ourselves to survive, with strict rules. We became death to live. But these death unicorns are defying our laws. They've already attacked my sister and her chief mate. It seems they are targeting you both next.>

Nightstalker scoffed. <Why should we believe you?>

Ironfire stepped forward to stand next to her embermate. <Because he's telling the truth.>

<How do you know?> He glanced at her.

<You said you trusted me. Trust me now.> Ironfire fixed Lirome with another stare. <Soul-friend. Yes?>

He nodded with a grunt. His mind and soul throbbed from holding back the onslaught of fear. Lirome was strong, but there were eight death unicorns closing in on their position. <Your highness, we need to get you two to the safe house. It's a block away. If you walk with me, I can get you both inside.>

Ironfire frowned. <And what about you?>

<I'll survive.> The bubble deflated another inch. <My sister is a healer. Don't worry about me.>

Nightstalker took his mate's hand, his expression guarded. <Tell us what to do.>

<Follow me.>

Lirome walked ahead of the dragons, forcing his protective field to hold firm as they moved toward the safe house entrance. Every movement caused him painful, heart-wrenching shakes that he did his best to hide. Perhaps this was the All-Maker's way of ensuring that he paid for the promised vengeance toward Ademis.

He dismissed the thought. Bonilus was never cruel. Lirome had made a choice to sacrifice his own needs for the whole, and he would bear the agony without further complaint. It was his duty.

Lirome froze as they turned the corner. Before them stood four death unicorns, two in skin form and two in hoof form, their silvery horns slick with black poison. Fear hit his protective field like a blow to his head. He staggered back into Nightstalker. The dragon stepped away.

<They're behind us, too,> Ironfire muttered, a breath of green smoke escaping her. <Another four.>

<Fewmets,> answered Nightstalker. <Your next idea, Ukerys?>

Lirome shook his head, trying to clear the throbbing that assaulted his entire body. Blood leached out from beneath his black fingernails and from the corners of his eyes. <We attack them, and

I'll extend the field as long as I can. As soon as you get a chance, the two of you run for the door."

<A foolish idea.> Ademis's strained mental voice belied his cocky words. <Unless I distract them as well and break up that damn field.>

Ironfire gasped in surprise. <Who are you?>

<An incredibly generous creature.>

Lirome rolled his eyes and swiped away the blood. <Are you serious, cat-dragon? Lives are at stake.>

<You and Maira are healers. Lives are always at stake. But I will do my part, as much as I'm able. At least one should make it to safety.>

"No. Both." Lirome said aloud. "They're embermates. They must both survive."

The rogue death unicorns stood, silently mocking them even as they poured all their power into the terror field. At least he was making them work hard.

<Both? That's a tall order. Five rodents and free rein to sleep on your dissecting table.>

<Done.> Lirome turned to Nightstalker. <Get ready to fight, and then run as soon as the moment arises.>

The dragon's eyes glinted. <Thank you.>

<All in a night's work.> Lirome smiled faintly.

As they stared at each other, a moment of understanding showed between him and the far younger dragon. Under less dangerous circumstances, they could be friends.

If they survived.

Nightstalker and Ironfire exchanged an intense look, then turned and nodded. <Notify the cat-dragon.>

<Already on it.>

With an ear-splitting screech, the cat-dragon dropped onto one of the death unicorns, shredding the beast's back with his claws. Then he leapt onto the face of a unicorn in skin form, breathing tiny spurts of flames into its eyes. Before either could react, he flew toward a third.

The blood-seeping tension left Lirome's shoulders as the terror field abated from literally heart-stopping to merely pulse-pounding. "Go!"

The dragons sprang into action, their movements deft and swift. True weapons of war, they ripped through the death unicorns with flames and claws. One beast went down on its knees, entrails oozing from its gut, its horn broken off and held in Nightstalker's grasp. Another swung at Ironfire with a knife, only to be flung into a wall with bone-shattering strength.

A horrific whinny filled the air from another death unicorn. <Traitor! You and Maira Ukerys are traitors to your own kind by siding with dragons!>

Lirome whirled around, facing his accuser, another death unicorn in skin form. "You are the traitor. The dragons seek to restore justice."

"There is no justice. Only vengeance and restitution by taking what's ours and protecting our own!"

The death unicorn's dark eyes flashed blood red, and he began shifting. Lirome moved faster, grabbing his foe's head and forcing two poisoned-filled darts into his thigh. He went down with a crash.

Someone leaped on Lirome from behind, their arms locked around his throat, shutting off his windpipe. Lirome stuttered a breath, then reached into that quiet, cold place inside him. Wolf claws emerged from his fingertips, and he sliced the arms with precision. The other death unicorn screamed, and blood spurted from his wounds as his hold loosened. Lirome whirled around and slashed at the death unicorn's throat. He gurgled, then fell silent.

Lirome sheathed the claws.

A deafening silence within his soul. Another life gone.

Another life he would have to save in the future.

A strange satisfaction filled him, one Lirome would never admit to the others in the herd. Causing harm and suffering was sometimes necessary, but it was never something delight in. Another reason it was easier to stand alone.

The death unicorns might have weaponized themselves, but Lirome? He'd gone further. Perhaps too far. All-Maker forgive him. It had always been in protection of others.

He wiped off his bloody hands on his dark tunic, then ran back toward the others. "Get in the safe house!"

But the dragons stood frozen in place by some unseen force. Lirome pushed between them and beheld a nightmare. A woman with icy pale skin and violent red hair held out her hands in front of her. Shadows curled around her body and spun from her palms, spewing fresh fear.

"Not so fast. We've just become acquainted." Her voice was polished silk over barbed wire. "I've always wanted to test my powers on dragons who weren't in cages."

Lirome summoned enough of his strength to push out a block barely large enough for the three of them, his body shaking from the effort.

<Can you get us out of here?> Zephryn's mental voice was strained. <Can you force her back?>

Lirome looked around for Ademis. The cat-dragon was nowhere to be seen. He had more courage than he let on, so like as not, he was wounded.

Leaving only Lirome. The fate of dragon leadership was in his hands. With the turmoil in his body, it would take everything he had.

So be it. If the All-Maker dictated, Lirome would die making sure those who had the power to effect change lived on. Perhaps saving these two would even out the many he had killed over the decades. At least he would rest among the other followers who had gone before.

<I will give you everything I have. On my mark, run for it.> He took a deep breath, steeling himself for a fight to the end. Maira had her husband back. There was no further need for him.

<Wait.> Nightstalker grabbed his arm. Lirome looked up. The dragon prince's face was shadowed. <You said you were the best physician alive.>

<Some say. But there will always be more doctors.>

Nightstalker's grip tightened. <You know how to heal those who have been experimented on?>

<That is a specialty of mine.> And one of the many reasons Lirome had traveled to the Scepter of Knowledge. A pity. Someone else would have to take up his duties. Someone else would have to give those unfortunates the kindness they deserved as living creatures with souls, created by Bonilus, the All-Maker.

<Are you able treat anyone? Human or shifter alike?>

<Yes. Especially in conjunction with my sister.> Why was the crown prince asking these questions? Lirome paused. <Tell her I'll be waiting for her in the Skies Above. And that yes, I did hide her favorite toy from her when we were children.>

<Unnecessary. You will see her again in this life.> The dragon shuddered under another onslaught of agonizing fear.

The red-haired woman smirked. "Such fun, thinking you can escape. Please, continue to do so. Your resistance only makes your fate sweeter."

On Lirome's other side, Ironfire gasped, her eyes widening. She glanced around, as if at unseen foes. Already locked in the terrors, her friendly face crumbled into horror.

Lirome shoved Nightstalker. <Go, your highness!>

The dragon's face was implacable stone. <Promise me you'll care for her.>

<You can't mean to—>

<Promise me!>

<I will do everything in my power unto my death. Which will be soon, because you both must be alive in order to survive! Your heartflames are bound!>

Nightstalker's eyes gleamed with what Lirome feared was delirium. Fear assaults did that. <If that were true, why would her uncle say otherwise? Why would he plan to have her bond broken so she could be mated to someone else?>

Lirome shook his head. He fought to keep his mind focused, energy nearly spent. <Because he's a mad scientist? They exist, you know.>

<Are you as smart as he is?>

<Smarter. Intelligence is my Talent.>

<Could she survive?>

His mind raced with the unwanted questions, compelled to solve the problem despite the dire situation. Damn his Talented intellect! <Theoretically, provided a number of factors were met and the timing was right, but this isn't some far-fetched science experiment! I don't want to see you both killed!>

<And I promised Kesia that I would keep her safe and get her

answers.> The dragon smiled grimly. <Farewell, Lirome.>

Before Lirome could reply, wings burst from Nightstalker's back. With an inhuman roar, he lunged at the red-haired woman, flames pouring from his throat and hands. The woman shrieked and sent more of the deadly smoke toward Nightstalker, consuming him in a cloud of shadow.

Lirome's jaw dropped. What was the dragon doing?

Then instinct took over. He had made a promise. Turning toward Ironfire, he scooped her up in his arms. She screamed and clawed at the empty air, her eyes seeking unseen foes. Such a strong reaction could only happen from someone who had already beheld far too many terrors.

"Rest," he shushed. Lirome surrounded her in a layer of protective soul magic, soothing the fears.

She quieted. Lirome gave one final look over his shoulder. Praying against all reason that the dragon prince had somehow survived. Stranger things had happened.

Through the smoke, he could just see the bloodied, gouged body of Nightstalker. Continuing to fight, even as his lifeblood flowed away.

Lirome's heart clenched, aching with the desire to try to save Nightstalker.

Yet he had made a promise.

Down the safe house stairs through protective doorways that no enemy death unicorn could get through. Down and away from the terror fields.

At last, they reached the medical room. Lirome laid Ironfire on one of the beds, smoothing her hair away from her sweat-soaked face. She would be dead soon. Dragons could not survive apart from their embermates.

What had Nightstalker been thinking, trusting in the theoreticals from Lirome's mind? Especially during a horrific fight.

A heart-breaking groan erupted from Ironfire, snapping him back into focus.

He could fret later. Right now, he had a patient.

Lirome pressed his palm over her upper chest, seeking out her heartflame, hoping to find a remnant before it snuffed out entirely as her other half slipped from this world. If the gods were gracious, he could attempt a connection with her that only the strongest healers could make, a connection that could keep Ironfire alive as her embermate had wished.

They had made some kind of soul-friend connection, however latent. That had to count for something.

He reached deeply into her soul, into the blazing heartflame that contained all that Ironfire was.

To his surprise, her flame was clear and strong. He blinked. Could Nightstalker be alive after all?

Ironfire arched up, coughing out streams of green smoke. One hand closed over his, pressing it harder onto her chest. Emotions consumed him as thoroughly as the green smoke. Fury. A bone-deep desire for vengeance. Paralyzing grief.

Need, shaped into an offering, as quiet and plaintive as the anger was vicious.

Lirome reached further inward, covering her gaping soul wounds with compassion and sorrow and matching rage at those who attacked them. Those who dared to harm the last hope for restoring the Scepter of Justice.

Fatigue drew him under like a wave, and he collapsed next to her, utterly spent, drowning in the losses of the night.

CHAPTER EIGHT

A woman laughed against his chest.

Shance blinked and took in the sharp features and dancing violet eyes of an incredibly attractive female with dark olive skin, black hair, and a small silver horn in the middle of her forehead. Maira Ukerys. The death unicorn he had spent the entire night with, not in his usual activities, but rather healing his crew and those who had attacked *The Silver Streak*. There were smudges of gray from where she had hastily wiped off her makeup as their worked finished, near sunrise.

She'd needed to rest, badly. Carrying her to his cabin had felt like the most sensible action in the world. Because she was his wife. They had married decades earlier and stood beside each other through countless struggles.

Even though Shance still struggled to remember the details.

Her lips curved. "Well, well. This is how we wake up? I guess part of you does remember me, Tyrius. Then again, you always were fond of sharing a bed with someone."

Her mocking was warm and gentle, with a dry edge. As natural as the drape of her body over his, the press of her curves against his torso. Shance enjoyed the sensation, although usually in situations like this, he and the woman were naked. In this one, there were definite layers of clothing separating them. But that didn't matter.

Even now, the closeness awoke something in him deeper than pleasure. Deeper than need. As if a part of his soul had returned, seeping good humor and determination into his heart. Instinctively, he wrapped his arms around Maira.

"You called me Tyrius. Who is that?"

The word sent an odd thrill through him, as though hearing something in a long-forgotten language, something that ran deeper than his own true name.

Am I Shance Windkeeper?

Who else would he be? Of course he was Shance Windkeeper.

"It's your birth name. To be fair, you always preferred the name Shance, and the Windkeeper name was given by the dragons. They give it to all dragon friends who have wind Talents."

He frowned. "The Lawless told me it was a family line."

"It was. One always served as the Chief of Council. You were included as an honor. But the others were targeted and killed early on in the war. Besides our son, you are the only Windkeeper left in Sekastra."

"The only one?"

Maira nodded. "Zilpath relayed what they told you in the Scepter of Commerce. Technically, the seat of Chief of Council is yours, or our son's. But there is no dragon-human council to confirm it. The dragons have their own council now among the Lawless." Bitterness leaked into her voice. "I doubt the dragons will support the chief mate of the death unicorns or a half-unicorn."

"Do I need their support in times like these?" Did he even want the position? He struggled with the layers of confusing memories. The old ones, the new ones, and the ones from an era and a land long ago. And yet, not. "What of my parents I spoke with? My family?"

"Imposters. Actors from within the Curious Intrigue. Which was why they seldom contacted you and why you rarely saw them in person."

Even as she spoke the words, they made sense. The way his relatives were always busy. The fleeting memories of other wind users, memories that were difficult to pinpoint. Now, new memories of the wind Talented prodded him, but they were different. Not his blood family. His friends.

More grief and anger filled him. His friends had died.

"Always trust the winds," he muttered.

A phrase his false father had said. But now, Shance knew it had belonged to another Windkeeper comrade. They had always used those sorts of phrases, and Shance had resisted them. Having been created to be a god by evil men, he could never stomach the idea of worshiping them or being worshiped. Although the god names themselves made excellent curse words.

Yet, for the last ten years, Shance had use those phrases and thrown tokens to the god-fountains. Had resisted the Four Corners religion, except for Zilpath's persistent friendship. Had lost everything he'd come to stand for, save a handful of principles and a strong dislike of violence.

Was the loss the result of brainwashing? His false family had also always invoked the gods and encouraged his belief. Maybe that had contributed.

How could this happen to his mind? How could he go back to being who he was—the chief mate, the mediator, the leader, the father—when this was what he had become over the last decade?

He held Maira more tightly, as a lifeline. Even though he didn't deserve her steadfastness, he needed it. More than anything.

"Did the Lawless know who I was?" More memories crashed into his mind. "Yes. They did. We told them when we entered Sekastra. Why didn't the Lawless tell me the whole truth in the Scepter of Commerce?"

"Would you have believed them at the time? Death unicorns and the rest? It was easier to accept your false identity and refer to Tyrius as a separate person. I don't approve, but I understand their perspective." Maira studied him, her fingers tapping his chest nervously. Shance remembered how she would often grab his hand or arm or shoulder and fuss with it when she was agitated with a new thought or a difficult decision. Or she would do it to let him know she was there and cared about him, that she was his, more than anyone else's.

Who else would she belong to?

He glanced at the timepiece on the wall. Eleven o'clock. Too early for a drink. But Fiarston, Shance could dearly use one. At least to blunt the guilt, anger, fear, and torrent of other emotions.

A beeping sounded from Maira's shoulder. She leaned away, flopping down onto the bed beside Shance, and accepted the call on her wireless commer.

An angry male voice spoke over the crackly receiver. "Where is he, Maira? Where is our son?"

Shance looked at her in astonishment.

"Son?" He mouthed.

She had a son with another man?

She held a finger to her lips. <Later. Kaliran can be difficult.>

<All right.> Mindspeak, just like last night. He'd gone from dismissing mindspeak to participating.

The throbbing was returning to his temples.

"Our son is unconscious, Kaliran." She sighed, worry paling her face. "I have done all I can at present. We are still trying to assess what was done to him. But he is in our care now, and his welfare is one of my greatest concerns, along with the others still held captive by the rogues that flourished in my absence."

"We are glad you have returned." The voice softened. "I had no doubt of your loyalty, my queen. And the chief mate is with you? We cannot sense him through the herd mind."

Chief mate? Shance sat up and looked at her. His mind was still spinning at the idea that she had a son with someone else. And now, *he* was her chief mate? What was that, anyway? The word seemed familiar, but he didn't understand it, especially not in this context. Maira shot him a glance that was both firm and apologetic.

"Yes, he is here. We are still conferring, and he has much to remember, but be at ease, Kaliran. The herd leadership is firmly in place and growing stronger. We will restore and protect what is ours, for the good of all."

"All stand with you and Tyrius Stormsong, the Descendant. I expect him to contact me and the other regents at his earliest convenience. There is much to arrange in the Lost Refuge."

Maira smirked. "Yes, I know how you've missed him."

"Only as much as a fly misses a swatter." There was an edge of humor to the voice. For a moment, Shance could almost picture Kaliran's face, a shade darker than Cadence's, split with a white-toothed smile and gleaming brown eyes full of good humor for anyone he didn't view as an idiot. Winning his trust had been worth the effort, but Shance couldn't remember why. "Until then, my queen. May your days be long."

"And may your nights be safe."

She sighed and pressed the wireless commer again. The lightness in her face vanished, replaced with fresh exhaustion and concern. Her emotions bled into Shance as water bleeds into cloth. He pulled her close to him again, trying to stifle his questions and curiosity.

But Maira knew. She could sense the tumult within him. She cared just as much for him as she did for every person in her herd, and far more, because Shance was her chief mate. Her husband. Her anchor, as necessary to her as she was to so many others. He was the first in her heart, and the only one with rights by her side and in her bed.

A part of Shance accepted the facts that appeared in his mind. The other was thinking that one drink wouldn't be enough. At least three would be necessary.

Even now, he could sense her doubts over her situation in her wry smile. "You still don't remember all this. I'm sorry. It always was complicated."

Maira's words were quiet with resignation, clearly sensing his turmoil as he desperately tried to keep up with everything that was happening. A day ago, he had been a single man with distant family. Now he was the husband of a woman who had children by other men. It was absurd.

Yet, every word rang true. Even the quiet melancholy in her voice. She had never chosen her fate. Everything in her life had been dictated. Even her death.

Until Shance had found her. So long ago.

"I always searched for the extraordinary. For destiny." A long, slow breath escaped Shance as he tried to process what he had heard over the commer. What was it Kesia had said? *You assume she hasn't been having sex as well.*

Her cheeky words had real implications that settled heavily within him, as more memories surfaced. The Glorious Destiny, a movement made of humans who wanted to be gods—so they made it so. They stole magic from others, amplified their own Talents, and manipulated the kingdom to their whims. Then gods had targeted unicorn women in order to destroy all descendants that could resist their rule. By the time unicorns had regrouped as deadly and powerful weapons, only a few females remained. Maira had formed political alliances with the leaders of the fractured unicorn herds—her regents—giving each of them children with her powerful lineage and bloodline.

He remembered her words, spoken long ago in determination and fading hope. *Romance and monogamy are luxuries for those who aren't trying to prevent their people from being extinguished. The good of the herd comes before all else.*

The words had aroused jealousy and anger long ago, as they did now. Maira's mates might not be in her bed anymore. The situation might only be political. But it still rankled that she was involved in it.

Still, beneath the anger was understanding, and compassion. For her and for her herd. Their herd.

A herd, a family he had forgotten. Had been made to forget.

He paused as guilt mingled with love settled in. "I'm unworthy of giving it, but I offer you all I have."

"And I accept. All of you, as I always have."

Her face twisted, and her shoulders shook. For a moment, her strength and playful ease crumpled into the weariness of a woman who carried the weight of a people on her shoulders. It evoked more recent memories of how he and Maira had spent the night, caring for his injured and traumatized crew until exhaustion left them snatching a few hours of rest just before dawn.

Another memory stirred Shance. "Cadence. Cadence Folham is your son with Kaliran Ukerys."

She nodded, her face tightening with worry. "Yes, although Folham was his alias last name. He is also your herd-son, under your protection as well as mine. Even if he doesn't want it right now."

Her voice trailed off in a despairing whisper that resonated with Shance. Last night the young man had resisted Maira's efforts to connect with his mind and remove whatever brainwashing had occurred. Eventually, they'd had to render him unconscious before he caused himself harm by bashing his head against the walls of his cell. All out of devotion to this mysterious Lady Lurien.

A lady who still held Brennar Ukerys Windkeeper in her thrall. The heaviness inside Shance grew until it was an anvil pressing him into the mattress and leaching tears from his eyes. Brennar, his son. A young man who viewed him as a faithless traitor who had abandoned everything for a shiftless life with the Congruency and High Command, dishonoring every vow he'd taken and every bond he'd made.

His captors had turned Shance into a fool.

Holding Maira close, resolve strengthened him.

No more. By Bonilus, no more.

"We'll get him back, my love." He gently tucked a strand of hair behind her pointed ear. "I don't care what it takes. We'll rescue him and Cadence."

"I know." She swallowed and gave him a sharp smile, her eyes flashing blood red. "It's the only way."

<If you are going to get anyone, start by getting yourselves out of that bed and joining your brother with the dragon.>

Shance jumped at the crisp, overly-precise voice in his mind. He sat up, looking around the cabin for the owner, while one hand summoned the winds. "Who are you?"

93

<Don't you recognize me? I am impeccable in either form.> A large orange cat with dragon wings, a dragon tail, and golden scales speckling his fur landed on the foot of the bed. <However, this one showcases my excellence far better. My unicorn requires a skin form presence sometimes so she doesn't get herself killed.>

"You of all shifters should know how hard I am to kill, Ademis." Maira shook her head, easing off the bed and rummaging through a bag on the floor. "What did the dragon, Tiers, name you in the Scepter of Commerce? Freckles? Perhaps I should call you that as well."

The cat-dragon fixed her with his bright green eyes. <Only if you want your face clawed off. I allowed those two to use that name because it was preferable than deigning to speak with them. Such as they are, moderately useful to the cause.>

<Naturally you could never bear them true affection.> Maira rolled her eyes. <And here I was afraid you wouldn't come back to me.>

<Always will I return to what is mine, in due time. I suppose now you must be shared again with the human on the bed gawking at me.> Ademis turned to him, his tail flicking back and forth. <Are you quite finished?>

"Am I … are you…?" Shance shook his head. "How is it that I can hear you?"

<You are honored to be accepted by me in my great magnanimity.>

Maira snorted. "When you became part of my herd, Ademis had to accept you as well, Shance." She glanced at the cat-dragon. "Did you bring fresh clothes?"

He twitched his whiskers. <Now I'm considered your laundress?>

"Ademis." She folded her arms. "Enough."

The two stared at each other for a long moment. Shance wasn't sure either of them was breathing. At last, the cat-dragon sighed. <Yes, I brought enough for both of us. I trust Shance can sort out his own clothing matters, since this is his cabin.>

"Ah, yes. I'm able to do that."

Maira sighed. "Good. There's no time to waste. We're already late, as usual." At that, Maira pulled off her shirt and slid her leggings down to her ankles, revealing the deep curves of her petite frame and a reddish lightning scar emblazoned across her chest from her neck to below her generous breasts. Heat spread through Shance, and his words were stolen away. She was exquisite.

And she was laughing at him.

"Come on! No time for mating now." Her eyes glinted, and she tossed her hair. "After all, there is the matter of all those other beds you've been in over the last ten years, albeit with the excuse that terrible people filled your mind with lies. I might need more persuasion to have you in mine again."

From any other lips, the words would be condemning. From Maira's, they were full of rueful humor, laced with forgiveness. Already trying to make light of their situation and clear away some of the guilt that consumed him.

Truly, she made their relationship so easy. Even when she had every right to withhold.

He didn't deserve her.

Shance grinned at her. "Persuading you will be one of my greatest missions, my dear."

<Augh, this flirting nonsense again. Why either of you find copulation necessary is beyond me.> Ademis made a hacking sound. <Disgusting habit. And it produces offspring who pull my

tail and ears and, most displeasing of all, my wings. Especially that Brennar fellow.>

His words, bold and only half-teasing, caught Shance like a bolt to the chest. Maira's eyes filled with tears and her body shook with sudden, choked sobs. It was the intense sorrow of a woman who had lost her husband, her children, and her entire family. He strode over and enfolded her in his arms, tracing her scar, reminding her of how much it displayed her courage.

He hadn't acted as the chief mate of a death unicorn queen should have. She honored him with full rights to her bed and equal say in all her dealings, standing up for him against her own kind. He repaid her loyalty with shameless exploits while under amnesia.

A fool and a wretch. That changed now.

Shance glared at the cat-dragon. "Watch your words, or they will be your last."

<Tut, tut. So explosive.> But the cat-dragon hopped off the bed and wound his way around Maira's ankles, vibrating with a rusty purr of apology. <Now then, no more of that, my dear. All will be well. You know I'll give my dying breath for you and all that sort of thing. I helped you get Shance back, didn't I? After the funeral, we'll get the tail-puller back along with any others in this mysterious lady's captivity. I promise.>

She swiped at her eyes and gave a firm nod, stroking his back. "Of course we will. Together." She quickly pulled on fresh undergarments and pants. "You need to get dressed as well, Ademis."

Shance raised his eyebrows. "What do you mean?"

The cat-dragon gave a peevish meow. <What do you think it means?>

Realization dawned on Shance a moment before the cat-dragon shifted, his fur and scales vanishing, his form growing until he stood half a foot taller than Maira, back in skin with ginger hair and an expression equal parts regal, bored, and mischievous.

And very much naked.

"Ah, that!" Shance averted his eyes and began changing his own clothes. For some reason, dealing with Ademis was old practice. "No matter how clever you claim to be, you still haven't figured out how to shift with clothing on since we last met. Disappointing. After all, you had ten years to figure it out."

Not that it was possible, but the cat-dragon deserved to be teased.

Ademis sniffed. "I had far better things to do."

"Like terrorizing small dogs?"

"Only when they start it. Why are you dressed like that? The stockings look ludicrous. Don't you have a uniform that looks slightly less absurd?"

Shance scowled over his shoulder. "Yes, but sometimes I don't want to be noticed as military personnel."

"So have Maira strike up an empathic disinterest field. She has to be good for something—ow!"

Maira snorted. "Ask me what I'm good for, and you'll be sleeping out in the cold."

"A horrid repayment for decades of devoted service."

"Service when you felt like it."

Someone knocked at the door. By the three firm raps, he knew it was Tegan. That, and she had warned him she wanted answers.

"Captain Windkeeper? We need to talk, sir."

"I'm aware, Commander Tegan." Ducus take the stockings! Shance grabbed black trousers, a dark blue shirt, and plain black tabard. Without his captain insignia, it would be standard off-duty attire for a Congruency airship top deck officer, and far more comfortable. "However, right now I have an urgent meeting to attend."

"Yes, you're already running late for the funerals."

"Funerals?" He paused, and sorrow gripped him afresh. "Lieutenant Vale and Airshipman Yulrit. Of course."

She nodded. "Yes, although those will be quick shipboard affairs. A Lawless vessel will transport the death unicorn corpses to their hometown in the eastern part of Sekastra."

"I thought we didn't kill them." He had tried not to.

"They chose to commit suicide rather than be captured. For the honor of their lady. Except for the one called Cadence, who is still unconscious." Tegan's mouth thinned. "You'll have to travel to the Edgefell Peaks for the other one. There's another Lawless vessel in port which will take you and the death unicorns, and I'll stay here and monitor ship repairs."

"Why wasn't I notified about the trip to Edgefell?"

She sighed. "Sir, this is what I am doing now. Sir."

He sighed. "Granted."

"And you are running late. Sir."

<Only a matter of perspective> Ademis hissed, straightening his bright green cravat. Maira chuckled quietly in agreement. Shance smiled despite himself. If he had come from another country with different customs, it made his tardiness to meetings a lot more understandable.

He finished pulling on his boots and opened the door. Tegan stood there, her face as weary as everyone else's. Even Ademis's. Beneath his smug attitude, the cat-dragon's skin form seemed gaunt. And were those scabs and scratches on his face?

Tegan cleared her throat. "In regards to the death unicorns, sir?"

"I assure you, Commander Tegan, I will inform you of all I can after the funerals."

"I've already contacted the Lawless, sir. They confirmed the bare necessities of your alliance with the death unicorns, and your apparent age." She frowned. "Although why they would keep such secrets—then again, I suppose we all have them."

Shance raised his eyebrows. This acceptance was unusual from his first officer. He lowered his voice so only Tegan heard. "No arguments about the wisdom of trusting the death unicorns?"

"Oh, I have many of those," she returned in kind. "And I still don't understand how you can love her so easily after so long apart. How you can get used to all of this," Tegan made a small, vague gesture, "talk of magic and whatnot. But she healed the crew. That's enough for me, for now. You need to leave." She raised her voice. "I'll draw up a full list of repairs and schedule the crew as I can. Virna insists on Ironfire being aboard to assist with repairs. She says, and I quote, 'That damn dragon is worth ten normals.' I'm not sure if offense was meant—"

"It probably was." Shance sighed. Kesia's Talents for shapeshifting and manipulating materials, along with the dragon's natural gift for mechanics, made her and the chief engineer comrades. Which meant they would both be in the bowels of the ship cursing at everything, while Zephryn skulked around and read or did something else completely useless. The dragon prince seemed at loose ends when he wasn't researching or trying to kill someone.

Tegan paused. "I'm sure Ironfire will be willing to come as soon as she feels able, given the circumstances."

"The circumstances?"

Maira peeked around his shoulder, interrupting his conversation with Tegan. "Don't push the crew too hard after last night.

Even with my healing Talent, there is no replacement for rest."

"Yes, ma'am." Tegan cast a questioning look at Shance, but he only shook his head. Explanations about his true past—and why Maira felt so free to order around his crew—could best be left for later.

"Is that all, Commander?"

"Yes, sir." She saluted him and left.

The fact that they would have to travel on someone else's airship bothered him more than he cared to admit. He turned to Ademis and Maira. "I don't suppose either of you have acquired a teleporting Talent? It would save the other airship captain the trouble of taking us to the dragon funeral."

Maira shook her head. "No, that Talent is our daughter's, not mine."

"Daughter! What?"

She smiled slyly. "I'm kidding! She's our herd-daughter, and she is safe with her father in the Lost Refuge."

He sighed and ran a hand through his hair. "You're trouble."

"Always. And you still don't like traveling on anyone else's ship."

She winked and slipped around him, walking through the door and moving across the deck with a playful confidence that belied her five-foot-two frame. Even more of his heart went with her as he took in every inch of her body, remembering how it had looked earlier in his cabin.

He followed her out of the cabin. Other memories flooded his mind. Memories of woman after woman he'd bedded, always seeking someone who would be the one. Guilt stole some of the heat from him. Maira might be his wife, but he was unworthy of her.

He would change that.

Ademis shook his head, skirting around them both to take

the lead. "Come. I left Lirome with the unstable dragon lady who won't rest. We should meet them soon at the vessel."

Something in the cat-dragon's words finally clicked in Shance's mind. Maira had sent for Lirome, but he hadn't returned. And Ademis continued to speak as if there was only one dragon when there were two. There had been two—Zephryn and Kesia—leaving for their safe house only the night before, Kesia's merriment contrasting with his seriousness, but each devoted to the other.

The bottom dropped out of his stomach.

It couldn't be them—but who else?

"Ademis ... what about the dragon man? Zephryn Nightstalker should be coming with the dragon lady."

The cat-dragon's playful expression grew solemn. "He's dead. There was an ambush last night. A raging fear attack. Lirome's not sure how Kesia survived her embermate's death, but he believes it may have something to do with the experimentation she endured. Lirome is helping her as well."

Maira glanced up, her expression concerned and speculative. "How is Lirome helping her?"

"You know. The usual bond. What you death unicorn healers always do for someone suffering a loss. Might work even better since they're soul-friends."

A loss. A death.

Zephryn was dead. The crown prince of dragons was dead.

A brief, violent whirlwind buffeted the cabin as anger and sorrow flooded Shance. He'd only known Zephryn a few weeks, and the dragon had been curt for most of that time. But he'd been Kesia's lifeline. Their embermate bond had withstood so much.

Now he was gone. All because a mysterious villain was turning death unicorns against good people, shifters and humans alike.

More guilt saturated him, twisting with grief and fury in his gut. He followed Ademis's quick pace through the ship.

First Cadence, then his son, then Zephryn.

Shance clenched his hands into fists.

Not again.

CHAPTER NINE

Emptiness consumed Kesia. Still bearing the shadows and memories of an essence that had tasted of peak pine and hot coals, now turned to ashes. Gone. Vanished with the fear and darkness.

Oddly vibrating darkness.

She smiled. <Who knew darkness could vibrate, Midnight?>

Silence answered her. Perhaps he was asleep. Sometimes Zephryn slept so deeply that her thoughts couldn't penetrate his unconscious mind. No matter. He needed to rest after the attack.

The attack.

A fist squeezed her heart, and her eyes snapped open. She lay in a small bed, underneath a blanket in a dressing gown, in a small room with plain brick walls. Not her room but a different one, used for medical treatment, judging by the bottles, herbs, and implements that lined one counter.

Next to her lay a large furry creature about the size of a cat. No, it *was* a cat, with a vibrating purr. Though it had odd golden scales in its orange fur and a scent of flames about it. Like a cat-dragon.

Kesia stroked its fur absently. The beast seemed oddly familiar, as if from a dream.

Or a nightmare.

She shuddered. Tired or not, she needed the comfort of her embermate.

<Zephryn?>

The cat-dragon lifted its head and looked at her. Profound pity glinted in its green eyes. <My dear, you need to rest more.>

<What?> She sat up in shock. <How can you speak? And where is Zephryn? I want to see him. Now.> Confusion and panic rippled through her as she reached out with her mind to find her embermate. She shut her eyes against the dread rising in her soul, trying to recall the truth through the haze of terror.

She remembered walking next to Zephryn, trying to tease him into revealing the mysterious research he refused to speak of until he "knew enough concrete facts rather than speculation." A figure showing up to help them ... somehow...

Absolute nothingness. The gaping hole within her, filled with a strange presence.

Zephryn wasn't asleep, was he?

Her breathing shallowed.

"Where. Is. He?"

The cat-dragon's tail twitched. <Lirome, you need to handle this. I only do the purring.>

<Coward.>

<I'm not the one who is hiding outside.>

<She has no reason to trust me.>

"Someone tell me what happened!" Her voice echoed off the walls of the small room. Kesia heard a sigh, and the door across the room from her bed opened. A tall figure walked in slowly, wearing only a pair of black pants, his chest lean and muscled. His violet eyes never left hers, and his long black hair was disheveled, as if he had endured a long night. Weariness and grief lined his dark olive face.

The small silver horn, black fingernails, and pointed ears marked him as a unicorn, like those who were supposed join them in the Scepter of Knowledge. Lirome Ukerys. She remembered him. Remembered seeing him by the Niversill Falls and feeling the odd connection of what he called a soul-friend. Remembered staring into the darkness in the street, certain that someone stared back at her.

Fear and anger turned her stomach. There had been other unicorns the night before, at least eight of them. Lirome had tried to warn her and Zephryn about the ambush. A searing memory overtook her mind, and she was lost to the past.

Zephryn squeezed her hand, his cobalt eyes fierce, eager for battle.

<We will show them what happens when you try to trick dragons.>

He slipped into his Cloak, his Talent that made him invisible to the naked eye, although the death unicorns still sensed his location through emotions. In turn, Kesia breathed out a blast of smoke, the fumes combining with the perpetual mist that wreathed the Scepter of Knowledge and obscuring her from sight.

One of the unicorns gave a neighing scream as Zephryn sliced through it, while another perished under Kesia's flames and claws.

Bones cracked.

Unicorns fell.

Then the scent of sulfur choked the air.

The eyes of her foe turned blood red. Alarm jolted through her. Nula had warned her about these signs. They meant something terrible, something that the unicorns she'd sent had never spoken of.

Zephryn's voice spoke to her through their private link.

<Rose-Wing, get out of here.>

<No, I'm not leaving you! You're the heir, the last hope—>

<As are you. One of us must survive, and you can. You will. You

are equally worthy to be saved. Go!>

She froze.

Dark smoke and fear laced around her, as dangerous and powerful as when she had stood in the great hall of the Pinnacle, naked and alone, awaiting her doom. Terror coiled around her heart and soul, suffocating her from the inside.

She was no longer in the Scepter of Knowledge. She stood in the cold, menacing hall as the Pinnacle elders circled her in the dark, waiting to strike.

She swallowed and screamed. Again and again, her muscles aching from tension, her throat raw from ashes and fright.

Then something snapped within her.

Emptiness entered. Aching loneliness.

Zephryn's last words pierced her mind. <Fight! Fight for us. Fight for yourself.>

In her last moments, she reached out. Asking. Pleading for something she didn't understand. Begging for anyone to hear her, see her.

All was dark.

Kesia swiped at the wetness on her cheeks. She was in bed once more, and the cat-dragon's purr filled her ears so she could hardly hear Lirome's words.

"I'm sorry. I did the best I could. He insisted that I try to save you. I gave him my word to do whatever I could."

Her hands shook, but somehow, her voice remained steady. It was as if someone else spoke through her, someone who was stronger. Whole.

Kesia clutched the voicelator pendant around her neck and looked up at Lirome. "How am I alive?"

The unicorn shook his head. "I don't know. I formed a healing bond with you in a last-chance effort, allowing you to use my life force. It's an emergency measure for temporary relief."

"But it isn't the same," Kesia whispered numbly.

"No, I imagine it isn't, considering you had an embermate bond."

She frowned. "Yes, but … it's different somehow. It doesn't feel…"

Her voice trailed off. The bond didn't feel temporary. Lirome's presence within her was guarded and cautious, far from the open connection between embermates. But it was more than a simple, fleeting link.

"Ah yes. The soul-friend connection," Lirome said.

"What does that mean?"

He shrugged. "Merely that we have some parts in common that give us a friendly affinity, as was said before."

"You're a unicorn. I'm a dragon. You're the brother of a queen. I'm the niece of an evil madman. What could we have in common?"

Lirome shrugged again, although she sensed something. A thread of deception. Kesia groaned internally. She still had no idea what to do with those feelings, those sensings.

The unicorn only continued. "Maira, my sister, examined you while you slept." He ran a hand through his hair. "Usually we ask permission, but this situation was too extraordinary. However, we have no leads as to why you are still alive. There's too much data to parse right now, and she has her own troubles."

"I understand." They wouldn't discover anything new. Dragon caregivers had studied her multiple times and been bewildered. Better to think about something else. Kesia paused. "The unicorns. There was sulfur. Fear. Their eyes turned blood red."

"Yes. They can do that."

"Why? Can you?"

"An interesting thought at a time like this."

Kesia lifted her chin. "I remember you telling us something about unicorns. About *death* unicorns. What does the 'death' part mean, again?"

The unicorn's face turned very still. "It could mean a great number of things."

His cautious tone flamed anger within her. She glared at him. "I am alive when I shouldn't be, bereft of my embermate, and alone in this world without any family and only a handful of friends that I've known for a few weeks. You will answer me honestly, unicorn. I deserve that much."

Lirome held her gaze for a moment, then nodded. Regret seeped from him.

"You're right." He sighed. "I'm sorry. I was going to tell all to the crown prince, and then, I could only give you a rushed explanation."

"Of course you were going to tell him," Kesia snorted. Zephryn was always the important one. She was the liability.

"But with his passing, you are next in line for the throne."

She shook her head. "No, I'm not."

"Yes, you are. Considering how you've been kept in the dark about much of this, willfully or otherwise, how about you trust my knowledge, and I trust your strength? I will tell you more about dragon inheritance later, but first let me answer your question about unicorns."

She didn't have energy to argue. "Go ahead."

He leaned forward. "I am a death unicorn, as are those who attacked you. Unicorns are by nature empathic healers. Users of soul magic for the benefit of others. There was a genocide against our kind ninety years ago. The slaughter was devastating."

"Nula told me the revolution that overthrew Glenalis in Elotrin was over fifty years ago."

"The revolution was when Shance and Maira overthrew Glenalis, and it was sixty-three years ago. The genocide occurred earlier and hasn't been reported. After it occurred, the unicorns who remained alive chose to be experimented upon. My people weaponized ourselves in an attempt to overthrow our oppressors. We survived."

Kesia's breath caught. "You *willingly* experimented on yourselves?"

His voice was steady, with an undertone of steel. "To survive, yes."

"Did your enemies survive?"

"We don't think so. Maira and Shance took care of that."

"And what were you doing while they stopped your enemies?" Something in her couldn't stop challenging the unicorn—the *death* unicorn. Maybe it was his offhand tone, or a curious ease that must come from the soul-friend connection. "Were you taking a nap?"

Next to her, the cat-dragon gave a rusty chuckle.

Lirome laughed shortly, violet eyes wide. "No, at that time I was trying to escape being burned alive."

"Hm. One torture that hasn't been an issue for me."

"I would imagine not. Little did my captors know that, thanks to some tinkering, it wasn't trouble for me either."

Tinkering. As if the physical form was an engine, instead of belonging to a person. She couldn't handle the notion. Kesia's levity died as quickly as a snuffed candle. "So, the death unicorns last night are rogues?"

"Yes." Lirome's expression had also sobered. "When I sought to heal you, you were surrounded by green smoke. An unusual color for a dragon. I assume these are aspects of your experimentation? Your hair strands and scale color also indicate as much."

"Yes. Unlike yours, mine was involuntary." She rubbed her fingers on the greenish scales on her hand. They were a far darker shade of green than before, with her older red tint on the edges. Fewmets.

She had lost Zephryn. And she was losing herself.

The certainty sank deep within her, a leadstone of her fate.

<So here I am. Abandoned. A reject.>

An indignant meow emanated from the cat-dragon. <If you are alone, have I suddenly become a ghost? You insult me.>

Kesia smiled weakly, and Lirome rolled his eyes. "Forgive Ademis. He has the manners of, well … a cat-dragon."

"I've never seen anything like him."

<I'm the only one like me, and I was kept in a cage far longer than even you, I'll warrant.> His whiskered face bore gentle reproof. <If we are comparing loneliness, I think I win.>

Kesia scratched his head. "This isn't a competition."

<Good. You fear my victory as the most unique creature here.>

The animal thought it was set apart? She could prove him wrong. Sort of.

Kesia continued to stroke the cat-dragon as the familiar tingle of pre-shift came over her. <You say you're alone? There's none other like you?>

The cat-dragon observed her with a trace of mournfulness in his green eyes. <It's not possible. The laboratory only created one of me.>

Empathy twisted her heart. <I'm sorry.>

As the words left her mind, she shifted, casting off skin for fur and glimmering gold scales. She crawled out of the dressing gown and gave her tail a flick with a sigh of satisfaction. Tails were fun. She yawned, blinking her eyes and giving her paw a lick before looking at the cat-dragon. He was staring at her, hissing and spitting bits of flame, his back fur standing up on end.

<Wha-what? What did you do?>

<I have two Talents. Shapeshifting into any animal is one of them.> Kesia gave a rusty meow. <However, it doesn't last. A few hours to a day at most.>

She shifted back into skin form, remembering to pull the sheet around her in case death unicorns cared about that sort of thing. She needed to learn more about them. Zephryn had tried, but the books in the Scepter of Knowledge had held precious little information about unicorns in general, much less their deadly descendants. Still, he had insisted it was easier to see the biases in books than in people. And then she had argued that people were easier and far more interesting to read. His eyes would glint in challenge.

Except he wouldn't do that anymore.

Grief and tears pricked her eyes.

"Fascinating. Your genes must be incredibly adaptive." Lirome fixed her with an intent stare. "I wonder if that has something to do with your experimentation. There must have been more to it than spewing green smoke."

"No." She pulled the sheet up closer, her throat heating. "I don't want to discuss this anymore."

He held out his hands. "I mean no disrespect. At another time, in the future. But the Lawless know you're alive, and they'll want to know how. And you wonder yourself."

Kesia frowned at him. "I have been poked, prodded, and examined enough. No one has been able to discover anything."

"They aren't me."

"You mean arrogant?"

His mouth quirked. "Intelligence is my Talent. And I'm skilled in areas of medicine and magic. Dragons are still blind to things like magic and spirit and soul. I am not."

His words tugged at her curiosity. Zephryn had said she would survive. How had he known? The question had to be satisfied.

But not right now.

She swung her legs to the side of the bed, wrapping the sheet the rest of the way around her and tucking the ends into place. Her soul might be brutally wounded, but her body wasn't. And she didn't need more people pointing out her differences and flaws. Even if they shared them.

It was too much to consider right now.

"Maybe later. I want to see him. His … corpse."

"Of course." Lirome paused. "According to the dragon leaders in the Lawless, Zephryn Nightstalker's body should remain covered and wrapped until the formal cremation ceremony."

Shock filled her. "I'm his embermate. Or I was. I deserve to see him."

"Yes, they were also very concerned about how you managed to survive." He paused again, leveling a measuring stare at her, as if weighing his next words. "Considering his stature—"

"Yes, I know. The crown prince. The valued one. I understand." Anger and grief consumed her. "I tried to save him! I tried to tell him he was more important, but he wouldn't listen!"

Flames streamed from her mouth. The cat-dragon leaped off the bed with a yowl, his tail smoking. Hot tears flowed down her cheeks, and she shut her eyes tightly. Would this be another thing she was blamed for? A broken experiment who couldn't stop the one person who mattered most from getting killed?

Would they put her in a cage again? Would the Lawless turn against her? Or would they simply abandon her as unfit?

<I'm worthless.>

<Kesia.> Lirome's voice was in her mind, calm and sure in the storm. The presence in her soul strengthened, tentatively easing deeper. Dimly, she felt his hands closing around hers. <You are broken, but you are not worthless or unwanted. Remember your friends and allies.>

<Who are they?>

He sighed. <I know Nula Thredsing counts you as a friend, and so does Shance Windkeeper. As do I.>

<You do? Why?>

<We are soul-friends. You are important to me in some way, and we unicorns trust such urges. Besides, I know what it feels like to consider yourself necessary only for someone else's sake.> A deep strength filtered through her. Not binding or intrusive, only offering and then retreating, quiet and gentle and a little uncertain. Then, humor threaded in. <And you singed Ademis's tail. I love that cat-dragon dearly, but he needs to be kept on his toes.>

<I heard that, you cruel boy. May mice defecate in your bed.>

A laugh escaped Kesia, bringing her back to the present. She opened her eyes and looked into Lirome's face, a mixture of earnest concern and a strong, anchoring peace. "Boy? According to your file, you are over eighty years old."

"I rescued Ademis when I was a child, and he had already lived at least ten years. The Glorious Destiny made him their favorite experiment, a dragon shifter within a cat—although he doesn't admit his dragon origins. I don't think he remembers them."

"You seem to make a habit of rescuing others and healing them."

"When I can. I failed in the case of your embermate." A shadow passed over his face, and she sensed tendrils of sorrow from him. "As for you, you were determined to live. You're powerful."

"No, I'm not." The words came out softly. Kesia instinctively reached out in her mind for the strength he offered. "My other half is dead."

Lirome sighed, and she felt him offer more strength. Barely enough. It was just as well. No matter her gut feelings, the death unicorn said the bond was temporary. There was no reason to get attached. "I don't know enough of dragons to offer any further advice. We'll be traveling to the Edgefell Peaks for the funeral pyre. I can only hope the dragon caregivers there will have additional insight. In the meantime, cling to my strength and to what you know is true. You have been made by Bonilus the All-Maker, and you are worthy of standing." He stood. "Now, if you would like, I can take you to see the body of your husband."

"Yes." The word took her last ounce of energy.

Without a word of warning, Ademis leaped into her arms. <And so, the vastly underappreciated, long-suffering cat-dragon selflessly overlooks the dragon's trick and offers comfort in time of need.>

Her arms curled around him, fingers lingering in his fur. "You're assuming I'll need it."

His mental voice turned serious. <My dear, sometimes we all need it.>

Kesia followed Lirome through the doorway and down a short hallway to a nearby room, heart thudding painfully in her chest with each step. The far corner was segregated by metal panels and an oilcloth curtain.

Lirome parted the curtain and stepped aside, allowing her to enter first. "Do you want some time alone?"

"Yes."

Kesia set the cat-dragon down and crept inside.

Zephryn lay on a metal table beneath a cold, white sheet. His bronze face was stern in repose—it always was. He scowled far more than he had ever smiled. Yet when he did smile, it was as if the sun had burst through a storm, fierce and merry.

He had smiled for her. A hand squeezed her heart.

<Midnight?> She traced the cobalt scales on his forehead, his cheeks, and down his neck. Stroked his hair, black as a raven's wing. <Midnight, come now. This is absurd. Come out of this. How do you expect me to survive without you? You know how I get into scrapes and difficulties. I'm too impulsive, too eager to explore.>

There was nothing. No twitch of his lips. No warmth of irritation and humor in her mind. No mental voice, sharp and edged with firm, unyielding devotion.

Silence, in a room made for sterilization.

<Zephryn! You can't be gone. People need you. Our dragons need you. What am I supposed to do? No one even regards me. Without you...>

Fresh tears blurred her eyes. One hand clutched her voicelator pendant, while the other clenched into a fist. Zephryn's final words echoed in her mind.

<One of us must survive. You are equally worthy to be saved. Go!>

He hadn't said that he loved her in that last moment. At least, not with words. He had said it with every moment he gave her. He had said it with his last breath at the mercy of those foul-hearted death unicorns. He had sacrificed himself for her, somehow knowing she would live.

Now.

Gone.

Her legs gave out from under her, and she fell to the ground, shaking with flames and sobs.

She was alone.

Strong arms caught her up and surrounded her in a cocoon of strength amidst the agony that ripped her heart in two.

Faintly, she wondered how Lirome survived her flames. What he had done to himself to make it possible. Why she sensed hot tears streaking down his cheeks.

But at that moment, none of it mattered.

All that mattered had died, leaving her there to pick up the pieces.

CHAPTER TEN

No matter how many funerals Maira Ukerys attended, it never grew easier. Especially not a stark, serious dragon funeral, bereft of the warmth and sustaining power of a herd. Maintaining a stable emotional balance among death unicorns was often troublesome and frustrating, but it meant that when there was a loss, all shared in both the grief and healing.

Here, grief was experienced in solitude. A funeral pyre holding the body of Zephryn Nightstalker rose in the center of the cliff top. The dragons in scale form on the cliff top emanated sadness, their faces grave and wings tucked back, standing isolated from each other. The gray one, Lord Urun Direclaw, and his crimson ember-mate, Lady Hiera Brightstriker, and the golden pair Lady Birana Dayflier and Lord Polias Sunscaler. These were the dragon founders of the Lawless, and together they formed the dragon council, representing and supporting the dragon leadership in the absence of the monarchs. Next to them stood Tiers Sunscaler, Zephryn's only dragon friend, there to honor the passing of the crown prince.

But who was there to comfort to his widow? Seeing how removed the dragons were from Kesia Ironfire, Maira knew there was no one to fill the role. Her heart twisted, remembering Elestel's funeral. The communal grief over the loss of one of her mates, even if a political alliance, was wrenching. Of course, the dragons wouldn't know of a widow's grieving. They hadn't expected Ironfire to survive.

Ironfire stood on the edge of the funeral pyre, apart from the rest, near where Lirome and Maira stood in hoof form, and beside Maira, Shance. Ironfire's scales gleamed an odd greenish-red color in the light of the torches and burning pyre. Thanks to the odd mixture of healing bond and soul-friend bond, it was easier to read the dragon woman. Bone-deep sorrow. Anger. Shame—at what? At her survival when embermates were meant to die together? Yes, and there was a bright thread of curiosity and a desire for justice. Comfort at Lirome's presence.

A rather strong comfort. Maira tilted her head to the side. She was familiar with the healing bond and had occasionally made them herself to stabilize someone's spirit until they awakened. But it was unusual for that bond to remain in place for so long. Both Lirome and Ironfire should be feeling the strain, especially Lirome. The healing bond was a one-sided offering and a soul-friend bond only went so far. He should be exhausted, especially since he'd spent quite a bit of time in proximity to Kesia on the voyage over. Yet all she could feel from her brother was strong dedication. Some fatigue, but that would be expected from sustaining a—

Maira shook her head. <No, it can't be.>

<It can't be what?> Shance asked next to her.

She looked down into his curious expression, wishing he could read her countenance and follow her thoughts, as they once could so effortlessly even when she was in hoof form. Her heart sank.

They would be that close again.

Which meant she needed to be open with him. <My brother

and Kesia Ironfire. I'm curious about their connection.>

Shance studied the pair and raised his eyebrows. <My memories are still returning, but I don't remember your brother being quite that conscientious with his other patients.>

Maira snorted. <He's always conscientious.>

<Yes, as an uncle and a cousin and a physician. This looks different.> Shance shrugged. <We could be reading into the behavior.>

Maira shook her head. <I don't think so.>

He stroked her flank. <You can't possibly be thinking of matchmaking now. Kesia just lost her embermate. She needs time to grieve.>

Maira sighed, stomping her foot lightly on the ground. <Human women do, or at least that's what their culture says. Kesia is an exception as a dragon widow. That puts her in a unique position. I am merely being mindful of possibilities. And she could use someone to stand beside her. Do you see how the other dragons treat her? At best, she is an oddity for them to protect. Even through their scales, I can sense a desire to keep her locked up for her own protection. There is some regret that she is alive at all.>

<Maira, your eyes are red. You're glaring at the dragon council.>

Her outrage flared. <You're not?>

<I am, but not as obviously.> Shance continued stroking her, pressing down hard so she would feel it. <Just take care. I don't remember much of their politics, but I know that we must tread carefully. Our people are allowed here on certain conditions, one of which is non-interference with dragon affairs.>

She whickered, stomping her front foot quietly. <Agreed. Although I will speak with them afterward.>

<Yes. But not alone.>

Maira gave another whicker, sending a pulse of affection toward

Shance. She had missed her husband. If only their reunion had come at an easier time.

Given how and when they had fallen in love, easy times had never been part of their lives. And they wouldn't have any hope of ease while the Curious Intrigue remained. There were too many other problems to focus on. At least Shance had started to remember her now. All-Maker help her, she would keep forgiving him. It wasn't easy when they hadn't been able to spend much time together. Even on the voyage over, Shance had been occupied with maintaining the wind speeds, and she with healing others.

They would find time. They always did.

At last, the dragons turned and walked toward the cave entrance behind them. Kesia followed them, her shoulders hunched. Lirome moved to accompany her, but she turned and shook her great dragon head.

<They will not permit any others. Only me.>

<Why not?> He tossed his head and snorted. <Your situation is still uncertain.>

<You yourself said I was physically well. That I am strong.>

Troubled feelings emanated from him. <Just because you are strong doesn't mean you have to face anything alone.>

Maira stepped forward. <I agree. Considering that I am the death unicorn queen representing the Lost Refuge, where many Lawless have been healed when none else could aid, refusing me entrance would be politically unwise of them.>

Kesia studied all of them, her sharp teeth showing in a slight smile. <All right. I wouldn't mind the company.>

A rush of relief filled Maira, relief from Kesia, from Lirome, and from within her own heart. She might not be able to assist her other family, but she could offer support to this dragon. Especially since this particular dragon was peculiarly important to Lirome, whether or not he would admit it.

As they entered the hall, the dragons shifted into their skin forms, scales patterning their bare flesh and corresponding colors threading their hair. Large wings emerged from each bare back. A basket of clothing lay in the corner, but they all ignored it, and Kesia did likewise. The other four dragons on the council surrounded her in a square, their wings outspread, leaving the unicorns, Tiers, and Shance on the outside. Dread emanated from Kesia again, and unless Maira misread, Lord Sunscaler and Lady Dayflier had looks of compassion on their sharp faces.

So some of the dragons cared.

Shance groaned quietly next to her. <Oh great. This is one of those 'bare all to show you speak truth and carry no weapons' moments, isn't it?>

<From what I saw earlier, you have nothing to fear in terms of your appearance, Tyrius.> Maira winked at him and shifted into skin form, as did Lirome. Shance rolled his eyes and stripped his clothing until all were on equal footing.

She didn't fault his awkwardness. Humans had no idea how to respond in these situations, where to look and not to look, and how to manage their own body language. They often acted like colts and fillies just come of age. Although even death unicorn adolescents understood the customs.

No matter. She would trust Shance to handle the situation. He had in the past. Hopefully some memories would surface and make it easier. And he would be able to follow along, for all would be in spoken word as part of the tradition of clarity and openness.

Lord Direclaw spoke first, his gray-bearded face solemn. "I see you have invaded our private meeting, Queen Maira Ukerys."

Maira put her hands on her hips. "The decisions made here affect dragon, human, and death unicorn. Such meetings should not be private."

The dragon never turned away from his part in the formation. "Hm. And Shance Windkeeper as well?"

Next to her, Shance cleared his throat. "It was the Lawless who told me that as a Windkeeper, I had a noble leadership duty as Chief of Council. Pardon me for taking them up on that offer."

"Our council is not the dragon-human council of times before." Lord Direclaw breathed out slowly. "Nevertheless, you are permitted. For now." His tone gentled. "Ironfire, I am truly grieved for your loss and absence from your embermate's side."

Kesia's expression remained carefully blank. "He chose to sacrifice his life for mine, Lord Direclaw."

"Now he must face the eternal fire alone, without hope of his spouse by his side. Truly a terrible situation. A loss for everyone here."

Irritation seethed within Maira. Elric's hooves! This dragon truly did wish Kesia had perished. All for the sake of dragon superstitions. Not that this was a time to quibble over beliefs, but the dragon woman was going through enough! She held in a breath. Now was not the time to speak.

Not yet.

Lirome cleared his throat. "Well, she is alive and in excellent health."

"Yes, she is." Lady Brightstriker frowned at Kesia. "A most curious dilemma. We aren't entirely sure what do with you, Ironfire. You still carry half the heart of Zephryn Nightstalker within you, a part your flesh and flaming brightly, according to the caregivers. At this point in time, you are the only living heir to the throne."

Kesia tilted her head, resignation overtaking her features. "You do not refer to me as 'princess,' Lady Brightstriker. Given that the only remaining member of my family allies with the Curious Intrigue, do you intend to disown me and place me in captivity again?"

Maira's muscles tensed as she waited on the answer to Kesia's question, ready to speak up if necessary.

"No." The firm response came from Lord Sunscaler. "There was some debate, especially considering the oddness of your situation," he said, his golden eyes flashing at Lord Direclaw, "but you are free and will remain so. We are not the Pinnacle, and your actions have more than proven your loyalty to the throne and to justice."

Maira breathed out imperceptibly, and Lirome's face relaxed a fraction.

Lady Dayflier spoke up. "Three questions remain undecided, questions you must assist us with."

Kesia gasped, and a wisp of greenish smoke escaped her mouth. "You're going to allow me to decide?"

Lord Direclaw breathed out smoke. "Well, it is irregular—"

"We are not the Pinnacle," Lady Brightstriker said, with a glance at her embermate. "No matter how convenient a unilateral decision would be, honorable dragons do not operate as such."

Kesia nodded, crossing and uncrossing her arms over her chest and finally placing them at her sides. Perhaps she was trying to appear confident, even in her frailty. "What are these questions?"

"First, do you wish to take up the mantle of leadership from Zephryn Nightstalker, with all the responsibilities that position entails, including representing the Scepter of Justice in the cause to stop the false war and the Curious Intrigue, as well as seeking out any remaining members of the royal family?"

"Yes. It's the least I can do."

Kesia's expression was certain. Good. She would need that in the coming weeks. Maira remembered the loss of Elestel. Twenty years later, her mate's death still sent a shot of pain through her, and they had not even been soul-bound.

"Will you seek out the murderers of the crown prince and their leader and bring them to justice?"

Fire flamed Kesia's throat. "Yes. With everything in me."

"Very well."

Lord Sunscaler spoke next. "In dragon law, two must always rule as king and queen. The roles are treacherous, for they are our first and last line of justice in the most harrowing situations. They seek out the most dangerous of foes, they face the most perilous of quests, and they serve all, from the least to the greatest. Much is demanded of them, and only together can they succeed."

Kesia fell silent for a moment, then swallowed hard. "I could attempt to find another embermate. I know in the past two dragons have been compatible with the same mate. It is possible I have another mate as well."

"You are willing to do this?"

Kesia nodded again. "I am willing."

"I don't know that you have much time to search." Lord Direclaw frowned. "Your heartflame weakens, despite what the death unicorn has done to sustain you."

Lirome stepped toward the square of dragons, his expression serious. "I can do more. We share a soul-friend affinity. This is a stronger bond that will ensure Kesia Ironfire is supported in the interim."

"A soul-friend? How is this possible? You are not a dragon."

Her brother's jaw worked, and Maira winced. Only she knew

how much that wasn't quite true. But there was no way her brother would admit it here. He had barely admitted it to her decades earlier.

Finally, he spoke. "I have much experience in treating those who have been experimented on like Ironfire. I have my own methods, if you could trust me."

Maira sensed the mental background noise of the dragons conferring privately. Their expressions clearly showed their suspicion. Lady Brightstriker spoke first from her section of the square. "Lirome Ukerys, it was your kind who struck down our crown prince. And this after the Scepter of Justice welcomed death unicorns in as refugees from Elotrin. How are we to trust you?"

"I saved Kesia's life. My sister and I are willing to seek out the rogue members of our people and bring them to justice."

"Wasn't it your responsibility to ensure these rogue elements were prevented? Were those not the terms set between your queen and agreed to by the dragon royal family?"

Next to her, Shance cleared his throat. "You are well aware that my wife and I were taken captive. We are here now, and we will support the crown princess."

"Yes, but even you have spent a decade out of contact. And Ironfire herself knows nothing of what Garishton Razorclaw did to her—"

"Zephryn Nightstalker, my embermate, trusted Lirome Ukerys." Kesia's voice was soft but edged with steel. Her amber eyes flashed. "And I trust him. He fought the rogue death unicorns alongside us, at personal pain. I will honor my embermate's trust, and my own."

Surprise flickered through Maira. Strong words for the dragon woman. Within, Maira could sense that Kesia only stood with great effort.

Still, it showed promise for a leader.

Another moment of quiet conference occurred among the dragon council. At last, Lord Direclaw spoke, his expression solemn. "All of this is highly irregular and without precedence." He turned to Lirome. "Do you seek to serve as her interim mate?"

The death unicorn shook his head. "At this time, I think she needs a friend and ally more than a lover."

"What do you think a dragon mate is? Or do you imply that a dragon is unworthy of a death unicorn? Not that you would be considered for the role, even if that were possible. Not after the behavior of your kind."

Maira sensed irritation in her brother, but his face remained impassive. "I am declaring that I will stand by Kesia Ironfire during this time of grieving. If she agrees."

Relief showed on her face. "I do."

Surprise ran through Maira. She had considered offering Kesia Ironfire a place in her herd once the dragon's bond-wound had healed, but what Lirome was suggesting was far more intense. He spoke of a period of devotion, walking alongside her through her grief. Among death unicorns, it was called the amshal, and between compatible pairs, the amshal often led to a mating bond after the mourning period was over. Kesia and Lirome were already soul-friends.

Kesia was a dragon. The amshal could be platonic—but who could tell? Her brother was always so reluctant to make bonds with anyone. He never did.

Then again, they were soul-friends.

<Lirome, are you certain? The amshal?>

<Yes.> His tone was dismissive. <I am only doing my duty.>

<Your duty may require more than you are willing to give.>

\<I know what I'm doing.>

\<Does she?>

\<Part of her does, or she wouldn't have agreed. Trust the flow of magic, sister, and let me think.>

\<Don't you use my words on me!>

\<Silence. I'm making a vow.>

Lirome focused on the dragons. "Rogue death unicorns attacked the crown prince and princess. It is only right that I should aid her in seeking justice. I will be at Kesia Ironfire's side as long as she chooses, by the All-Maker and all that I hold dear."

His words rang out in the empty air. Unless Maira was mistaken, Kesia seemed more relaxed. A quietness settled on her features.

She needed someone. Whether she needed Lirome after the amshal, and whether he would admit it, would be interesting to note.

"Very well." Lord Direclaw said. "The final question. Kesia Ironfire, do you agree that any children you have, regardless of your mate, will carry the Nightstalker surname to continue the honor of that line?"

"Yes."

Again, strong and sure in the face of the monumental agreements she had just made. If Maira remembered correctly, this entire exchange would be all that was required to certify the inheritance of power. The ceremonies she remembered from the Scepter of Justice had been for the benefit of others who felt the need for such grandeur. Dragons themselves were remarkably pragmatic and minimalist.

"Lirome Ukerys, as her devoted ally, stand in the center next to Kesia Ironfire," intoned Lady Dayflier.

The dragons' wings flapped once as low thunder, and they all breathed out flame. A great gust of fire and wind flowed around Lirome and Kesia, and their hair flew back away from their serious faces.

"Kesia Ironfire, bearer of the heartflame of Zephryn Nightstalker, this council of dragons hereby acknowledges and names you anew Crown Princess Kesia Ironfire, heir to the throne of the Scepter of Justice and defender of all dragons. May you serve in a worthy manner, bring justice to the darkest of places, and die an honorable death."

The dragons beat their wings a second time and blew another gale of flame. Then all fell silent.

Maira's heart twinged. Dragons were always so aware of death. Even those who followed religions which promised an afterlife for all of the faithful.

Judging by the gravity on Kesia's face, she felt the full weight of the blessing bestowed upon her, along with the burdens of leadership far too heavy for someone so young.

Suddenly Maira understood why the dragons worried about her lack of embermate.

Beneath her bravery and confidence stood a dragon who didn't even know why she was still alive.

CHAPTER ELEVEN

A stirring in his soul awoke Lirome. The same plaintive, word-less aching he couldn't fathom. Nothing had ever felt so empty and void of purpose.

Kesia. The lament had every sign of her peculiar magic.

He got out of his bed and slipped into a pair of pants and a loose shirt. She had her own room in the library district safe house, as was appropriate for the circumstances, but his room was next to hers. Surely he could stop by and calm her, even just by standing outside her door and being present. There was no need to make more trouble for her by unnecessary contact. The dragon council had made their suspicion of him clear.

Lirome left his room and stood noiselessly by her door. It was half open, and inside he could hear Kesia speaking to someone. Good. She hadn't woken up engulfed in angry flames for him to absorb like she often had in the past two and a half weeks. Another curious occurrence. He knew his blood tinkering had made him fireproof, but absorbing her flames was rather unexpected. It could be some aspect of the soul-friend bond. A matter for further con-sideration. Still, he was glad he could help, even if he lacked the satisfaction of understanding why.

Her soft laughter broke through his thoughts. Through the half-open door, he saw her leaning over a clipse-mirror, her brown hair loose over her shoulders and her graceful body hunched and weary in the tunic and trousers.

"Nula, it isn't as simple as killing her."

"Why not?" Nula Thredsing's rich voice came through. "She killed your embermate. You're the hand of justice. You just told me that dragon royals don't get involved in local affairs except in official matters of state. Rather, you skulk around like an official vigilante, observing the wicked and the good and dealing justice in cooperation with human authorities, as possible. Then you report to the dragon-human council and weigh in on large decisions. Which, by the way, is a strange way to run a government."

"I don't mind the idea. The Scepter of Justice was meant to be a fair and open city, not tyrannical. It seems fitting that the highest rulers should have to handle the lowest tasks and be accountable to others."

A smile tugged at his lips. It didn't sound terrible at all. Far better than Maira's endless negotiations and meetings. Lirome had envied the previous dragon king and queen their autonomy.

Kesia sighed. "I just wish I wasn't doing it alone. It feels odd."

Nula's voice gentled. "Zephryn seemed to think you were more than worthy."

"Zephryn also never told me why."

"He loved you."

"And what else?" She sighed. Wisps of smoke escaped her lips. "I still don't know what I am, Nula. Zephryn and I escaped the Pinnacle because my uncle wanted to sever our bond. He assumed I would survive. We thought he was mad, but … here I am. What does that mean?"

Curiosity pricked Lirome, then he shook his head. He'd fallen too easily into eavesdropping. This wasn't his conversation to hear. If Kesia wanted him to know something, she would tell him.

He turned to leave.

"You'll find it. Lirome's there to help you, right?"

Lirome turned back to the door at the mention of his name.

"He's here to monitor my health and ensure I stay alive. Which ... I sometimes wonder why that's important. Surely the dragons would be better served with someone else in power. Besides, Lirome must have far better things to do than stay with me."

Her words stung him. How could she think he didn't care? He'd given all he had to get her and Zephryn out of danger. Guilt shot through him. The dragon crown prince. He would have died for them both, if the damn dragon hadn't extracted that promise. Then, Lirome had given up his own freedom to stay with Kesia during grieving.

How could she think she was unvalued? Alone?

Her plaintive, heart-rending ache resounded through their bond. An ache he had no idea how to answer. It made him certain he needed to spend more time observing and caring for her as long as necessary. The dragon council seemed intent on finding her a new embermate.

Yes, a full dragon would be appropriate for her.

Nula had started talking again. "Kesia, you need to listen to me. I know you were beaten and abused and lost everything. And now you've had to give up even more. But you are stronger and braver than you know, with or without Zephryn. You have a purpose."

The dragon woman cracked a thin smile. "You sound like the priests and priestesses at the Four Corners temple."

"Lirome has you going to those meetings?"

Kesia shrugged. "I don't mind them. It's something new, and I don't really have much else to do other than heal and research and try not to set the safe house on fire. And … they accept everyone. I know I'm broken. I shouldn't be alive. What they say makes sense—which is odd, because I didn't think much of it earlier."

"Well, the Four Corners might be the best thing for you. A lot of them are caring people. Even though I don't hold to everything they teach, and I dislike many of their rules."

Lirome stifled a snort. Of course Nula would.

Kesia shrugged. "I've had to obey cruel people for years just to survive. I don't mind obeying the rules of a religion that is so accepting and willing to understand."

"If they're so accepting, then why have so many rules?"

She blinked. "You can be accepting and still have rules. The two ideas aren't opposed. Good rules are a kindness. I wish the Scepter of Knowledge had more rules on electro-car creation. Maybe there wouldn't be so many crashes."

"Fools. Why don't they use groundcars? I'll never understand it." Nula hmphed. "Anyway, you know I have a taste for futures. Someone's up there orchestrating those futures. It can't hurt to get closer to that person."

"So you see organized religion as a way to gain political favor with a deity?"

Lirome grinned. The dragon certainly had a deft mind and wit to match it.

Nula chuckled. "I never said that!"

"You didn't have to."

"Well, put that perception to good use and find the evil woman who murdered your embermate and kill her. I'll keep my ear to the ground about a new embermate for you. It helps to be married to a dragon spy. As long as he has the wisdom to give me useful information."

Kesia smirked. "Naturally, that's the only reason you married him."

"What can I say? Whoever is up there destined me an ideal husband." Nula sighed. "You won't be working alone forever. Who knows? Maybe it's Lirome, the confirmed bachelor and heart-stealer! I know she won't say anything, but I believe Zilpath had a soft spot for him when they first met over twenty-five years ago."

Heartstealer? Lirome shook his head. Exaggerations. He simply knew how to use his soul empathy to learn what pleased others and turn it into a mutually beneficial connection. It wasn't a special skill. More like a special trickery. Zilpath herself had told him it was dishonorable for a follower of Bonilus to behave in such a manner, even if it was traditionally acceptable for death unicorns. It was one of the many reasons he had ceased even minor flirtations.

And one of the reasons he was certainly unsuitable for Kesia.

The dragon sighed. "Well, if the indomitable Zilpath couldn't turn his head, I'm not about to. That isn't how I want it to work. Even with Zephryn, I had to initiate matters of romance. Repeatedly. It would be nice if it weren't all on my shoulders."

"I understand. Just know that sometimes, men are stupid and need help."

Lirome swallowed a snort. Help was the last thing he needed. Continued faithfulness, temperance, and focus? Yes, he needed all of those. That was all.

"I'll take that under advisement."

Nula tsked. "I notice you're not wearing the voicelator pendant anymore."

Kesia's hand flew to her throat. "Well, we don't really need to hide dragon resonance in the Scepter of Knowledge, and they don't use tepstone. The device isn't necessary anymore."

"You don't want to keep it for sentimental reasons?"

"Why? It only reminds me that Zephryn is gone. I'm already well aware of that. And I can remember him quite well without an object. He only gave it to me a month and a half ago."

The half-dragon gave another tsk. "I can't fault your logic. But I recommend wearing it for a little while anyway, at least in public. You're trying to win the hearts of humans who have a very different grieving process, and win the hearts of dragons who looked to Zephryn as a symbol of hope in the old kingdom. If you leave off the pendant, it would seem like you're disregarding him."

"Even though the dragon council is apparently already seeking a new mate for me?"

Nula sighed. "Even so."

"Very well. Good night, Nula."

"Try to get some sleep, Kesia. You'll make it through this."

"My survival has already been proven. But thanks."

The call ended, snapping Lirome back to his own thoughts. His face heated. Despite his misgivings, he had continued to listen. All-Maker forgive him.

Should he own up to it? Naturally, he should. But Kesia might not respond well. It could break her trust, and it seemed as though she already didn't trust him much. Which wasn't atypical. Maira had always been the twin to win over others. Lirome could, when he chose, but thankfully it had rarely fallen to him to do so.

Yet the idea of failing Kesia devastated him.

Of course it did. He had already failed her and her former embermate once. That could be the only reason.

Then amber eyes stared at him, closer than they had been before. Kesia stood at the door, which was open far wider than it had been a moment ago.

She raised her eyebrows. "Couldn't sleep either?"

Well, there was nothing for it now.

He cleared his throat. "I overheard you speaking, and I was curious."

"I figured as much." Her tone was matter-of-fact. "I'm used to not having privacy, Lirome. And you're already sensitive to my emotions and have seen me in other difficult times recently. Thank you for being honest, at least."

"I'm sorry." There was nothing more to say. "It won't happen again."

Kesia slipped past him. "Sensing my emotions, or eavesdropping on my conversations?"

"The second." He ran his fingers along the back of his neck. "I should go."

"Wait." She folded her arms over her chest, studying him carefully. Not the winsome or shy persona Kesia showed to others, but a more blunt, sincere side. It made him feel curiously ... seen. Just as it had the first time they'd met.

Lirome hadn't decided if that was a good thing or a bad thing.

A faint smile curved on her lips. "What is the human phrase? 'Turnabout is fair play.' You've heard my fears and vulnerabilities. Your turn."

"My turn?" He took a step back. The dragon couldn't be serious.

Kesia nodded. "Yes. You've committed yourself to helping me, and I don't know why, other than duty." Her index finger was set ablaze as she ticked it off. "You tinkered with yourself, your blood, and I don't know why or what you can do." Her middle finger joined her index finger. "You understand my grief, yet you've never lost a mate." Her forefinger made the flaming digit collection a trio. "And you have a longer tea-making process than anyone else I've met."

She waggled the four burning fingers at him. "I want answers." Kesia's tone grew quieter, and she collapsed the flames into a fist, then shrugged. "Please. I'm tired of so many people treating me like an untouchable. A last choice. And I don't want to go to sleep to more nightmares, waking up furious over events I can't change. If I can think about, learn about, care about someone else, it makes it easier to face the dark. Besides, I trust you. Aren't we supposed to be soul-friends?"

The plaintiveness in Kesia's voice echoed in her soul's cry. Lirome's mouth dried. There was no defense against this. Not when he understood her words so deeply.

Untouchable. Experiment. As he had made himself, so she had been made against her will. In the end, the results were the same. Isolation.

Then her face fell. A moment later, the sadness was quickly replaced by a tight smile and resignation. "It's all right. You're doing more than enough by coping with my night terrors. Speaking of which, I'll probably ignore Nula's advice and stay up to train. I might as well—"

"Kesia." He placed his hand over hers, projecting warmth. "Your words have value. Why did you assume I would dismiss them?"

She breathed out slowly. "So many have. And you have no reason to answer my questions. It isn't part of your duties."

Her bitterness was palpable. For once, Lirome regretted keeping her at a distance. Only giving her professional support, when she wanted understanding. A part of him longed for understanding as well. Enough to keep speaking. "It isn't. But … I want to. As I can. I'm not used to…"

"To speaking about it?" Kesia smiled wryly. "I understand that."

"Yes. You do. Which is remarkable." He paused. "I can answer two of your questions tonight. That's all."

Her face lighted with sudden glee and amazement, a shocking change from her sadness. "You will? That's fine. That's enough… for now." Kesia winked. "All right. Are you always called death unicorns? Why not just unicorns?" She froze. "Wait, I didn't mean for that to be one of them—"

Lirome chuckled. "I can answer that easily. We keep the name of "death" as a memory of the genocide. It isn't merely a symbol of becoming weapons. It's a reminder of the loss of so many of our people."

His voice caught. So many of their women, targeted and killed to end the unicorn race. So many children unborn, perishing in the womb. Children never conceived because their future mothers had never lived to meet their mates.

The reason why he and so many other death unicorn men, even now, would never find their mates. Connecting with a human was incredibly rare, and few in Sekastra were open to those soul bonds. Lirome's intellect was brutally honest in that regard. The percentages, the odds, were strongly against him.

An untold grief filled him, a grief that had no logical place. It was senseless to grieve a mate who had never existed in the first place. The All-Maker always had a plan. His plan simply involved Lirome being denied what others took for granted. Other male death unicorns had had to cope with the same fate.

Strong, delicate hands clasped his. He stared down into Kesia's face, saw her reflecting the grief, even if she didn't understand the source. The soul-friend bond. Her own all-too-recent loss. It had to be. He squeezed her hands back. For a moment, they stood locked firmly together.

Then as one, they released. Lirome cleared his throat. "Well, for the other questions?"

She nodded. "Yes. You tinkered with your blood and genes. You're fireproof, which has obvious benefits. What other things can you do?"

Ease filled him as the conversation changed to a lighter topic. "Come with me. I'll show you. As long as you're ready for a fight."

Kesia raised her eyebrows as she followed him to the large sparring room adjacent to the main meeting area in the safe house. The space was bare except for lights flickering in sconces and weapons lining the walls and secured in a large cabinet in the far corner. The safe houses were open at all hours, so the lights were always lit.

Lirome strode into the room, then turned to face Kesia.

There were two ways of releasing the pain within him. One was tears, which he had no use for, despite the death unicorn culture's emphasis on herd emotion-sharing. The other was combat.

Combat was something he only sought with a trusted few, normally wolves. But Kesia's calm acceptance of her predator nature disarmed him.

"Try and attack me."

She tilted her head, hands on her hips. "Lirome, I'm a dragon. You might be fireproof, but my strength far outmatches yours."

"If you can use it." He allowed a grin to stretch across his face, and activated the adrenaline and other chemicals in his body. The ones natural to a sealshifter, accelerating their reflexes and perceptions beyond all other shifters. "Strength can be redirected."

Kesia took up a fighting stance. "As you say. But I'll keep my claws sheathed."

"You don't have to. I may not heal as quickly as my sister, but I heal fast enough." Lirome twitched his fingertips. "Besides, then I would have to sheathe mine."

He allowed his wolf claws to emerge, for once unashamed of them. It was impossible for shame to live amidst the amusement that filled him at Kesia's stunned expression. His claws were shorter than hers, but they could still cause damage.

She breathed out smoke. "How did you—"

"You know the answer. I experimented with donated blood from other shifters. The blood manifested in a handful of traits."

"Yes, but that's—"

"Impossible? When you stand alive before me?" Lirome shook his head. "Now I think to get your final question answered, you'll have to defeat me in combat."

Her eyes turned slitted, and she bared her teeth in a grin. Something that here, for a moment, he could answer. Knowing that Kesia wouldn't tell a soul about his secret. His muscles twitched, anticipating a proper sparring session.

She didn't move. Only stared at him expectantly, her eyes gleaming. "Go ahead."

"You first."

"Very well."

Kesia came at him with a series of quick feints, swiping at the skin on his chest and right bicep—then brought her left elbow in for a swift blow to his gut. Only it never got there. Lirome caught her arm and redirected the energy to the side, throwing her off-balance while grabbing her from behind.

She grunted and easily twisted out of his grasp, bringing her heel down against his foot. He muttered a curse and stepped away. Kesia whirled around and regrouped in an instant, immediately aiming a low kick at his shins.

On and on they went. Both of them holding back from true harm, the sparring a martial dance. A mixture of intellectual challenge and pure movement and speed.

Invigorating. Freeing.

Until at last, they both were locked in close again. Lirome's claws managing to get inches from her throat, while Kesia held them fast with indomitable strength he couldn't match.

She chuckled. "All right. I think my other question will be about the tea."

"Tea sounds delightful."

"So you say."

They released each other, backing away. Lirome's muscles burned, and his stomach heaved for breaths. He thought sparring with wolves was difficult, but dragons were another matter entirely. The sheer discipline of Kesia's attacks was incredible.

Elric's hooves, *she* was incredible.

"You're a great fighter yourself," she said, wiping sweat from her brow.

He frowned. "How did you know—?"

"Oh, I just … sense things, sometimes. Little things. It's been happening for a few weeks now." Kesia smiled ruefully. "You know what your experiments did to you. I still don't know what's happening to me."

"Hm."

Her sensitivity could be due to the soul-friend bond. Yet why would she sense other things besides him? Lirome would have to think more on that. Right now, refreshment sounded good. Water, preferably, but he could always drink tea along with it.

"You wanted to know why I take so long making tea?" He headed for the doorway, and Kesia fell into step beside him.

"Yes. It seems absurd to have all those steps of sifting and steeping and stirring."

"Far from it." He shook his head disapprovingly. "It is the only way to get a perfect cup."

"As you say."

"I do." Lirome gestured her over. "Watch and learn, oh doubtful dragon."

As his fingers went about the familiar task, an odd peace filled him. At least, in some way, he had helped the grieving dragon to smile. He had succeeded in that task.

She had made his burden a little lighter.

It couldn't replace the grief, or end the war, or even reveal the mysterious red-haired woman who had killed the crown prince.

But for a fleeting moment, the plaintive aching from her was gone. There was peace. And tea.

And Kesia's teasing voice, that for some reason settled him like nothing else had.

That concerned him most of all.

Chapter Twelve

There had been a time when Kesia had craved books. She'd dreamed of poring over them and learning everything she could, just like Zephryn enjoyed doing. During their imprisonment, he had told stories of the marvels to be found in books.

But now that she stood ten stories in the air in yet another room filled with books, all she wanted to do was burn them. No, that was unkind. Perhaps only burn the dull ones. The research books, filled with endless histories, records from meetings that people in this Scepter seemed to call at every opportunity, minute societal data—all should be consumed with fire.

Lirome gave her a sidelong glance. He'd opted for clothes more appropriate for blending in, which included a plain gray waistcoat, jacket, and breeches. His black hair was pulled away from his face. He wore none of the death unicorn mourning makeup that his sister wore all the time. Kesia felt a twinge of curiosity to see what it would look like on him, accompanied by an urge to apply it to him herself. Especially to his lips.

She immediately shut down the impulse, but her throat flamed hotter.

"I don't recommend acting on your irritation. Although, if

you're going to set this place on fire, wait until I've put a few books in the book dumbwaiter with a note to deliver to the tea shop near the safe house."

Kesia raised her eyebrows and turned to him in disbelief, swallowing the flames. "You found worthwhile books in the recent civil records tower?"

"A few older medical journals. It's amusing to see the mistakes of others, but studying their ideas, even if misguided, can yield new solutions." He shrugged. "Besides, if they don't help, you can use them for kindling in your flame training."

"I have been running out of targets. Good idea."

"I have those occasionally." He disappeared behind another bookshelf. Intent on their search for evidence of the red-haired woman and the death unicorn presence in the city affairs.

She smiled despite herself and tried to focus on the book in front of her. This was the first time she had entered one of the libraries where she and Zephryn had worked. Finally, Kesia had felt she could do so. She hadn't woken up engulfed in flames and tears for five nights in a row. That had convinced Lirome she was ready to be around others again, and he'd agreed to them leaving their underground confines.

She had also been able to continue her training and research work while in the safe house. She regularly spoke with Nula and Shance. And she'd learned more about Lirome's medical pursuits and started to assist him. It was his suggestion, so she wouldn't fear examinations so much. Resting in the safe house was a far cry from imprisonment. She'd even been able to taste the local cuisine, since her death unicorn ally enjoyed sampling new foods and was concerned over her appetite. Which had been getting better. She was back to eating a serving more than typical human females. Now,

Kesia just needed to double that.

She stared at the dusty tomes as Lirome did his part to find fresh research among the stacks. There was no tall, stern figure sitting across the table to eye her with a knowing look. No voice in her head, making sharp comments on all that she said or did.

Her stomach twisted over the bread, fruit, and meat she'd eaten that morning. Suddenly, she wished she hadn't eaten anything.

She could almost hear Zephryn's words in her mind, almost see his faint smile. She remembered one conversation as if it were yesterday.

<Burning the books would be a very bad idea, considering that the shelving and buildings themselves are made of wood.> Zephryn glanced at her, his cobalt eyes fierce and tired. <But I understand the sentiment.>

<Oh? You seemed quite engrossed.> She tapped her fingernails on the table, shifting them into claws just enough to leave tiny indentations in the wood.

His hand clasped hers, and his boredom floated clearly through their heartflame bond. <Only because I've learned to force myself. Couldn't you tell how I was feeling?>

<Usually I can, but when you're focusing that hard, it almost shuts me out.>

Concern filtered through their link, and he squeezed her hand. <Why haven't you mentioned this before?>

She shrugged, enjoying the touch of his skin. <When I was imprisoned, anything I could sense of you was a beacon of hope. I'm only getting used to the differences now.>

<Ah, I see.> He frowned. <When we were imprisoned.>

<You weren't held with chains wrapped around your wrists and neck. You were permitted access to the libraries and the meetings and

the halls.>

Zephryn held her gaze a moment more, then sighed a faint breath of smoke. <I know. I don't like thinking of it. You are so very important, Kesia.>

"Kesia? Kesia!"

A hand grabbed hers, but it wasn't Zephryn's. It was strong and lean, yet it was the wrong shape, the wrong kind of grip. It lacked heat but offered support to her soul. She blinked and looked up into Lirome's violet eyes, bright with concern. "Your throat is burning."

"Oh." She swallowed and yanked her hand out of his. "I'm sorry."

"Maybe we should have stayed in the safe house longer—"

"No. I've spent enough time cooped up there. Continuing Zephryn's research is my responsibility as crown princess. I'll keep better control over my heat." Kesia strode over to the glass window and stared out into the foggy streets below.

The perpetual mist of the Scepter of Knowledge condensed over everything it touched.

She remembered how it had fused with the terrifying shadows made that fateful night, turning into something else. Something that had consumed her, even as the fear had done. It almost killed her. Still, she had remained alive while Zephryn, the crown prince, had died. Zephryn, in skin form, with the dark blue scales visible on his forehead, cheekbones, along his neck, and so many other places. She knew where every glimmering scale had been.

No more. Now, there was nothing for her. The dragon council claimed to search for an embermate, but who could ever care for her as Zephryn had? Her words to the dragon council had been spurred by impulse and a desire to serve. Not a real expectation.

Perhaps there was no one else out there. The embermate bond only came about from a full alignment of values, purpose, and mutual attraction. There weren't many dragons to begin with, even fewer since some still sided with the Pinnacle.

Could any relate to what she was?

Even Lirome had indicated on multiple occasions that it was only duty that kept him there. Never mind how easy it was to speak with him. To trust him. Soul-friends only.

She picked at the high collar of her blouse and stiff corset. Shifted in the tall boots that had far too many buttons. Her hair was swept atop her head in a tight bun, pinched with an excess of pins. It was the ideal cover—an average woman in the Scepter of Knowledge.

She wasn't average. She wasn't even a human woman.

Why wear this clothing?

She exhaled a long plume of smoke that was greener than it had ever been. Zephryn had insisted she could own her experimentations. But where was he now?

Her chest tightened with a flame-choked sob. No. There was no time for tears.

To divert her attention, she focused on the view outside the window. The dark, narrow streets were rimmed by strips of sidewalk in paler gray. The Scepter of Commerce had wide lanes and a sense of flow, but here, tall wood and steel buildings crowded every block. Street vendors and debate callers clustered on every corner, demanding that others take notice of their words. She'd sometimes paused while walking with Lirome to listen and discuss.

Even more fascinating than the people were the wires strung from poles and cars with lightning rods affixed to the tops that cluttered the skies and jammed the roads. The Scepter of Knowledge had clipse-mirrors and wireless commers like the other cities in the Congruency, but they preferred innovation, which meant finding ten ways of doing the same thing, even if the initial problem was already solved. Hence the electro-carriages on lightning tracks.

Some said the vehicles were safer and better for the environment than groundcars with their fumes. But in the six weeks since Kesia had arrived at the Scepter of Knowledge, three electro-carriages had burst into flames from an electrical surge. The first time, she'd thought the burst was another dragon. She knew better now. Kesia wanted to find the erstwhile inventor of the electro-carriage, singe a few hairs off his head, confiscate his blueprints, and use them herself to solve the explosion issue. Maybe then she and this inventor could discuss other innovations in the Scepter of Knowledge. She wanted to explore and figure out how this place worked. Perhaps break into some new places and spy on people. Maybe meet some new humans.

"Are you sure you're all right?"

She huffed. Couldn't the death unicorn leave her alone with her thoughts? "I am unharmed, if that's what you mean. You said so yourself."

"I said physically you were unharmed. You're currently steaming the window and nearly melting the glass."

"Fewmets!" Kesia turned away from the window, wiping her hands on her skirt and glowering at the unicorn. "Why aren't Shance and your sister here yet? Wasn't the cat-dragon supposed to summon them?"

Lirome met her glare with a quelling look. "Yes, but neither of them have the Talent of teleportation."

"More's the pity."

She turned back to the window. At that moment, a glimmer of

sunlight broke through the clouds, turning the ceaseless rain into a myriad of sparkling, iridescent drops.

Kesia inhaled. "It's beautiful."

"It's rain."

She fixed Lirome with a dirty look, but he only answered with a half-smile. The sort that suggested he agreed with her and only wanted to tease. "I'll remember your callous dismissal of rain the next time you're thirsty."

His violet eyes glinted. "An empty threat, since I prefer tea."

"Tea happens to be made with water. Unless you prefer something else, like acid or oil?"

His voice remained deadpan. "I am always interested in new flavors."

Kesia chuckled. Lirome's eyes widened as he surveyed the outside. The beams of light had grown brighter, dancing among the droplets in a brilliant reflection.

"You are right about the rain, at least." His voice deepened with awe. Ever so gently, he rested his hand on her upper back. One of his usual gestures of comfort.

"Are you glad you didn't ignore me?"

He turned and studied her seriously once more. "Skies rue the day that I ignore you."

She held his stare, caught in the quiet sincerity that seemed to promise more than he was aware of. More than she could hope to decipher. She'd had a hard enough time deciphering the intentions of Zephryn, and they had been bound for ten years. Kesia didn't have a chance of understanding Lirome. Especially when she could sense him blocking her, and couldn't even trust that sensation.

She sighed and broke eye contact. "I was just thinking of a recent conversation with Zephryn, where he insisted again that I was somehow valuable."

As one they began walking back toward the table. "He mentioned that your uncle sought to break your bond for some ulterior motive. Garishton thought you would survive."

"Yes, and be broken enough to mate with someone else. Apparently, he knew what he was doing." Bitterness laced her tone. Kesia sat down on the tabletop for a change. A fresh idea came to mind. She hated it, hated even thinking about the experiments she'd endured. But there might be answers. "Is there any more information about Garishton Razorclaw in the Lawless?"

Lirome shook his head. "If there were, they wouldn't release it to me."

"Why not?"

"Dragons are first and foremost trying to restore the Scepter of Justice. The fall of the old kingdom was very messy."

Kesia nodded, recalling what she had been told by the Lawless in the Scepter of Commerce. "Garishton loved Zephryn's mother, but so did the crown prince. The crown prince merited precedence because of his status. The dragon-human council had judged he needed an embermate more."

"And they took steps to make sure it would remain so." Lirome frowned, rubbing his forehead. His expression turned distant as he recalled the past. "I'm not privy to the details, but I know they segregated Garishton Ironfire from the rest of your kind, perhaps making him vulnerable to the Curious Intrigue."

Segregated. The word was cold. Hard. Evoking the loneliness she was accustomed to. Her uncle had felt isolated, and he had cursed her so she would be isolated too. Anger flamed within her. Her hands closed into fists.

Lirome sat down in front of her, his hands covering her fists.

She looked down into his eyes. Seeing within them understanding, deep and complete, that he still wouldn't explain, except to say that they were soul-friends.

It didn't feel the same as earlier. Something was changing, slowly enough that Kesia wouldn't have noticed if the wound in her soul hadn't been so sensitive. But she couldn't hope to put it into words.

"There is another place to look for answers," Lirome said. "The Four Corners temples."

Kesia tilted her head, confused. "I enjoy the Remembrance gatherings every nine days. My very survival is impossible, and that opens me up to other possibilities as well, even the beliefs of a Creator. And I like that I can ask questions about everything. But how would they hold answers about my uncle?"

"He was devout at one time."

Bile rose in her throat. "Here I thought you were trying to make this religion appealing."

Lirome gave her a cutting stare. "The Four Corners didn't turn him to evil actions. They keep their doors open to all, and it is possible he told them something that he told no one else. Even secret information or documents."

"Would the priests or priestesses allow that?"

"If he invoked the Rite of Consolation, they would have no choice. The Rite stipulates that only comfort and advice may be given to the person being consoled."

Kesia frowned. "Couldn't the priest or priestess use some kind of judgement?"

"They are only mediaries in keeping the rituals. They cannot give absolution." Lirome's expression turned thoughtful. "However, there are ways priests or priestesses can alert an outsider if they truly think someone is a danger—or in danger. And the Rite of Consolation narrows it down, because it is only administered by someone of the same gender. We'd be searching for a priest." He yawned. "This is a large city without restrictions on the number of worship houses. There are at least ten temples of various sizes, most of them outside the official Temple district. There are even more lay meeting areas."

Kesia nodded. "Would those be kept in the civil records?"

"Most of them would."

"Then let's search!"

If they couldn't learn anything about the rogue death unicorns, at least they could figure out what Garishton had done to her. It was a partial solution.

Without waiting for him, she headed to a shelf and began browsing. Finally, something that could lead to answers. Something that would enable her to understand her embermate's final words and perhaps justify his sacrifice.

After browsing for a short while, she carried a high stack of thick books over to the table.

"Lirome? I'm not bothered by the weight of these books, but I would appreciate help looking through them."

A snore answered her. Kesia blinked. The death unicorn had fallen asleep on a book that recorded the civil tree harvests for the last thirty years.

She raised her eyebrows. He looked far less regal and much sillier when his mouth was half-open making a sound like a wood saw. Such was his self-proclaimed dust affliction. He probably shouldn't be sleeping like that. It was probably bad for his back. A flicker of humor warmed her.

Sometimes, she let sleeping death unicorns lie. But this wasn't going to be one of those times.

What would be the most amusing way to wake him? Not cruel or something that would inflict physical injury. Never that.

Her eyes rested on the stack of books she carried. Kesia inhaled quietly and prepared to deposit them next to the death unicorn's head in one resounding thunk.

It wasn't as if she was doing anything too unusual. Really, he should know better by now.

Her muscles tensed, ready to drop the books.

Lirome's wireless commer chirped loudly. He jerked up, tapping at the small square. At the same time, the stack of books slipped out of Kesia's hands and fell to the ground. She skidded off-balance into one of the shelves. It rocked back and forth precariously. Fewmets! Alarm shot through her. She reached out and set the massive shelf to rights.

"Scale mites, Lirome! You had to wake up *now*?"

One of the death unicorn's hands shot out, grabbing her arm and steadying her, while the other silenced his commer. He gave a small smile. "You would have been disappointed by the results."

Kesia studied him, her fear calming under his touch. "How so?"

"Unicorns are able to sleep through anything when our souls are certain they rest in a safe place. Your emotions gave you away." He smirked. "You really thought I wouldn't catch on by now?"

That statement deserved to be ignored. She huffed. "Didn't we discuss you reading my emotions when I can't read yours?"

"Yes, but this wasn't intentional. It's sometimes a hazard around others who aren't able to contain themselves."

Kesia paused. "Are you saying I lack control?"

"No, that isn't your trouble at all."

"Is it part of the soul-friend connection?"

He frowned. "Maybe. You are something altogether different. Equal parts grief and laughter, yet entirely at peace. It doesn't make sense. A death unicorn would still be in the depths of sorrow."

She swallowed. "I do grieve. But Zephryn is dead. He isn't coming back. He's gone, and I'm here, working to make the best of the situation alone."

The last word stung as she spoke it, echoing a deep disquiet she had tried to ignore. It was an unvoiced cry of longing that had no place, for there was no one to answer it.

She huffed again. "I'm not fond of being deconstructed and analyzed."

He glanced down at her, his lips twitching into a knowing smile. "If you persist in studying others, don't be surprised when you are studied in return. Are you always conducting experiments on your surroundings?"

"Your snoring begged for examination."

Lirome's wireless commer chirped again. He sighed, released Kesia's arm, and began helping her pick up the books while answering the call. "Yes, Maira?"

"We're on our way."

"And you couldn't mindspeak because—oh, never mind. I remember."

"I'm healing as fast as I can, brother dear."

"I know." A mixture of compassion and irritation flashed over his face. "Why did you call? It's dangerous for you. Someone could intercept this communication."

"Life is dangerous. We've been delayed by two different electro-carriage accidents. Begin the briefing without us. How is the dragon?"

Kesia finished putting the last few books on the shelf and leaned toward the commer. "She's alive, and she can hear you. And she heard your brother snoring."

Lirome made a face at her as the commer responded. "I'm glad to hear he's getting rest—"

"Maira snores as well," Shance's voice broke over the commer.

"I do not!"

"My memories haven't all returned, my love, but I remember that. Only when there's sufficient dust, though."

Yet another voice sounded. "Shance speaks the truth!"

"Silence, you two!"

Kesia's mouth curled into a grin. The distraction pleased her.

Lirome chuckled. "Fine then. Come soon. Long days—"

"And safe nights. I know. Don't have an aneurysm. You need your brain."

He pressed the commer again, and Kesia sat back down on the table, tilting her head.

"Your sister tends to run on her own schedule."

"Yes." He sighed with a rueful look. "I am glad she's alive. After all, I spent a decade searching for her. But the leadership of our people weighs heavily on her, which means sometimes, she fights back with carelessness."

"Yes, Zephryn did the same." She paused. "If your sister is the queen, doesn't that make you a prince?"

Lirome shook his head. "Our society is strictly egalitarian, except when necessary for authority. My sister is the queen by virtue of birth and need. Shance Windkeeper, her chief mate, has his own mediatorial responsibilities, and her other mates operate as regents. I am considered no different than any other death unicorn. Utterly unimportant."

"I would say you're very important." Kesia frowned. "Why did you offer to help me?"

Lirome exhaled through his nose and placed a hand lightly over hers. "I made a promise. It was the right thing to do."

His touch sent waves of warmth through her. Odd. His skin should be cooler because he was not a dragon, even though he had trace amounts of dragon blood.

She pushed off the table, closing the distance between them. "But why not another death unicorn? Why not call up someone from the Lost Refuge?"

His violet eyes darkened. "I was the one who made the promise. I will stand by it."

"I see. Very logical. Thank you." Understandable, given the circumstances. Never mind the odd feelings that swirled around her.

Besides, Lirome would be leaving as soon as she found another embermate. Or as soon as it was convenient for him. Yes, he had said he would remain as long as she chose, but those were only words. Since when had her choices mattered anyway? She moved away from him, ignoring the pang of sadness that came from she knew not where, and leaned over the table.

"So, I've discovered a few books to look through."

Lirome sighed and rolled up his sleeves. "Very well. But these must be assessed after our tea break."

Ah yes. One of the best habits Lirome had introduced. Kesia let herself be pulled into pleasanter musings. "Which shop shall we test out today? You're still not going to convince me to enjoy it."

"We'll see about that."

A raucous sound cut off her retort.

"Another campaign rally?" Kesia muttered. "What is it about this time?"

Silence descended between them as they listened to the cries and the shouts.

Lirome's expression sobered. "The disavowal of the Lawless and the need for the war. Even at the expense of attacking the Scepter of Commerce for their cessation. My instincts say we should get down there."

"All right. These can wait."

Kesia slapped the book shut and strode toward the door.

At last, something was happening.

Even though it was negative. She was used to negative.

CHAPTER THIRTEEN

The streets were thick with people. A heavier than usual mist had blown in off the bay and settled among the tall buildings and electro-carriage wires. For one hour a day, all motorized transportation in the Scepter of Knowledge came to a halt to allow anyone and everyone who wanted to shout their views or opinions to do so. One could usually hear diatribes on the merits of everything from anarchy to an all-vegetable diet. The latter would have appealed to Lirome if he didn't have a fondness for bacon.

But today as he and Kesia pushed their way through the crowd, there was only one voice intoning above the masses. One sweet, lyrical voice amplified by a large audiceptor in front of the speaker on the platform. The woman was of average height with deep red hair falling over her shoulders and brilliant blue eyes set in a pale, unblemished face. She wore a silver-gray dress that flowed over her figure. Around her stood a number of men and women who stared out into the crowd as if they guarded a prized hoard of treasure. Many in the audience looked similarly enraptured.

All Lirome wanted to do was kill the woman where she stood, for she was the villain who had swallowed up Zephryn Nightstalker and broken him with fear. Next to him, Kesia had frozen in place. Lirome took her hand, sending out as much reassurance and strength as he could.

<I'm here, Kesia. I'm here.>

Anger poured from her. <I know. I don't want *her* to be. And why does my head ache?>

<May I intrude a little to check?>

She nodded impatiently. Lirome slipped into her mind and perceptions, comparing them to his own. The red-haired woman was exuding soul magic, turning the minds of the crowd. Somehow, Kesia sensed that as well.

Impossible. Dragons couldn't perceive soul magic.

<I don't understand.>

She nudged him. <Listen!>

The woman opened her mouth to speak once more.

"The Scepter of Knowledge is a great city, filled with marvels of the mind and an innovative and philosophical spirit." She smiled at the applause, then her tone turned serious. "But there are those who threaten this livelihood. Corrupt and evil dragons circle the skies and would quench the fires of intellectual improvement as easy as they lit the Pinwoods ablaze a few years ago. Or have you forgotten the terrible inferno that nearly decimated your—our beloved home?"

Murmurs of agreement filtered around Lirome and Kesia. Even though from the books he'd reviewed, the blaze had only affected a small portion of the Pinwoods. According to Kesia, it would have been considered a failed mission on the part of the Pinnacle.

Lirome winced. The slurry of tainted adoration around him turned his stomach. He mentally pulled away from Kesia's perceptions, and together they made their way over to where Shance and Maira stood. There was a hardness to the captain's face and a sharpness in his eyes. Maira stood beside him, resting her hand on his arm.

Lirome exhaled in relief. They seemed to be reconnecting again in the four weeks since Nightstalker's death.

The villain continued to speak.

"For too long has the Scepter of Knowledge stood idly by while so many have suffered! The Scepter of Commerce has already been deceived into inaction, leaving many more vulnerable to this war."

A lie. The Scepter of Commerce had a standing military engaging the true enemy. They were paying for siding with the Lawless. The attacks in their airspace had been brutal, and perilously close to the city itself.

"Do not follow the folly of the city-state to the south. Take the final steps necessary to win this war. Stand with the Curious Intrigue. We are on your side. We desire to lift the veil on true knowledge and science to further all of humanity."

The red-haired woman's face filled with grief and outrage. Kesia gasped, rubbing her forehead. <Others feel pleasure. Of course, I'm the one feeling pain.>

<Feeling pain is not a weakness.> He studied her with concern. <The most important thing is to acknowledge it, allow it to pass through you into its place, and do what you know is best in spite of it. No matter what.>

She smiled despite herself. <Thank you. Even though you're still reading my emotions.>

<It is my job to assure your well-being, Kesia. Why is it so hard for you to accept that?>

<Maybe because it's embarrassing to be someone else's duty all the time!>

With her words, she dropped her internal barriers. Rage, grief, frustration, and that singing need consumed him for a moment. He blinked and shifted backward. Kesia gave a tiny grin. Across from her, Maira stifled a chuckle.

Lirome glared at his sister. <Do you have something to share?>

<Nothing at all regarding your disagreement.> Her face quickly turned serious. <But this woman is lying and twisting the crowd. Something must be done about it.>

Kesia nodded. <There are rules for opening a discussion for an opposing opinion. But I'm only a junior elocution acolyte. I can't challenge solo.>

Maira's face turned grim. <I'm whatever I say I am. And I am more than capable of handling whatever this wretch can throw at me. Do you know the official words?>

<Yes.>

<Then get up on that stage and say them with your full dragon resonance to sound appealing. I'll be right behind you when I see an opening. Trust me.>

<All right.>

While Lirome's mind was still catching up, the dragon lifted her chin and raised her voice so as to carry over the crowd.

"I challenge for right of dissension and counterpoint!"

Around her, the boisterous crowd dulled to handfuls of whispers and murmurs. On the platform, the red-haired woman blinked in exaggerated confusion. "Dear me, did anyone hear a sound, like a little mouse?"

Anger flared within Kesia, filtering and mingling through Lirome. He felt her channel the emotion and summon more energy deep from within herself. Elric's mane, she was strong.

Her voice rang out, along with a plume of greenish smoke.

"I, Kesia Ironfire, challenge this view with my right of dissension and counterpoint!"

At her final words, the crowd fell silent, their attention fixed on Kesia. Fortunately, her outburst of smoke had dissipated into the fog quickly. She glanced over at Shance, who winked at her. His wind Talent at work. Good.

The red-haired woman narrowed her eyes at Kesia. A second later, Lirome felt the terror surrounding the dragon, threatening to render her immobile. Such horrible focus and precision. But he wouldn't let it come near his … charge. Patient. Soul-friend.

The dragon woman was right. None of those quite fit. But now wasn't the time to worry over it.

He sent a steady peace through Kesia's mind and siphoning off the worst of the fear. Her eyes drifted over to him, and her lips curled in gratitude. Lirome gave a half-smile in return. <Only leveling the playing field. Please, rip her to shreds with words until we can do so physically.>

Lirome felt her surprise. Vengeance was not only for dragons.

The red-haired woman stepped to the edge of the platform, her devoted entourage moving with her. Her face was pinched in suspicion, even as her voice remained sweet. "Let me see the outsider who challenges the truth claims of the Lady Lurien."

More words flew out of Kesia's mouth. "There are no titles of "lady" in the Scepter of Knowledge. Are you a representative of the Meritas—or the Meritas herself?"

It was bait. The reigning Meritas was a man who had campaigned under the premise of maintaining neutrality in the war. He was also known for the Talent of indomitable will, much to the dismay of many who tried to sway and bribe him.

Kesia walked to the edge of the platform and climbed up the stairs. She was every inch the composed speaker, carrying the weight of maturity borne from hardship.

"Alas, I am not yet the Meritas, though if these fine ladies and gentlemen agree with my words, my ascension to that august position will be forthcoming. Still, Lady Lurien Alistil is my chosen name for this situation. But what do we have here? A mouse after all."

Lurien gave Kesia a critical glance. Kesia stared right back at her.

"My apologies if you misheard my two very recent statements. I am challenging you—"

"Yes, yes, I know. You are well within your rights to do so. It seems you have the attention of the crowd as well." The red-haired woman made a sweeping gesture to those gathered around the platform. The crowd watched the two women as if observing a heated firefight. "Most ... *curious*, indeed. You seem to be a woman of singular Talent, Kesia Ironfire. Or perhaps plural?"

Dread filled Lirome. His voice filled her mind. <She knows about you.>

<Don't worry. I will make sure I know about her.>

"So, Ironfire—such a very flame-filled name—when will this debate commence? While we're on the subject, what are your credentials?"

"My credentials?"

"Oh yes, my good woman. You see, I am an experienced senior elocution master. By this little pin on your collar," Lurien made another gesture with a surprised expression, "you are only a junior elocution acolyte. Only a senior elocution acolyte can face me in a debate of this magnitude. You are seeking to overturn my entire campaign. We are an intellectual meritocracy, after all. You must show your mind worthy of the task to unseat one such as I."

"You seem to have memorized the official guidelines as well."

"Haven't you, oh one of bold voice? So very bold and with much resonance. Very interesting. Will any in the crowd speak for you? Otherwise, you are just another loud voice among the masses."

Kesia's face tightened. <Maira, I think your time is now.>

<Agreed.>

The dragon sucked in a breath. "It seems you have a poor opinion of the people in this city, Alistil, to refer to them with such disregard."

"My apologies. It seems that you still have no sponsor, Ironfire. Your words mean nothing."

The triumphant statement sounded a knell of embarrassment along Lirome's link with Kesia. Anger and deep-set insecurities warred within her.

"She does have a sponsor." Maira's voice was clear and strong. She strode up to the stage and ascended quickly. "I will sponsor her in the debate to unseat your position in the Scepter of Knowledge."

Lurien's eyes widened as she turned to face Maira. The death unicorn queen strutted around her, carrying her short height like a crown. "And just who are you?"

"Maira Ukerys. I am as fit to join this debate as you are, as well as to legally unseat you forever from this city, and send you back where you came from. I'm sure your own ... family will be most relieved to keep you close." Maira flashed a winsome grin through her black lips. "Please, I welcome any opposition you may have to my statements. After all, you seem quite good at holding others captive with your words. Among other things."

Lurien gave a shaky laugh, her fingers playing with her hair. Clearly she was unnerved at the presence of the death unicorn queen herself. Lirome snorted. She should be.

"Unseat me? The stakes have been raised, I see. I accept, Maira

Ukerys. Nine weeks from now, at the Celestis Festival, the debate will commence. If I win according to judge and vote, the Scepter of Knowledge will enter the war."

"When you lose, you and the Curious Intrigue will be banished from this city forever." Maira studied her as if she were a terrible infection. "Do you accept these terms?"

"Yes. I will present them to the Meritas jury at once."

Kesia leveled a glare at her. "*We* will present them, after both parties approve of the documents."

"Of course." Lurien focused on Kesia once more, her lips curving into a pert smile while her eyes flashed blood red. "Until next we meet, little mouse."

There was the confirmation they had been waiting for. The redhaired woman was another death unicorn. The leader, and a very powerful one.

Kesia nodded shortly. "Until then."

She and Maira turned and began walking away. They had just reached the edge of the platform when Lurien made a sudden, dramatic gasp. "Oh dear, I forgot one minor part of this. As a junior acolyte, Ironfire has the advantage with a senior acolyte as a partner and lead. Shouldn't I also have a partner?"

Maira turned back, sighing reluctantly. "It seems only fair. Whom do you choose?"

"Well, since Ironfire has implied that I think less of the masses, it should be someone from this very crowd. Someone of the people, as a sign of good faith in the wit and intellect of the populace. I think I know just the man."

Her eyes flitted around—and lighted on Shance Windkeeper.

CHAPTER FOURTEEN

The moment Shance realized Lady Lurien was going to choose him, he instantly regretted his presence at the rally. He should have taken Maira, Lirome, Kesia, and his ship and flown away to figure everything out. He should have stayed in the shadows. He should have ducked into a building.

He should have done anything possible to flee the moment the death unicorn who held his son enthralled focused on him as her next prize.

Shance knew she was a death unicorn. He could sense it as surely as he could feel the frosty fire on his skin. Naturally, since he was a sensitive—the Elotrin word for someone with death unicorn heritage, of which he had a scant amount from Efluria and Elric in his family tree. The Lady Lurien, if that was her true name, was enrobing the crowd in sympathetic soul empathy, a tactic that had worked well until Kesia breathed out her greenish smoke and Shance dispersed it among the people.

Did the smoke now rid soul manipulation of its power as well? Unheard of. That was innate shifter magic. But the green smoke couldn't have shown up at a better time. From Kesia's stricken expression, she likely thought the smoke was another slip-up. Hopefully one of the death unicorns would illuminate her.

Lady Lurien seemed far less oblivious. The expression she turned on Shance was pure calculation and triumph.

"I call Captain Shance Windkeeper as my second."

The crowd turned toward him. From the platform, Maira's eyes burned into his. Next to Shance, Ademis hissed.

<One word of leave, and I will shift and burn and shred that woman.> The cat-dragon said. <And her dress. And then the audiceptor. That device has been a devious enemy since its invention.>

Maira shook her head slightly. <Be at peace, Ademis.> Her face was resolute. <Shance, she can't force you to do this. You have many acceptable reasons for withdrawal.>

<Not the least being that Lurien is trying to grab herd power.> Lirome added, his face implacable with thought. <You are Maira's chief mate. No death unicorn should hold any authority over you.>

<Unless...> His wife paused. <Stall her. I need to think.>

Shance cleared his throat. "I am an airship captain, not a public speaker. I'm woefully underqualified to assist you."

"Then it shall be fair as we take on a junior and a senior acolyte. Your skill in conversation must be as strong as Ironfire's, since she has no achievement medals to her name."

Kesia's mouth tightened, but otherwise she remained impassive. Next to her, Maira may as well have been carved out of stone.

"You know how to flatter a man." Others around Shance chuckled, and he held up his hands. "I have responsibilities to my ship and crew. I cannot commit to a debate of such significance, especially one with an uncertain outcome."

Lurien's red-painted lips curved into a smile. "Hardly uncertain, I would say. And I do appreciate your commitment to your responsibilities. Brennar, come here."

Shance's heart stopped as he saw his son emerge from the crowd, ascend the platform, and walk eagerly to Lurien's side. From there he waited at attention while she studied him in approval, as if appraising a beloved object.

"As you see, I have others who lack experience who could serve just as well to handicap me against my foes. After all, I cannot win too easily." Lurien gave a theatrical sigh. "Still, I thought that understanding the opportunities at my side would open your mind to the idea. Perhaps it would release other parts of you as well, if you so choose."

Another wave of frost fire unicorn magic pressed lust and enticement upon him as thickly as mud. Shance shook them off with a grimace. No matter what women he had slept with over the last decade, he was quite certain Lurien had not been one of them. She was as desirable as rancid engine oil. Nevertheless, she held his son and who knew how many other death unicorns in her thrall. Perhaps by accepting the position in the debate he could infiltrate that thrall, convince them to resist, and return his family to the herd.

As he gave Maira a sidelong glance, he could tell she was considering the same venture. The regret and steely determination emanating from her revealed how little she liked it. <If you go with her now, any and all death unicorns she holds enthralled will see it as a critical loss on my part. To lose my son and others in my herd is one matter. But to capture the attention of my chief mate?> Maira shook her head, her eyes flashing dark red. <She will be cocky and sure.>

<Which could be exactly where we want her.>

She pressed her lips together. <I know. By the gods, I know! She twists the minds of many against the central rules of our people. She

must be stopped. If you infiltrate, it will give us additional insight on how to bring her down.>

He could feel Maira pushing down every part of her that cried out against the injustice of losing her chief mate once more. There was a familiarity to the moment that told him they were used to making sacrifices for the greater good and returning to each other afterward.

But during those other times of separation, Shance had been faithful to Maira. Only the amnesia had defeated him. For that, and many other reasons, he refused to fall prey to Lurien.

His focus would be reclaiming his herd, his son, and the heart of the woman who stared down at him. Shance sensed the barriers that remained between them, the same barriers that kept them apart at night. He knew she felt his desire, and if he made an overture, he knew she would respond. She was a queen who knew her responsibilities and cared deeply for those caught up in this situation. Yet nothing in Shance's marriage to Maira had been out of duty or responsibility. She was worthy of love and pursuit, and he would make sure she knew that all over again.

Publicly.

"Are you sure you want me on your side? After all, there is a slight conflict of interest."

Shance strode up the stairs to the platform, right past Lurien, and over to Maira. Heedless of who was watching, he reached out and traced the edge of her cheek down to her chin. <I will return to you. I promise. I will return to you with what we have lost.>

"I know," she whispered fiercely. A swell of stalwart belief flowed through their still-mending bond. "You are a good man. Know that I have forgiven you. Resist any lies that tell you otherwise. You are mine, and I am yours."

She stretched up on her toes. He instinctively moved down to intercept her lips and pulled her up into his arms for a deep kiss that blocked out all else. He drank in her taste, her scent, the feel of her body in his arms. A body he dearly missed, as well as the rest of her. Getting their son and their herd back would be a fitting recompense. There could be no better way of showing that he was no longer the shiftless man of the last ten years. Take this mission, and he would be a man ready to claim his wife and his rightful place by her side.

"If you're finished, Captain Windkeeper?" Lurien's tone was lazy. "Considering your history of conquests, I have no concerns about your fraternization with this trollop. After all, it hardly involves your mind. What is your final response?"

He pulled away from Maira and glared at Lurien. As a death unicorn, she knew exactly how great of an insult that was. He wanted nothing more than to slaughter her for the offense to his wife, but he remained calm. Lurien had to think she'd won.

He reluctantly set Maira back on the ground. Then, squaring his shoulders, Shance walked over to Lurien, each movement of his legs heavier than lead.

Finally, he faced her. "Despite your remarks, I am curious to see how you plan on winning, Lady Lurien. Your confidence is compelling."

She grinned. "I assure you, Captain Windkeeper, I am far more than my feminine wiles. Still, I won't complain about you noticing them."

Viorstan, the woman deserved to be gutted right there on the platform in front of everyone. Instead, he gave a faint smirk. "Considering how garishly you put yourself out there, I could think of little else."

"Always the charmer." She gave his arm a playful swat, then turned to the crowd. "Ladies and gentlemen, barring any issues from the Meritas, we have a debate! Please do read to the newspapers for further details."

The crowd burst into applause and cheers. Shance didn't dare look at Kesia or the cat-dragon in the crowd below. Anything of the sort would ruin his resolve.

He kept a careful expression on his face, but inside he sent out a plea—to whom? Not to Viorstan and Fiarston. But to the All-Maker? The great deity who had allowed Shance to endure ten years of faithlessness and now suffer the shame from that?

Bitterness coiled in Shance. Maybe not.

He glanced at his son. Brennar was entirely focused on Lurien, as if she were a beacon of hope in his universe. Anger rose within Shance, stirring up winds that he forced down. How could he maintain control while in close quarters with that vile woman?

The bitterness diffused, enough to send out a prayer after all.

Shance needed all the help he could get.

CHAPTER FIFTEEN

Bureaucracy was always the same. Droning on about specific rules. Insisting that you follow the letter of the law when all you wanted to do was kill the woman standing across the table. It would be a terrible move for Maira, the death unicorn queen who sought to bring healing. The young dragon woman with her, however, could do so with impunity. In fact, it was her duty.

Kesia smiled faintly. <At the right time, I will kill Lurien. I have my own protocol to follow, if we hope to capture the city for the Lawless instead of simply incite a riot.>

<Such a shame.> Maira raised her eyebrows. It was unusual for a dragon to be perceptive of death unicorn emotions. Unheard of, in fact. Yet that seemed to be typical of Kesia. <Have you aged so quickly that you've lost your sense of fun?>

Her amber eyes brightened. <Oh, I'm still quite set on burning the endlessly dull library books I have to research.>

<Along with those constricting clothes, I'd imagine.>

Kesia sighed. <I need to blend in.>

<Why? Blending in makes us as deceptive as Lurien, who is clearly a death unicorn masquerading as a human. There are others in the Scepter of Knowledge who wear different fashions. Just be prepared to

be noticed, should you choose to dress more comfortably.>

<Being noticed is rarely a good thing for me.> Kesia's face became a blank mask. She turned back to the gentleman speaking over his high, stiff collar.

Ah. That must have touched upon a sore area. It made sense. The dragon had been raised believing she was the worst of criminals. Being noticed doubtless led to punishment. And the dragon council had hardly given Kesia reason to think she was valued for anything other than being alive. But if Kesia kept denying her right to speak for herself, it would only perpetuate her feelings of worthlessness.

Maira sighed, and moved on to replaying the rules of the debate through her mind. The Festivals of the Three Centrals—hearkening back to a time when the majority of people in this Scepter worshiped the sun, moon, and stars—would occur within the next nine weeks. The Solaris Festival would take place within three weeks, and the rest would follow at three week intervals. The debate would be held during the Celestis Festival at the end of the ninth week. Until then, both sides were welcome to campaign by speaking in small groups in private settings, but no public forums could be held by either party. The debate would be projected throughout the city via their system that connected audiceptors to a larger version of a voice horn. A vote would commence right after, with polls open for a day. Thus the fate of the Scepter of Knowledge would be decided in favor of the Lawless or in favor of the Curious Intrigue and their false war. The winner would also immediately be able to petition for a debate to win the role of Meritas.

Maira and Kesia had no interest in that role. Lurien had far too much.

Nine weeks. It should be more than enough time for Shance to connect with Brennar and the others under Lurien's thrall, and for

Kesia to find proof of Lurien's misdeeds. It was absurd that Kesia should have to find additional proof when she was a witness to the attack that killed Zephryn Nightstalker, but the only other witness had been Lirome. Considering his soul bond with Kesia and his own shadowy doings as her unofficial assassin, her brother was hardly an objective witness.

Gods-cursed bureaucracy.

Maira signed her name on the contract next to Lurien's. Then Kesia and Shance signed as well. Shance. She had been deliberately ignoring him this entire time. There was no need to give Lurien more fodder.

But as she rose to leave, she made eye contact with her husband once more, taking in his square jaw with trimmed beard, determined blue eyes, and sandy blond hair. She couldn't help but acknowledge his nicely muscled form that she always found more reasons to appreciate.

Even as she did, she knew he was studying her just as intently, haunted by his missing memories yet staying true to her.

Lurien pursed her lips as she watched them, her face triumphant. "Glad you had your fun with him. Now he's mine, as everyone else will soon be. Your highness."

"Your delusions are not my concern."

Maira pivoted and left the room with its pinwood and polished slate floors. She soon exited the state building, where Lirome and Ademis stood waiting. The cat-dragon was decidedly peeved to still be in his skin form. As for her brother, his eyes quickly skirted over her and focused on Kesia with relief.

The fool still hadn't spoken with Kesia about their soul-friend bond—and whatever else lay beneath the surface. The tension between them was obvious, and it wasn't pleasant. Maira's shoulders twitched. <For someone who claims to be direct and honest, your withdrawal from your feelings is dishonorable. Even hurtful.>

<Keep to your own matters, sister. There is already one Zilpath in this country, and that is more than enough.>

<Oh yes, my dear friend Zilpath. I really should contact her sometime. Then she can deal with your conundrum.>

His face darkened. <You wouldn't dare.>

<Try me.>

A laugh interrupted their mental conversation. Maira looked over to see Ademis making a face at yet another bystander with an audiceptor. Kesia's shoulders shook with mirth. "It isn't a threat. It's just mechanical."

"You don't know that for certain. There are many evil things in this world."

"Yes, there are, but that isn't one of them."

Ademis huffed and turned to Maira. "Shall we go now? I'm quite ready to be done with this human nonsense."

"Fine. To the safe house." She turned to Lirome. "Will you be joining us?"

"I have a prior engagement. There's a bakery that has new varieties of scones that apparently must be tried."

Kesia's face lit up. "Including needlesap!"

"Though it might taste foul. They certainly smell that way."

She grinned. "We won't know for sure until we taste them ourselves."

Maira watched her brother's face reflect Kesia's glee. For a moment, he looked like he had before worries and hard choices had turned his heart cynical. He made a short bow. "As you see. Very urgent business."

"Indeed." Maira shook her head. <Talk with her.>

<Don't bother me.>

<Then handle your own life.>

She turned back around and started walking toward the library district safe house with Ademis, taking his arm. While Maira preferred staying with Shance aboard their airship, she appreciated having a room within the city as well for times when she needed to rest. Such as now.

As they made their way through the Scepter of Knowledge, she wore a pleasant expression on her face and smiled at others. Meanwhile, her mind wandered toward Lurien and the way she had seemed so confident of getting Shance on her side. She thought of Cadence, who still hadn't awoken. Of Kesia, so fragile beneath her light, careless exterior.

So much. All-Maker, there was always so much.

"Maira! Wall!"

She looked up to see a doorframe inches away from her. Ademis jerked her arm quickly, pulling her to a stop. Maira glared at him.

"What would it matter? I'd heal quickly anyway."

"Yes, but you'd be cranky the whole time."

She sighed as Ademis pawed at various parts of the wood until he released the catch in a seemingly flat wall in the side of a building, revealing a small opening. "Thank you. For once."

He returned her smirk. "See if I assist you ever again. Please tell me you were projecting the field of disinterest?"

"Oh, Elric's hooves, did I forget that?"

"Maira…" His voice echoed as they descended into a large underground chamber lit by flickering oil lamps.

She sighed. "You know I always maintain the empathic disinterest field." A far more benign use of unicorn empathy. It simply made bystanders oblivious to any unique details about the projector.

"I don't understand why you simply can't project the field sufficiently for me to be in my other, far more estimable state of being." Ademis plucked at his waistcoat with disfavor, even though earlier in the day he'd been quite proud of it.

Maira rolled her eyes as they reached the last steps and began walking across an enormous room. Old pieces of rusted machinery and rotten bookshelves covered the dirt floor, reinforcing the disguise of an abandoned service tunnel turned rubbish collection point. "You know why. If I need your help during an altercation, it is far easier for you to shift into cat-dragon form from skin form, rather than the other way around. Especially with the clothing issue."

"And why would I want to help you?"

She leaned up and pinched his cheek, then gave his hair a ruffle. "Because you are an exceptionally generous and caring cat-dragon who knows that no other being could put up with you as well as I."

Ademis smiled. "That has not been proven."

They reached the second secret entrance. Maira pressed a few key places on the wall, triggering the opening.

"You've had more than enough time to discover such things. Yet, here you are, at my side again."

They walked down a narrow hallway that opened into a second cavernous chamber. The floor was polished wood, and the room was lit with electric lights in sconces on the walls. A central table with long benches on either side bisected the room, and the walls were lined with cupboards and a waist-high shelf. Well, above-waist-high for Maira. She'd long been used to living in a world of tall people.

"Much of this world has yet to be explored, unicorn girl." He shifted and began preening his scale-speckled orange fur. Maira knelt and picked up the pile of clothing.

"There isn't much left to explore, except water," she retorted. Everyone knew that Fylorn only had two major continents. Sekastra occupied most of one, except for the northern ice deserts. Elotrin covered the other. The rest was the vast ocean.

Another member of the Lawless, a man with thinning white hair and a portly figure, motioned to her from the kitchen. "Your grace, someone's been beeping at your clipse-mirror all morning."

"All morning?"

A curly-haired woman rifling through a shelf of manuals next to him wrinkled her snub nose. "Yes. A very persistent individual."

Trepidation and annoyance filled her. Chances were good it was several persistent individuals. News must have spread about the discovery of Tyrius Stormsong, and her regents wanted more information. They had every right to know, considering his ten-year absence. It was an almost unpardonable transgression for one who was supposed to protect the herd and govern her other mates.

Ademis made a dismissive chitter as they headed to her bedroom in the safe house. <You could just get rid of all of them and run away.>

<Another useful piece of advice. How did I ever manage without you?>

The cat-dragon stalked into the simple room ahead of her, staking his claim on her bed.

She paused and smiled at the humans. "I'm sorry for any trouble. Thank you for telling me."

Their amiable expressions returned. Maira followed the cat-dragon into her room, her smile fading into exhaustion, worry, relief, anger—all the emotions she kept tightly controlled. Within these walls, her posture and countenance could reveal the truth, though she still kept a tight rein on her empathy, lest she bombard bystanders with unwanted emotions.

What she wouldn't give for a few hours with the herd, able to express pain and receive comfort. To run freely on four legs, thinking only of the presence of her people, and nothing else.

To be held in Shance's arms, only as a woman desired by a man.

Her heart sank. Just a short time ago, she had allowed her chief mate to enter the lascivious domain of their enemy, all to free their son and the others the rogue death unicorn had ensnared.

At least she'd had a few weeks to reconnect with him. There remained vast plains between them, formed by the distance of time and lost memories, but they had begun to close the distance.

Maira had mates. But Shance was her husband. He always would be.

Ademis gave a rusty mreow. <Are you going to answer that beastly thing, or shall I knock it from your desk and break it?>

The beeping from her clipse-mirror finally pierced through her thoughts. Maira grimaced, peeled off her outer coat, and dropped it over the cat-dragon.

He hissed. <I will burn this thing with fire.>

<Go ahead.>

He sniffed and curled up inside the garment, with only his scaly, pointy-tipped tail visible and twitching. Maira walked to the desk at the foot of the bed and sat down. Best to get through the calls, at least the ones to her mates. She breathed out slowly, centering herself, and allowed her unicorn traits to surface. The pointed ears, black fingernails, and the rest. She paused for a few moments of prayer to Bonilus the Beneficent, then touched her palm to the mirror suspended between two bronze stands, allowing it to read her handprint.

Another quick swipe revealed the signal origins of the missed calls. A useful trick only available to the elites in Sekastra, but easily modified thanks to Ademis's knowledge of the old kingdom in Elotrin. The cat-dragon was remarkably good at tweaking devices, provided it meant he could destroy parts of them in the process.

<Enough dallying. Make the damn calls, and then we can nap.>

She sighed. "It's not even midday."

<All times are suitable for naps, and you're already exhausted.>

Maira flicked her forefinger off the tip of one of her pointed ears. Ademis mrowled at the rude gesture. Then she turned various dials and knobs to reach Kaliran, her oldest mate. Also her most reliable political ally and by far the most opinionated.

Of course, he was sitting at his desk, as if waiting to receive her message. His dark eyes gleamed with relief. "My queen. What is the news? Where is your chief mate?"

"I told you, Shance is still recovering his full wits."

Kaliran's face creased with concern. "How long will that take? It has been a month."

"Considering how he spent ten years with his true nature and memories repressed, giving him grace would not be amiss."

"Hmph. This is not the time for indulgence." Yet by the expression on his deep umber face and golden eyes, she knew he understood. "Cadence's situation?"

"Our son remains in an unconscious state. He is under surveillance in a safe location. I will give you more information when it is available."

He nodded. "Good. I appreciate that, and I greatly desire your return to the Refuge, my queen. The other regents and I have done our best to maintain the peace, with the help of your brother, but we are eager to be reunited with our leader."

"I look forward to that as well." As long as it wasn't endless work, and she was able to see their children. Maybe, after all this time, Kaliran had found someone else, as he had been free to do when Maira had married Shance. The soul bond outranked the others, and while the political side of her mating with Kaliran had to remain intact for herd stability, any other parts were strictly separated. Then again, if Kaliran had found someone, that would be additional, polite jockeying as Maira and the other woman sorted out who occupied which areas of authority. Maira stifled a groan. One of the few perks of being in a coffin for a decade—there had been no worries about managing her time or delicate situations.

She closed the call with Kaliran with a few more pleasantries, spoke briefly with their other son, learned the news about her grandchildren, then moved on to the next message.

Weirad. Her other living mate. She was surprised he had contacted her, given that he minded the farthest reaches of the Lost Refuge and was often in the wilderness for weeks at a time.

A heavy-eyed man with long brown hair, a ragged beard, and light olive skin answered her call. He blinked. "Maira? Are you still alive, then?"

"As far as I know, Weirad. I assume you are as well." She couldn't suppress her grin. Weirad had never been one to stand on ceremony. Kaliran had sought the alliance to stabilize his own authority, but Weirad had been the third son in a badly-depleted herd, very wayward and stubborn. Maira quietly believed that Weirad was glad their alliance required such little maintenance other than semi-regular updates, the odd council meeting, and occasional adventures into the wilderness to assess his work.

"I'm inside a house instead of wandering the plains freely, so 'alive' is a generous word. Hisen and Kisen are on patrol so I can speak with you." His lips quirked.

"You're half-alive, then."

"Or half-dead." His voice trailed off, and he cleared his throat. "In any case, I wanted to let you know that a package has been dispatched to your location. A variety of dried herbs and various spices I've grown that should replenish your healing stores. Plus the one leaf that brews that beverage you like."

Maira chuckled. "The one that allows me to stay up longer? Lirome will hate you. He's always trying to make me sleep."

Weirad smirked. "Good thing I'm not in any way responsible to him."

"Thank you. I really do appreciate it."

"Yes, well, your contact with Kaliran keeps him from trying to boss me around. Shance was even better at keeping Kaliran away."

Another downfall of her situation. Weirad and Kaliran did better the less they saw of each other, something the other death unicorns worked hard to ensure for the sake of herd sanity. Shance had been particularly good at keeping the peace, especially when he teamed up with Elestel.

Her former third mate.

She ended the call with Weirad and moved on to the final message. Amarel Ukerys showed up on her screen, her orange eyes sparkling, and her face framed by wavy brown hair.

"Hello, Mother. How is Brennar?"

"We're working on getting him back. There is a rogue death unicorn in this city, as you suspected, and she is holding many enthralled." Amarel was her only child with Elestel Ukerys before he had been killed over twenty years earlier. She was her eyes and ears in herd communications. Her light brown face and pale orange eyes were a clear reminder of Elestel, but her mild, caring temperament and iron will were entirely her own. Upon Elestel's death, Amarel had taken the place as Maira's third regent.

She was also the closest thing Brennar had to an older sister.

Amarel frowned. "I thought so. Do you know who it is? I only have suspicions. There are too many of us to track that carefully."

"I'm not sure who it is. This unicorn has a Talent that hides her true appearance in some way. But she already knows who I am, and who Shance is, as well as Brennar. Very politically astute. She seems to have been building up to this for years."

Maira's daughter shook her head. "I will coordinate with Weirad and Kaliran and see what I can find. I've already ruled out the oldest generation. Those that are alive remain loyal to you."

Maira sighed in relief, loudly enough that Ademis stirred on the bed.

<Foolish girl, are you still entertaining the notion that your own herd despises you?>

<At any point, anyone can turn on you. Even a herd. That's what Father and Mother taught me.>

Ademis gave a mreow of disagreement. <Considering the location of their final resting places, I wouldn't trust them as the final authority.>

<You mock my pain and their deaths.> Heedless of her daughter on the screen, Maira turned and glared at the cat-dragon. He stared back resolutely.

<No, I'm pointing out that they were far less connected and devoted to the herd than you, and you spend far too many of your waking hours concerned with your people. Another good reason Shance is back, though it's a pity he has to be away right now. He was always good at calming your excessive people-pleasing.>

Amarel's voice interrupted Maira's next thought. "Cat-dragon being an accurate pest again?"

Maira turned back around. "Yes, but don't say it too loud, or his head will swell to monstrous proportions and there will be no getting him out of this room."

Her daughter laughed. "I have missed your humor, Mother. May you have long days."

"May you have safe nights."

With a loud sigh, Maira sagged against the chair. There were still so many to contact. Other children and grandchildren and perhaps, by this point, great-grandchildren. The death unicorns had been encouraging large families for the last fifty years or so to increase their population, and it had worked.

With the abundance of children and a few death unicorns even marrying humans, the days of multiple mates had ended with Maira's generation. For that, she was thankful.

She checked the timepiece on the wall, then reached out for her chief mate before realizing that she couldn't communicate mentally with him without line of sight. The bond between them needed to be strengthened before that could happen. Still, she felt sure of Shance's actions in her heart. Experience had laid the foundation of trust that mental communication did not.

Next, Maira reached out for Lirome on the wireless commer.

"Maira? Did you arrive at the safe house well?"

"Yes, and I've spoken with Amarel and the regents. They are looking into who this death unicorn could be."

"Very good. Always so clever."

She smiled at the compliment. She and her twin brother might not always see eye to eye, but he had always been supportive of her. Being restored to him was a blessing from Bonilus. His voice continued. "And it seems you survived contacting everyone."

"Yet again." Maira blew out a thin stream of air through her teeth, eager to change the subject. "Concerning Lurien. We know she targeted the crown prince, hoping to take out both of the dragon heirs. I think she recruited Shance for a very specific reason. We saw how he was able to disperse Kesia's smoke with his winds. He'll be capable of far more once his other Talents emerge."

"But they still haven't, so the jest is on her. Although there still is a risk involved."

"No, there isn't. I trust him. I felt his utter derision for her."

"Yes, but I also know the mind needs time to heal. He was gone for ten years."

Maira scowled. "That is hardly a moment, compared to the rest of his life."

"Even so, those memories and that identity will haunt him. You expect too much from him."

"And I give him my full heart and love in return."

Lirome hmphed. "Just take care that you don't give your heart and strength to so many people that you die from lack of love yourself."

"Don't be melodramatic."

"I'm not."

She lay back on the bed, rolling her eyes. "Ademis won't let me die in such a manner."

The cat-dragon flopped next to her in a sprawl. <I make no promises. I'm only here for the adoration of my magnificence. As well as the opportunity to destroy things that beep and hiss and crackle.>

Maira snorted. <You hiss and crackle. Does this mean you're going to self-destruct?>

<I do NOT beep.>

"Well, I intend to rest until you and Kesia reconvene at the safe house."

"Please do. We've stopped to purchase some of the latest papers."

"How were the needlesap scones?"

Kesia's voice came over the speaker. "Excellent!"

"Or disturbing, considering your preferences."

Kesia chuckled. "You're lying."

"How would you know that?"

Maira snorted. Likely because the dragon woman wasn't a fool and had seen Lirome lie before. "Endure bravely, brother."

She pressed off the wireless commer. At least the two were friends. That was good, although Kesia would need more. Maira wasn't as astute about dragon perceptions, but she knew that dragons fully committed to their bonds.

Maira pulled the pillow over and tucked it beneath her head, settling next to the warm, furry lump of Ademis. The long night of healing and the scant hours of sleep caught up to her and stilled her into slumber.

It seemed like no time had passed when Maira was awakened, not by a particular sound, but by two strong bursts of emotion. One was from Lirome, filled with cold fury and anger. The other emanated from a fierce heartflame that threatened to singe her empathy and scald her numb.

Kesia.

Riddled with fear.

Chapter Sixteen

She was alone. She always would be. They wouldn't stop coming after her. The fear would never end. Not even Lirome could protect her.

At least the death unicorns couldn't see her. And if they couldn't see her, they couldn't direct their terror toward her, no matter how much they pursued. Kesia curled up tightly into a corner of the abandoned box and wrapped her tail around her. Not a mouse, but a similarly-sized moss-skinned hopclaw, a rodent with elongated legs that could leap great distances and float in water using special air sacs on its sides. It was native to Scepter of Knowledge and well-suited to the damp climate. A far more useful shape than a mouse.

Now if only the jolts of fear would stop sending her into a downward spiral toward hibernation. The last thing she needed was that animal urge.

She tried to distract herself with thoughts from a few minutes earlier.

The needlesap scone had tasted sharp, with an edge of honeyed sweetness. It had invigorated her after the exhausting amount of paperwork she had filled out to set up the debate with Lurien. New things were always refreshing.

Lirome had smiled across the table from her, teasing as usual, and that made her feel even better. The death unicorn had a nice smile with a sly edge, and he had offered it more readily over the last few weeks. Other than his evasiveness about the nature of the bond he'd made with her, he was a pleasant companion and astonishingly easy to work with. That was a mercy from the All-Maker himself, if she could believe in the deity.

But the ever-present emptiness inside consumed her. Lirome's presence seemed to hover around the singing void, never willing to quite fill it. No matter how she might privately long for it.

It was hardly her place to speak to him about the emptiness. If she spoke up, and he didn't understand her, it would shift the precarious balance they had struck as soul-friends. Besides, he was a death unicorn. He had said it himself. They were different than dragons.

No sooner had she dismissed her thoughts when the fear had struck like a hammer to her heart, slamming her from all sides. She had been so startled that she'd breathed out green smoke in the bakery, far too public of a place. Standing out was never good. Safety came from hiding. The death unicorns were after her. Getting away from civilians was vital.

She'd run down a side alley, slipping out of skin form and into hopclaw form, scurrying into a pile of boxes in the tiniest spot next to the wooden wall and waiting for the fear to cease so she could escape.

Footsteps sounded nearby. Far too near. Her tiny teeth chittered, and a squeak escaped.

"We know what you can do, dragon. There will be no escape."

Someone knocked away a few of the boxes. She shuddered.

Where was Lirome? Why wasn't he fighting? Kesia's fur-tipped tail twitched. Well, why would he? He was simply her healer, responsible to fill the hole inside her temporarily out of duty and honor and a desire to give recompense. That was all. There was nothing in his vows spoken before the dragon council that suggested they were long-term partners of any sort. She only wanted to see it as more because—

The death unicorns were nearly finished with the boxes. Terror squeezed her heart.

She was on her own. The reason didn't matter.

Another form pushed out of her body, lengthening and slimming it. Oily fur disappeared into dry scales, and her eyesight worsened. The vibrations of the death unicorns' search were now unbearable through her skin.

Yet as a small glass snake, she could deflect ambient light and escape. Moreover, she bet that a reptile wouldn't be as vulnerable to fear from adrenaline as a mammal. In her core dragon form, she certainly wasn't as naturally fearful. The calming of her heart proved her right. She just had to get away.

Quickly, she slithered down the alleyway. To where, Kesia wasn't sure. She'd left her clothes behind. Fewmets!

Why wasn't Lirome's voice in her mind? She had always been able communicate with Zephryn, no matter what her form. But Zephryn had been her embermate. Lirome was only a soul-friend. She flicked her tongue out, measuring the space around her and darting down another alley, this one filled with burlap bags of old grain. And a few real hopclaws. The predator in her wanted a snack.

Not now.

The fear dissipated, and she paused, focusing on the vibrations through the ground. The death unicorns hadn't followed her. Kesia sighed internally. If there was an All-Maker, she would thank him. As it stood, she was just glad to have escaped unscathed.

She waited for a few more minutes. Suddenly new footsteps thudded down the alley. A hiss escaped Kesia, and she coiled up, ready to strike with her crippling venom.

"Kesia, it's me."

She blinked, trying to place the vibrations and the amorphous shape through her snake eyes. Something deep within her soul was certain it was Lirome.

Very well, then.

Kesia shrugged her shoulders, feeling the scales slough off her as her form suddenly stretched out. Scales were overtaken by skin, limbs emerged and grew, and she stood, brown hair flowing down her back, arms crossed over her chest.

She blinked a few times, bringing Lirome's face into focus. His violet eyes were tight with worry, and his lips were set in a frown. He kept his eyes on her face, as expected, and held out her clothes to her.

"Do you make a habit of running off alone and dismissing your garments?" His dry voice held an edge of irritation.

What cause did he have to be irritated? *She* had been the target. Kesia grabbed the clothes and begin slipping them on, immediately regretting her decision to do so. The confining fashions were even worse than she remembered. She was *not* putting those damn hairpins in again.

"You're a death unicorn. I figured you weren't the target, and that you could handle yourself." Kesia tried to lace the corset and gave up. For now, the skirt and blouse would have to be enough. "Besides, getting into a fight in a public area is unwise."

"So instead of speaking to me, you run off? You know I can

shield you from them. I thought dragons were trained in battle strategies. What strategy recommends refusing communication and going rogue?"

Prickles of his annoyance filled her. Part of her felt some contrition at his words but not enough to back down. "A strategy formed when you're raised a convicted felon and your only ally is your embermate, who isn't always around to help. Who isn't around at all now."

Kesia's voice only caught slightly over the last sentence.

He snorted. "You're not a prisoner anymore, Kesia."

"I don't have an embermate either." She glared at him. "If I'm constantly dependent on you instead of being seen as an equal, I might as well be."

The words came out bluntly, crying out her loss. For the gap that remained in her soul. For someone to fill it.

She swallowed hard, just as Lirome spoke. "You should be more careful."

"Careful? A few hours ago you praised my impulsive actions on the debate platform and commended me for seizing an opportunity."

"Yes, but that was a different situation."

She put her hands on her hips, stifling the urge to bare her claws. "This is the second time I've been attacked by fear. I had to do what I thought was best and what would cause the least amount of harm to others."

"What about yourself? You're the crown princess of dragons. The only living heir. You need to learn to value yourself and trust me."

"Which is why I ran away! I trusted my instincts!" Kesia huffed a stream of smoke. "And how can I trust you? You still dole out information sparingly. I understand you need time to think, but then you never choose to reveal much at all. That isn't honest. You're just so earnest and stubborn that you get away with it."

He stepped forward. "I have spoken as much as is fitting for every question. Information is a valuable commodity, and I've seen it abused too much to speak freely. Especially—"

"Especially to a young crown princess who is only a temporary patient until I find another embermate and have a child." The words came out bitingly hard. For some reason, Lirome's words felt like a slap to the face, far beyond his usual quiet arrogance over what he thought she did and didn't need to know.

She knew he was being dishonest, even if she couldn't articulate why. The sense of his secrets, of his wariness, itched at her skin, causing her scales to rise to the surface.

He stared down at her intently. "My vow is true. I remain at your service until you choose to release me."

And again with the calm, studied expression. As if something was wrong with Kesia for breaking first. Rage coiled within her— and she didn't even want to be angry!

She flung up her arms. "What does that even mean? Just another vague death unicorn phrase that you won't explain, because why explain anything to me? You keep everything from me until you feel like sharing!"

"Yes, well you talk too fast!" His shout echoed through the alley.

Kesia swallowed.

Words spilled from him. "I didn't mean it like that." He stepped toward her, his face filled with confusion and frustration and... something warm and strong. Desire. "I meant that all of this is happening too fast, and I don't know what to do with it. I don't want to be dishonest with you. You're unlike anyone I've ever met, and this situation is unlike anything I've ever encountered, and it's unnerving to me how much I want to be around you!"

His every word jarred her. Kesia stared past his shoulder. She somehow couldn't close her mouth. Could barely breathe.

"I'm ... I'm sorry," she finally managed. "I didn't mean to disrupt your existence."

"But you did. That's nothing to apologize for." He sighed, his breath cool on her cheek. "I should have spoken earlier. I see that now. I didn't realize you thought so little of me."

"I don't. I'm not rejecting you, Lirome."

He reached out, fingers hovering over her skin, almost touching her face. "Neither am I. Everything is complicated. I don't know enough."

Kesia hesitated, then shook her head and stepped away from him. "In that, you are entirely like Zephryn." She sighed. "Maybe I'm the fool for thinking differently of you."

He opened his mouth, but she continued. "Don't tell me. You need more time to think. Alone. Because while I must share with you, you can't share with me." She turned away. "I'm going back to the airship to do something I'm good at. Something where my impulsivity won't disturb your need to think through everything and exclude others."

She shifted into a local sea-hunting bird with glimmering turquoise feathers underlaid with gleaming violet. Lirome could get her clothes again. Better yet, he could leave the pile of discomfort there for the moths and hopclaws to destroy. She had the wind in her wings, the open sky around her, and *The Silver Streak*'s engines to investigate. Something simple and straightforward.

She'd thought Lirome was simple and straightforward. An

effortless connection. Then that stupid sense within her expected more, and somehow, that bothered her more than anything else. It was as if he had wronged her by shutting her out. As though something else was required of him. Perhaps it was a pesky side effect of the soul-friend connection and the healing bond.

Kesia gave a loud trill and dove through the air. Less thinking about those matters. She had a long flight in store before she took up residence in the bowels of the ship. It made no sense to fret over something that might all be in her mind.

Even though she was sure it wasn't.

CHAPTER SEVENTEEN

Lady Lurien Alistil looked far too pleased with her collection of men.

That was the only word Shance could think of for the retinue of humans and death unicorns who surrounded her as they rode in an electro-carriage to her residence in the northwest part of the city. A well-dressed, well-maintained collection of men who seemed to have their faculties intact, except that when she gave the slightest glance, they jumped to attention. A finger snap from her may as well have been a shout.

She had attentive women surrounding her as well. They seemed far less infatuated, though still adoring and considerate, as if each of them counted themselves lucky to have Lurien as a friend.

The overall effect kept Shance's stomach in constant turmoil, even with the advanced turbulence dampeners on the electro-carriage. The fact that Lurien continued to exude the scent of rancid motor oil didn't help matters.

She reached out a slender hand to trace the edge of her bodice, where the top of her breasts rose. Shance fixed his eyes firmly on her face, just in time to catch a smirk. "Already entranced with me, Captain Windkeeper?"

"More like amazed at your astonishing array of suitors. How do you keep them satisfied and free from jealousy?"

"Oh, a woman has her ways." Lurien gave a musical laugh that fell on his ears like clanking sewer pipes. "At least, I certainly do. Consider it a cultural need they are happy to serve. You of all people should know about surrendering everything for the sake of a powerful woman."

Her brilliant blue eyes dared him to say more. Shance clenched his teeth and refused to answer her. He had enough memories to know that having multiple spouses was permitted but rare among death unicorns due to the emotional difficulties it brought to herds.

Maira's situation was uniquely political, and he could see how much stress balancing her mates and maintaining political peace brought her.

He looked at the other figure in the car. The one who'd refused to speak to him, having eyes only for Lurien or the occasional glance outside the electro-carriage window. Brennar. His son.

Part of Shance longed to speak with him, to reach through the hostile indifference and connect with the defiant young man who had Maira's thick black hair and blue eyes identical to his own. Those eyes evoked faint memories of a young child running across the deck of an airship, eagerly asking questions and...

The memories faded. Shance's heart squeezed, then filled with guilt. He couldn't even remember his own son. Not enough. Who was he to attempt a connection with him? To bring him back?

Yet he had to, even if he only remembered scant details about the young man.

Heaviness weighed on him. *All-Maker, you might not care about me, but help me free my son, at least. Do that much.*

Shance clenched his hand in his coat pocket and felt the small square and transceiver nubs of a wireless commer. He knew it wasn't his. Lurien had plucked Shance's commer from his lapel, dismissing it as outdated and unnecessary. Both lies, but ones he had to acquiesce to in order to infiltrate her ranks.

Who had put it in his pocket? Was it a trick? Lurien was too flamboyant to resort to subtlety. She enjoyed displays of ownership and would offer him her choice of communication tech on her timetable. Kesia had been on the other side of the negotiation table, so it couldn't have been her. But Lirome had brushed by him on the way into the state house, his neutral expression the perfect cover. The death unicorn had always been good at sleight of hand. Shance hadn't had much time to reconnect with his brother-in-law, considering the events of the past few weeks. Still, the support the commer implied steadied Shance's nerves.

Maybe Bonilus was looking out for him, at least this much.

He had a wife. He had a family. He had friends and a crew. He might have let them down in the past, but he wouldn't let them down now.

Lurien raised her eyebrows. "Ah, there's the rakish Windkeeper smile. What's so amusing, Captain?"

It was time to see what this death unicorn upstart could reveal. He returned her stare. "I'm just curious how you've managed to convince my son that you're a more worthy ruler than his own mother. I might have failed him, but she never has. The only reason she was away was because your beloved Curious Intrigue held her captive in a coffin to drain her magic."

"That's not true!" A gust of wind blew through the electro-carriage, and Brennar's eyes blazed. "My lady told me the truth."

"Your lady told you that your mother was dead. That's what you claimed earlier when we … met on my airship."

"No, that's wrong. I never said that!" Brennar's voice rose. "My lady has now told me the truth of mother's disappearance. It was the Lawless who turned against our people and kept her imprisoned. The Lawless used her and created lies about her death. And now, Mother supports them, so she cannot be trusted."

Brennar's voice grew softer with his last few words, his ire weakening as if he didn't quite believe them, no matter what the machinations of the wench beside him. Understandable, considering Lurien couldn't even keep her own lies in order.

Lurien glared at Shance. "You upset him. Do you think to win your son back with such gross untruths?"

"In terms of winning others over with untruths, I think you have beaten me." Shance leaned forward. "Still, he trusts you so deeply. What herd are you from?"

She stuck her chin out, for a moment looking more like a petulant child than a polished performer. "The old herds are weak and unnecessary. They have imposed unfair restrictions upon us. They say we came here for freedom, but all I knew was defeat until I seized the offer given to me and took what was mine."

"You mean stole it." Shance kept his voice level and watched Brennar's face grow increasingly more livid out of the corner of his eye. "Stole and tricked and coerced it from others, even from those you claim to favor most."

"Silence!" Another blast of wind shook the electro-carriage, scraping it against the electric line and sending violent sparks through the interior. Lurien shrank back in her seat with a few muttered curses and shoved Brennar into the pathway of a large burst.

No!

Shance leaped in front of Brennar. Pulses of lightning jolted through him with breathtaking speed and excruciating pain. His body was a frozen block of agony, trapped by a million needles of heat.

Someone was shaking him.

"Father? Father! You need to wake up."

He couldn't breathe. Not even to acknowledge Brennar's words. No, it couldn't be Brennar. His son hated him.

Someone was pressing on his chest, forcefully. Over and over. Pushing through the numbness.

"Wake up!"

A shot of air forced its way out of Shance's mouth with a scalding gasp. A series of chest-shattering coughs followed. Every bone and muscle in his body ached. He curled up on his side on the electro-carriage floor, wanting nothing more than to be free of the pain. Strong arms surrounded him. He looked up into worried blue eyes and a light olive face set in a firm expression.

Brennar's mouth curved into a small smile. "After abandoning me for ten years, I'm not letting you die that easily."

His words held no venom, only gentle humor and relief. Shance managed a faint smile in return, his chest now aching for an entirely different reason.

"I'm sorry," he whispered through dry lips. "I'm so, so sorry."

His son's eyes softened, and he opened his mouth to speak. An overpowering wave of death unicorn magic, frosty fire with sulfur undertones, filled the air. Brennar's expression dulled to his usual animosity, and he jerked away. Shance's heart sank.

"Good job, Brennar, my dear." Lurien's voice was as smooth as silk and poisonous as a glass snake. "I knew I let you off-leash for a reason. We can't let your father die when there's still so much to do. After all, he's an essential part of the entire plan."

Brennar gave a cruel smirk. "As your will commands, my lady."

"Get on your feet, Windkeeper. I consider the lightning accident fortuitous. Your body is designed for far more than wind, and it's high time you remember that, or you'll be no use at all."

Shance pulled himself back to his seat. The electro-carriage had stopped in front of a large stone edifice on a high cliff overlooking the Cresida Inlet. One of Lurien's servants held the door open while she and Brennar exited. Shance followed slowly, every part of him feeling as if it were made of rusted tin. Yet the pain was already fading.

As it was meant to. Doldrums, why couldn't he remember faster? Now, he was at the mercy of Lurien's knowledge. But he had the wireless commer. There would be opportunities to talk with his wife.

In the meantime, he wanted to wipe the cocky look off Lurien's face.

"We know what you're doing, Lurien," he said, summoning his old ease. "You think having Maira's chief mate and our son will give you some kind of leverage."

She shrugged. "You're right. It will."

Lurien turned and began walking up the polished stone pathway to the house, Brennar attentively at her side. Others walked out of the house to join him.

"Do you really think you're going to get away with this?" Shance called from behind her.

She stopped and turned around, a bright smile on her face.

"Why, yes, I do. You see, I've had ten years to play this game, Windkeeper. Or should I call you Tyrius?" She pursed her lips, then gave a breathy giggle. "It doesn't really matter. I've already taken out the prince of your pitiful little group. All you have left is a frightened convict and two broken death unicorns. You see, my plan is like this house. For everything you see, there is twice as much you don't."

Lurien stalked closer. She reached out to trace his jaw with her finger, evoking a shudder in Shance that was mostly revulsion, with a despicable thread of attraction. Her soft lips quirked.

"So please, Captain Windkeeper, remind me of my plans. It's delightfully endearing. Just as endearing as it will be when you fall to my charms."

Shance stepped back. "That will never happen."

"We'll see. There is one difference between me and your precious Maira Ukerys. She's a woman who has so much and treats it humbly, granting others freedom. Me? I've learned from her mistake." Lurien's blue eyes hardened. "I'm a woman who knows what I want. I want everyone. And with a little magic, or a lot, everyone will realize they want me too."

She spun on her heel and strode back up the path. Shance shook his head and took a deep breath of the fresh, cold air off the bay. He clutched the wireless commer so tightly his knuckles hurt.

Viorstan. Lurien was a nasty piece of work.

But he would not let her take his family from him.

Chapter Eighteen

The All-Maker had a sense of humor, but at the moment, Lirome Ukerys did not appreciate it. Especially when it involved his relationships.

As soul empaths, death unicorns were prone to emotional outbursts. Maintaining a solid equilibrium was vital for herd stability. Lirome's natural temperament predisposed him to manage others quietly and keep order because excessive dramatic displays annoyed him. One reason he had taken so naturally to Kesia was that, despite her outgoing nature, she had an equally level temper. Extraordinarily so for a grieving widow.

Which was why the scene in the alley was so deeply disquieting. He'd sensed enough of her emotions to know that she was upset at having argued with him as much as she was annoyed with him for his reticence and supposed dishonesty. Had he really been that difficult to speak with earlier? They had gotten along so well.

Lirome sighed and rubbed his forehead. Over the last few days they had spoken as little as possible. She had ignored him in favor of working on *The Silver Streak*, reading quietly, speaking with others, and contacting the Lawless to learn more about her role as the crown princess and the status of the ongoing war. Which was well enough. Lirome could keep himself occupied with healing injured soldiers and Lawless agents. Healing was one area where death unicorns were expected to contribute when they could. The Lost Refuge still took in the most injured of the Lawless, caring for them and releasing them with the command to tell no one of the refugee town.

Even then, he had grown used to Kesia assisting him with the healing procedures. She was a quick learner and seemed to enjoy helping him. But now, as he bandaged the unconscious man on the bed, she didn't enter. There was only that singing ache from her that echoed within his own soul. A soul-friend connection shouldn't produce this side effect.

None of it made sense.

The dragon council assumed she needed a mate. Well, that certainly couldn't be him. If she were a death unicorn, Lirome would assume she had need of a death unicorn mate. But she wasn't a death unicorn. She was a dragon. The only dragon widow. Biologically, he and Kesia were hardly alike.

Lirome sighed, washed his hands thoroughly, and left the infirmary room. Kesia sat at the central table, playing with bits of metal and wires. Curiosity stirred within him. What was she creating?

Then she looked up at him, her amber eyes guarded. All he could do was stare and wish he was somewhere else. Or that he could take her in his arms.

This was absurd. He wasn't socially unskilled. He could navigate major events and quiet conversations with ease. Managing conflict was not an issue. It was exhausting after a while, and he needed time alone to rest, but he could resolve issues.

Except around Kesia. Everything he did was wrong, and that in and of itself was wrong. Especially because it was incredibly easy to relax around her. The morning in the library had been full of the moments of banter that he'd grown to enjoy.

The natural connection of soul-friends. Yet in all his years, Lirome had never seen a strained soul-friend link cause this level of unease and anguish.

He cleared his throat, quickly made a cup of tea, then retreated to his private room. There was nothing he could say.

Kesia. I miss your smile and your laugh. I miss understanding the deep grief and loneliness you carry. I have felt the same way for decades. The last thing I want is to leave you alone as well.

Lirome grimaced. Well, nothing that he felt comfortable saying. Not until he understood the urges. Then he could speak quite freely.

For now, he had to keep searching for answers. He couldn't sleep anyway.

He frowned at the words on the page in front of him. Yet another folder filled with data from Kesia's prior examinations. Various papers fanned out over his desk in the small room he'd taken over in the safe house. Next to the papers were a plethora of books on dragon physiology as well as some of his own private journals from decades of practice on humans, death unicorns, wolves, and even seals.

Nothing made sense any more than it had weeks ago when he'd first begun investigating and analyzing. Kesia was utterly unique, defying all known standards.

It was one of the many reasons why he adored her.

Lirome sat up, blinking. Adored. That was even more absurd. They were soul-friends. She was still grieving. That was all. Even with death unicorns, the mourning period was a minimum of three months. He and Kesia had only known each other for a month and a half.

Besides, she was a dragon. He was a death unicorn with traces of other shifters. Lirome had already calculated that his odds of finding a compatible death unicorn mate was three hundred fifty-seven thousand one hundred fifty-nine to one. A dragon would be impossible.

He reached for his cup of tea to settle himself. As his fingers touched the handle, an orange paw pushed the half-filled vessel over the edge of the desk.

"Elric's mane!" Lirome lurched out of his chair and grabbed the cup, glaring into Ademis's green eyes. "Why are you troubling me right now?"

The cat-dragon bared his teeth in a lazy grin, oblivious to Lirome's frantic clean-up efforts. <You're keeping Maira awake with your worries. When she doesn't sleep, she tosses and turns, which means I lose the most comfortable nap in the airship. You need to get your emotions under control.>

"They are under control!"

<Then why are you yelling?>

Lirome gritted his teeth. <Because of a cat-dragon who needs a shave and a muzzle.>

<Watch it, or I'll tip over the ink well.> His pointy, golden-scaled tail waved dangerously near the small pot.

"Fine." Lirome cleaned up the last of the spill with his shirt and started setting aside the afflicted pages to dry. "I might have been projecting somewhat. Maira is gracious enough to guard the herd when I do."

<As if she doesn't already have enough to do.>

"Well, she's doing too much, and I am apparently doing too little. We are quite the sibling pair."

Lirome sat back in his chair just in time to see Ademis flop on his papers. The cat-dragon gave a rusty meow. <Indeed. Though she was less internally dramatic than you are when she was falling in love.>

"What is that supposed to mean?"

The cat-dragon popped out his claws. <I've known you since you were eleven. If you lie to me about your feelings while I'm in the same room, I'll shred every last paper. With great satisfaction.>

Lirome sighed, setting down his tea. "What do you expect me to say? I can't have feelings for Kesia. It isn't biologically possible."

<She isn't an ordinary dragon.>

<I'm well aware of this.>

<She's an experiment. She's been treated as a criminal her whole life, expected to do the worst by everyone around her. And now, you're treating her as if you expect her to explode.>

<Technically, she did explode a few days ago. She was quite angry.> Lirome paused. <So was I. It was terrible.>

<So fix it! She feels awful!> By the time the cat-dragon had finished, his fur was standing on end and his tail twitching. Able to empathize for once in his self-centered existence.

When Lirome finally spoke, it was carefully and slowly. "I don't mean to treat her that way. But I must be cautious. The last thing she needs is to follow false positives into false hopes."

The cat-dragon hissed again, his ears flat against his head. <A death unicorn foal is more vulnerable to emotions than an adult. Do you remember that?>

"Yes. They have to be taught to create shields and control themselves."

<Kesia is feeling things from others around her.>

"She's sensing things, yes. A peculiar intuition I've been trying to understand." Even as he spoke the words, Lirome's mind began to work.

What the cat-dragon was suggesting was … not impossible. But highly improbable.

His breathing shallowed and his stomach knotted with concern. And an odd, inappropriate hope. She was a new widow.

The dragons are already seeking a mate for her. Lirome thought back to the singing need within her. *Perhaps she is as well.*

Ademis stared at him. <You are a death unicorn, but you are also fireproof, manifest wolf claws, and move as quickly as a seal. I am a cat-dragon. I'm not fully a cat, and I'm not fully a dragon. I am both, but I am also unique.>

Lirome pushed his chair back into a leaning position. "Yes. And Kesia has two Talents, inherited from both parents. Matter-shaping from her mother and shifting from her father."

The cat-dragon studied one of the pages. <It says here that her father was experimented on as a shifter. She confessed to killing him in self-defense as a child. He'd been turned into a monster with many different attributes.>

Lirome's heart sank. That was something no child should have to go through. He understood how that sort of trauma changed someone. It had changed him when he'd gone on raids at the age of eleven to sabotage the gods of Elotrin and their Glorious Destiny.

"You're suggesting that Kesia's animal shifting Talent was tampered with, using the green smoke. Which is why that is part of her."

The cat-dragon sniffed and stalked to the edge of the desk. <I'm no scientist. This conversation is already boring me. But she was able to match my shape perfectly, just by touching me. She was affected by Lurien more than anyone else, on multiple occasions—

because she couldn't block her. I'm cat and dragon both. You are a death unicorn with wolf claws. Why couldn't she be the same?> Ademis leaped off the desk, dispersing papers with a final swoosh of his tail. <What do I know? I'm just the cat-dragon who will rip your eyes out if you don't settle down and allow Maira to sleep. Good night, boy.>

Lirome stared at the desk for a long time after Ademis left. Could Kesia have the genes of other shifters lying dormant within her? For what purpose?

For what purpose, indeed. Garishton Razorclaw had been trying to create a weapon. Someone who could master and outwit the other shifter races—seal, wolf, and unicorn—with their own magic and attributes. Someone who could rule them.

Lirome only manifested one trait from each race. With Kesia's adaptable genes, she could do far more. She could become each race at her choosing. Perhaps even manipulate their innate magic with her green smoke, as she already interfered with Lurien's soul magic.

A danger, perhaps. But also a great asset and gift.

He well understood how that worked.

The hope within him flared brighter than it had any right to. Yes, the connection between them had been that of soul-friends. Of course it had been. She had already found her embermate. But upon his death, she needed someone. Soon, if the dragon council was to be believed. She was not made to live alone.

And so, Kesia had reached out to him, without any knowledge of doing so. How could she know? Her aching and silent despair could be a natural response to him ignoring what they could have together. For a death unicorn, the greatest need after the loss of a mate was a friend to bear the weight of grief.

For a dragon, apparently that individual was also a new mate.

Shame and anger filled him. If that were the case, he was the greatest fool for denying her. She needed to be examined more thoroughly, more blood taken for testing, in order for him to be certain. They needed to speak, and explore the bond between them.

The knots in his stomach twisted. She didn't want anything to do with him. Lirome couldn't blame her. He'd denied her truth and comfort—and she had done nothing but trust him all this time. He'd felt her insecurity and worry over her own place in the world, and he had been a source of that anxiety.

He groaned a wordless prayer to the All-Maker, then sighed.

He needed to open conversation with her and speak honestly and directly. It was all she had wanted from the start—deep communication without any dramatic flourishes. Remarkably sensible of her.

Yes, he needed to reconcile with her as soon as possible.

Right now, Lirome owed his sister a good night's sleep, unbattered by his emotions. Which meant one final cup of tea with just the right amount of sleeping herb. Otherwise, there would be no rest until Lirome saw Kesia again.

And apologized.

CHAPTER NINETEEN

At least she could fix an engine. Even one as cantankerous as *The Silver Streak's*. The damage from the most recent attack had been mostly structural, but some of the issues on the top deck had impaired the "dellercate innards" of the engine. The chief engineer, Virna, wanted her engine in perfect condition, even in the smallest areas. Which meant that after more than four weeks of work, Kesia was still scurrying around in various tiny animal forms, scoping out the damage better than the zeroscope setting on Virna's goggles.

It was a relief to be a beetle or a mouse, crawling around and figuring out what parts needed repairs. To be able to fix the problems, working with her mind and hands in the company of Virna's abrupt little comments and mumbles. To take a break after a few hours so she could breathe in the fresh air on the top deck and fly a few laps in sun-dove form.

All of it was preferable to being cooped up in the safe house or library with someone who couldn't be honest with her. To be fair, Lirome was skilled at more than just research. He had assisted with improvements on the ship, which meant they'd had to interact in some respects, and it had been…

Kesia sighed. Terrible and unnatural. And quiet.

The quiet had been her fault, which was odd. She was used to pushing down the barriers that Zephryn had put up. In this case, she didn't want to speak first. Not again. She could sense some of Lirome's emotions as he studied her. She could feel the half-finished words simmering behind his stare. Kesia had even been tempted to give him a piece of paper to see if writing things down would help release the tension between them. But hiding behind such things was silly.

Here was someone who wanted to speak with her, even if the words were difficult, and he couldn't find them. She should make an effort to speak back instead of pushing him away because of one unpleasant moment. Goodness knows she had given Zephryn seventy times seventy chances, if not more. She'd certainly overlooked minor squabbles with Shance and Nula.

Besides, even if he wouldn't explain himself, she missed Lirome. Better his company with secrets than no company at all.

If that meant Kesia didn't value herself, at least the emptiness inside her wouldn't hurt as much. Grieving was hard enough when she was around Lirome. Without him, the sorrow was an insuperable barrier, separating her from the joy of life. That made her angry.

Anger and sorrow only made for more nightmares.

So when Virna announced a break, Kesia made sure to remain on the top deck in the area where she knew Lirome took his break. It had only been a few days, but he was a creature of habit, which made him remarkably easy to find.

She sighed, leaning against the railing of the ship. There was freedom here in the suspended dock. The breeze carried the scents of fresh saltwater and brine, and undertones of rich loam from the Pinwood forest to the north. The electro-carriages might be less stable, but Kesia didn't miss groundcar fumes one bit.

Lirome neared. His familiar swirl of emotions slipped through the cracks of a solid, calm facade. Shock flitted through her. How was she sensing him so clearly? It couldn't be the soul-friend connection, not when Kesia was a dragon. From what she knew, only death unicorns should be able to feel emotions like that, even if Lirome was opening his heart to her.

What was happening?

No more running away. No more pretending he didn't get under her skin. Kesia needed answers. More than that, she wanted conversation with him, which was somehow better than conversation with anyone else. Because she liked him, wanted him around, more than anyone else.

The realization came quite suddenly but settled naturally into her gut as if it had always been there. It was a soft, gentle lapping, deeper and deeper, like walking slowly into the waves along the shoreline.

Then, Lirome was next to her. She felt his presence, even as she stared out into the city and the Cresida Inlet in the distance.

"I see you've taken my sister up on her suggestion of more comfortable clothes."

An easy topic to start with. She could go along with that.

"Yes. Maira was most helpful." Kesia smiled. The death unicorn queen had only asked one question: how had Kesia endured the local fashions for so long? "I'm not sure how she even found some of these items. I checked the shops in the city. They carried the boots, yes, but the trousers and this sleeveless tunic?"

She gestured to the crimson fabric of her shirt, secured by a far more comfortable corset that laced up on either side instead of stifling her in the back. Coupled with a slim, short coat and her hair tied loosely away from her face, Kesia felt more at ease than she had since arriving in the Scepter of Knowledge.

Lirome chuckled. "Maira has her ways. She's had to clothe many children over the years, both her own and her grandchildren. We understand the discomfort human clothing can bring."

Kesia nodded. It was odd picturing the petite death unicorn queen managing so many mates and children as well as leading the herd in Sekastra. Yet Maira seemed to do it easily, with such confidence.

A confidence Kesia had begun to sense deep within herself. It was only a flicker, but grew stronger in ways she didn't quite understand. Lirome somehow fed her newfound confidence, and she knew, without speaking, that it was more than that. More than enjoying each other's company.

To broach that subject, she needed to apologize first.

She took a deep breath and exhaled slowly. "I'm sorry if what I said harmed you—"

"Why are you apologizing?" He gave a dry, gentle laugh. "You were right. I should have spoken sooner. To be honest, I didn't have much to say, because I've been confused as well. But I should have made that clear."

"But I accused you of things—"

"Out of a place of pain and loneliness."

Kesia pressed on. "I'm usually more controlled."

"So am I. That doesn't seem to be the answer." He laughed again. "We're mortal, Kesia. I'm told by my sister that we're allowed to be irrational sometimes." A shadow crossed over his face. "I'm not used to working with someone else deeply, but I will try. I will improve."

Lirome's words settled in her heart, easing wounds that ran deep and replacing them with something even more fragile.

Hope.

Hope that she wasn't alone. Hope that she wasn't creating something out of nothing. It was a hand extended toward her, holding respect and perhaps something stronger.

Silence fell between them, pierced by the cry of sea birds and the squeal of electro-carriage cables far below.

Finally, Lirome spoke. "Among death unicorns, there is a tradition of the bereaved waiting three months before seeking a new mate. This is called the amshal, the Time of Recalling, in which the memories of the mate are pondered, shared, and savored before setting them to rest. Another death unicorn walks with them as a friend—the amshalir or amshalla, someone innately called to stand by and care for the soul of the bereaved."

Kesia pressed her lips together. "You tell me this because we are soul-friends."

"I tell you this because … I think we are something more. And unless I am very much mistaken, I think you realized it far earlier than I did.

"I see." Kesia paused. Something in his words itched at her, causing her to wonder at his allusions. But she didn't have the energy for skirting around topics anymore.

She looked at him. "Would the 'something more' be a potential mate bond between us?"

Lirome stared at her. "How did you guess?"

"I like guessing. Sometimes I even get to be right."

"In this case … I think you are." She felt a trickle of rueful humor from him. "Would you like to hear my reasoning?"

Kesia nodded. A part of her was stunned that the death unicorn had agreed with her. That they were having this conversation.

What will the dragon council think?

She pushed the fear aside.

"First, tell me what you sensed at Lurien's campaign speech?"

"Sense? Fear. So much fear, until you shielded me. And then…" She paused. "I breathed out the green smoke, which was bad. But when I did, the crowd … I thought they seemed less devoted to her. I wasn't sure."

His eyes widened. "You think your green smoke may have lessened her empathic hold on the crowd?"

"Yes. It's only an idea."

"It's right. Maira, Shance, and I—we all sensed it. You cancelled her empathic manipulation. Another question, if you would. What does my magic feel like?"

What kind of question was that? "Nothing. Just magic, I guess? I can tell you're doing things."

"Other races, when they can sense death unicorn magic at all, say it feels like frost fire. Even the Descendant, who has a drop of unicorn blood, has noted this sensation. But death unicorns don't perceive our magic like that. It's just natural." Before she could ask about this information, Lirome continued. "You said your father was experimented on. That he seemed to be a mixture of many different creatures when you killed him."

The memory of her father flashed in her mind. Kesia swallowed bile, hands shaking. "Yes. Though I never understood why he was so mixed up."

Lirome's hands closed over hers, calming her and providing a feeling of safety. "What if your uncle was trying to combine other shifters into your father? And then…"

Kesia blinked. "He succeeded with me? Lirome, are you saying that I have death unicorn blood?"

"I believe so, and a significant amount, along with the blood of the other shifters. I don't have conclusive proof, but circumstantially, it's the only answer. It would explain how we connected as soul-friends. And when Zephryn died, your heartflame sought a compatible mate. Although considering my behavior, I'm not sure if that was a good thing or a bad thing."

"Good thing." The words rushed out of her.

Lirome raised his eyebrows. "Even with my snoring?"

"A minor inconvenience."

"I see." He smiled, his teeth bright against his olive skin, enhancing the high cheekbones she wanted to trace, if he hadn't already been holding her hands. Then his expression fell. "I would never wish this scenario on you, Kesia. I would have traded places with Zephryn in a heartbeat to save you both. I tried to!"

For the first time, she felt his answering grief at her loss. His anger at being unable to save them both. The emptiness within her was slowly filled with the depth of his own grieving. Creating, strengthening the new bond between them, as they found understanding and caring within the other.

Kesia stepped closer to him, wrapping her arms around him. Offering her own peace. <It isn't your fault. You cannot keep blaming yourself.>

A ragged sigh escaped him. <But if I had only—>

She held him tighter. Leaned into the bond.

<Zephryn ordered you to save me. He gave his life for me. It is done. Continuing this line of thought is stupid and hurtful to you. Stop.>

He chuckled. "Interesting words of comfort."

Kesia glanced up at him. "Did I do it wrong?"

Lirome stroked the edge of her jaw. "Actually, no. I prefer directness, which has set me at odds with my own people at times.

You are ... more than perfect."

Her face heated as they parted. Still standing close, holding hands.

His expression turned earnest. "In all my years I have never felt ... this. For anyone. I assumed it would never happen."

"You've never had sex, then?"

Lirome laughed. "I've explored mating rituals. There is another unicorn tradition, the autumnal and spring vigils. The boundaries between unmated unicorns and humans are nonexistent during those times, and any mating behavior is considered noncommittal. I was a very traditional sort in my youth. Over the years, and out of greater commitment to the Four Corners, I have chosen to abstain from that tradition."

"I see." Kesia pushed down more questions about this tradition—for the moment—and opted for another one. "So, what happens now?"

He stared at her, concern and adoration warring on his features. "I would ask you the same question. Death unicorn mate bonds are connected through soul, but always governed by consent and choice. A death unicorn widow or widower is expected to remain unmarried for three months as part of the grieving process."

"But dragons are part of their embermates upon sight. And then shortly after, their heartflames are bound." Kesia swallowed. "You and I can't do that."

"No, we can't. But Maira can weave together my soul and your heartflame using her soul magic. She's done it once before with Nula and Tiers." He paused. "It seems we are already building that connection ourselves. Death unicorns do this as a lead up to the official bonding. I didn't know dragons could. From what I've studied, four weeks for a dragon is an eternity."

"Well, I'm not a typical dragon." Kesia sighed. "Being around you helps me grieve. Process. Find beauty in life again."

He nodded. "Likewise. And as long as your heartflame is preserved, none of this has to be rushed."

"Agreed." But her worry also matched his. "The dragon council is wary of death unicorns."

"That's putting it lightly." He sighed. "I don't blame them. But I highly doubt they want their new crown princess being bound to a death unicorn. Which, I presume, would put me into a position of leadership over dragons. They would assume I took advantage of you in your grief."

Kesia rolled her eyes. "Yes, because I am helpless and incapable of challenging others." She grimaced. "Well, until recently, maybe I was."

"You're growing and moving on from a past of horror and abuse. If I'm not allowed to blame myself, then neither are you."

She snorted. "Just because you're ancient—"

"I'll have you know that for a death unicorn, I'm not even middle aged yet."

Kesia smirked, enjoying their teasing again. "So we keep this from the council. They will want conclusive proof, which we don't have. There's still the mission to stop Lurien. Since our bond is different than a normal embermate bond, I think we can wait."

"I wouldn't mind a little more time to adjust. Death unicorn bonds are not made as quickly." He hesitated, sadness once more showing in his violet eyes. "It is a challenge to move on from my own grieving over a mate."

Kesia raised her eyebrows. "You've lost a mate?"

He turned away from her slightly, his expression distant. Through their fragile bond, she felt the old wounds of grief and separation. "In a sense. I told you that I didn't expect to find one. The genocide killed so many of our women. I knew, as so many other death unicorn males did, that I would never find someone. And yet…" His jaw worked. "All shifters are meant to have a mate. It is part of our instincts to expect one. Impossible to entirely quench. To live with that urge to keep seeking, to see others finding their mates, knowing that your destiny was killed before they even had a chance." He shook his head. "You learn to harden yourself."

"So that's why you understand." She reached out and gently stroked his face, feeling another aspect of their bond settle into place, as surely as she felt his embarrassment, his shame over comparing his loss to hers. Kesia sent back reassurance to him. "It isn't foolish. Your loss is real. If the All-Maker set our lives this way, then I'm glad we met each other."

"I as well."

Then he pulled her into his arms. Never mind who saw them. This time was theirs to share. To grieve together. Rest in each other.

To find some measure of wholeness.

At last, they parted. Kesia swiped at her face and sighed. "I'm sorry, in advance, for the difficulties that will come with figuring this out. I still don't know what I'm doing."

He nudged her. "You need to stop apologizing. We'll figure it out. Intelligence is my Talent, and you are remarkably clever. I've never seen anyone adapt so fast. We'll discover it together."

His expression was so certain, so sincere. His words connected deeply with the part of her that wanted to learn everything she could about those around her and discover how to work with them. The part of her that saw life as a series of adventures and challenges, not something to be feared.

Her heartflame flared within her. The alignment of values and passion. The shared experiences. Everything was there.

Kesia snorted. "So intelligent, yet you didn't think I would challenge you on our mysterious connection?"

"Well, you are a natural at diving into trouble." His eyes glinted. "And although I like to think I take more care in my decisions, I have a fine appreciation for trouble myself."

"I see."

Lirome must have sensed her uncertainty, because he leaned closer, his long black hair framing his face. "Never be afraid of your strength, Kesia."

She inhaled, stirred by his words and his ease.

"Well, the first item to figure out is how to get you to mind-speak to me when I'm shifted into another form."

"Agreed." Lirome smirked. "Or you could simply communicate with me before running off on your own."

"Well, now that you're open to sharing things with me, I'm happy to reciprocate. Shouldn't we be about new discoveries?"

"Yes. After tea."

Kesia wrinkled her nose. "More of the hot leaf-water?"

He looked at her in mock-disapproval. "No sneering, my Fire-breather. This shop has twenty-six different varieties, and an impressive array of newspapers, puzzles, and live musical entertainment."

She tilted her head. "As opposed to dead entertainment?"

"Come and see for yourself. Even you will find a flavor to enjoy. And we can discuss our plans."

"Very well. I don't have any more engineering tasks. Although I'm certain I could be useful somewhere—"

"We both could. This is wartime, even if this Scepter doesn't acknowledge it. But if we can't acknowledge tea, then what are we stopping the war for?" He tugged at her hand. "Come along, then. The best tables will be taken by mid-afternoon. We don't have much time."

Lirome sped across the deck and down the gangplank. Kesia grabbed her cloak and ran after him. Apparently, once the death unicorn was certain about something, he didn't hesitate.

It was refreshing.

Besides, she was curious to see if he could coax her into enjoying tea. With the additional work for the debate weighing on her shoulders, it felt good to fixate on a small exploration.

Maybe she could bring some of it back to Zephryn. She reached out with her mind to ask him—then paused.

No. He wasn't there. She could imagine the conversation they would have had—they had held similar ones in the past.

They never would again.

Kesia sighed and rolled her eyes, blinking away the wetness that had formed. She brushed her thoughts aside. Lirome was a few paces ahead of her, slipping easily in and out of foot traffic, but she could feel his attention on her, not smothering, but watchful. He stopped and glanced over his shoulder at her with a hint of impatience and far more concern, sensing her repressed sorrow.

She flashed him a carefree smile, hoping he would take the hint. She didn't want to face any more difficult emotions today. Catching up with Lirome—her embermate, or bondmate, or whatever they would call it—was all that mattered.

Capturing a bit of enjoyment amidst the darkness.

CHAPTER TWENTY

"Lady Lurien summons you to her presence."

Shance heard the implied 'again' in the servant's statement, along with a note of disdain. Toward the order or toward Shance, it was unclear. Perhaps it was both. From what Shance had observed, not all the servants had been emotionally twisted into her service. Some of them had been blackmailed or bribed into their positions. If this servant was one of them, he could be useful. Shance gave the gray-haired man a smile as he rose from his chair. "She seems very needy. It's a wonder you continue to work here, Mr.—"

"Cortin. Ezra Cortin." The servant raised his bushy brows with a veiled sneer. "I work here for the pay, same as many others. I'll not say anything against her ladyship, so if you're expecting me to betray her—"

"I would only expect you betray her to if I did so first. Otherwise, how could I make you into a comrade against her?" Shance flashed him another smile as he tucked his clothing into place. When facing Lurien, it was best to make sure every button was fastened. "In case you are out of touch with the rumor mill, let me reassure you that I have no interest in Lady Lurien except to see her head on a spike and her soul-slaves freed. Including my son. If that displeases you, it will be difficult for us to be friends. Otherwise, I'm glad to meet you, Mr. Ezra Cortin."

Shance offered his hand. The man's lips curled slightly. After a moment, he shook it quickly, and went back to his formal posture, stiff in white livery. "Now, sir, the lady awaits."

Shance exhaled as he followed the servant down the hallway lined with cream wallpaper, pinwood wainscoting, and thick gold carpet. Bronze chandeliers suspended from the ceiling gave it a warm, sensual glow. He had made his first ally in the domain of his enemy. There were many more to sway, but one was a start. Hopefully, Cortin would alert the other servants in the estate that Shance was here to help, not to be Lurien's next toy and bedmate.

Something Lurien herself needed to be reminded of. Again.

Three hallways to the left, up one set of stairs, and he was in her private suite with its roaring fire and plush seating. A veritable banquet of fruits, cheeses, meats, breads, and superb wine lay on a side table. In the center was Lurien, sprawled on a lounge, her deep red hair streaming down her back, every inch of her alabaster skin on display.

Shance immediately focused on the wall behind her, fixating his mind on something repetitive. Like the handful of verses he remembered from the Holy Scrit. If they happened to be the verses about fencing laws, so be it.

"If the fire is too hot for you, my lady, call one of your slaves to bank it to a tolerable level."

"I could. But I find there is great freedom in exposure." The sound of her voice drew near him. "Due to your prudishness, you must look away, whereas I can look all I want. What a foolish thing, to deny yourself the privilege of studying your enemy's weaknesses."

Shance ground his teeth and summoned enough wind to create an unbreachable barrier between himself and Lurien. "In the end, you are the whore who is exposing herself for greater affection."

"A whore?" She gave a little giggle. "My dear Captain Wind-keeper, is that any way to address a lady? I thought you knew how to show a lady she was … special."

Her velvety words pierced through the wind barrier, carrying with them the smell of rancid oil, and beneath it, a beguiling floral scent. She continued to speak. "Come now. The past haunts you so. The memories, the responsibilities. Sharing your wife with other men. Oh, not her bed, but her responsibilities as she cares for these children that are not truly yours. Why would you put yourself through that again? Why not take the pleasure offered now?"

"So I can join your harem instead?" A part of him found the idea appealing. The rest of him found that part nauseating. Shance shoved away the mire of thoughts, pressing out more with his winds. "You who enslave and collect others to suit your whims?"

"I release them to enjoy their passions, free from condemnation!" Lurien sighed. "I'm offering the same to you. A place by my side. To be my mediator and the first in my bed." She tapped her finger to her lips. "Otherwise, if I cannot have the father, I will take the son. In front of him. Oh, Brennar?"

"Bren," Shance whispered.

Despite himself, he glanced around for his son. He stood in a corner of the room, equally unclothed, his face set in the artificially serene expression that Lurien so desired. But his eyes—his eyes were trapped.

Lost. Trying to seek an answer.

Lurien's mouth curled into a triumphant grin. "You, or him? I must say, I prefer you. I've had your son so many times, it grows dull. Maybe, if I had you, I would allow him to go free. You could rescue your son from my supposed enslavement and rescue me from dreadful boredom. What say you, Shance Windkeeper? Do we have a deal?"

Frost fire and sulfur crawled over his skin. For a moment, he wavered. Perhaps it would be better to do it now before his memories fully returned, before he remembered Maira and their past together. While he still viewed himself as disgraced for abandoning his family and herd. He certainly wouldn't enjoy the experience with Lurien. Didn't that count for something?

Brennar made a small sound, clearing his throat barely enough that anyone would notice. Lurien certainly didn't. Her attention was entirely on Shance.

But then his son shook his head. Only slightly.

He was there. He fought.

Maybe praying to the All-Maker was useful after all.

Giving in would help no one, but Shance knew what would. And it would hurt equally as much—and play one of his few cards.

Outright rebellion.

"As thoughtful as your deal is, Lurien," Shance said, "I'm afraid I will have to pass."

She pouted. "Such a shame."

Lurien tossed her hair, then turned toward Brennar.

"I do have a recommendation."

"Which is?"

He raised his hands, summoning a gale that shook the room. "Don't threaten me when I have too much to lose. I tend to act irrationally."

Winds blasted through the room, sending the table of food crashing into the chairs and whipping the fire into a frenzy of heat and smoke. The gale knocked Lurien and Brennar to the ground, and Shance pinned them in a corner with chairs.

"Brennar, stop him!" Lurien shrieked.

A new gust swirled into the room, pushing back the furniture. A furious bolt of wind struck Shance into the chest before he could block it. He hit the ground, unable to breathe. He pushed himself to his feet only to face a pistol, held by his son, aimed directly at his heart.

"Pathetic. You could once command storms, and now you can only upset a room? I understand why my lady prefers fresher blood."

Shance swallowed, staring into his son's eyes. "Brennar, you don't have to do this."

"I'm afraid he does, Captain Windkeeper." Lurien scoffed. "And I'm afraid I must return you to your room without food or water until you learn how to treat a woman properly. Cortin!"

The servant appeared, stoic and displeased as usual. "Follow me, sir."

Shance gave Brennar one final, beseeching look. There was only spite in his son's eyes. "This isn't over."

"Oh, I believe it is." She licked her lips, pulling Brennar close to her.

Shance turned away, biting back words, and followed Cortin down the hallway once more. One of his few moves to play, and he hadn't even stirred his son. Wasted.

As he reached the door to his room, Cortin shoved something into his hands. A tiny flask.

Shance looked up. The old man shook his head. "It's a bit stronger than water—I'll see you get some water later. But if my son treated me like that, I know I'd need a drink."

"Your son?"

"Haven't seen him or my grandchildren since Lurien hired me. She offered very good pay to the servants, then threatened our families if we left for any reason." Cortin grimaced, his dour face wrinkling further. "I can at least see to it that anyone who stands against her gets a bit of food. Now get in there before anyone suspects! This place is full of her spies."

As soon as Shance was inside, the door slammed behind him, leaving him to what was truly terrible whiskey.

And a faint glimmer of hope.

CHAPTER TWENTY-ONE

Sleeping alone had little appeal—so at times, Maira simply didn't. The leaves from Weirad had arrived, which meant she could get by on four hours of sleep. In the meantime, she strode through the decks of the ship, from stern to poop, aimlessly running her fingers over the recently-repaired framing and chatting with the crew.

After all, the crew should learn to be comfortable with her as well. Many of them already were, since she had healed them from the turmoil of the death unicorn raid. And her short stature was an advantage. No one thought danger came in a petite, youthful-looking package with a touch of matronly cushion and a confident smile. All the better for her. Maira had learned to charm others early. It had made her position as queen of the death unicorns a bit easier.

She simply added Shance's crew to her herd, without the actual empathy bond. The ones who openly disliked her, Maira treated with more kindness. After all, she had the benevolence of the All-Maker. Her life was improving, even if she didn't have her chief mate around right now. It didn't take much to improve over ten years in an electrified coffin.

The pang of longing her heart contradicted her thoughts. Her people needed guidance and her mates were restless and some gods-cursed upstart was trying to claim her title through perverted soul magic. She needed Shance. Yet, she had to let him infiltrate Lurien's home, for the sake of their people. Just as she'd given up so much in her life for the sake of her people.

By Lady Allandra, sometimes I wish I could run from all of this and shift into something easily-hidden, like that young dragon woman.

Kesia Ironfire. She would soon learn the burden of responsibility. Although perhaps it was different for dragons. At least she had Lirome standing by her. It seems they had both stopped tiptoeing around each other and admitted the mate connection between them, which was better for all concerned. There would still be issues with the dragon council. Maybe she could see to that.

Gods. Shance was right—Maira was a busybody, worse than Zilpath. Oh, Zilpath would be good to contact for some conversation.

Maira rounded a corner and nearly ran into the stocky figure of Commander Annabel Tegan. Tegan's feelings of concern and curiosity flowed from her more easily than those of the rest of the crew. Elric's Mane! She had forgotten the minor herd bond she had made with Tegan on the night of the death unicorn raid. That oversight would not do. She would have to find a moment to quickly cut the soul connection without alarming the airship officer.

"Your majesty, do you ever sleep?"

Maira sighed. "Commander, I told you that aboard ship, the title 'your grace' is sufficient. Especially when noting my chosen sleep habits, which are not your concern. Is that clear?"

"Of course, your grace." The other woman's face closed down. "By your leave."

Of all the times for Maira to lose her temper.

"Wait." Maira placed her hand lightly on Tegan's arm, and her emotions increased. For a moment, the woman's face seemed to fluctuate and shift like a sheet fluttering over a very different visage.

To her credit, Maira didn't flinch.

"Your grace? Is something wrong?"

"What? I'm sorry, Commander. My mind wanders, sometimes. I wish I could blame it on the wakefulness tea, but that would be a lie." She smiled ruefully but didn't release Tegan's arm. "Perhaps it was a trick of the light, but I was certain you looked rather different just now."

Tegan's brow twitched. "I'm sure I don't know what you mean, your grace."

"I'm certain you do." Maira squeezed her arm, quietly severing the herd bond, then released the limb. "But you can keep your secrets if you like. Just know that I'm quite good at keeping them as well."

"It would do no good. Although—" Tegan eyed her speculatively. "Perhaps, if you would explain more of what you did to my mind that first night? You cleared it somehow. I want to know how. A secret for a secret."

Ah, clever. Maira nodded. "Agreed. You first."

"Do you question my honor?"

"No. I can sense your fear. Fear of the unknown has a way of breaking honor, even if you have the best intentions. Even if, like me, you are serving a deity who mandates honorable behavior."

Tegan nodded. "I don't adhere to the Four Corners. Or anything, really. I'll throw a few coins into the air god's fountain in passing. But," she glanced in either direction, "as you insist. My Talent is creating illusions. Few know this. They assume my Talent is unremarkable, and I want it to stay that way."

"Why?"

Tegan sighed. As she did, the veil of illusion fell, revealing a very different woman. No longer middle-aged and stocky. She was younger, with defined, attractive features, crisscrossed with patches of silvery scales. Her flesh puckered and twisted where scales met skin. The eyes that stared down at Maira were mismatched: one human, and one dragon. Her hands were likewise covered in scales.

Grief twisted Maira's heart. The work of the SPU, the Pinnacle's Scientific Protection Unit. They had continued their human testing as well as their experiments on other shifters. She sighed. "Well, I can say that you are one of the most beautiful survivors I have ever seen."

"Really?" Tegan's lip curled derisively. "Tell that to the dead dragon they ripped apart to make me into this. Tell that to my family, who have shunned me. The Scepter of Pleasure is unforgiving toward who are ugly." She shook her head. "No, this is a minor curse compared to others. But I thought, since you were a healer… well, I've seen what you've done for the crew. What you did to my mind. Could you fix this?"

"No more than I can my own." Maira stroked her collar bone where the lightning scar spread across her chest. "I won't lie and tell you there is nothing to fix. All in Bonilus's world are subject to the trials of decay that we mortals brought into it. When I touched your mind, I simply created a bond to remove the fear. A bond that I broke, just now, since I made it without consent, for which I am sorry. Your scars show that you have healed physically, but your heart…" She shook her head. "I could coerce you to joyfully accept your fate through a different bond, but that would be no better than the slavery Lurien is imposing on those in the Scepter of Knowledge."

Disappointment and resignation flashed across her features. Tegan gave a short nod. "Understood, your grace." The veil snapped back into place, and her expression became businesslike once more. "I ask you not to tell anyone else. Also, I'm called Pryenil Slightshadow by dragons. A name given to me by the woman whose scales I now wear."

"Thank you for sharing with me."

Maira searched for something else to say. There was so little comfort to give survivors, especially those who chose to separate themselves. Perhaps she had made things worse by broaching the subject.

Her wireless commer chirped. She acknowledged the call with no small relief.

"Hello, my love," she opened. "I wish you were here."

"Likewise. Let's hurry up and take out this wretch so I can return." Shance's words through the crackly speaker warmed her soul. Never mind that Tegan was present. Maira would take any comfort she could get. Shance's words of open affection had always been one of his best qualities.

"That won't be easy. Lurien is confident she has every detail planned. Either she's overly-arrogant—"

"Or she has contingencies we haven't yet discovered. I wish it were the former, but somehow, I doubt it. Have you gotten through to Brennar again?"

"No. Lurien's hold over him grows stronger each day. If only I could have another near-death experience with lightning." Shance's tone was wry, but she could hear the underlying desperation. "I don't remember a regular death unicorn being able to subvert the bond between family like this."

"It shouldn't be possible. I've been speaking with Amarel. She says there is no one among the herd who could attempt such a thing, much less succeed to the extent Lurien has."

Tegan cleared her throat. "Another experiment from the Curious Intrigue?"

Maira nodded. "It must be. Though I'm not sure they have the subtlety to alter soul magic this much. I suspect some sort of chemical intervention as well. She must be using some kind of serum or potion to soften the minds of her targets and make them more pliable. Which means she could very well warp yours as well, Shance. Be careful what you drink."

"Viorstan. Maybe this was a bad idea."

"No. As you rise to full power, you should be able to resist more and more. You said yourself that she never managed to seduce you into her bed, even at your weakest."

He snorted. "Apparently it is a point of great frustration for her."

A thrill of triumph shot through Maira. "I'll work with Lirome to develop a serum to awaken your memories more quickly, and hopefully, with them, your full Talent. Perhaps something to increase your resistance in the meantime. I can't have you falling prey to her now."

"I won't." Hard and resolute. "You are the only woman I want." His voice turned playful and sultry. "I suppose that makes you my prey instead."

Maira's face heated, but she couldn't resist a response. "You are welcome to try. You have quite a game to play to catch me this time."

"I think I can handle you."

Tegan rolled her eyes. "Can you please keep the flirtation to yourselves? We're discussing business right now."

Maira sighed. "Always with the children interrupting." She gave Tegan a wink. The commander replied with an inappropriate hand gesture, then left, walking down the corridor once more. Maira added. "Such rudeness."

"I need to leave anyway," Shance said. "It's difficult to find time alone with her soul-slaves everywhere, ready to report my every move."

"Annoying and disturbing. I'll meet you at the Solaris Festival."

"Will you be in disguise?"

"I don't believe I will, considering I'm leading the charge against you."

"If you're against me, I might not be able to resist. Please, be against me."

She giggled. "We will have to manage that as well. Long days—"

"And safe nights."

She pressed the wireless commer with a satisfied hum. A mind suddenly invaded hers.

<Maira, your unconscious child is shaking and disturbing my sleep!> Ademis had been doing his nomadic napping rounds since Maira hadn't wanted to rest. <Come fix him!>

Fear gripped her heart. She spun around and ran for the healing bay, her heart slamming in her chest. Maira sucked in a breath and forced down the worst of her emotions before they affected the crew around her. No one else needed to suffer just because she did.

She was dimly aware of alarm from Shance. So he *could* sense her, even at this distance. He should have been able to feel her soul-state deeply and offer her comfort, but he had not yet returned to his full potential.

All-Maker, fill me with your strength.

She ran into the room and saw Cadence, fallen from his cot and laying on his side, breathing shallowly. Ademis sat next to him in skin form, a blanket about his waist, his normally mischievous expression quiet and concerned.

"He's come out of it, I think," Ademis said. "I had to shift to make sure he did all right. The damn guards wanted to hold him down." He shook his head. "Humans and their misinformation."

Maira ran her fingers through Ademis's hair. "Thank you. You can return to normal now."

"Good."

A few moments later, the cat-dragon curled up beside her, purring comfort. Maira breathed out slowly, trying to settle her thoughts. She needed to be as calm as possible to read Cadence's soul.

She gently placed a hand on his chest. Discord filled her, a chaos of confusion and bewildered dreams accompanied by a curious relief. The shadows from earlier were gone.

A kind of withdrawal, then, from Lurien's grasp. She would have to run additional tests, but something in Maira's soul was certain this was a breakthrough. They were closer to a solution. If Lurien's enhanced soul magic relied on chemicals, all they had to do was locate them and take away her source of power.

For now, all Maira had strength to do was sit next to her son and the cat-dragon, cling to the thread tying her to her husband, and pray to the All-Maker.

CHAPTER TWENTY-TWO

The electro-carriage stopped with a burst of lightning. Lurien exited first, followed by Brennar, another death unicorn named Cervin, and Shance. He deliberately delayed his movements, lest he seem too eager for the Solaris Festival. Lurien would question that, and while he could deflect her words, the fewer questions, the better.

The first of the three festivals, the Solaris Festival, was held on the southern edge of the Cresida Inlet to the west of the Scepter of Knowledge. Three broad stone bridges spanned the inlet, each one lined with displays and vendors; one decorated with golden banners and ribbons, one with white, and one with silver. The crossway bridges darting between them allowed for orderly traffic. Below, low boats made their way on the easy current, rowed by guides who charged three times as much for pleasure rides during the festival. All three bridges intersected into a broad platform that allowed for live performances, music, and dancing.

"Ah, such a lovely, vigorous time. To think, when I rule this city-state, all days will be as such, as long as the citizens know what is good for them." She turned toward Shance, her parasol firmly in place shielding her head, and her red lips curved in a beckoning smile. "Are you certain you won't allow me the honor of taking your arm as you lead me onto the dance floor?"

Her tendrils of empathy magic reached out to him, trying to entwine with his soul. Shance pushed away the urge to say yes. Lurien might still smell like fuel oil, but the taint was lessening and turning into a perfume the longer he was around her. He needed to find his friends and crew.

Especially Maira. Who hopefully had a serum by now.

Shance returned her smile cordially. "I would sooner keep company with a python in the endless void of Ucurit, my lady."

"Still so stubborn. You have outlasted all the others, including your son." She patted Brennar's shoulder as if he were a beloved pet. "But everyone comes around eventually. You'll find it far more enjoyable to surrender willingly rather than by force."

"Surrender always comes with a price." He thought back to his most recent conversation with Maira about Cadence's rough convalescence. Lurien would pay for that as well.

"Yes, it's such a sweet price." She shrugged. "If you are unwilling to enjoy what is before you, I shall have to accept the arm of this handsome young man. He takes after his father in many ways, I'm sure."

Shance fisted his hands. The death unicorn was quite open about the lovers she took to her bed, all of whom were entirely devoted to her pleasure. Thanks to her soul compulsions, no doubt. Sickening.

It was made infinitely worse by the look of complacency and snide triumph on Brennar's face. As if escorting the foul woman was a great boon instead of an enslavement.

Shance must have had hopes and dreams for his son involving acts of valor. He didn't remember those dreams, but he was quite certain none of them involved Brennar being kept like a pampered lapdog by a psychopath. A controlling wretch with hair as red as crimson sun and a face of delicate alabaster, set off by a flowing golden dress that clung to her slender figure in all the right ways.

He blinked and shook his head. Damn it. He couldn't let the death unicorn's seductions get to him. Not now, not when he would soon rest eyes on his beloved. Shance tugged at his golden cravat, letting the rigidity around his neck snap him into focus. He took a deep breath and surveyed the scene around him.

Lurien flashed him a warning look over her shoulder as she walked toward the golden-draped bridge. "I have eyes everywhere. Many you see, and more that you don't. Consider this your furlough, as it were, but don't wander off or they will ensure you pay for reneging on your bargain as my second in the debate."

"As always, your threats and warnings of pure violence are music to my ears." He flipped her a disrespectful salute. "Until sunset, my lady."

"Until then, you fascinating rogue of mine."

"Never yours." Anger tingled within him, along with the sharpest flickers of something brighter and more dangerous than the winds he controlled so easily. Something that heated his blood like electricity, sounded like music, and tasted of ozone.

A storm. What had the Lawless records called him? Tyrius Stormsong. Master of wind, water, lightning, thunder. But Talents didn't work that way. They called upon a single element, force, or power, not the combination required for a storm.

Yet Kesia had two Talents—matter-shaping and the far rarer animal shifting ability. Did Talents in Elotrin work differently because of their open acceptance of magical energy? A part of him knew it was so. And he could even fake enough confidence around others.

But when alone, the gaps in his memory were all too ominous.

Shance shook his head. He needed to find someone to talk to. Someone who wasn't actively trying to get in his pants. He scanned the bridges and spotted a familiar brunette on the edge of the silver bridge.

Kesia. She looked far more at ease in pants and a loose tunic cinched by a side-lacing bodice and a neckline that dipped below her collarbone. Conservative for the Scepter of Commerce or Scepter of Pleasure, but nearly scandalous for the Scepter of Knowledge. Likely Maira had something to do with the dragon embracing a more comfortable fashion.

The dragon woman knelt beside a display of an engine prototype, which was propped on a table. She was engaged in an animated conversation with the vendor while her fingers poked and prodded one of the metal table legs.

"So you see," she said. "All you need to do is adjust the dampening valve from the electrical converter and tweak the exhaust vents, and you'll be able to control the rate of combustion far more easily."

The gentleman frowned thoughtfully. "If I make those changes, I'll need a larger body to house the whole thing."

"Not necessarily. Tweaking the vents will funnel more hot air away from the engine's core at a faster rate, which will allow you to compress the structure of the engine and do away with such large frames. Unless you want more protection from other vehicles in electro-carriage accidents. Also, accidents will happen less if you can control the combustion rate."

She finished fiddling with the table leg, smoothing the metal as though it were clay. "And the table leg is as good as new! Better, actually, because I reinforced it with the melted remains of those leftover screws."

The engineer nodded. "Good thing you stopped by my table, Miss. I would have been in real trouble if this thing had broken down. This is my first prototype. Although after your suggestions, I might have to rework the blamed thing."

Kesia paused, clearly uncertain about the human customs. "I'm … sorry?"

"Oh, don't be. Honestly, you probably should have charged me for an in-depth critique like that." The engineer gave her a smile. "All that, and you're pretty as well."

She shrugged. "I would still be capable if I wasn't pretty."

"Yes, that's what I mean." He chuckled. "I bet you have a husband or sweetheart around here somewhere."

"I had a husband. He died."

Shance winced. Most humans would have politely evaded the question, but dragons never saw the point of that. The engineer winced. "I'm sorry to hear that, Miss. That explains your get-up."

"My clothing? I suppose." She gave her all-black outfit a quick glance. "Black was Zephryn's favorite color." Realization flashed across her face. "They are human mourning colors. Yes. That's right." Kesia gave the engineer a smile. "Don't trouble yourself. You didn't know he was dead. It was over seven weeks ago."

The engineer sputtered at her sweet, factual tone, probably unsure if Kesia was heartless or simply making a bitter remark at his ignorance. A good time for Shance to intervene, since his dragon friend was without her death unicorn shadow.

"Oh, there you are, sister. I was worried." He took her by the arm and gave the engineer a bright smile. "Very sad for all of us, but grief assails everyone differently. It's time we met up with our mother and father by the mid-cross bridge."

He turned and directed Kesia toward the bridge, and they walked away. Kesia strode with him easily at first, then pulled free. "I should find Lirome. He was getting us beverages, but then I saw that man's table about to fall over, and I had to help." She paused and stared at Shance. "You have odd particles around you."

"What? Have you been in the sun too long?"

"No! And they're not like the green smoke particles. They're sort of … clear. Yes, clear. I can draw out the green smoke, so let me see if I can draw these ones out as well." She closed her eyes and took his hand in hers. A tingle filled him as though she were sifting through his cells with a million tiny knives. Shance tried not to flinch.

After a moment, she opened her eyes, which glowed with a greenish tinge. Green scales splayed across her face and hands. "I think I got most of it. But you need to be careful. Whatever Lurien is doing, whatever she's using to enhance her soul magic, it's sinking deeply inside you."

Shance nodded his thanks. "You've learned even more about yourself."

"Too much at once." Kesia shook her head. Her scales vanished with the action. "Sometimes I wish I had fewer mysteries within myself."

"I'm with you there. Although … I can't imagine losing a spouse."

She gave him a sideways look. "Isn't that what it's been like without Maira for ten years? You were always seeking someone to fill that space. Even me, as ridiculous as that was." Kesia gave him a wink. "Now you have her back. Except you don't. You will."

Hopefully very soon.

"Yes, I will." Shance studied her. "And what about you?"

Kesia shrugged diffidently. "The dragon council continues to search for an embermate for me. Which seems like a waste of time, considering the war."

"They want to keep you alive."

"Yet, they don't trust me." The dragon woman pursed her lips. "I've solved the problem of a mate in the meantime."

Before Shance could follow up, a smile spread across Kesia's face, aimed at a figure who had just appeared. "There's the lost unicorn now."

Lirome, clad in plain, dark gray clothes, held out a cup with an aggrieved look. "Oh, am I the person who is lost? Please, tell me the tale of the lost unicorn. What happens next after he hands an errant dragon her strewsberry ice and scolds her for vanishing on him again?"

Kesia grinned slyly and took the polished metal cup, giving the death unicorn a pat on the cheek. "Me, vanishing? That would be a fun trick. But not one of mine. I'm only guilty of caring too much about the misfortunes of others, which was why I was assisting that engineer back there with his table. Some people find altruism a desirable trait. You and Maira recommended that I used my problem-solving instincts to help others. It's fun!"

"Always with an excuse. It's a wonder I keep you around." Lirome's lips curved, and he tugged at a lock of Kesia's hair. "Great job. Did he need any other help?"

"I informed him of five possible improvements to his engine. Two of them he said he would implement after the festival. He paid me a compliment, and judging from Shance's expression, I didn't handle it as well as I should have."

Shance stood and watched the two in disbelief. From memory, Shance knew that Lirome was capable of flirting, but Kesia? Was this what she meant about a mate? He managed to find his voice. "Just remember that for humans, the traditional mourning period is six months to one year."

Kesia shrugged. "I'm not human."

"The vast majority of this city is. And unless you told him you were a dragon, he probably thought you were heartless for dismissing Zephryn's death after only seven weeks. Or he suspected that you had planned his death."

"I would never!" Her eyes flashed into slits, and flames appeared around her free hand. "How dare he think—"

"No one is thinking anything. Be at peace." Lirome grabbed her hand in his, engulfing the flames. Viorstan! Shance fully expected to smell the scent of roasted death unicorn, but there was only a flash of shadowy magic. What was going on?

Judging by the look on Lirome's face, Shance would have to wait to question him. At that moment, the death unicorn only had eyes for Kesia.

She sighed out a plume of smoke. "Well, I was under control."

"Yes, and you still are." His voice was straightforward but unusually gentle. "You are doing the best you can. The All-Maker will see to the rest. As will I."

"Indeed." Her face lit up. "Did I tell you what I was able to do to Shance? There were these particles, and I removed them!"

Lirome's eyes narrowed. "Particles?"

"Yes, deep inside him. I think they were affecting him--"

A familiar longing tugged at his heart, interrupting their words. "Maira," he breathed.

Shance turned away from the two, and began walking across the bridge. Pushing through others around him, drawn by the woman striding toward him, her violet eyes sparkling. Unlike Kesia, she had chosen to follow the Scepter of Knowledge fashions. Her crisp white blouse set off her dark olive skin. The black corset she wore enhanced her curves, and her black-lipped smile said she was fully aware of and appreciated his attention to both of those areas. That the physical distance that had lingered between them in bed was over.

If there was one thing Shance could genuinely thank the All-Maker for, it was her.

Maira spoke first. "I see you managed to escape Lurien."

"Sometimes I wish I'd never let myself get caught." He swept her up in his arms and breathed in deeply. Never mind Lurien's spies—let them see what true affection looked like. "You are in my thoughts continually."

She chuckled, her fingers tickling his hair. "As you are in mine. Although this current position is quickly becoming intolerable with this corset cinching me."

Shance set her down and fixed her with a serious gaze. "My dear, we must see about removing it then. It won't do for you to be so uncomfortable."

"How generous of you to offer." She flashed him a grin as they made their way across the bridge and into the crowd on the other side of the inlet. A faint taste of frost fire revealed the presence of death unicorn magic. Maira was producing an empathic disinterest field. "How is Brennar? Has his true nature emerged since Lurien attacked you?"

Shance shook his head. "No. Unless I wish to suffer another near-death experience, he will remain entrapped. How comes the serum?"

"I'm still working with Cadence's withdrawal symptoms. Lirome is helping when he can—and, surprisingly, Kesia as well."

"She has knowledge of medicine?"

He turned them down a side alley in the quaint dockside village. There had to be a suitable place somewhere around here for a tryst.

Maira continued. "Lirome is teaching her. She has an adept mind and can sometimes point out when Lirome and I are talking past each other, producing a new solution simply by piecing together what we're saying. There is much untrained potential in her."

"Indeed. She seems to be holding together, thanks to Lirome. Your suspicions about them might be correct after all."

"Yes. I've noticed it more and more lately. I doubt the dragons will be happy."

"Well, your herd wasn't happy about me, and we survived. At least Lirome isn't on the side of the enemy."

Maira frowned. "The dragons might think he is. Do you believe they envision an heir who is half death unicorn?"

"True." He was vaguely aware of how odd it was to be speaking of Kesia as if she were so much younger, when less than two months ago he had assumed them to be far closer in age.

Still, the dragon was in good hands with Lirome.

And Shance had a lot of time to make up with Maira. He finally found a small, respectable inn of wood and white-painted brick and secured a room. Just as he had opened the door, Maira leaped into his arms, wrapping her legs around him and capturing his mouth in a deep kiss.

Damn, he'd missed her.

Heat spread through him as they made their way through the door. After a brief pause to lock it, the stifling cravat and tight corset were the first things to hit the floor. Shance and Maira fell easily into the familiar taste and rhythm of each other, body and soul.

There were so many unknowns. So much to make up for. But in these moments, they only needed each other. The sharpness of electricity filled Shance again as he kissed his way across her lightning scar, evoking a soft groan in response.

Then Maira's hands gripped his shoulders and pulled him down. All was lost to sensation and the heady, indescribable euphoria unique to death unicorn soul bonds. Every feeling, every part of their essence, pain and joy and fears and hopes, becoming one even as their bodies united.

Lightning. Wind. Frost fire.

Afterward, as they lay dozing in the late afternoon sunlight, he traced her scar again. "What is this? It seems … familiar."

She studied him with disappointment in her eyes. Then she smiled faintly. "A long time ago, you and I made a choice. We joined, impossibly, to destroy a horrible kingdom."

"The legacy of the Glorious Destiny."

"Yes." He brushed back the soft black hair that framed her face. She continued. "There were unexpected side effects. But no regrets."

"No regrets," Shance repeated. He knew the words were true, but the source of that certainty remained a mystery. "I'm sorry. I should remember so much more."

She traced circles on his chest. "You will. I'm sorry I don't have the serum yet. I will soon. I promise."

"The sooner, the better."

Maira's brow wrinkled. "It isn't an ideal solution. The mind is meant to heal slowly, Shance. Forcing knowledge and memories to surface all at once won't be easy for you."

He picked up her hand and pressed his lips to her palm. "I can weather any pain to remember."

"You'll have to." Ah, the candor she used when trying to cut through his bravado. "I can't tell you what it will be like to remember so much, so quickly. And I'll try to be with you, but I can't promise—"

"You're worrying too much, my dear."

She snorted. "So what would you suggest?"

"Hmm, since speaking isn't helping…" Shance gently kissed her face and forehead, using extra care around the sensitive base of her small silver horn. Her pointed ear tips and sharp, delicate jawline each had their turn. "Perhaps we should have a repeat performance."

Maira pursed her lips, aware of his distraction, yet unable to resist. She leaned over him, her skin smooth under his touch. "The sun is setting soon, and you must return. There isn't much time."

"Are you offering me a challenge?" He found his way to her neck, nuzzling down the scar. "Because I accept."

Getting lost in his wife was preferable to the alternative of brooding over the serum or facing a past he couldn't fully recall. He didn't want to know just how far he'd fallen in the last ten years.

Or how much he'd failed.

CHAPTER TWENTY-THREE

The platform loomed in front of Kesia. Not the stage of a meeting hall, like she had faced with Zephryn nine weeks earlier. Now, such public forums were forbidden by the accords of the campaign. But this speech Kesia would give to the Lawless members in the safe house was even more terrifying.

In this speech, she would reveal her scales. Assert her authority as the crown princess. Offer herself officially to the Lawless of the city. A small test of her future as the dragon leader.

And she must do it alone.

Kesia sucked in a breath and sent up a prayer to the All-Maker. She stepped onto the wooden dais and faced the audiceptor and, beyond it, humans and dragons, all ready to judge her. For once, she understood why Zephryn hated public speaking. She would rather be facing a score of dragons and airships on the battlefield than making this speech.

Then a peace came over her.

She could do this. Zephryn had saved her for a reason. She wouldn't let his death be in vain. Nor would she let down Lirome, who watched her from the shadows.

"Agents and members of the Lawless. Thank you for joining me this evening." Kesia's voice shook over the last word. She gritted her teeth, and her eyes caught Lirome's. He gave her a nod, violet eyes gleaming with assurance.

They might not be able to speak over a private link yet, but she could sense his belief. His understanding. He too, had difficult parts of himself to reveal. Now, he shielded her from the emotions of the crowd, lest they overwhelm her.

She could do this. She wanted to do this. No matter what happened to her or how the people reacted. Hopefully she wouldn't say anything wrong, like she had in conversation with the engineer at the Solaris festival two weeks ago.

"As you can see, I'm alone." Kesia clutched her voicelator pendant, just as Nula had advised her. "My embermate, crown prince Zephryn Nightstalker, was murdered nine weeks ago by Lurien Alistil, an ally of the Curious Intrigue. According to everything we know about dragons, I should have died with him, and Lurien would have succeeded in eliminating the royal family of the Scepter of Justice, once and for all." Kesia's lips twitched. "I am sorry to disappoint."

A few uneasy smiles and coughs followed her statement. She breathed out. It felt good to speak honestly. With those few words, more came. "Zephryn Nightstalker was, above all else, a servant of his people and a protector. He believed saving me was the best choice to achieve those goals. I disagreed with him, but he proved just how stubborn the Nightstalker line was. My goals are to continue his legacy and ensure the Scepter of Justice is restored for all."

Now was the time of revelation. Showing her scales, which were more green than ever. An open sign of what had been done to her.

What was hers.

"As you know, the Curious Intrigue conducts many brutal

experiments. I was not immune to this treatment—in fact, I received especially cruel attention. A favor from my uncle, Garishton Ironfire, now Garishton Razorclaw." Kesia allowed the scales to surface on her hands, her arms, her face, until they painted a pattern over every exposed part of her, shimmering a deeper hue of the green smoke that caused so much damage.

Whispers and gasps flickered through the crowd. Even without sensing their feelings, Kesia could clearly see the pity on many faces, the curiosity on others. Even revulsion on some, most notably the dragons.

Her gut clenched, but she soldiered on.

"One of Zephryn's most passionate arguments was that I not find my identity in how I was mistreated. I was harmed. I am different from a normal dragon in ways I am still discovering. But I am still a member of the royal family. I am still deserving of justice and protection, as is every human, dragon, and other shifter who has been mistreated. Restoring the Scepter of Justice only has value if we stand with those who have been mistreated, tortured, and violated, not against them."

The room was silent. She lifted her chin.

"And so, as the crown princess of dragons, I will give every last breath and flame to undo the hideous schemes of the Curious Intrigue and restore the Scepter of Justice. No more war. No more worrying what new horrors will be created by mad scientists in a laboratory." She gestured to her face. "Though perhaps, if you grow tired of your current scale color, they could be of use. As long as you don't mind losing your Talent or your life."

There were a number of scattered chuckles at her grim humor, and a few more faces in the crowd settled into security and loyalty. She smiled back at them, making sure to keep the right amount of eye contact without lingering so much it disturbed them. *Zephryn, if only you could see me now.* The familiar sadness tugged at her heart, and her throat tightened.

She caught Lirome's eyes and felt the warmth of his presence. A smile curved his lips. He gave a small nod, encouraging her to finish strong for Zephryn's sake and for her own.

Kesia had friends who cared. And a mate.

Yes, she would finish well. She spoke her final words into the audiceptor.

"So I tell you, fellow members of the Lawless, and all the free people of the Scepter of Knowledge who stand here tonight: there is hope. Zephryn Nightstalker did not and will not die in vain. You are not alone. The Scepter of Commerce remains strong and free. And in four weeks, at the grand campaign debate, the Scepter of Knowledge will also be free!"

A smattering of applause and cheers filled the room, along with more whispered conversations and discussions. Words supporting her speech. Words against it. Doubt and fear, which trickled through Lirome's shields guarding her new sensing ability.

She set her jaw against the whispers. Right now, she had another appointment. Lirome had discovered a lead on a priest that had spoken with Garishton Razorclaw. Finally, they might be able to get some answers on what he had done to her. All she had to do was get free of the swarm of people.

She remembered to wave, descending the makeshift stage to the side where ropes created a pathway for her to walk through the crowd. Across the room, she could sense Lirome nearing her position. She breathed a sigh of relief, then threw back her shoulders and started walking, shaking hands and exchanging brief greetings with those she passed.

One woman fixed her with a firm stare. "It's good to see an honest, straightforward speaker after all of Lady Lurien's smoke and mirrors. I'm glad you're there to keep the death unicorn queen honest. Your type of leadership is just what we need from the Scepter of Justice."

"Thank you." The words were automatic, but Kesia marveled at the woman's response. She was happy. Excited.

There was no way this would last. Especially since the woman distrusted Maira. What would she do when she discovered the crown princess had a death unicorn mate?

Kesia continued down the roped-off aisle, hearing similar positive statements. Another person stopped her. A dragon man, his eyes narrowed and his mouth a slit. "You might have convinced others here with your smooth words, but it remains to be seen if you will restore the Scepter of Justice or destroy it."

"It's already been destroyed. Doing so again would be a waste of time."

"Even so. We'll be watching you, Ironfire."

A deliberate omission of her title. She swallowed hard, then flashed the dragon a smile that bared her teeth. "I expect so. That's why I was on the platform."

She turned away from him, shoving down the anxiety his words caused. Kesia kept walking, holding her head held high even as she longed to be free of the noise. She was nearly to the end of the suits, dresses, and hats, where Lirome stood waiting for her, his tall, plain-clothed figure a welcome relief.

Someone grabbed her hand, and her skin heated with the warmth of a dragon heartflame. Kesia looked up into the intense face of a dragon with pale skin and copper scales across his defined features and copper strands threaded through his waves of dark brown hair. "Princess Ironfire. An excellent oratory. You are truly showing honor to your fallen mate."

Kesia nodded. At least one dragon believed in her. Well, two if she counted Tiers Sunscaler. "As I should. And you are?"

"Arthurim Flamemaster, at your service." His ice blue eyes regarded her with fervency. "I have dwelt in this city for many years as a double agent after the loss of my embermate."

Kesia's mouth dropped open, and she stepped closer to Flamemaster. "What? I thought I was the only one."

"We had not yet bonded when she was captured. Her loss was difficult but endurable." He sighed out a soft plume of smoke. "It is rare, but it occurs. When the dragon council informed me of your loss and your continued state of solitude, they encouraged me to introduce myself."

"Of course they did. They are seeking an embermate for me."

"Indeed." His heartflame beckoned to her, sharp with pain and fascination, but not as Zephryn's had. It was a quietly emotive echo, a seeking need.

But Kesia had Lirome. Although right now, Flamemaster didn't need to know that. He had been sent by the dragon council, which meant he would likely report back to them.

"Your solitude grieves me. And my bloodline, while not royal, has always been faithful to the crown."

She frowned. "Thank you. I'm hardly in a place of solitude. I have the companionship of Captain Windkeeper's crew as well as the death unicorns Maira and Lirome Ukerys."

"Ah yes, those two. Hardly a replacement for your own kind. You are admirable in your willingness to endure them, however, particularly Lirome Ukerys's healing bond."

Now he'd gone too far. Kesia lifted her chin, her throat heating.

"My own kind kept me imprisoned, shackled, and trapped in the Pinnacle towers. My own kind were suspicious of the name Ironfire because of my uncle. Some of my own kind still expect me to suddenly become a traitor."

Regret passed over his features. "All unfortunate actions and attitudes. But you offer a new way for them. For all of us. I merely wanted to say that you need not settle for the ground when you can take to the air." He stepped forward, pressing into the edge of the rope. "Tell me, when was the last time you flew or hunted, Princess? Doesn't your heart long for the open skies? Only a dragon can offer that to you."

His words wove a spell in Kesia's mind. She *had* missed flying and hunting. Those were two activities Lirome could not join in. Yet there must be other ways for him to take to the air. There had to be. Even if there were not, she would not abandon Lirome. He had admitted to her that emotions didn't come as easily to him as they did to other death unicorns, yet he understood her. They were connected.

Arthurim spoke again, and she pulled her hand out of his. "The council would very much like to see us make this work, Princess. Dragons in my position are rare—and being allied to a good family such as mine would increase your credibility with your people, just as Zephryn's presence did. I noticed how many dragons in the audience recoiled at your scales."

Anger rose within her. Did he think to coerce her? "Flamemaster, if my scales and lineage disturb the dragons, then their hearing is apparently also an issue, because they didn't listen to my speech."

"I did." The other dragon met her gaze. "But not everyone is as accepting as I am."

He considers himself accepting? *When he acts as though he offers me a favor by bonding with me?* Kesia's claws pressed at her fingertips.

"Are you all right?"

Lirome's voice cut through the fury building in her mind. Kesia blinked and stifled her claws. "An interesting conversation, Flamemaster."

"Arthurim, Princess Ironfire."

Kesia nodded. "Yes, so you said."

He shot the death unicorn a look of disdain, then his expression altered to one of longing as he focused on Kesia. "I dwell in the southeast corner of the city, near the Dryside District. Contact me if you want to share a flight."

Kesia raised her eyebrows. "Thank you."

"Indeed." Lirome fixed Flamemaster with a watchful, suspicious gaze, then glanced at Kesia. "We have other matters to attend to tonight."

His violet gaze returned her to full control. Her soul-friend—amshalir—was quite right. They had another mission.

"Until next we meet, Arthurim."

"Until then, Princess."

Kesia gave the crowd a final wave and followed Lirome out of the safe house into the electro-carriage that waited outside.

"Temple District," the death unicorn told the driver. He studied her in the dim interior lighting of the carriage. "You anticipate seeing this new dragon again?"

"Anticipate? No." Kesia settled back against the cushioned seat, glad for the quiet of Lirome's presence across from her and the absence of the crowd. "It seems likely our paths will cross. There aren't many unmated dragons in the Scepter of Knowledge."

"I doubt he's eager to remain that way."

Amusement filled her. "Were you reading his emotions?"

Lirome snorted. "So were you. His intentions were clear, Kesia."

"True, but it wasn't as if I was immediately drawn to him and no other. That is how dragon embermates find each other." She leaned forward and took his hands in hers. "I am quite certain about where I want to be. Thank you for interrupting us."

He smiled. "Just doing my duty, Princess. You clearly wanted to be elsewhere. Or to rip Flamemaster's throat out."

"Your duty, hmm?"

"Well, and I had nothing better to do."

She grinned. "I see. Arthurim did try to lure me away with the skies."

Lirome frowned. "Oh?"

"Yes. I admit, I do enjoy flying. I have wings, after all." She missed the open air beneath her wings. Turning and wheeling, untrammeled by the limitations of a skin form or the short-lived enjoyment of an animal shape. "I want to fly sometime soon. I think I'm ready now. Speaking tonight helped process the grief."

Lirome rested his hand on her shoulder. "Then you should."

"But you can't be there with me."

His hand moved down to rest over her heart. "I'll be here in your soul. You shouldn't deny yourself your birthright simply because I can't join you physically."

Kesia sighed. "I know. If only … well, you can build things. I can think of new things. Perhaps together—"

"What?"

"We could make you wings. Or a saddle."

A grin transformed his serious face, and he laughed. "You are incredible."

"And I like seeing you smile."

"Likewise, my Fire-breather."

The electro-carriage came to a halt. Kesia didn't move. Neither did Lirome. Between them, the air was thick with something warmer. Flickers of desire, playing between their souls. Still new and fragile.

His fingers moved up from her heart, sliding up the line of her neck. Kesia shivered, drawing closer. Needing to be closer, feeling the same need from him. She studied his violet eyes. His lips, so near to hers.

Heat filled her.

"Oye, back there!" The driver's voice barked out. "You gonna get out and pay? I don't have all night."

They broke apart.

"Until later." Kesia sighed. Perhaps it had been for the best. Perhaps it was still too soon.

"Agreed."

How soon was too soon? She pushed aside the thought. They had more important matters to focus on.

Lirome exited the electro-carriage, keeping the door open for her. They had stopped in front of a square edifice in the Temple District, a place where all religious organizations were permitted to hold whatever services they liked, as long as they didn't cause harm to the public. Some of the places of worship were three or more stories tall, while others were scarcely larger than a shed filled with small idols and incense. There was even a small copse with fountains and gardens for the elemental deities, including Viorstan and Fiarston that Shance and other airship sailors offered devotion to, as well as the three Centrals, still revered by a scant number of humans in this Scepter.

Kesia turned to look at the square, richly-carved building that was the Four Corners temple. Four lamps burned along the edges of the small courtyard in front of the building. Its large double doors were always open, night and day, with acolytes and priests on hand for prayers.

"Another temple to test." She and Zephryn had never set foot in this area of the city, much less this temple. While studying the religion out of curiosity, he'd once joked that the Four Corners seemed to be the cult that caught the dregs of the land, so open were their policies regarding who could join.

Ironically, that was one reason Kesia found comfort there. Although the temple customs themselves varied, according to the traditions of each subset, the main principles remained constant. And the principleof welcome meant that Kesia couldn't be turned away, no matter how much of a hideous experiment she was.

But that also meant that even Garishton Razorclaw was allowed inside any Four Corners temple. The thought curdled her stomach.

Lirome nodded. "The priest was certain about having spoken with Garishton on more than one occasion some time ago. Mediary Evoris will only speak with you, as a direct relative."

"Hm. Well, let's go in and learn more, then."

"Indeed. Follow me."

They walked up the steps and into an open reception space. There were benches and lampstands scattered around the room and staircases branching off either end. This late at night, there were only few devout there, eyes closed in prayer or placing food or objects in specific areas around the room. In front of her, Lirome visibly relaxed, breathing deeply the fresh incense and mist wafting through the air. "One of my favorite kinds of temples."

She nodded. "I like these larger ones. No one notices you're at the afternoon meetings every nine days. Sometimes, it's good to fade into the background."

Especially with her mission as the dragon leader.

He nodded, glancing over his shoulder at her and half-smiling. "Look above us."

"Above us?"

Kesia looked up to see a many-paned glass dome with a hole in the center. Incense emanating from a carved central pillar in the room passed through the hole and out into the city. Amazement filled her. Most temples only had a small hole in the ceiling.

"Our dome is one of my favorite parts as well." The voice was calm and pleasant, and belonged to a priest who was making his way toward them. "The All-Maker doesn't care about the smoke itself, but he does care about our obedience to his words, even when we don't understand them." The clergyman smiled at her, his hooknose crinkling and his thin shoulders hunching together. "Mediary Evoris. How can I help you?"

Kesia glanced at Lirome, but he returned her look with a quiet expression, observing. Never forcing his way into any part of her journey. Always believing her to be capable.

Part of her was grateful to him. Another part wanted a break from speaking, having already talked to a crowd and assumed other such duties of public office earlier that evening.

She sighed and found more words. "Mediary, I'm told that my … uncle, Garishton Razorclaw, came to this temple several times and spoke with you."

The priest nodded. "Yes, the scowling dragon. I was surprised he continued to come back, but pleased, of course. Although sadly, it hasn't seemed to alter his course of action. Have you seen him recently?"

"He went into hiding after I destroyed his tower."

"I see." Mediary Evoris studied her shrewdly.

"He tried to kill me first. After abusing me and experimenting on me for over a decade."

"This does not surprise me." The priest paused, fidgeting with the lapel on his simple brown coat.

He clearly wanted to speak. It couldn't hurt to ask. "Lirome said he spoke with you regarding his private matters. What were they?"

"I'm not at liberty to say. His words were spoken in the strictest confidence."

As expected. But it didn't quell the anger within Kesia.

"I'm his niece!" Her words echoed through the chamber, eliciting a few disapproving glances. Fewmets. All she wanted was answers. She lowered her voice. "I've recently lost my embermate. I have to help restore the Scepter of Justice. And right now, things are happening to me as a result of his experiments. I need to know what he said." Her voice lowered. "Please."

Mediary Evoris shook his head. "Nothing is more sacred than the Rite of Consolation."

Frustration tore at Kesia. Next to her, Lirome cleared his throat. "Mediary, I have full respect for the vows the sons of Olosael and daughters of Allandra take, but in this instance, can you make an exception?"

"I'm afraid not." He paused, sympathy clear in his eyes. "There is something I can do for you. Garishton gave me something for safe keeping. He made no specific requests about it, only that it not fall into the wrong hands. Considering what his goals are, and what yours are, I think if you happened to find this notebook, it would not be breaking my vows."

Surprise and relief filled her. "Yes. Please. Where is it?"

"I can't tell you where it is." Mediary Evoris raised his hands. "All truth is found in the Four Corners, where the wind blows."

A clue.

"Where the wind blows…" Kesia glanced around the room. She focused on the hole in the ceiling. <Winds … But he couldn't have put it on the dome in the ceiling.>

<What about beneath the altar?> Lirome gestured toward the steps that radiated from the altar like pond ripples from a single drop of water. <The crack at the base of that one has been upsetting my mind since we entered. It makes no structural sense.>

<Let's go!> They ran toward the crack, falling to their knees and pressing and prying at the stone. Finally, the stone gave way, and Kesia lifted it easily. Beneath the stone was a small, leather-bound notebook. She grabbed it and quickly flipped through the pages.

It was filled with messy handwriting and diagrams. The words were hard to read, but from her quick skim, it discussed experiments and … yes. Warys Ironfire. Kesia's mother and Garishton's sister. <This is it.>

She stood and turned toward the priest. "Thank you, Mediary."

The priest stood there frozen, his robed back to them.

Lirome frowned. "Mediary?"

Kesia walked around to face the priest. His eyes were hard, and his mouth was open in shock. No, not shock.

Fear.

A clinging, choking terror wove around her soul and squeezed. *Run.*

It was what Kesia had always done when threatened. It would be so easy.

Except the fear was blunted by the death unicorn who steadied her with his gaze. <Remember your training. Remember what I

taught you.>

Kesia nodded and reached into her mind, finding the part of her that responded so strongly to the fear and locking it off. She breathed in, centering herself in the scent of incense, then breathed out a thick cloud of green smoke that engulfed the priests and the surrounding devotees.

The devotees gave cries of alarm. But Mediary Evoris only set his jaw and gave a little shake. "You're able to stop the attacks?"

"Yes. The smoke won't hurt your Talents."

"A gift from the All-Maker then." He grimaced. "Lurien's rebels. They know better than to attack. A desperate move. You must be making progress in your opposition, Princess."

"My name is Kesia. And we will see at the debate."

"True. Our temple prays for your success. Right now, I think the two of you should take the back exit." He nodded to the journal in Kesia's hand. "May it aid your quest. For what it's worth, your uncle loves you. I could see that clearly. But his heart is twisted, and that can produce the worst kind of affection."

An understatement if ever Kesia heard one. "What of the death unicorns? We can't leave you here defenseless."

Mediary Evoris shrugged. "The All-Maker gave us magic, Talents, to use for good or ill. This temple is a sanctuary for good. A memory of the time of perfection, a legacy of perseverance, and a beacon of future hope." He smirked. "My Talent might only be exact measurements, but that includes exact measurements of fallewsfree, which should make the death unicorns extremely uncomfortable."

Lirome tilted his head. "How did you manage to get that noxious herb here?"

"Long and careful cultivation. And I only have a little, to use at greatest need." He paused. "I believe this qualifies as a time of great need. With that green smoke clearing the air, I think I have enough wits to burn some at the entrances. You have truly been gifted, Kesia Ironfire." The mediary gestured toward one of the staircases. "Press the panel at the very end, and you'll enter a tunnel. Follow it, and you'll be safe."

"Thank you." Lirome nodded at the mediary and took Kesia's hand. Before she could think, they were running toward the staircase.

Anger flared in Kesia. She was running again? Lurien could be outside the temple right now. Kesia had eliminated the fear—why not turn back and bring justice to her embermate's death? "We should turn back. Tear apart these death unicorns so they can't harm anyone else."

Within Lirome, she felt an answering need for vengeance and justice. Something he kept buried deep from the detection of death unicorns, lest they judge him. His eyes turned blood red, and the scent of sulfur emanated from him.

Then he shook his head. "Not right now. We have Garishton's journal. Studying it will help us learn about you, and might even give insight into how he harmed others. We need to get it to safety. The death unicorns can wait until another time."

She stopped short, fixing him with a scowl and yanking her hand away. "Lest you forget, I am here to seek justice for the crown prince."

His wide face and high cheekbones were stone. "We both are. When there are opportunities for just killing, I will be the first at your side. But this is not one of them. We must wait."

"I'm tired of waiting! Tired of staying on the sidelines." Flames flew from her throat. "I'm a dragon. I'm stronger than you, Lirome. You can't stop me."

"No, I can't. But you will have to go through me first."

No arguments. No fierce reprisal. Only a quiet resolution and a sadness that both infuriated and quieted her. She could kill him. Rip apart his body, or try to. Considering how they matched each other in sparring, it would be a terrific fight to the death.

Her words struck her heart, crushing her resolve. Why would she ever want to kill her own mate? Kesia sucked in her flames through a veil of tears, sending out a wave of remorse and apology and allowing herself to be pulled into Lirome's arms.

For a moment, she clutched him like a lifeline. So much for her newfound devotion to the Four Corners. So much for operating with a clear head.

His understanding almost made it worse—would have made it worse. Yet Kesia needed that anchor.

"Very well," she whispered.

Lirome stroked her hair. "We will stop her." He pulled away, a twinkle lighting his eyes. "For now, we see if you truly are faster than me, you overconfident fire-breather."

Kesia laughed shortly. "Challenge accepted, you horn-headed ass."

As she sought the hidden panel, his amusement filtered through her mind. They may have to run, but at least they had Garishton's notebook. That was something.

They were one step closer to answers.

CHAPTER TWENTY-FOUR

Maira stared at the death unicorn towering over her in hoof form. His violet eyes met hers defiantly, and he stomped the ground, letting out a screeching neigh. The scent of sulfur filled the air around her.

It would have been paralyzing to anyone else who happened to be in the room besides herself and Cadence. Maira had anticipated this reaction on his part and kept the room clear. Even Ademis watched them through the window. The cat-dragon was immune to most death unicorn chemicals, but they made him sneeze fiercely.

She focused her attention on her son. "Cadence, this isn't helping."

The death unicorn threw back his head. <All you need to do is give me the joy potion. You and Uncle Lirome are clever enough. I know you can make it.>

"It won't help you." Speaking the words aloud would hopefully anchor Cadence in the moment and distract him from his cravings. "The joy potion was only an enhancement Lurien used to augment her powers. She numbed your mind and made you susceptible to all sorts of soul-enslavement."

"But I need it—I need her! You don't even care if I die."

264

Maira sighed and swallowed. Part of her role as queen was standing between others and their own pain. All death unicorns knew the best way to show strength and leadership was to protect the herd from outside threats. It was worse when those threats were from inside one of their own.

She let out a slow breath, allowing her mind to distract her from her son's pain by making plans. Kesia had done a thorough sweep while Cadence slept, drawing all the green smoke particles from him that she could. Clearly, he needed another pass, perhaps several more. The dragon was new at using this ability, and Cadence had been intensely drugged by Lurien's soul magic. Maira could only wonder what Brennar was like. He bore the blood of a god, not a human. Perhaps that would make a difference.

Then again, withdrawal was withdrawal, regardless of genetics. And Lurien had woven a potent elixir of soul magic and chemicals.

Cadence still glared at her, but she could sense his heartbeat slowing. Good. "I love you, Cadence. Your father loves you."

<Where is he, then? Where is the herd-father?> The death unicorn shook his head. <Lady Lurien was right. She is the only one who truly cares for me.>

"A lie. She cares for no one but herself. Your father, Kaliran, is safeguarding our people at the Lost Refuge, something he has done faithfully for many years during my captivity at the hands of Lurien. This is the truth." Maira took a step forward. "And your herd-father is working to free your brother, other unicorns, and humans."

Cadence snorted. <He'll never be able to. Just like you'll never be able to free me. She's irresistible. The sun, the moon, and the stars in the sky are hers, and on the final day, she will breathe joy upon the ground.>

His final phrase was something devotees of the three Centrals spoke over each other. Was Lurien trying to use the religion somehow? It was a nominal system. Common as figures of speech, but nothing Lurien could use to coerce anyone. They didn't even have an official temple of worship, as the adherents claimed the sun, moon, and stars could be venerated anywhere. And their monuments had recently been taken down for repairs.

"What are you speaking of?"

He stared at her, then began to shake violently, his hooves skittering off the ground. Alarm shot through her. As she ran forward, he started to shift into skin form, but stopped midway through and shifted back with an agonized scream. Maira flung her arms around him, pouring out all the healing magic she could muster.

Cadence reared back and forth. Maira's feet slammed into the ground, then his hoof smashed into her toes. Pain ricocheted through her. Still she clung to him, praying desperately to the All-Maker.

"Cadence. I'm here. I love you. I love you so much. I'm here."

The defiance in him snapped in an explosive emotional release that buffeted her soul. Finally, he began shifting again, until it was the weight of her taller, larger son in skin form leaning on her much smaller body. <Mother … I'm sorry…>

He went limp. Even Maira's death unicorn strength could barely hold him upright. <Ademis!>

<What, again?> The cat-dragon's arms were around Cadence in an instant, lowering him to the ground. Ademis patted his cheek. <Come on, young one. I actually like you. You always sneak me the best treats behind Maira's back.>

"I knew that was him. You awful cat-dragon." She wiped away the sweat and tears that coated her cheeks. As she stepped away, fresh agony pulsed from her foot. She fell backward onto the floor. "Gods! Why isn't it healing?"

Ademis glanced at her from where he knelt, covering Cadence up with a blanket. "You gave him so much of your healing Talent it made my tail stand on end. You'll need to rest for at least half a day to heal like you usually do."

"Nonsense. I need to be at the Lunaris festival in a few hours to give Shance the memory-boosting serum."

"Have Lirome or Kesia give it to him. They'll be there anyway."

Maira shook her head. "No. Kesia needs to be here to help Cadence. From what I could sense, his last outburst was a breakthrough for him. If Kesia can siphon out the rest of the chemical Lurien is using, he'll be on the mend for good."

"I don't feel like arguing with you. It's your pain." Ademis stood and strode over to her. "Come on, let's get you up to your room."

She raised her eyebrows. "After you throw a blanket around yourself."

"To cover what? I'm a cat-dragon."

"And I'm a death unicorn." Maira glared at him. "You know how humans are about nudity, even if you are a eunuch." The scientists of the Glorious Destiny had castrated Ademis once they realized he wasn't compliant, but the work had been minimal to allow for other experiments. "Shance's crew are beginning to trust me, and I won't jeopardize that. Cover up."

"Humans and their ridiculous customs." He sighed, rolled his eyes, and snatched a blanket off the bed. Once it was wrapped in place, he helped Maira to her feet and upstairs to her room. She kept a pleasant smile on her face and gave the crew good reports about Cadence as they passed. There was no need to alarm them with her own injury.

Besides, it was only her foot. She had been through worse.

At last, they reached the captain's cabin. Ademis steered Maira toward the bed, but she protested. "No, not the bed. The desk. I need to use the clipse-mirror."

"Are you somehow allergic to rest, my dear girl?" he scoffed.

She shook her head. "No, but I need to contact Kaliran and give him an update on our son. Then I need to contact Kesia. And I've been negligent in speaking with Zilpath…"

The cat-dragon gave an exaggerated sigh and tapped a wireless commer on the table. "Kesia? Be here as soon as possible to deal with Cadence. He blew up again today."

The dragon's voice crackled over the speaker. "Literally?"

"No, not literally. Don't be daft."

"Don't be cryptic. I've had my fill of that."

Ademis smirked. "Lirome?"

"Garishton, actually. I have another mark against my uncle. The organizational pattern of his notebook defies logic. What happened to Cadence?"

"I need you to come over and perform another siphoning treatment while he's unconscious and monitor the results with Lirome. Maira thinks Cadence is finally free from Lurien's influence."

"That's wonderful! We'll be over shortly, after tea."

"You like tea?"

Kesia's voice turned sheepish. "Lirome found a tea made from strewsberry leaves. It's not terrible at all. I might even enjoy it. But he doesn't need to know that yet. No need to make him more arrogant."

Her sarcasm was clear, and Maira smiled in spite of herself. The two grew closer by the day. It was refreshing to see her brother with a woman who could match his unique attitude of compassion and aggression. However, they were still keeping their relationship from the dragon council. Well, they were adults who could handle their own matters.

And she needed to handle hers. With a nod from her, Ademis silenced the wireless commer. He raised his eyebrows. "Do you really need to contact either of the others right now?"

"I don't want to cope with the fallout of you talking to them."

"I don't know what you are inferring. I am quite adept at managing Kaliran." He blinked innocently.

It wasn't a good idea. Kaliran and Ademis mixed as well as oil and fire. But Maira's eyelids were heavy, and her foot throbbed incessantly. Another reason she needed Shance back. She could trust him to handle all forms of communication on her behalf without mucking anything up.

She paused briefly before giving in to the cat-dragon. "The majority of the news is good. Telling Kaliran of every minor difficulty would only distress him. Here—" Maira wrote a quick note. "Give this to someone to send on telewire. That should suffice."

"Good idea. As for Zilpath?"

She sighed. "I can contact her after I rest."

"Excellent choice."

Maira hobbled to the bed, wound and set the alarm on her timepiece, and fell asleep, only vaguely aware of Ademis curling up next to her in his fur form.

She awoke a few hours later, her foot and body still aching, but recovered enough to don the formal clothing necessary for the

Lunaris festival. High-necked blouse, cameo pin, white-accented corset, and a pearlescent white skirt. The usual make-up on her face and the serum hidden in her corset.

If she clenched her teeth hard enough, walking was no trouble at all, which was exactly what she told Ademis before entering the electro-carriage. Unlike the first festival, the cat-dragon insisted on attending this one. It was held on the north side of the city at dusk on a broad plain. All of the vendors were arranged in concentric circles, their booths festooned with mirrors and other glimmering objects. Pearly lanterns were strung on high poles to light the evening's events. In the center of the circles was a large dance floor with a mirrored surface.

There had been dancing at the first festival, but the second festival featured it far more. Most prominent among the festival-goers was Lady Lurien, swaying seductively in a shimmering white gown, her lips set in a smile as pleased as poison. Maira's stomach turned. Of course the wretch was pleased—she danced with Shance. Whether his attention to her was feigned or whether it was a sign of him falling prey to her attentions, that attention had to end.

Now.

The resolution settled in her stomach like steel.

Ademis nudged her. "You can't possibly be thinking of dancing out there to catch his attention."

She squeezed his arm. "You know how to dance."

"And you're still hiding a limp."

"Are you saying you're afraid, silly cat-dragon?"

His eyes glinted. "No, but you're even more of a fool than I thought. And I've known you for over six decades, so that is impressive."

"Dance with me, or I will find someone else." Maira stomped

her foot in emphasis, and pain lanced through her. That was a mistake. Stupid death unicorn habit.

"Very well. You owe me."

She flashed him a smile. "Don't I always?"

"Yes."

They entered the swirl of dancers, all stepping and swooping in a graceful, orderly fashion. The steps were familiar enough for Maira to pick up on. She and Ademis quickly made their way toward Lurien and Tyrius. By the end of the dance, she could almost touch his arm.

She did so with a disarming smile. "Pardon me, dear sir, but I believe I must have this dance."

Lurien stared down her narrow nose at Maira. "Pardon *me*, dear woman, but you overstep yourself. Such a request can only be made by a man."

"You are one to lecture about traditional roles." Anger freed Maira's tongue. "You're a hypocrite as well as a usurper."

Next to Lurien, Shance studied Maira with open appreciation. Elric's hooves, his shimmering white waistcoat did not suit him. It matched Lurien's outfit, to be sure, but her husband's blond hair, fresh blue eyes, and broad-shouldered figure would look far better in blue or silver. But as usual, Lurien only used others to complement herself.

Lurien leaned close to Shance. "Such silly, pathetic insults, don't you think?"

A slow smile spread Shance's face. "I think you need to leave, because I have a dance with my queen."

"Be careful." Lurien ran her hands over his jaw. Maira wanted nothing more than to break those fingers. "I would hate to have to do anything murderous to my sweet Brennar. He does so enjoy his time in my company."

Shance's jaw worked, and something like lightning flickered in his eyes. That was an encouraging sign, but Maira knew that he was not strong enough.

He needed the serum.

The next song started. Ademis had vanished, as he was good at doing when he was utterly uninterested in a scenario. Maira breathed deeply, stabilizing herself and preparing her foot for more injury.

It was worth it to spend a few moments in Shance's arms. She only wished it could be longer. Soon, it would be. Soon, he would remember who he was, and what his place was in the world.

Hopefully the memory serum worked like Lirome thought it should, and Shance's mind wasn't irrevocably damaged from the strain.

Such encouraging thoughts.

He whirled her around, then pulled her close. "Are you all right, lovely one? It seems your foot is causing you some difficulty. And sadness clouds your heart."

A sigh escaped her. As usual, Shance saw through her facade, and he knew she worried about her family. As he always had known, right from the start. He'd always seen her as a woman, not only as a powerful queen and ally, and he had always treated her as such.

She wouldn't allow an evil wretch to take him away.

"Cadence's withdrawal took a painful turn. But he's doing better, and so am I. I think I've almost figured out how to counteract this 'joy potion' Lurien is dosing herself with. The tide is turning." She rested in his arms for a few beats longer than the music called for. Relishing their shared relief at the progress. "I have the memory serum. Drink it as soon as you are able."

He nodded with that earnest, focused expression she knew so well. The one that revealed how much he was still taking this situation on trust, and not on his own knowledge. "Are there any special instructions?"

"No. I've never created something quite like this, and neither has Lirome. I don't suppose you could sneak away to *The Silver Streak*, or find us a place to rest like you did at the last festival?"

A frown shadowed his face. "Lurien's noose has grown tighter. However, her hold over her servants isn't absolute, especially within her own estate. I've been able to learn some things and gain allies. Nothing conclusive, but enough to worry her. This dance will most likely be all I can spare."

Another turn in the dance, this time requiring a pivot on her hurt foot. Maira hissed through her teeth and forced another smile. "Well, then, it seems this serum comes at the perfect time. Make sure you are in a secure place of rest."

She slipped it out of her corset as the song neared its conclusion. Shance pulled her close, running his fingers through her hair. "Only if you do the same."

"I'll be fine."

He smirked. "We used to play a game where every time you brushed off your problems, I gave you a kiss. Why do I feel like if we played that now, I'd never stop?"

"Go ahead and try."

Shance swept her into his arms and kissed her deeply, his hands wandering over her body. She could barely release the vial into his hand, craving his nearness more than anything else. Wanting nothing more than for him to carry her off the dance floor and come home. To be with her, once and for all time. As it should have been.

As it would be.

A lyrical, cutting voice filtered into her ears. "My, my. You two will need to breathe eventually."

Lurien.

Anger fueled Maira's passion. She took a quick breath, grabbed Shance's collar and pulled him in for one final, deep kiss, lingering on his lips as he reluctantly set her on the ground.

She turned to Lurien, a myriad of insults ready in her mouth.

All-Maker, help me. She's not worth it.

Maira inhaled deeply and gave a faint smile. "A city built on treachery soon falls. I should know. I caused a city to fall."

"Oh, I remember. Don't worry, *little* queen." She sniffed. "I remember very well."

Something in her tone slithered inside Maira, evoking more fear. She could only trust in the plans of Bonilus.

And pray Ademis found her before her foot gave out completely and she had to crawl to the damn electro-carriage.

Chapter Twenty-Five

Lady Lurien had been unusually quiet that night. Sure, at the dance she had done her best to show the public that she and Shance were a star-crossed couple preparing for the upcoming debates, but there was nothing exceptional to that. She tended to get insecure when she saw Shance with the woman he loved. He had mastered the art of fending off her advances while not drawing her ire so much that she harmed Brennar or one of the other people she commanded.

Still, considering how openly Shance and Maira had kissed, Lurien should have done more than leer and condescendingly tell him "off to bed with you now" as if he were a stubborn child. She was up to something.

And they still didn't know what it was.

Shance huffed, running his fingers along the wood paneling as he walked to his room. The death unicorn was always up to something. Enhancing her soul-magic. Altering the perceptions of others, so much so that Brennar and Cadence had both believed they saw their mother die. Charming everyone she could to her side. All terrible things. Yet she was doing something much worse, and the fact that he couldn't see what it was—that none of them could see it—made Shance mad enough to want to get in her face and challenge her.

It would do no good. And she would likely find it thrilling that he was so close to her face.

All-Maker, if you're all-powerful, can't you simply strike her down where she stands? Right at this minute? That would be preferred. And I rarely ask these things.

He sighed and gave the guards on either side of his room a friendly greeting. They studied him with their usual stoicism in their black and gray uniforms, electro-pistols, and sharp pikes. Lurien went overboard on the soul enslavement of those she called "expendables."

All because she honestly, madly believed in her cause. Part of her was already driven insane by it. Like so many others were. Nula's parents. General Brody. Lurien wouldn't be the first politician to be driven mad by their convictions.

Shance stepped inside his room. A large canopied bed presided over the space, with only a few narrow chests and a mirror lining the walls. One window on the east wall highlighted the rushing waters of the Cresida inlet. He stripped off the ridiculous clothing from the festival and left it in a pile on the floor, sitting cross-legged on top of the bed in only his pants. Then he held out the small vial Maira had slipped to him and wished with everything in him that she could be there.

They belonged together. It had always been so, from the moment he'd laid eyes on her. Shance was certain of that, even though he didn't remember laying eyes on her for the first time. Just one of many memories that lay buried within his mind. The silvery liquid in his hand would either fix everything or make everything worse.

He sighed. "Who were you, Tyrius Stormsong?"

Scattered memories and feelings surfaced. Strength far beyond what he could have imagined wielding. A purpose deeper and stronger than he had ever possessed in his years in the military.

An image came to mind. *He sat in the center of a vast room of polished white marble, singing a song in a foreign tongue and playing an instrument.*

He had played instruments? Absurd. Shance had always been fascinated by the music quarter in the Scepter of Commerce, but that didn't mean he wanted to be a performer. Well, he did, but he had no training or talent.

Or did he?

Shance clenched the vial tighter.

Tyrius Stormsong. The 'song' part of his name explained the musician. But if that's who he was, then how could he be a ship's captain? Would that part of his life be cast aside once his memories manifested? Would he care about his crew anymore?

He sat back on the bed, rubbing his forehead. This was far too much to deal with. All he wanted to do was be in the skies, breathing in the fresh air and feeling the freedom the heavens offered. Except the damn window was locked, trapping him with mindless men and women he had no way of helping because he didn't have access to the memories and knowledge he should have. He didn't have the magic he should have. Even if he were to blow open the window with a blast of wind, what would it help? He still wouldn't be able to connect with a son he barely knew or a people he barely recalled.

Shance stared at the vial of silvery liquid. One easy shot back. The most significant shot he'd ever take in his entire life.

He would remember everything. For good or ill.

His wireless commer chirped. Shance pressed it and silently began measuring out the time. The commer could only be used for ten minutes before it would be noticed and tracked by Lurien's communication-monitoring slaves.

"Maira?"

"Not quite, sir." Annabel Tegan's clear, no-nonsense voice sounded in the room. "I wanted to give you a report on the crew."

"A report?"

"Yes. On *your* crew, sir."

Shance stood and walked over to the window, looking out as if he could somehow see *The Silver Streak* suspended in dry dock. Viorstan, his ship was as trapped as he was. "Go ahead, Commander."

"All of the crew are fully healed from the injuries sustained during the death unicorn attack. The ship is also in good working order and ready to sail at your command. In addition, enhancements have been made..."

She droned on about the various details of the ship. No doubt about it, Tegan was a good first officer. He knew he had misjudged her. She had remained loyal after their escape from the Scepter of Commerce, and even through this whole death unicorn issue. It was commendable of her, but why had she done so? He knew if he asked her directly, Tegan would give one of her practiced answers. Better to approach the situation from another angle.

"Tegan, how is the crew adjusting to the presence of Maira and Lirome?"

The wireless commer fell silent for a long moment. "As well as can be expected, sir. And better, I would say."

"Better?"

"Yes. Although the initial introduction was ... less than ideal."

"You mean flame-cursed terrible."

She chuckled. "Yes, that. Even so, both of the death unicorns have gone above and beyond to establish good relations with the crew. Lirome has assisted in the rebuilding efforts, and your wife continues to give every free moment to connecting with each crew member. In other circumstances, I would be concerned about her presence, but I must say, she is admirably supportive. Although she needs to rest more."

"Yes, that's always been an issue with her." Another statement, spoken confidently out of a past he didn't remember. Shance sighed. Tegan knew about the memory serum, and he had to talk with someone. "After I drink this vial, Tegan, I don't know how I'll change."

"I can't imagine it would be for the worse, sir."

He wiped away some condensation from the glass. "Oh?"

"You were Shance Windkeeper before. You might have been born Tyrius Stormsong, but Maira Ukerys said you chose the name Shance yourself. So who you are as Shance Windkeeper are parts of that person, not the other way around. According to the declassified Lawless records, you supported the Lawless, but also refused to use your powers for bloodshed. Instead, you functioned as a mediator and facilitated captures, not kills. I can only say that returning your memories would be an improvement, not a detriment, because you would have more power at your disposal."

Shance frowned. "Very logical, Tegan."

"I try, sir. Your crew is here. Your family is here. We aren't going to abandon you." She paused. "So pardon my bluntness, but take the flaming potion already. Sir."

He shook his head and gave a faint smile. "Your thoughts are noted, Commander. Good night."

Shance turned off the wireless commer and stared out the smudged window.

There was nothing to do but drink.

All-Maker. Lady Allandra, Lord Olosael. Whoever is listening. Please let this help. I want my son back. I want my family back. I want my life back.

"Here goes."

One quick swallow. The liquid tasted like water and metal and light with an aftertaste of frost fire. It zipped down his throat, sizzling like electricity. The next moment it shot through his veins and set his heart beating madly. Shance pressed a palm to his chest and sparks shot from it, tingling into his skin and sending him to his knees.

Sparks?

Through the stuttering in his mind, he recalled his first trip to the estate in the electro-carriage. The lightning arcing through his body. Brennar waking up for a moment, just in time to force Shance awake.

Now, there was no one. Only shuddering arcs of electricity through his body. He convulsed on the ground as image after image, emotion after emotion flashed through his mind.

<Maira. I love you.>

Darkness consumed him.

A storm erupted in her mind, swift and sudden. Consuming Maira with the memories beneath the surface of a soul that had slept far too long.

Her beloved. Her Shance.

She stood at the edge of a white marble hall, round and wreathed in shadows that curled around ornately carved pillars. All of her attention was focused on the man on the platform at the center of the room. His blond hair reached his shoulders and hung in his face in defiance of the polished order of this place, where humans had elevated themselves to gods and flaunted their superiority. Loose robes of dark gray and silver draped over his shoulders. He played a chordistrom in a manic, wind-wailing tune that stirred the heart to dance and mourn at the same time. He looked just like he had when she had been paraded in front of the gods in chains. The young death unicorn queen, captured at last.

And like then, she stepped out of the shadows, drawn by the emotion and passion in his song. The gods had dissected their souls to the most usable particles and disregarded the rest. They were the cold-hearted. The soul-dead.

Yet, Tyrius Stormsong played as one possessed by the rain and the winds. Furious storms and arcs of lightning were channeled through his body as easily as breathing. The power took no toil on him, for it was anchored in his soul and not from without, as the rest of the gods used their enhanced Talents. For Tyrius was in truth the last Descendant. Always an outsider among his own people, bearing a drop of the ancient blood of Elric and Efluria, the first union of unicorn and human. Those who had, for a time, ushered in an era of peace between their peoples that had never been seen since.

In that moment, Maira had had no knowledge of his origins. All she had known was the storm and rage and irrepressible joy in his eyes as he stared at her. When their eyes met, nothing mattered but the whirlwind of music that entrapped them both, even as they were enthralled with each other. Their doom had been appointed and set.

Awareness dimly filtered through her. There was another figure in the hall. Shance Windkeeper as he was now, hair shorter, trimmed beard, and wearing the military uniform of an airship captain. Even in his state of soul-slumber, he had remembered that the skies were his home. He glanced at her briefly in the same state of astonished wonder. Then his eyes locked on to Tyrius Storm-song, and the room exploded in flashes of lightning and swirls of images.

She saw herself dressed as a royal slave in manacles and a choking collar being claimed by Tyrius and loathing him for it. Not realizing until later that he married her to keep her from the brutal bed of Pulaeus Breathlife. She saw the evenings where she gradually opened up to his kindness and introduced him to the stories of his ancestors.

His first introduction to the death unicorn herd. Leading away the refugees of Glenalis after its destruction. Going through the rites of unity and acceptance. Enduring strife as her people looked upon Tyrius with suspicion and upon her as a traitor. Seeing him tirelessly labor to earn the respect of the herd and the loyalty of her other mates, until all accepted him as equal.

Seeing him take part in raising their herd-children, particularly after the death of Elestel. Throwing his energy into establishing relations with the dragons of Sekastra, the death unicorns' new home, until all recognized him as worthy to be her chief mate and the protector of the herd, even as she was their soul keeper and leader.

And then ... Brennar. Their own child, after so long. Such a difficult time, carrying the child of a god and a death unicorn. But what joy when she finally bore their son! Another heir. It would be up to the herd to decide who would rule after she was gone, especially as Cadence was the eldest and Amarel the eldest female. But the child of the queen and the chief mate was a sign of hope and further confirmation that Tyrius Stormsong was a god only in biology. In heart and soul, he was Shance Windkeeper. Bearing the soul of a death unicorn and the name of a dragon.

Her husband. Her ally.

Her closest friend.

A final image, veiled in gray misery. They had been traveling to the Scepter of Commerce. Brennar was supposed to stay on the airship, but he had begged to see the Trebbian Seas and the mosaics of the Central Market. It was meant to be a short trip—no one should have been able to see them.

But someone had.

Lurien, her red hair gleaming in the bright sunlight, her mask of friendliness replaced with a triumphant smile.

Dragging Brennar and Maira away. Encasing Shance in a cold, dark prison and twisting his mind. Shutting Maira in the depths of the coffin.

The memories vanished, along with the music. Maira turned. The platform was empty.

"Tyrius?" Her breath caught in her throat. "Shance?"

The room fell away, and she stood in the night sky, surrounded by stars. Alone. Her nightdress swirled around her.

How had she gotten here?

Maira fought back her fear. Unlike most death unicorns, heights didn't send her into a terrified frenzy. This situation had to be a result of their minds, their souls, meeting once more.

"May I have this dance?"

She turned. A man coalesced out of the breezes and held out a hand to her. Her husband, clad in a loose tunic and pants, his hair the length of Shance Windkeeper, but his eyes the stormy blue-gray of Tyrius.

Whole.

She couldn't keep the smile off her face. "Only if you tell me your name." She tossed her hair. "It's rude to dance without being properly introduced."

"I am Shance Windkeeper, the name given to me by the dragons, the name approved by my herd. I am yours, my love."

"And I am Maira Ukerys. Always yours." Maira took his hand, letting him pull her into spins and steps in the heavens, through the gentle caress of the winds.

Everything was filled with laughter and joy and starlight. A moment of precious peace in the midst of turmoil. A moment that stretched into many as they vanished into the winds and appeared in their bed in the airship, enjoying and experiencing each other anew.

At last, fully one in soul with her husband. Past, present, and future. Of one accord. Of one heart.

Maira awoke alone. The window was open, the air filled with light breezes. She reached over to the vacant spot in the bed, feeling emptiness within her. A marvelous dream they'd shared. That was all.

When she turned her focus inward, she could sense their bond, stronger than it had ever been. There were only three weeks until the final festival, but she knew that Shance was now healing to full strength.

Lurien was in immense trouble.

Maira's clipse-mirror chirped. Most likely Kaliran.

Now, she had the best news to satisfy him.

"Cadence is healing. And the chief mate has returned."

CHAPTER TWENTY-SIX

Even three months after his death, Kesia still missed Zephryn's faint smile as he read. The gleam of his cobalt eyes. He had been her embermate and life without him passed oddly, no matter how close she grew to Lirome.

But at this moment, what Kesia missed most were his research abilities, because Garishton Razorclaw's journal was a dense collection of meaningless gibberish. There was likely some intrinsic order to the notebook, but it baffled every attempt of her and Lirome to solve it. Judging by Lirome's sighs next to her at the table in the safe house, he felt the same. The feelings trickling through their bond confirmed it.

Garishton Razorclaw might be a brilliant scientist, but he was very difficult to follow. They had been able to confirm that Kesia had blood from all four shifter races in her veins, but no idea of how much, or how it would manifest, or a myriad of other details.

She tapped her finger on the table hard enough to leave dents. Then sighed. Paused. Shifted in her seat and turned her eyes back to the journal.

The words blurred on the page.

She nudged Lirome's shoulder with hers. "Do you need a cup

of tea?"

He gave her a knowing smile. "Is that ever a question?"

"Coming right away."

Kesia got up and walked over to the kitchen, putting the kettle on to boil and pulling out the silken pouch that held the loose gavbrush leaves. It was his preferred beverage when he had that particular look of focus on his face. Her mind unwound as she went about the familiar task. Bring the water just to a boil, pour it over the leaves, steep for ninety seconds, add a dash of lemis rind. Stir well.

After a moment, she poured herself some strewsberry juice from the icerator cooling cabinet and added some tart lemis rind. Then it was back to the table, setting both mugs down.

Lirome looked up at her, his violet eyes glinting as he sipped the beverage. "Thank you. You make tea perfectly for someone who only likes one flavor."

Warmth filled her at the words. She was still getting used to compliments. Dragons simply didn't give them, and humans mostly gave them to curry favor.

But Lirome gave them well. As if he knew she needed them.

Considering he could sense her emotions, he probably did. In turn, she understood his need for tea.

"Making tea is soothing." Kesia shrugged, returning his smile. "And there is always the possibility of enjoying different types. You're the one who insisted that."

"And I maintain it."

A quiet silence passed between them for a moment. It was easy. Comfortable. She knew exactly where she stood with Lirome. Slow. Relaxed, as they figured out the bond between them, as they grappled with their own sorrows together and supported each other. No pressure to move ahead into uncomfortable areas.

Yet … sometimes she just wished she didn't have to sleep alone. That she didn't have to stand up in front of others alone. And then there was Arthurim Flamemaster. He had shown up at her other small group speaking engagements with the Lawless and other sympathizers in the city. All of them the same mixed bag of encouragement and suspicion. Kesia had managed to avoid and otherwise delay the dragon without revealing her and Lirome's connection.

It annoyed her to do so.

She studied Lirome. His silver horn visible, along with the rest of his unicornshifter features. Shirtless, as he always was when in the safe house, although he would throw on a shirt to appease any humans who were uncomfortable. Silly humans.

Being shirtless suited his lean muscles and dark olive skin immensely. The long black hair spilling over his shoulders didn't hurt the view either.

Lirome's lips twitched as he bent over the journal. "Are you perhaps distracted, fire-breather?"

Fewmets! Kesia's face heated. *Slow, Kesia. You are both going slow.* She cleared her throat and sat across from him at the table. Searching for something to say.

"Oh, um … why do death unicorns have a three-month mourning period?"

Lirome looked up at her, confusion creasing his face. "You wish to know that?"

"Yes. Why not?"

"Very well. Individuals in a herd share their emotions with the whole group. The individual grief of a death unicorn is enough to paralyze a herd. So the amshalir or amshalla goes with the grieving death unicorn into the wilds, away from the herd, where they can project all of their sorrow for three months. After that, we judge the hardest times to be over. For the remainder of mourning, the grieving individual needs to be with the herd, and all need to start moving on."

Kesia nodded, leaning forward on the table, pressing her hands into the wood. "It's been three months since Zephryn died."

"So that spurred your question?"

"I suppose." She shrugged. "It is part of your culture. I want to know about it."

Lirome stared at her, violet eyes intent. "Since you are curious … should a death unicorn and their amshalir or amshalla fall in love with each other, herd recognition and even marriage is permitted after the three-month period."

Heat filled her again. Not solely her own, but also coming from the death unicorn across the table. Her mate. Which meant, eventually, they would begin to act like mates. In all ways.

Kesia swallowed. "Well, that is … interesting. Although I would never want to expect anything neither of us is ready for."

"I certainly concur." He reached out and traced the tip of his finger along her hand. Up to her wrist. Lingering on the sensitive underside of her arm. Causing her scales to surface. Leaving a trail of heat and desire, tempered by caution. Respecting her recent loss.

For some reason, that made her want him even closer. How close, Kesia wasn't sure, but closer than they were now. She eased up from the bench, propping her knees on it so she could lean farther across the table. Her face was inches from Lirome's as she traced a fine line of flames up his arm and bare shoulder.

He inhaled sharply. Tension radiated from him, a mixture of passion and care.

She whispered near his lips. "I'm ready for something."

"Likewise."

Their lips met in a gentle, teasing kiss. Then another, deeper and stronger. Filled with an intensity and fervor Kesia had never dreamed Lirome possessed. Her own heart rose to match the feelings, as their emotions merged and amplified through the soul bond. She kissed him again, her fingers tangling in his hair, and his fingers trailing down her jaw and neck—

An odd series of rattles and knocks broke through the moment. Startlement filled them. The regular visitors to the safe house knew better than to cause such a commotion.

<Intruder.> They thought as one. They parted. Kesia called flames to her hands, while Lirome reached for a knife and a pistol, his eyes flashing blood red.

Then she scented the air. A dragon.

Arthurim.

"Is everything all right? The outer chamber is filled with smoke." The voice was crisp with an undertone of confusion. Arthurim stepped into the room, his mouth curled. He was clad in the usual stockings, breeches, waistcoat, and long coat of the Scepter of Knowledge, and he looked about as comfortable as any shifter did wearing human clothes.

Kesia swallowed, stifling her flames. "Yes, we're fine. We were only experimenting."

<An interesting term for it.> Lirome's voice muttered over their private link, another aspect of their bond that had recently emerged. <You play with fire.>

<I wasn't the one kissing a dragon.>

Arthurim frowned. "Isn't the green smoke dangerous? It eliminates Talents."

"Well, the smoke I produce varies in the results. That particular type does not prevent anyone from using their Talents. After all, you found me here." Kesia flashed him an innocent smile. "How can I help you?"

The other dragon glanced between the two of them, his face bearing a touch of skepticism. Surely he couldn't sense anything unusual. After all, the healing bond accounted for their connection. No one had questioned it thus far. And dragons were blind to the growth of a soul bond.

Finally, Arthurim spoke. "I was merely recalling our previous conversation about the last time you shifted."

She lifted her chin. "I can shift into animals whenever I want to."

He shook his head. "Not the shifting of your Talent. Shifting into your scale form and taking to the skies."

"Not since..." Kesia's throat swelled. Not since the funeral had she shifted into her scale form. She hadn't felt ready. Lirome's first priority was her healing, not an arbitrary dragon deadline.

Although lately, she had been longing for the skies.

"You should do so." Arthurim strode across the room, ever the predator, but more graceful than Zephryn. Zephryn had been raw power, and he'd worn it openly to represent his lineage and to protect her. Arthurim carried himself as someone who fought for a noble cause, not someone who'd fought for their very survival.

If ever a dragon could be a dandy, that was him. The human term fit him perfectly. A dandy who, for all his proclaimed humility, still thought offering a mate bond to her was a grand gift.

Lirome studied Arthurim quietly. Keenly. His expression had become cryptic as he communicated once more over their private link. <There is no question. He seeks you as a mate.>

<We knew this already.>

<Yes, but that doesn't mean I like it any better.>

She focused on Arthurim. "Speak plainly. Are you seeking my company out of kindness, or are you also seeking to see if we are compatible embermates? Because if it's the second, I will say plainly that I am not drawn to you in that way."

"Yes, but we're both in unique situations. The bond could grow through familiarity, rather than be immediate. Although kindness could also be part of the equation." His icy blue eyes glinted. "Dragons are capable of kindness, Princess. You've certainly shown that. If a unicorn can be deadly, a dragon can be altruistic."

"Yes, but that doesn't mean they are."

"Have the caregivers treated you unkindly?"

"No. Not them. Others." The dragons at the Pinnacle had been another matter entirely. And the dragon council, while distant, clearly showed their opinions of her by sending a persistent dragon to offer a mate bond. Doubtless the council thought they were only being logical. They certainly wouldn't accept a death unicorn mate.

Although she didn't know that for sure. Lady Dayflier and Lord Sunscaler had seemed more sympathetic than the other pair.

This was not the time for speculation. All she knew is that Arthurim wanted something from her that Kesia had no interest or ability to give—and she couldn't tell him quite yet, because it wasn't his business. She inwardly groaned. She'd rather return to her former activities with Lirome, no matter how the connection shocked her. At the same time, her heartflame was eager to shift. The open skies, wind beneath her wings, the sheer freedom beckoned her.

Lirome spoke again over their private link. <Go, my Fire-breather. This is the first time you've really felt compelled to fly. You should enjoy it.>

<And leave you to suffer through that cursed journal?>

A mental shrug. <If it becomes too difficult, I'll find a stronger

beverage than tea.>

<Reasonable. I'll be able to test our ability to mindspeak from a distance.> She sent to Lirome.

He gave a slight nod. <As you choose.>

"All right," she said to Arthurim. "I need a break anyway. And I'm sure Lirome would like a break from me."

The death unicorn chuckled. "Your unorthodox methods have certainly given me much to consider. Regardless, I think some quiet should enable me to sort through these materials and make some sense of them."

Kesia smiled at his words. "I'll meet you later at the tea shop. Usual time."

"I'll hold you to that."

She made her face a mask, daring a tease. <You could hold me to other things as well.>

<Yes, like the stove. It would save money for the safe house.>

<Aha, I knew there was an ulterior motive to our bond.> Kesia turned to Arthurim. "Very well. Let's go for a flight."

"Thank you."

She raised her eyebrows. "You use niceties?"

The dragon gave a short laugh. "You really do think all dragons are ill-bred, don't you?"

"No. But we are direct and forthright as a rule."

"I'm direct with my niceties. As part of my directness, I must confess that I'm also on reconnaissance duty for the Lawless. It will guide the direction of our flight patterns."

"Aha." Kesia smiled. "As it happens, I'm quite good at recon work, in my own way."

Hopefully this time it wouldn't lead to an airship exploding.

Half an hour later, they were on the outskirts of the city, stashing their clothes in a thicket at the edge of a clearing. By the time they shifted and took to the air, Kesia had learned the specifics of Arthurim's mission, how his Talent for tracking and locating tied into his work as a recon agent, and how long he had been involved in the war. His parents had been loyal to opposing sides, and in order to preserve their bond, had withdrawn from the conflict entirely, retiring to the Ashdown Peaks in the north of the Scepter of Industry. Arthurim had known little of the war when he had met his embermate, a member of the Lawless. But shortly after their meeting, she had been captured by the Pinnacle and then killed by SPU experimentation. Arthurim only had a few memories and the despair that his destined partner had died before they could bond. He had taken up with the Lawless to honor her and seek justice for her death.

A story with haunting echoes to Kesia's own. Part of her resonated deeply with the loss in his heartflame, although her own loss was greater from having been connected with Zephryn for ten years. Still, the majority of those years had been spent as close friends. They had only begun relating to each other as spouses within the last few months.

Despite her annoyance with him, Kesia could imagine having a sort of friendship with Arthurim. Once she got past his intent to mate with her. It would be similar to Shance.

No, it was easier to get along with Shance than Arthurim.

After she shifted to her scale form, all she knew was the sheer freedom of flight. The satisfaction of open space around her as she glided on massive wings. And as she flew, she felt fresh sadness.

Lirome was a death unicorn. He would never be able to join her in the skies in this way. He would never know the freedom of flight, just like she'd never know what it felt like to race across the ground.

Perhaps she could. After all, she'd turned into a cat-dragon. Was it possible to turn into a death unicorn as well?

Even if she could, Lirome could never reciprocate and become a dragon.

Resolve filled her. There was more to life than sharing a single activity. Lirome was her mate. He had stood by her faithfully, and she him. They carried each other's souls.

She still chose him.

A flicker of flames scattered across her tail. Kesia yelped and wheeled around, glancing over her shoulder, expecting an enemy. But only Arthurim was there, his tail flicking back and forth.

She glared at him. <Was that you?>

<Me? Tease a princess? Never. Especially not on a recon mission.> Humor colored his tone, and he flapped coppery wings. <Unless you choose to take part rather than continue your brooding.>

She huffed out a stream of smoke. <I'm not brooding. I'm simply waiting for you to let your guard down.>

<Why is that?>

Kesia shot a stream of flame directly across his snout, then flew ahead with a roaring chuckle. They were over the northwestern plains now, skirting the edges of the Pinwood Forest. A safe airspace, compared to others. For a few moments, there was only the game.

<I'm glad you're flying.> Lirome's voice filled her mind. <You needed the chance to explore freely.>

<Someday you should come with me. You can ride on my back.>

<I would like that very much. For now, I am trying to decipher whether this scribble is a word or an attempt at artistry. Carry on.>

She chuckled. <You as well.>

Suddenly a familiar taste filled her mind, something like acrid poison and fresh leaves, like ozone and gloom. Darkness surfaced in her mind. Smoke choked her with terror and hatred.

Athurim's voice cut through her panic. <Kesia, behind you!>

She spun around. Dragons! More and more, wheeling around her and Arthurim, scorching the skies with rage and flames. She dove down beneath the circle, skimming the tree line, then shot up behind the attackers and sent a blast along their backs. More fire sizzled along her wing. A screech escaped her as another orange dragon tore into her tail. Kesia whipped her tail around, shaking him off.

A roar of pain echoed from her left.

<Arthurim!>

Three dragons hounded him with fire and fear. He twisted and turned in the skies, trying to escape their grasp. Blood dripped from a gash in his snout, and one of his legs hung limp.

Her mind screamed at her, telling her to shift into something smaller and disappear. But that would make her more vulnerable! Besides, she couldn't leave Arthurim. She didn't owe him anything, but he was a fellow dragon, and she couldn't abandon him to his fate.

She soared high into the air, pain slicing up her shoulder with each frantic beat of her wings.

Lirome's voice echoed in her mind, calm and peaceful, though she could sense his deep concern. <Kesia? What's happening?>

<We're under attack. Ten dragons. They came out of nowhere.> She faced a cloudbank of shadows, forming into a snarling face and lethal form with additional barb enhancements. Garishton Ironfire. Her blood chilled. <Lirome, my uncle … he's right in front of me.>

<You're filled with fear, Kesia. Did anything happen before the dragons attacked?>

<Darkness in my mind. I smelled smoke…>

Garishton loomed closer, gaping jaws aflame and claws extended.

<Did any of the other dragons mindspeak with you?>

<Only Arthurim.>

Peace filled her, strengthening her soul and anchoring her mind, despite the looming threat of her dragon uncle. The wounds on her tail and wing faded to nothing.

They weren't real.

None of this was.

Lirome's voice continued. <You know what to do. You did it at the temple. The attack isn't real, but Arthurim's fear is. Save him. Clear out the smoke.>

<I'm in scale form. I've only practiced in skin form.>

<You are always *you*, Kesia, no matter your form. Now clear out that smoke and find the source. I'll be right here with you.>

Lirome was right. Garishton couldn't resist taunting her through mindspeak. He never could. This thing in front of her was an illusion that warped her perceptions. And she could get rid of it.

Kesia breathed in deeply and exhaled a massive cloud of green smoke. It coiled around the image of Garishton, eliminating him to wisps of nothingness and traces of fear. She inhaled again and blew out more streams of smoke. Each of the dragon attackers disappeared.

Now to free Arthurim.

She flew over to where he still struggled against his attackers. <Arthurim, they aren't real.>

<Tell that to the blood pouring down my back.>

There was no blood, or wounds of any kind. <Let me show you.>

Kesia exhaled again and covered him with clouds of green smoke. The remaining dragons faded. Arthurim whirled around, his icy eyes blinking, the crest on his back flaring up and down.

<How did you do that?>

She breathed out one final gasp of smoke. <As I told you, my green smoke isn't always bad. Lirome has been teaching me how to use it against those who would harm us.>

Respect showed on his face. <So death unicorns might be useful after all. They did make the problem. It's only fitting that they should solve it.>

<Not all death unicorns are bad. Not all dragons are good. Garishton Razorclaw is a dragon, but he is part of the Curious Intrigue.>

<True.>

Kesia rolled her shoulders, releasing the tension. She waved her tail toward the Pinwood Forest below. <There must be some kind of secret facility down there that released the smoke. We need to investigate.>

Arthurim studied the area intently for a moment, taking in the lay of the land. <Good. I'll be able to find it from the ground now. We should go in on foot.>

<I could shift into a bird and fly down there myself.>

<No.>

<No,> agreed Lirome in her mind.

She gave a low roar. <Why? Because I'm the princess and somehow unfit for reconnaissance?>

<No, because there's a reason a king and queen always rule together. They watch each other's backs and keep each other safe.> Arthurim's feelings turned rueful. <At present, your only options are myself and the death unicorn you seem so fond of.>

Fewmets! Did he suspect?

Did she even care anymore?

Kesia didn't have time to worry about Arthurim's suspicions. Right now, there were bigger problems somewhere below them in the forest.

<Very well. We'll reconvene with Lirome, then investigate further.>

She turned and flew back to the city, eager to be in the presence of her mate once more and ready to locate this secret base.

And if necessary, utterly destroy it.

CHAPTER TWENTY-SEVEN

It didn't matter that Arthurim was there. It wouldn't have mattered if a hundred dragons had been present.

As soon as Lirome saw Kesia walking across the clearing at the northwest edge of the city, tugging her tunic into place, he only had eyes for her. When she ran into his arms and buried her face in his shoulder, he welcomed it with all the happiness and relief he could muster.

\<You did wonderfully,\> he said. \<I am so proud of you.\>

She sighed. \<I couldn't have done it without you.\>

\<Yes, you could have.\> He pulled away enough to see her face. \<And you might have to, in the future. But I will be there as long as I am able. I am honored to be with you. Always.\>

\<Always.\> Kesia repeated, her amber eyes filled with affection and resolve.

Arthurim cleared his throat. "We need to get on with the investigation, Princess. Should I say 'Prince' as well?"

There was no mistaking the accusation in the dragon's tone. A knot formed in Lirome's stomach. He leveled a glare at Arthurim, but the dragon only blinked, adjusting his boot laces.

"You might have others convinced that you've made a healing

bond, that you're only soul-friends, but I know a mate connection when I see it." He sighed. "This explains why your heartflame didn't respond to me, Kesia. Do you know how the council will receive this news?"

"The council doesn't need to know yet." Kesia folded her arms. "And what could they say? The bond exists."

"The world is greater than you, Princess. Sometimes sacrifices must be made."

Anger filled Lirome, and beside him, Kesia growled. "Never speak to me of sacrifices. That is an order as your sovereign. Now, as to the investigation, I believe going on foot will take too much time."

"Perhaps on two feet it will, but on four?"

Lirome secured his clothes in the thicket and shifted, feeling his hoof form as a second skin. He stood balanced on four legs in a body made for running. He stomped his foot in satisfaction, then returned to the clearing It had been too long.

Kesia smiled in approval. <I can shift into a horse form—or perhaps, even into a unicorn form.>

<You want to attempt that now?>

<Yes. We're already mates. I want to try.>

<Very well.>

Kesia reached out and stroked Lirome's hair, down his face and the velvety hair on his nose. He leaned into her touch.

Then she slipped into the edge of the thicket. A moment later, she stood before them on four legs with a silvery horn emerging from her head and a flowing black mane. She pranced around a few paces, her limbs strong and lean, her head arched proudly.

Lirome trotted over and nuzzled her neck. <You look magnificent.>

Happiness filled her. Another emotion they shared. <Thank you.>

Arthurim studied her. <Remarkable. Are you able to run yet?>

<Usually, it takes me a little to get used to it, but this feels… natural.> She whickered.

<Why is that?>

Kesia paused and looked at Lirome. Should they reveal their theory about her mixed shifter blood?

Lirome shook his head. Not yet.

She gave a short neigh, ignoring Arthurim's question.

<Well, shall we be off?>

Lirome stomped his front hoof on the ground. <Yes. Arthurim will ride on my back. Come on, dragon. We don't have time to waste. Can you hold a seat without a saddle? I do not wear those.>

<Yes, quite well, actually. Comes from living among humans more than most.> He vaulted onto Lirome's back.

<I see.> The extra weight was annoying, but it wouldn't be the first time. He glanced over at Kesia. <Follow my lead.>

They ran into the forest. The pinwoods rose up around them, exceptionally tall, spindly trees with tufts of fluffy leaves on thin branches. They often grew entwined in thickets, turning the sunlight greenish. The density of the trees reminded him of the forests of Elotrin, although there the trees were thicker and the leaves broader. Still, it was refreshing to have a good gallop. Even with the dragon's body weighing on his back, Lirome relished racing around the trees and leaping over obstacles in accordance with directions Arthurim gave. Kesia kept pace with him, and Lirome could feel her enjoyment, though he also sensed confusion.

<Why do I feel as though I must ride abreast? It's more logical to follow behind you. Arthurim is leading the way.>

Lirome mentally chuckled. <You're a leader, Kesia. In death unicorn herds, that means you would want to take the lead.>

\<Ah. But I can't. You are necessary in that place.>

\<Instincts are their own masters, sometimes. I don't mind that we're side by side. Just don't freeze.>

\<I never freeze.>

After a few hours of travel, Arthurim squeezed his legs together around Lirome. \<Up ahead.>

\<I see it. Next time, just speak. I'm not some dumb brute that you have to signal to like that.>

\<Understood.>

Lirome and Kesia slowed as they neared the location. It was a large, cleared area that looked like a construction site, with lumber, metal, and stone scattered about, along with various tools and instruments. Not at all what he expected a hidden base to look like.

Indeed, for some reason he felt curiously relaxed and at ease. Even ready to throw his head back and laugh.

Lirome quarantined the emotion, instinctively pressing out a barrier around them. The strange feeling had to be from another death unicorn using soul magic. But no one stood in the clearing, and they hadn't detected anyone in the pinwoods.

Kesia shifted into a large hound and sniffed the air. \<Some kind of smoke. Like Lurien's. It's coating everything in this place. But I'm not afraid.>

Then she shifted to skin form and breathed out green smoke. The exuberate feeling vanished entirely. Lirome dropped the barrier.

\<No, fear was not the emotion,> said Arthurim. \<Until a few seconds ago, I felt strangely giddy. Did your smoke clear it out?>

\<Yes. Lirome's barrier helped me to focus.> She scratched one floppy brown ear, then set her large, wet nose to the ground. \<I smell ... fresh glue. New wood. Other building materials. Lirome?>

He understood Kesia's query. He knew far more about construction. <Get off my back, dragon. I can't see as well in this form.>

As soon as Arthurim complied, Lirome shifted and crept through the trees. Large structures lay in pieces around the construction yard. He mentally pictured the pieces together. Three large, narrow cylinders. A circle shape with spikes around the edges. A crescent shape. And a pointy star shape.

A sun, a moon, and a star?

Lirome relayed his thoughts to the dragons. Kesia frowned. <But what for?>

<Three large monuments used to stand on the outskirts of the city,> Arthurim said. <The three Keymarks, celebrating the three Centrals. They were taken down months ago to be remade.>

<By whom?> Kesia tilted her head.

Arthurim's face paled. <Lady Lurien Alistil.>

Lirome turned to face him. <When will the monuments be replaced?>

<At the Celestis Festival, to coincide with her debate. They were meant to be unveiled at a later date, but she changed it.>

He nodded. <Three monuments, customized by Lurien herself, reinstated during a critical debate for her that relies on public votes. A time she needs everyone to love her.>

Lirome frowned. <Possibly she modified the monuments to emit and pulse an invisible smoke that could enhance her soul empathy and make people more responsive to her.>

Kesia broke in. <Some variant of this "joy potion" that has so many of her entourage ensnared. Only now she could ensnare a city.> Kesia made a low whine in her furred, jowly throat. <I'll be at the debate—maybe I could choke Lurien with green smoke? Or just kill her outright?>

Kesia was half-joking. At this point, Lirome was almost inclined to agree with her, or even take out Lurien himself. Legality be damned.

<I'll assist with finding the Keymarks.> Arthurim said. <And I'll need to attend this debate as well. Considering the behavior I've witnessed, further observation of you and Lirome Ukerys would be prudent.>

So much for a slow and steady relationship. He and Kesia had agreed to that, and the bond between them had seemed to cooperate. But if Arthurim was going to continue skulking around, they might need to rethink the plan.

Would Kesia oppose an elopement? From their kissing earlier, she had seemed open to the idea of getting closer. Yet this close, this quickly?

<We should go.> He shifted back to hoof form. He dearly needed a run to consider this. And to motivate himself to call Zilpath Irudha should he and Kesia need a lay-order temple ceremony.

If only he could tolerate how many times Zilpath would sign, 'I told you so.'

And convince a priest that cooperating with the saucy old woman was a good and necessary idea.

Chapter Twenty-Eight

The dragon needed to speak faster.

Arthurim Flamemaster might be gifted at tracking, and as such he was an asset to them, but he was far more long-winded than Maira preferred. Especially when he was delivering valuable information that could get her husband back to her sooner. At this point, it couldn't be soon enough.

Ademis shifted in her lap, his ears twitching. He spoke over their private link. <Stop moving around! Do you need a dose of catnesper?>

<No, and neither do you. At least not in a place where you can roll off anything or set anything on fire.> She stroked his head. <You could always nap somewhere else.>

<Nonsense. This is part of the arrangement. Your chief mate will return soon, and I'll have to share you more. I am fine with that because his presence makes you less moody, but it also means I need to hold your lap captive while I can.>

Soon. Ademis had said soon. And he wasn't an optimistic cat-dragon. Maira shifted her focus back to Arthurim's debriefing. They were on the airship, so they all chose to speak aloud for the sake of Tegan, who stood close to the door, keeping an eye on the crew while listening in.

"And there is evidence that suggests these old versions of the Keymark statues are being used to create new versions for nefarious purposes," Arthurim said.

Kesia nodded in agreement from where she sat between Arthurim and Lirome. "Arthurim and I did some reconnaissance on the proceedings. The new statues are being installed the day before the festival and will be guarded closely. It will be difficult to gain access to them."

"Difficult, though not impossible," Lirome put in, leaning forward on the table, his shoulder brushing Kesia's. Interesting. "Still, Lurien is clever. By making this an official gift, she is put into a position of great favor as a philanthropist honoring the history of the Scepter of Knowledge."

"Which means something must be amiss," Maira said. She sighed and rubbed her forehead. "This … it's the same pattern that led to the rise of the Glorious Destiny a century ago in Elotrin. Offering gifts and benefits to humans and unicorns alike, before turning those gifts against them. Back then, we were simply unicorns and had no mark of violence upon us. But the noose tightened, and the self-made gods struck out against us."

Kesia paused. "If you don't mind me asking, struck at you how?"

Maira exchanged a look with Lirome. She opened their twin link.

<Should we tell them now?>

He nodded. <Yes. We need their support.>

It was time.

Maira started. "The Glorious Destiny was a movement started by a league of human scientists over seventy years ago in Elotrin.

They wanted to make themselves gods and dominate everyone else. They started finding ways to siphon ambient magic. They also released different chemicals into wells and other water supplies to limit who would get Talents, because they saw common citizens having Talents as an unnecessary encumberance." She shook her head. "We unicorns were an asset and a threat to them. They wanted our blood for their initial experiments, and they feared our soul empathy, because they knew we would sense their plans. After years of good relations between humans and unicorns, the Glorious Destiny implicated the unicorns for a crime we didn't commit. They claimed we were using our soul empathy to manipulate and harm the human population, bending them to our wills. Such things are against the most fundamental tenets of our people. But we have always been quiet about our Talents and abilities. The self-made gods used that secrecy against us. And then…"

Grief and outrage tightened her throat. The memories weren't hers. By the time Maira had been born, the genocide had already occurred. But race memories were strongly kept among the herds, and she had inherited terrible ones in full measure as the leader of her people.

Lirome reached across the table, took her hand, and continued her story. "At first, our human allies didn't believe the words of the gods. After all, we had proven ourselves for centuries. But the gods framed us. They had tortured several of our own, enough that they were filled with hatred and pain, ready to project those emotions upon everyone around them like mindless beasts. The gods released these tortured unicorns into public. The results were devastating. All these humans, cowering in fear or lashing out in hideous malice. It was a massacre, emotionally and physically." He paused. "None survived."

Maira squeezed his hand tightly, working hard to maintain control so neither of them would emanate the strong grief roiling within them. In her lap, Ademis purred like a rusty motor, giving her strength and giving himself relief from her feelings through their bond.

At last, she spoke into the silence. "All humans turned on us and went to the gods for their salvation. Determined to end unicorns once and for all, the Glorious released a toxin into our largest forests, a poison that targeted unicorn women of childbearing age. Those who were pregnant died within days. Those who were not had a one in five chance of surviving. The men who encountered the toxin were rendered sterile. Only one herd in the farthest northern reaches of Elotrin, the herd of my parents, remained untouched. We were considered the least educated, the wildest. And we became the only chance for survival.

"And we did, by arming ourselves. We became deadly in ways we could control. Flashing red eyes and the scent of sulfur to make ourselves appear more dangerous. Glands around our horns in hoof form that produced black poison. Paralyzing smoke, guerilla warfare techniques, advanced healing methods so we could recover from wounds more quickly." Maira gave Kesia a look of pity. "My parents tried to ensure that we would never stoop to acting out of bitterness and hatred, but it was seeded in many hearts."

Silence fell as the others in the room processed this information. Kesia turned and nudged Lirome's shoulder with her forehead. Maira could sense the hum of private mindspeak between them.

After a moment, she cleared her throat. Time to move on.

"My daughter has researched and found no one named Lurien Alistil. But she did find an Otressin Alistil, who disappeared long ago, perhaps a decade after we arrived in Sekastra. He strongly opposed any connection, any alliance, with outsiders. Death unicorns for our own kind only. His description partly matches Lurien's, except he had darker skin and hair."

Tegan frowned. "Yet she allies with the Curious Intrigue? Didn't you say they were following in the steps of the Glorious Destiny?"

"It's odd to me as well. We have watched the Curious Intrigue carefully. It has been one of Lirome's chief missions."

He took up the conversation. "They are also interested in self-improvement and glorification. But they are less organized. And they allow shifters into their ranks, which the Glorious Destiny never did."

Maira added, "Also, from what I've learned, Otressin is dead. Perhaps Lurien is a relative? In any case, she is determined to take over this city. Now that he has his full wits about him, Shance will be thoroughly investigating her house."

Kesia nodded. "Good. We only have two days until the debate."

"I'm well aware," Maira snapped. She exhaled. "I'm sorry."

"You don't need to be. You're separated from your husband. I understand."

The quietness and openness in Kesia's tone undid Maira. "And I understand your loss. I pray to the All-Maker that you will stand strong."

The dragon woman laughed shortly, expelling green smoke. "Right now I'd settle for making it through the next few days. Pray for that."

Lirome gave her a faint smile. "A worthy goal, and one we will achieve together."

"I know." She squeezed his hand again, then returned his stare.

"All in the power of tea."

"Oh, yes."

Irritation flared from Arthurim. Maira turned to him as he cut in. "I'll see about tracking down the creator of the new Keymark monuments. Their scent is everywhere. Lurien must not be used to dealing with a tracking Talent. It isn't as common as others."

"But very useful and welcome." Kesia flashed him a smile. "Thank you for your help."

His icy eyes glinted. "It is the least I can do for the crown princess. You seem to make enough of your own trouble."

Arthurim's gaze fell on Kesia and Lirome's joined hands. Maira's heart sank. He would be sure to report to the dragon council. Maybe Maira could spin Lirome and Kesia's bond as an alliance?

"Indeed." Kesia stood. "But right now, it's important to focus on the tasks at hand. Maira, is there anything more I can do to assist you? Have you written your final speeches?"

Maira shook her head. "No need. I have enough notes and enough life experience. The key to these speeches is to undermine the other side as much as present your own. I destroyed the Glorious Destiny. I think I can stop the rise of an errant death unicorn. Just learn your parts and be ready to leave as soon as you can."

Kesia nodded. "I will."

The dragon woman's eyes fell on Lirome, and some unspoken words flew between them. He smiled and stood up abruptly. "We'll make sure the monuments are taken care of, sister. You deal with this false queen."

"I shall." Maira cleared her throat. "Keep communicating with each other. Lurien has taunted Shance repeatedly about planning far more than he knows. We only have two days to figure out what that is."

"Agreed," Kesia said.

The dragons and Lirome departed the ship. She could see a faint storm cloud of emotions hovering around Lirome. She could hardly blame him. The idea of a dragon and unicorn marriage was already complicated, and it had become more complicated with Arthurim in the mix. There was no doubt who the dragon council would demand Kesia bond with.

Speaking of storm clouds. She tapped her wireless commer.

No response.

Maira's heart raced. She pressed it again.

Only the crackling chirp of empty static.

She forced herself to breathe. Shance might simply be in a place where he couldn't contact her safely. The wireless commer might be out of range. Or perhaps it had broken. Those were all perfectly logical reasons why she couldn't hear from him.

Never mind the foreboding in her gut.

She pressed the wireless commer one more time.

"Hello, dear one. I've been waiting to hear from you." His voice was calm and sure, filled with a richness that thrilled her. She could listen to him speak for days, listen to him sing for weeks. Hopefully he remembered how to sing now that his memories had returned. "My time is very short."

"Shorter than me? Hmph." Ademis rrowled in annoyance at her lame joke. "Have you discovered anything new?"

"Only that Lurien is more suspicious than ever. And smug. It's as if she's tremendously pleased about something."

Maira frowned. "Do you think she knows that you have your memories back?"

"Yes, she must. But she hasn't said anything or insisted that I leave."

"I wish you could leave." She paused. "Why can't you, again? I know we had good reasons, but I can't seem to remember them. Especially when I consider sleeping in an empty bed tonight."

Ademis scratched at her. <And what am I?>

<A scaly fluffball who enjoys napping, but that's about it. You hardly measure up to Shance.>

<Hmph. Your pillow will suffer the consequences for that statement.>

She flicked his ear.

Shance spoke. "I would love to ensure you didn't sleep until late tonight, but I'm finally making some connections with the servants, and they've indicated a secret passage that might lead to her laboratory."

"Lirome and I have already figured out how to counter the joy potion. Although that was on single individuals. For Lurien to release that potion city-wide, she doubtless made some changes. It's going to dissipate and lose effectiveness, so she would have to make it even stronger."

"I'll look for this new potion. Anything I can get and bring back to you will help. I have to try. Besides, I'd hate to waste the connections I've built up. These people really do want to help take Lurien out."

Maira sighed. "Glad to see your old palace charm and wiliness coming back."

"Who, me?" She could picture his roguish grin. "I only tell people what they want to hear—and then tell them the truth when they aren't paying as much attention. Using the skills the All-Maker gifted me with."

Maira smiled and leaned back in her chair. "You must realize the longer you stay on this commer, the more I'm tempted to use my queenly authority to order you to ride the winds over here and take care of me."

"And I also know you're too self-sacrificial to say the words."

"Elric's mane! You know too much."

"Only about you."

The words sent pleasant chills up her spine and nestled deep in her heart. After so long, she was known. Understood. To have her husband of so many years speaking with her, understanding their private jokes and shared memories, brought an overwhelming sense of relief.

"I won't be long." The commer went dead.

Maira sighed. "Don't be."

There were many tasks to do. There always were. But for a moment, she just stared at the commer, praying that everything would turn out all right.

For once.

Chapter Twenty-Nine

Shance smiled and thanked the servant for holding the door open.

"Always at your service, my lord. For whatever you require."

Cortin's tone was laden with hidden meaning, and his hand clutched a small knife hidden in his coat pocket. His eyes flashed with a loyalty that Shance had reinforced over the last few weeks.

All of which served Shance's advantage, if he could keep the servants in check until the right time.

Soon.

He gave the servant a short nod. "Nothing as of yet, my good man. Just keep this area clear, if you would."

"It shall be entirely vacant, my lord."

Shance strode through the door and walked a decent pace down the hallway. Then he winced and rubbed his forehead.

The headache had returned with a vengeance. The sharp spikes of pain almost overrode Shance's commitment to keep his wife free from worry. If anyone could free him from the agony in his head, it would be her. But she was already using so much healing magic to help Cadence and expending herself to assist his crew and create a counteragent to Lurien's joy potion. He suspected she was drinking that special tea Weirad sneaked to her.

Shance shook his head. He could get along with her two other mates just fine, and he remembered years of familiarity with the marital situation Maira had to navigate. But while she was her mates' ally, she was Shance's wife. His especial care. And she pushed herself too hard.

As soon as he finished freeing his son and the others from Lurien's hold, Shance would ensure Maira could get the rest she needed. In the meantime, he could cope with the headache on his own. It wouldn't be the first time he'd had to swallow discomfort for the sake of the greater good.

Regaining his memories had only proven that the humiliation of the last decade was just one of many trials he'd endured in serving his queen and Bonilus. All he could do now was persevere onward.

He continued down the hallway, calling lightning to his fingertips, and feeling only the faintest flicker. Still dormant. Viorstan. Even so, it was enough to use as a sensor, as he had in the past. Lurien had to have a secret lab somewhere, a place where he could locate whatever chemical enhancements she used and relay the information to Maira.

Shance glanced warily back and forth, checking the hallway. All clear. The servant was as good as his word.

He scanned the paneled walls, pressing his palm along the wood grain until he felt something cold and hard. Flickers of lighting prickled his palm like needles. His storm magic interacting with the world around him.

This was the spot.

Now if only he could get it open. He pulled out a pair of goggles another servant had slipped him and turned on the infrared setting. Nothing. Elric's mane. He switched to the magnification setting, studying the wall surface for the slightest crack.

It had to be here somewhere.

Someone cleared their throat behind him. Shance jumped and pivoted, his muscles tensed for action. There stood Brennar, the usual sardonic expression on his face. So damn smug for a young man enslaved to an evil death unicorn. It wasn't a good look for him, although that was hardly the main reason Shance was seeking to free him. Still, it was one reason.

"May I ask what you're doing, Captain Windkeeper?"

Shance's mind raced for a response.

"You may. Of course, I'm not completely sure myself. You could help me find the hidden doorway here, or report me to your mistress. Perhaps interrupting her from a tryst with one of her other men."

"What my lady does is her business and for the benefit of all." Brennar's voice dripped with mindless obeisance, his gaze never wavering. Winds swirled around him. "Anything you are looking for will only disturb the good she seeks to do."

"You're wrong. Can't you see that?" He reached out and grasped his son's shoulder as more twinges of lightning flooded his hand. He pressed the winds back at his son, using them to amplify his voice. "You are Brennar Ukerys Windkeeper. You are my son, and I never meant to lose you. It was a trap."

Brennar shuddered under his touch, a frown of confusion breaking through his smug expression. He blinked. "What are you—you're tricking me!"

"No. I'm trying to save you. I'll die trying, if I have to." Shance released him and turned back to the door. "You're welcome to assist me. Or you can turn me in, or kill me. But I'm going to keep searching."

He flung out his arm, releasing a finely concentrated line of air to find the space. He began to find the tiniest of cracks around the door, just enough for his winds to slip in. Where his winds could get in, they could break in with violent force.

Shance concentrated even more, using every bit of control he had, his jaw tightening with the effort. Then he noticed a second stream of air joining his, outlining the other half of the hidden entrance.

He glanced over to where Brennar stood, his light olive face a mask of concentration. Surprised lifted Shance's heart.

"You're helping me?"

"Don't get excited," he said. "I'm only using this as an opportunity to learn more of your techniques so I can master them and overtake you more easily."

"Of course you are." Shance flashed a smile. "Carry on."

"I don't answer to you." Brennar's lips twitched in something closer to a genuine smile instead of his usual disdainful smirk.

After a few moments, the hidden entrance was shaking on its hinges from their combined efforts. Now to carefully push it open. Shance reached out and clasped his son's shoulder again. "On my mark."

"All right."

"Ready ... set ... mark!"

As one, they blasted the area with focused air, forcing the secret door inward. Just as quickly, Shance pulled back. Brennar followed suit a second later, although without as much finesse. The door smacked against the interior twice, the sound echoing down the hall. Shance winced.

Brennar strode forward with an impatient sound. "Well, are we going in or aren't we?"

"I didn't realize you wanted to come in."

"I don't," he declared. The words were belied by the curiosity in his blue eyes. "But someone has to keep an eye on you. It may as well be me. I can report to Lady Lurien afterward."

"Come along then." Shance brushed past him and pulled out a torch to light their way through the darkness.

He needn't have bothered with the torch A few steps in and recessed lights flickered on from of the ceiling. A quick glance told him all he needed to know. The lights were from Glenalis, the capital city of the gods in Elotrin. Technology from the old days. Lirome's report had warned about it creeping into Sekastra.

It seemed to have made greater inroads over the last ten years. Shame gripped him. Monitoring traffic in illegal tech had been one of his duties until his mind had been reduced to that of a young human male, obsessed with finding his perfect love. It wasn't unlike Shance's real experience at that age, although by twenty-eight, he had found Maira, a captive death unicorn woman he married in order to protect her from a worse fate, all the while falling in love with her.

Just as he had with Kesia during their false betrothal. Believing she was his destiny.

"Viorstan." The word echoed through the passage, and he quickened his pace. Would he ever live that down? How had Maira accepted him back so easily?

The answers floated through his mind.

Because the Four Corners mandated forgiveness. Because they had a son together. Because she honored her vows. Because she was Maira, his wife, and he didn't deserve her.

That didn't mean he was giving up.

Brennar scuffed his boots next to Shance. "Are we going anywhere, or are you wasting our time with a pointless secret passage?"

"Still asking if we're there yet?"

"...no. But we aren't anywhere except in a decrepit passageway."

Shance chuckled despite himself. "Just wait."

He hoped he was right. Ahead of them loomed a doorway of burnished bronze and iron, inlaid with a complicated set of gears and mechanisms. His heart sank. Of course. Another lock. Maybe this time he could short-circuit it with lightning. If he could summon enough.

Shance inhaled, trying to collect the remnants of what he once had been. Tiny sparks of electricity tingled around his right hand, and he stretched his arm out toward the door.

"It won't be enough," Brennar said over his shoulder. "You still can't do anything."

"Thanks for the encouragement," Shance grunted. "I don't remember you being this negative."

"That was before my parents abandoned me to the care of a psychopathic death unicorn."

Frustration set his veins on fire. "We didn't abandon you!"

Matching fury filled Brennar's voice. "Sure you didn't. You just left me alone while you and Mother faced danger in the Scepter of Commerce, never caring that I didn't have anyone else except you! That no matter how much I tried, I would never fit in with the herd without you there, among her other mates and children. Where were you then?"

Shance's arm flared white-hot with the blazing of the sun. "We made mistakes, but protecting you will never be one of them. And we never used you, not once. Not like that hideous woman who turns you into a simpering, sniveling fool every time she uses her twisted Talents and magic!"

Arcs of lightning flashed around him as he grabbed his son's arm. "Mock me for my failures. I deserve it, after all I've done or neglected to do. Trade your loyalty for a disturbing fantasy with Lurien if you want. But don't you ever question that I love you!"

Lightning flashed around him, bolts of it hitting the door and sizzling into Brennar. Oddly, Shance didn't care. Within seconds, the lightning had shivered into his son's skin and bones, as if nestling there. Of course. His son had inherited part of his storm Talent, which was why the lightning didn't harm him.

Brennar looked at him with triumph and relief in his eyes. "I knew it would work."

"You knew what would work?"

Brennar nodded at the door, which swung open. "That. I remember, when you grew passionate about something, you'd lose control of your Talent. I thought making you have a strong emotion would awaken it. Anger was the easiest choice for me right now."

"Spoken like a true eighteen-year-old." Shance sighed and started to let go of Brennar's arm.

His son held him fast for a moment, his face softening with memory. "I remember. Something in the lightning cleared her falsehoods. I remember … more of what's true."

Shance swallowed. Part of him wanted to grab his son in a fierce hug. The other part was wary. This could be another trick.

He settled for squeezing Brennar's hand. "It's good you came with me after all."

"Yes. But we need to move quickly. She'll be here soon."

Shance released his son and moved toward the doorway. "And why is that?"

"I lied. I alerted her before I came down here. She has me check in every half hour, like I'm her personal man-slave." Brennar chuckled sourly, running a hand through his thick black hair. "I suppose that's what I've been. Willingly."

"No, not willingly. Never let yourself think that. She targeted, lured, and brainwashed you. That's something else entirely."

Brennar's face paled. "And to think I was willing to see you in her collection. Even though I knew what she had planned—"

"That knowledge should be punishment enough without sharing it with anyone. Least of all with me."

They entered the laboratory. It was brightly-lit and filled with the usual mysteriously bubbling concoctions Shance never understood, even after years in the company of Maira and Lirome. He folded his arms, surveying the various tables and their assortment of objects. In one corner were shackles for ankles, wrists, and neck pinned to a wall. In another was a curious leather chair with more straps and ominous tubes and needles attached.

Shance finally asked, "I don't suppose you took after your mother in terms of medicine and chemical research?"

"No, although Lurien wishes otherwise. Apparently I've taken after you in more ways than just rumored reputation." He pulled at his collar. "That being said, I should apologize for the attack on your ship."

"Accepted. Now start pulling vials off of shelves and wherever else while I contact Maira."

He tapped his wireless commer. It crackled with static. Shance frowned and pressed it again. He had warned Maira it might be useless, but this soon?

"We're underground," he muttered. "There must be something in the walls."

Shance began grabbing as many vials as he could, securing them in a pouch at his side. An odd fragrance, engine oil mixed with fresh flowers, tickled his nose.

"Lurien?"

"Are you sure?" It was Maira's voice, with that dry, amused edge and sultry undertone she reserved for only him.

He looked up to see her standing there, her face flushed and her petite form dressed in the usual black clothing that suited her so well. Relief flooded him, but with it came an odd reserve. "What are you doing here? You're supposed to stay on the ship, no matter what. Lurien can't find you here."

"I don't care. I had to see you." She gave him a sly look. "Weren't we always the ones to break the rules for each other, my love?"

Next to him, Brennar's eyes narrowed, and he stepped forward. "Mother, I'm sorry."

"I forgive you. As I always do, for those who turn against me." Darkness threaded her tone and her violet eyes flashed. She turned her gaze to Shance. "I'd almost think you weren't happy to see me. But I know that can't be true."

Shance blinked. Paused. "I am ... but..."

"Maybe less clothed?" She toyed with a lock of her short wings of black hair.

Her hair. Maira's hair had grown long during her imprisonment in the Talent-siphoning coffin.

Realization chilled Shance. That explained the scent of engine oil, and the cloying, beckoning overtones of flowers trying to beguile his mind. He shook his head. "Nice try. But it won't work."

"What are you talking about?" The woman who was not his wife blinked.

"Elric's hooves! Enough, Lurien. The hair was an obvious mistake."

An exaggerated sigh shook her chest. Then she blurred in his vision for a moment as her perception Talent loosened its hold on him. After a moment, Lurien Alistil stood before him, her milk-white skin glowing against the wine-colored gown she wore, and her lips pursed in disapproval. "An oversight, I'll admit. But your journey down here was even more ill-advised. I see I need to inflict a stronger lesson to bring you in line, Captain Windkeeper. Come here, Brennar. Give your lady a hand."

"I don't..." Brennar's face paled, and sweat beaded his brow. "I don't ... want to."

Her delicate face pinched in a frown. "You don't? And why, dear one, don't you? After all, you know I'm the only one who truly cares for you. Perhaps I should show you again in my bed. Come here. Now."

Lurien's last word was rich with soul-command, hard and un-yielding. Her eyes flashed blood red, and the air scented of sulfur. Shance's stomach turned as Brennar slowly walked toward her, still clutching a vial in one hand. She smiled. "There now. Much bet-ter."

Then he brought the vial up and flung it in her eyes, the liq-uid splashing pale green over her face and hair. She screamed, but Brennar only smiled faintly. "There. Now. Much ... better."

"Ungrateful bastard!" Still scrubbing at her eyes, Lurien reached into her bodice. A flash of something sharp and lethal emerged. Shance's heart lurched, and he started forward.

He was too late. She had buried something deep in his son's gut. Brennar bent over, collapsing to the ground, his hands over a dark, rapidly-spreading stain on his waistcoat.

"Brennar!"

Shance ran toward him, but two guards emerged from behind Lurien, each one grabbing him by the arm. He grimaced. "Do you think they can stop me?"

Lightning flickered along his body, and fierce winds buffeted the laboratory. Brennar had proved he could withstand the blasts, which meant Shance could fry the entire place without a single qualm.

Lurien shook an elegantly pointed index finger. "Ah-ahhh. Careful. I'll slit your son's throat if you try any of that. You know I will."

Shance willed the lightning back into his body, praying his son still breathed. "What do you want?"

"Total domination over this city in revenge for what they did to my people. My father's people, I should say. Otressin." She shrugged, toying with the knife that dripped with his son's blood. "I am half human. A disgrace, he always called me. The result of his dalliance with a human woman, since there were not enough death unicorn ladies in his generation, and he never met his mate." Her lips trembled for a moment, then she pressed them together. "My mother raised me among humans, but I learned quickly that I could never be considered one of them. Nor would a death unicorn herd accept me." She shook her head. "So I decided to take control of my own destiny. I allowed the Curious Intrigue to experiment on me, enhance my magic, and teach me chemical secrets. Then I made a deal with them. If I killed the dragon prince and princess and stopped the Lawless from taking this city, they would give me the Scepter of Knowledge. Anyone from this Scepter who joins me lives—and anyone who does not will die. But I doubt many will be able to resist my charms."

She made a delicate gesture with her hand. "Guards, strip him and tie him up. We must teach him a lesson if he is to join us for the Celestis Festival."

Shance struggled against the guards to no avail. They were death unicorns, with the full strength of their unicorn forms. And every strain against their muscles put Brennar in danger. He gritted his teeth as they cut away his clothing and clasped him in the shackles. "What are you doing?"

"Hmmm." She tore her eyes away from his naked body. "Just as the stories say. An excellent specimen. Such a shame you're taken by such a pathetic wretch." She gave another exaggerated sigh. "And then that troublesome felon princess refused to die, thanks to her conniving uncle, no doubt. I always knew he was running his own agenda within the Curious Intrigue. Anyway, this city needs a special breath of air, as it were. With your mastery of the winds, you are the ideal person to disperse my lovely, persuasive concoction. A true monument to this city."

She chuckled over some private joke. Shance's mind raced. Could Kesia counteract Lurien's newest potion with her green smoke while Shance controlled the breezes?

"I see that conniving expression." She jabbed him in the bare chest, frost fire tingling over his skin. "Betray me, and your son dies. That is a promise."

He swallowed. Appease her for now. Revenge later. "I understand."

"You're a man of action, Captain Windkeeper." She traced patterns on his bare skin, raising gooseflesh. She leaned up and whispered in his ear. "So I think some action will serve to reinforce my meaning."

She stepped back and waved dismissively. "Don't harm his face."

As the heavy blows and harsh whip-strikes fell on him, all he could do was stare at Brennar's prone form, bleeding out on the hard gray floor. His son, who had so recently begun to return to him, fading before he'd ever lived.

Resolve filled Shance. Lurien would pay dearly.

Somehow.

Then all thoughts were consumed in agony and blood, running down his skin. Stealing his breath.

He fell to his knees, and everything turned to black.

CHAPTER THIRTY

There was nothing worse than giving a practice speech to the cat-dragon. Ademis stared at her, made snarky comments, then ignored her, his loud snoring accompanied by tiny wisps of flame.

Kesia sighed. She was already struggling to focus, and the obnoxious creature wasn't helping. Lirome was supposed to be there helping her practice, but he was busy at another Lawless infirmary in the Scepter of Knowledge, tending to wounded soldiers who had been brought to the city. Kesia had offered to help, but he'd said she needed to rehearse.

Tegan, Kesia's other usual evaluator, was occupied with shipboard duties.

Which left Kesia to the encouragement of the scaled feline.

Ademis snored on, sprawled on a wooden chair in the main area of the safe house. He lay on his back with his stomach up in the air and his pointy tail curling back and forth. Kesia rolled her eyes. So much for support.

Arthurim had offered to stay and listen, but Kesia had decided against that. She still wasn't accustomed to the new dragon's outgoing ways or his suspicion toward her and Lirome. Would he report them to the dragon council? Would the council do anything? What could they do to her?

Kesia didn't like any of the questions.

She and Lirome were still biding their time. The debate was tomorrow night. There was little time to think about anything else. Saving the Scepter of Knowledge and stopping Lurien trumped their own relationship needs.

What *did* she need?

Fresh grief sliced through her. Zephryn alive would be nice. But that wasn't possible. And she had met someone else. An image of the death unicorn flashed in her mind. Lirome's slow, easy smile. His off-hand jokes and sarcastic remarks. His comfort with social situations and enjoyment of solitude.

The taste of his lips and the feel of his silky black hair flowing through her fingers.

"How am I supposed to focus?" Kesia breathed in and exhaled slowly. Or tried to. A stream of flames escaped her, setting Ademis's chair on fire.

He leapt up with a yowl. <You idiotic scale-covered—>

Kesia ran to the sink and filled a bucket of water from the cold tap. "You have no room to talk! You were supposed to be listening to me, not sleeping!"

She flung the water at the chair, dousing one side of the cat-dragon. He hissed. <Listen to you over-practice and grow steadily more nervous and anxious? Why would I?>

A clapping of hands broke in, followed by a rich voice. "Freckles gets a singe. That seems appropriate."

The cat-dragon spat. <See if I ever cuddle you again!>

"Finally, you talk to me." A bright grin split Nula Thredsing's deep brown face, and she brushed off her turquoise corset-coat. "I'll cry my way to the arms of Tiers. But that would mean I cry, and I will never admit to such a thing. Neither would he, since he's an excellent secret-keeper and knows what's good for him."

A laugh broke from Kesia. She ran to embrace the half-dragon as Nula strode across the main area. Hugging was still new, but this time, it felt entirely natural. "You didn't have to come!"

Nula held her tightly. "You mentioned in our last clipse-mirror call that you wanted me to."

"Yes, but I didn't expect you to. No one does for me."

They pulled apart, and Nula shook her head. "Well, now you're proven wrong. And I thought I had issues with trusting others. This must be why we're friends."

"I suppose so."

They walked over to the central table and sat down. Ademis still meowed loudly in the background, spewing undertones of how terrible they were and how heinous the situation was. Kesia flicked her fingers and sent another burst of flame his way.

Nula watched in admiration. "I'm still trying to get the hang of those hand-flames."

"They take practice for accuracy. I can teach you, if you'd like."

"Eager to stop rehearsing?"

Kesia grimaced. "It only helps so much. If I study too much now, I might lose that … spark. Maira understands. She hasn't pressured me to practice." She snapped her fingers, creating a spark. "Besides, I was having trouble focusing. Between the cat-dragon snores and…"

No. Discussing Lirome was out of the question. Not even with Nula. So far, she had managed to at least keep that circumspect. Kesia stood. "Would you like something to drink? Some water or tea?"

"You *are* learning customs well. Water is fine." Nula studied her. "When did you start enjoying tea?"

"Lirome managed to find a few flavors I can tolerate." She paused. So much for not bringing up the death unicorn. But why not speak of him? She could certainly speak of him without exposing their bond. "It was a sort of quest we embarked on, though I maintain that I do not, in fact, love tea. So he hasn't succeeded."

It made for fun jesting. Yes, it was good to be able to joke with someone. To be able to go out with them for mutual enjoyment. And just for a little while, to not carry the burden of grief alone.

Fewmets, she wished he was here. They still needed to discuss how to best approach the monuments and disable them. Maybe they could even start tonight. Yes, it would be good to start tonight.

Maybe they could kiss again. Explore more of that incredible soul sharing.

Her fingers pressed into the glass, creating fingerprints. Fewmets! Kesia managed to contain her matter-shaping Talent and set the glass in front of Nula. Her friend's clear gray eyes bore intently into hers.

Kesia shrugged. "What is it?"

"Are you in love with Lirome Ukerys?"

"What?" Kesia started and sat back on the bench. She had to remain calm. "Why would I be? That isn't how mourning works. I've learned a lot about mourning. In death unicorn culture, you must wait three months before choosing another spouse, and all is handled within the herd. In human culture, there is a waiting period of at least six months to even be seen in the company of a male—"

Nula waved a hand. "I'm aware of my own customs, thank you very much. You didn't answer the question."

"The question is stupid."

Nula tsked. "Still not an answer."

"Why does it matter? I need to focus on the task at hand." Kesia shoved the thoughts away. "Such as teaching you how to master hand-flames. It's simply a matter of secreting a certain type of oil—"

"You need to tell him how you feel. Unless he already knows."

The half-dragon's voice was far too commanding for Kesia's liking. She stood up from the table, arms folded across her chest. "This is a pointless conversation."

"You're wrong." Nula stood too. "I might not enjoy dealing with emotions either, but I know that going into the public arena with too many emotional issues is asking for trouble. And you can stop pretending. I know you love him. You'd better feel something for him, since he and Zilpath are at a Four Corners temple right now talking some priest into handling your elopement."

"They're what?" Flames wreathed Kesia's throat. "How would you … how are they … what's happening?"

Nula chuckled. "Imagine how I felt, having to learn all this from Zilpath on the airship ride over here. She hates airships, especially when they have to skirt around the latest battle zones. The Curious Intrigue isn't happy with the Scepter of Commerce's secession. They've been trying to blockade our routes in addition to the usual wartime attacks."

"That's terrible!"

"We still have plenty of other routes. The local tribes really hate the Intrigue. Something to do with slave trafficking that cheats the tribe leaders as well. Not good for business." Nula scowled, but her eyes twinkled. "Kesia, I thought we were friends. Why did I have to hear about this from Zilpath?"

Kesia ran a hand through her brown hair, her pulse still jumpy.

"I'm sorry. I couldn't risk it. Lirome and I, we're trying not to tell anyone until after we sort things out with the dragon council."

"You've already had sex, huh?" Nula smirked.

"No. According to the Four Corners, that takes place after marriage."

"Yeah, but y'know, things happen. In dragon culture, you'd already be considered married."

"Tell that to the dragons," Kesia growled. She shook her head. "I'm fine with honoring the Four Corners. And also, I'm not sure I'm ready anyway."

Not for everything, when even prolonged kissing created intense soul intimacy. Revealing parts of both of them that had long stayed hidden. Slow was good. As long as they continued to move forward. She would like that. Kesia paused, touching her lips.

"You've at least kissed, from that gesture."

"Oh, yes. I enjoy that. And I would like to sleep with him."

Her friend raised her eyebrows. "Yes?"

Kesia flushed. "Literally sleep, Nula! We're still figuring out the rest."

"There's that smile. I knew something was going on between you two this whole time. Now I'm here to witness it."

Witness it? The words seemed absurd. This couldn't be happening. Lirome would have discussed it with her! Kesia glared at the absent death unicorn and reached out through their private link. <Lirome, an elopement? When were you going to talk with me?>

<Did Nula spoil everything?> The death unicorn's tone was wry. <I would have discussed this with you, I can assure you. I didn't plan on the injured soldiers this morning, and then other matters caught my attention. Are you angry? You sound angry.>

<I would have appreciated advance notice.> Kesia rolled her

eyes. <Is this event supposedly happening today?>

<Unlikely. Elopements are tricky to negotiate with the Four Corners. They usually have a nine-week mandatory waiting period of preparation. There are lay-order ceremonies that can be performed quickly, but only Mediary Evoris was willing to serve. As a member of the Daughters of Allandra, Zilpath can perform lay-order ceremonies with a priest, but she and Mediary Evoris are not on the best of terms. They are still arguing over the details right now.> His distress filtered through their bond. <Another reason I didn't want to bring up the idea until I was certain it was a possibility.>

<I understand.> Kesia sighed. <We will discuss this soon? Once you know for sure?>

<Yes. I'm sorry for any distress.>

<Just remember that I wasn't the one who ran off without communicating this time.> She sent a flash of teasing toward him.

<I'll have you know I walked. Zilpath doesn't run easily.>

<Noted.> Kesia shook her head. <I forgive you. Mostly. Enough to still consider elopement.>

<Good. I'll be in contact.>

Kesia focused back on Nula, who had poured herself a small glass of something strongly alcoholic from the icerator. She held it up. "I'm celebrating early!"

Celebrating Kesia's forthcoming marriage. The idea still seemed absurd. Even though, if she was honest, she was quite ready to be bound to Lirome. She needed a partner in her life. She needed him.

"And you expect me to teach you how to summon flames to your hands, after drinking?" Kesia snorted. Then laughed. Then folded her hands. Unfolded them. "Don't celebrate too early. I doubt this will happen before the debate. Mediary Evoris and Zilpath are still arguing about it. Also, the dragon council could find out."

Nula took a sip of the dark blue liquid. "I doubt the dragon council is going to come barging in to stop your wedding. Zilpath has been very discreet."

Kesia frowned. "They seem set on me marrying a dragon and very set against death unicorns. I can't blame them, after everything that happened, but still…"

"It's unusual. But they shouldn't be surprised."

"Surprise is not what I'm worried about."

Nula shook her head. "I've been researching dragon customs with Tiers. If a dragon loses their parents, they are placed in a new family unit within a week. Other dragons take responsibility for their welfare. If parents lose a child, they are permitted to assist in the rearing of other children, and they also do so within a week. My guess is that you have a few deep and necessary connections that must be filled in some way. You're not eloping until over three months later, Kesia. I'm amazed you lasted this long."

"So am I." Yet that was the nature of their bond. Kesia's mouth was dry as bone as she processed the rest of what Nula said. "I never had new parents. Criminals don't get such treatment. Not when you killed your own father."

"None of that talk. You killed your father in self-defense, after he had been turned into a monster. And you and Zephryn had an exceptionally close bond. Everyone saw that. It might have covered over everything else." Nula's tone softened, and she hesitantly rested a hand on Kesia's shoulder. "Just because you were denied one need of your people doesn't mean you need to deny yourself others. It's good to see you happy again. Especially because then you will teach me that flame-summoning trick."

"You'll have to set down the glass first."

Nula threw back the rest of the liquor. "Now that isn't fair.

Especially after I gave you such great advice. Teach me, or I'll take it all back and let you wallow in self-indulgent misery."

Kesia smirked. "I'll get another bucket of water. Hopefully the cat-dragon will know to keep his distance."

<You are both the worst creatures in the world.> Ademis flicked his tail at them, then abruptly spun around in a circle and ran into another room of the safe house.

Nula tsked. "I've heard that before. Come on, dragon princess. Show me how to set the world aflame."

The chair was dead.

It had already been singed from the incident with the snoring cat-dragon. It might as well be burned the rest of the way.

Nula grinned at the broken, ashy pieces strewn across the floor. Her right palm glowed with faint flames. "That was so much fun. I cannot wait to show Tiers. In more than one way."

"I imagine you will in bed." Was this the moment to wink? Yes. Kesia did so.

"Not bad, dragon. That euphemism almost sounded natural. Although how would you know about those matters?" Nula put her hands on her hips. "I thought you didn't speak about such things."

"We're becoming closer friends." Kesia shrugged. "In any case, you appear to be able to summon flames quite well. Just be careful you don't overuse them, or you'll have to stop for a time. You're half human, so I would think the effort would be more taxing.

"I understand." Her friend paused and put on the corset coat she had thrown over a chair, cinching it into place over her blouse. "That scenario would seem to leave the death unicorn out right away. You wouldn't want to set him on fire in the nether regions."

A flush crept over Kesia's cheeks. "We have a curious connection thanks to the bond. Lirome is already flameproof and we discovered early on that he's able to absorb my flames. It has proven useful in public situations. I'm not sure how it works, exactly. Lirome thinks it might have to do with soul magic and our soul bond." Truthfully, Kesia thought he was making guesses.

Nula wrinkled her nose. "Going on about magic again. In other words, he can synchronize with your shifter energy. I suppose it makes sense? Whatever he says, since he's the physician." Her face smoothed. "So there is nothing impeding you from having a good time—having sex—with him."

"Yes. When that happens. Right now, I would just enjoy being physically close to him."

"I'm sure you would."

Kesia fixed her friend with a look. Nula's expression turned serious for a moment. "I understand, Kesia. You've been through enough. No pressure from me on the rest of your intimate details. I'm just glad you're not letting the council push you around. Come on. I'll buy you dinner—as many courses as that dragon stomach needs."

<They've come to an agreement.> Lirome's mental voice was weary, but triumphant. <Get here quickly, before they change their minds.>

<On my way.> Kesia glanced at Nula. "No dinner yet. We need to get to the Four Corners temple. Now."

Kesia dashed through the two outer rooms, up the staircase, and out the door and onto the street. She waited impatiently for

Nula to catch up.

Her friend grimaced. "I did not wear shoes for this kind of adventure."

"Heels are never practical." Kesia sniffed, waving down an electro-carriage.

"On the contrary. They are very practical for impressing others and sounding threatening on tile floors."

"There are no tile floors in the Scepter of Knowledge. Only wood and slate," Kesia said as she entered the electro-carriage.

"Another reason why the Scepter of Commerce is superior," Nula huffed, pulling herself into the seat next to Kesia.

The ride seemed to last for a month, but at last, they pulled up in front of the Four Corners temple. Kesia paid the driver far more money than necessary and turned toward the steps.

<Lirome, Nula and I are here.>

Relief and joy poured from him. <Come inside. Zilpath is waiting to guide you to the private room.>

<Are you certain about this? You were the one who was concerned about the details.>

Calm flowed through their link. <Yes. We don't know what the debate tomorrow will bring, Kesia. Or what the council will try to do to stop us. I've seen too many years of politics to believe they will stand idly by—they might even undermine their alliance with the death unicorns in order to stop Maira from joining our souls together.>

<That would be barbaric! You and I are already mates.>

<Yes, but I'm a death unicorn. Bonding with me might be considered even more barbaric and unheard of. You've seen Arthurim's attitude toward us. We can still go slowly, but Kesia, will you marry me?>

His words made sense. Resonated with what she had seen from the dragon council. And what she'd told Nula was true. She really did want to sleep with Lirome. She craved that companionship in her bed each night. <Yes. I'll be right inside.>

"Hello, Princess."

Her heart sank. Arthurim Flamemaster. He couldn't possibly know what she was up to, could he?

She turned toward him. "Why are you here? I didn't know you were a follower of the Four Corners."

"I'm not. But I do know this isn't an official gathering. That happened two days ago." He turned a level stare at her, his defined face harsh and unyielding. "I also know that the death unicorn is a devotee who would insist on a Temple marriage before fully securing the soul bond."

Kesia's breath shortened. "I have an appointment."

"You can't do this. The dragon council knows, and they are in an uproar."

"You told them!" Her throat heated. It took everything in Kesia's power not to punch him. "What I do is none of your concern."

Arthurim advanced toward her, lowering his voice. "It *is* my concern. We are not death unicorns who can so easily replenish our ranks. Our people deserve a princess who hasn't been emotionally manipulated by one of them. They deserve an heir who isn't a halfbreed." He sniffed in derision. "Unless you are willing to take on multiple spouses, like their queen."

"No. Lirome will be my only mate. That is my choice."

"You would be so selfish? You're the only crown princess. You're the hope of all the dragons. You owe it to us to choose wisely—"

Anger boiled within her, along with a litany of words that suddenly wouldn't stay inside. "Two months ago I was a convicted felon. The only people who cared about me were the crown prince, who is now dead, and my evil uncle, who made me into his personal experiment." Kesia sucked in a breath. "Your perfect crown princess is nothing more than a reject from a disgraced bloodline. Wasn't that your very argument in marrying me? To 'cleanse' my bloodline with yours?" She huffed a stream of green smoke. "I am going to marry the man who has stood by me through all this and never asked for anything more than to help me stop Zephryn's killer and understand myself. The man whose sister has been working herself into exhaustion trying to rescue her family and protect this city. If the council has a problem with that, if all dragons have a problem with that, they can find another crown princess."

Kesia turned and stomped up the stairs to the temple.

Once she entered the reception area, Nula grabbed her hand.

"Where did that come from?"

At her words, tremors overcame Kesia. Relief. Shock. Surprise at herself. "I guess ... I finally realized what I'm worth."

Zilpath's wrinkled face appeared in front of her, her fingers waving around wildly. Kesia shook her head. "Zilpath, you know I still don't understand you."

"She wants you to know that picking fights with those in power leads to trouble," Nula said. "Especially when you have lost so much already."

"That's reassuring."

Zilpath gave a snaggle-toothed grin and kept signing. "And she wants you to know that she's on your side. You and Lirome should have as many children as you want." Nula chuckled. "Apparently she has a standing wager with him."

"I'd like to get married first."

As they walked through the rest of the Temple into the private room, Kesia's mind filled with Arthurim's accusations about her behavior. What would she do in the future? Could she have children with Lirome? Considering how much experimentation she had been through, could she have children at all? Would they even survive the next forty-eight hours?

But when she looked into Lirome's violet eyes as Zilpath and Mediary Evoris pronounced the ceremony, everything else faded. There was only the two of them, making their promises. Each dripping a single drop of blood into the basin of incense.

Uniting them in the eyes of the All-Maker, even if the dragon council disapproved.

At the end of the ceremony, Maira stepped into the room. The death unicorn queen's clothing was wrinkled, her face worn. But she managed a smile as she moved toward Kesia and Lirome and stood between them.

Maira raised her eyebrows, glancing at her brother. <You know that this won't solve every problem, right? I'm not only speaking of the dragons. The death unicorns will have many questions as well. You'll have to stand before them for the herd-joining ceremony eventually.>

Lirome shrugged. <I'm only your brother. The ceremony won't be that long.>

<Yes, and Kesia is the dragon crown princess, which means this marriage has alliance implications, whether you like it or not. Plus, the death unicorns don't trust dragons any more than dragons trust them.>

Kesia rolled her eyes. <So more people distrust me without cause? Tell me something new.>

Maira chuckled. <Just making you aware.>

She pressed her palms to each of their chests, above their hearts.

Kesia gasped as soul energy filled her, pulsing into her heartflame and traveling through Maira and into Lirome, joining Kesia to him. Binding them inseparably, quietly and gently.

Naturally.

His heart began to beat in time with hers, reminding her that she wasn't alone.

CHAPTER THIRTY-ONE

At least Lurien allowed him to get dressed before parading him around at the Celestis Festival. Clad in a gleaming silver waistcoat, black breeches, and a black and silver jacket, no one would guess his ribs had been cracked or that his arms and legs bore purple bruises. They even wrapped his feet after he had been forced onto glass shards; however, they had left the shards in his feet. Every step sent blistering agony through his soles. It was Lurien's additional insurance against him running off. Shance managed to keep enough wind beneath each step to allay the worst of the pain. A simple trick, now that he had regained his true Talents.

Conqueror of rain, wind, thunder, and lightning. One of the prized members of the Eternal Court of Glenalis, the city of the gods. He had willingly submitted to enhancements that elevated his wind Talent. He had become Lord Tyrius Stormsong of the air and skies.

Shance snorted. Even at the time, he had thought the titles overdone. All he'd wanted to do was play music, find good company, and maybe make life a little easier for those around him. Instead, they'd sent him on missions to destroy others.

Was it any wonder he'd accepted the Four Corners religion?

That he had assisted Maira in destroying the gods?

Just as Lurien wanted him to do tonight. To disperse her hideous smoke, and then take out any who opposed her. But she wasn't attacking tyrannical, power-mad psychopaths. She was twisting a city's soul to her will.

Yet if he failed to obey her, Shance's son died.

This isn't over. My wife, my family, found me. I'm not alone. I can still win.

He had no idea how.

Surely Bonilus wouldn't have brought him this far to leave him.

He surveyed the city from his seat on the platform on the Celestis Tower, the home of the astronomy and astrology libraries. To allow for superior star-viewing, the tower had platforms extending from every floor. And as tradition dictated, the tower was surrounded by airships, each of them the old-fashioned sort with silvery, gas-filled balloons above them instead of turbines. Each was draped with tiny lights and glittering silver bunting. They were clustered close enough together to create walking pathways for various dignitaries and those fortunate enough to buy or steal tickets to the event. On the streets below around the central square, the rest of the populace celebrated around large, coiled speakers shiny with wires and glittering decorations. Everyone would hear the debate and appreciate the cluster of three Keymarks, the monuments Lurien had so graciously donated.

Unfortunately. He sighed, wincing as his ribs moved. As the junior elocution acolytes, he and Kesia were expected to make short speeches, then turn the debate over to Maira and Lurien. For that, Shance was relieved. At least he wouldn't have to argue against his wife publicly, even if he would be forced to use his Talents against her.

In the end, it didn't matter that Shance had servants from Lurien's household infiltrating the party. It didn't matter that he had sowed seeds of doubt in her enslaved human pets. He couldn't do a damn thing about any of that.

He surveyed the platform before him. Silver lanterns flickered with brilliant lights, showing officials from the Scepter of Knowledge government, including the current head, Meritas Ovin. He stood proudly, his eyes shrewd, his bald pate shining, and his rather stout body straight and stiff. His Talent was simply indomitable will. No one could sway him unless he consciously willed it, no matter what their magic was. Not even the joy potion could alter him.

Lurien had been complaining about him on the way over. "After all this time, I still cannot persuade the Meritas to see reason. If only he would surrender—"

"To your overpowering magic that would rob him of his identity and independence?" Shance had grimaced. "Do you expect me to sympathize with you?"

The truth was, if Lurien mastered the rest of the city, all of the other government officials would oppose the Meritas and be all too glad to cede their power to her.

Now, he watched as Lurien floated among the guests in a billowing silver dress, her hair elegantly coiffed around her head in snakelike tendrils, and her charm and soul empathy at large. Maira also mingled easily, wearing dramatic black clothing and make-up with silver accents that made her violet eyes and olive skin gleam. She managed to win as many smiles as Lurien without resorting to the soul-twisting tactics of her counterpart. There was something about her that saw all of a person, instantly cared about them, and wanted to assist. She mentioned once that that was how she had been raised. Her entire life was lived in servitude to her people.

Only Shance could see her fatigue, how her hand trailed by her side, how her shoulders twitched almost imperceptibly. She shouldn't be facing this alone. They should be together, working as a team, winning over others.

But if he moved, the trigger holding back a knife aimed at his son's gut would release, and Brennar would die alone in a hidden room below the platform. Only when Lurien disabled it would he be free. And Shance knew she wouldn't until he had dispersed the noxious poison meant to subdue everyone in the Scepter of Knowledge, making them malleable to her will.

He was already stirring the breezes ever so slightly around the Keymarks. The people were already inhaling the irresistible fragrance that responded to Lurien's voice alone. All she would have to do was get up on the platform and speak to the people, and the Scepter would fall.

Shance still hadn't managed to get this new version of the joy potion for Maira and Lirome to study. Even if Maira had a counteragent for the old one, it wouldn't matter—or so Lurien had assured Shance during one of his beatings. She could have been lying, but why would she?

If nothing else, the rogue death unicorn seemed to pride herself on leaving nothing to chance.

The only remaining threat to Lurien was Kesia Ironfire and the green smoke she emanated. But how would Kesia know he needed her help? Who knew if she was in a place to do so?

Shance glanced over at the dragon. She sat on the other dais at the far end of the platform, clad in a crimson tunic, simple corset, trousers, and boots, with a silver ribbon braided into her soft brown hair. Upon seeing him stare at her, she gave him a wave and descended the platform, where she was swept up in the crowd.

He remembered over four months earlier when she'd wanted to learn more about human social customs. Both of them had been different people then—him without full memories or power, her still hiding and doubting herself. Now her amber eyes showed shadows of maturity and grief, and there was a firmness to her jawline.

They really needed to talk once this was all over. He missed his friend.

"Here. You look thirsty."

Shance straightened, his fingers clutching the arms of his chair. Kesia stood before him with a disarming smile, holding out a cup. "How did you—?"

"It helps to have a death unicorn as a husband. He's projecting an empathic disinterest field."

Shance blinked. Of course. He had seen Lirome earlier. Wait, Lirome was her husband?

She handed him an ornate glass that smelled like beer. "Here. Drink this and listen. We don't have much time before Lurien notices."

It *was* beer. Viorstan was looking out for him. Shance eyed her. "I warn you, Kesia. I'm no friend to the Lawless right now. They have Brennar near death at this moment. If I move, he dies. If I don't disperse her new joy potion, he dies. If Lurien senses me speaking with Maira on a private mindspeak link, he dies." Shance sighed, frustration rippling through him. "I don't want to betray anyone, but I will not do something that will kill my son."

"That complicates things." She paused, clearly conversing with someone else in mindspeak. "Unfortunately, we can't simply take down Lurien. We need to implicate her and drive her from the city.

Maira said you had made connections with discontented servants who would stand against Lurien. They would be an asset."

Shance nodded. "They won't speak up and testify against her until they are certain it is worth the risk. I can't guarantee that when I can't even protect my son."

"Granted. And if Lurien's joy potion is strong enough, even your witnesses will have addled minds. Fewmets." Kesia frowned, then a few other expressions flashed over her face. More mental conversations. Shance still found it rude when they happened in front of him—but now it was even more obnoxious because he should have been included through his link with Maira.

But he couldn't dare listen in. What if Lurien could eavesdrop somehow? Shance couldn't take that risk.

The death unicorn glanced his way. Her brilliant blue eyes narrowed when she saw Kesia.

"You need to go," Shance shoved her arm lightly.

"I'm not afraid of her. Not anymore."

He gritted his teeth. "Until my son is safe, I *am* afraid of her."

All of his knowledge, his power, and Shance was still brought under the thumb of despots. The organization changed, but the evil remained.

Sympathy showed in the dragon's eyes. "I understand. We're doing everything we can. We need to let the debate play out until Lirome and I can disable the monuments. It makes no sense for me to cancel out Lurien's manipulations up here when her joy potion floods the city. After they are disabled, I'll return and help you here. For now, let Lurien think she's winning."

"If you keep delaying, she *will* win!"

"I know," Kesia whispered. "But this is our only option."

She turned away and walked down the platform, disappearing

into the crowd.

Leaving Shance alone once more.

Shance was trapped. And there wasn't a god-cursed thing Maira could do about it except pray to the All-Maker and trust the last-minute plan she'd created with Kesia and Lirome. It didn't help that Lirome was irritated with part of the plan.

His displeasure prickled along Maira's skin. She made a tiny motion with her hand like she was swatting a fly. There were too many other matters to attend to without him fretting about the schemes of his new wife.

<This plan is madness. You must stop it.>

<Are you aware of who you're speaking to?> She smiled at the dignitary she was dancing with, a district manager of some sort. <I am the last person who is going to lecture someone else on safety.>

<She's right about that,> Ademis chimed in from where he was picking bits of meat out of the appetizers and leaving the crackers. <I agree that every part of this plan is dangerous, but Maira isn't going to assist you, Lirome. Look what happened to Shance and her after they got married. They both died!>

<That isn't comforting.>

<Well, they only died for a little bit. It turned out all right. I was coming to that final aspect.>

<Still not comforting.> Lirome glowered from where he stood off to the side, invisible in a disinterest field. Kesia had returned to her place on the dais, munching on a strewsberry tart and sipping a glass of water.

She intervened in the conversation. <It isn't meant to be comforting. That's the point, Smokey.>

<I don't understand. You called Zephryn 'Midnight.' I call you 'my Fire-breather.' And I'm dubbed 'Smokey'? You're the one who produces green smoke.>

<Then you can use the term as well. Dragon nicknames are often given based on color. You're the color of smoke. Besides, I'm still testing out nicknames.>

Maira caught her brother smiling through his annoyance. <We will continue discussing this later.>

<Yes, after my death.>

Lirome huffed. <And please add the word "fake" in your talk of death.>

<Merely enabling myself to produce a convincing performance.> She smirked. <You need to trust me, tea-minded.>

<Tea-minded?>

<I agree. That one doesn't work.>

A chiming of many bells interrupted their discussion. Maira's blood chilled. The debate was about to begin.

The crowd parted, allowing her passage to the dais. It had taken much convincing for Ademis to agree to remain near the food table rather than by her side. She should be comforted that he valued her over such choice tidbits.

In truth, she was. Despite his attitude, Ademis was the most loyal friend she'd ever had, apart from her brother Lirome. Now, she ascended the stairs with neither husband, nor brother, nor mates, nor the cat-dragon for support. Only Kesia, her new sister-in-law, stood beside Maira.

The red-haired wretch stood on the opposing dais, petting Shance's head in a proprietary way, her smug expression assuming she had already won.

Maybe she had. If Kesia and Lirome couldn't disable the monuments ... if Maira couldn't find Brennar in time...

Maira pushed down her dread and sat as Meritas Ovin, standing at a central podium, opened the debate.

"The debate that will take place here tonight will decide definitively whether the Scepter of Knowledge will formally join the war against the dragons and support the Curious Intrigue, or whether it will oppose the war against the dragons and support the Lawless. Both Lurien Alistil and Maira Ukerys have had nine weeks to privately inform you of their reasons, but for the interest of fairness and in honor of our Festivals of the Three Centrals, the official debate was scheduled for tonight. Each side will present their case, and then there will be two rounds of rebuttals. The debate will end with closing statements. Then the populace will have one day to vote in favor of the Lawless or the Curious Intrigue." Meritas Ovin took a deep breath and continued in an even graver tone. "Citizens of the Scepter of Knowledge, this is a historic moment. Your vote will change the destiny of our city. Choose wisely."

Applause thundered throughout the Scepter of Knowledge. After a moment, Meritas Ovin held up his hand for silence. "The junior elocution acolytes will speak first to introduce each argument."

Lurien affected a deeply grieved expression. "Sadly, my dear Captain Windkeeper is feeling very ill. While he stalwartly braves his condition to attend this most prestigious event—that I personally honored with the three new Keymark statues—he will be abstaining from his introduction of our side."

A murmur of confusion went through the crowd. Shance had not left his seat that entire night. Kesia had mentioned that he was trapped due to Lurien threatening Brennar's life.

Fury joined worry in the depths of Maira's gut. Lurien would pay for so much.

Lurien raised a pale, delicate hand in acknowledgement of the crowd's worry, the other placed across her breast. "I thank you for your concern, but I shall persevere and present my debate solo."

Meritas Ovin nodded. "Understood. In the interest of fairness, the introductory statements by the junior elocution acolytes will be removed from both debates. Instead, there will be a five-minute recess, after which Lady Lurien Alistil will be permitted to speak her piece."

Gods. Maira fought to keep a reaction off her face, while internally her thoughts whirled. Not only had they been deprived of the goodwill they hoped to evoke from Kesia's down-to-earth nature, but Lurien had the advantage of going first.

It was precisely what Lurien wanted, no doubt about that.

Maira glanced over at Kesia. At least it would make Kesia's grand departure even more shocking.

"Are you sure you want to do this?"

"Yes."

The dragon woman answered in a way only those who had faced death countless times could. Maira's heart softened. She truly was glad Kesia had bonded with Lirome, even if she risked everything to do so.

At that moment, Lirome started moving back through the crowd to the exit stairs. Descending the Celestis Tower to prepare for his next part in the plan.

"All-Maker be with us," Maira murmured.

Soon, the bells chimed again. Meritas Ovin smiled as the crowd quieted.

"It is time for Lurien Alistil to make her opening argument.

Lady Alistil, your time to speak starts … now."

Lurien glided to the center of her dais near the audiceptor, partly obscuring Shance. Convenient. All the better to hide his dispersal of the invisible smoke. From the rapt way the crowd watched her, they were already under her spell.

"Ladies and gentlemen of the Scepter of Knowledge, I want you to understand the great wealth of knowledge that lies within your grasp, if you only open your hand," she gestured dramatically with an open palm, "and accept the friendship of the Curious Intrigue…"

Maira tuned her out. It was the usual over-emotive rhetoric Lurien favored. Instead, Maira focused on the crowd. The winds picked up around them, slowly at first, then more and more quickly. A stirring breeze, fragrant with invisible fumes mixed with Lurien's potent soul magic. Their eyes slowly glazed over, and their responses were made in greater agreement. Their cheers grew louder with every melodramatic statement she made.

Maira's heart tightened. All of this, caused by Shance. The skill in the breezes, the vastness of them as they moved through the city, the edge of moisture that allowed the fumes to cling precisely.

The subtlety was beyond a Windkeeper, but not Stormsong.

Lurien was reaching the end of her speech. Her dress billowed behind her in the strong winds and her blue eyes gleamed with pleasure. The crowd was utterly in her thrall, except for Meritas Ovin, who merely noted the crowd's reactions in genuine puzzlement, scratching at his head.

Maira turned to Kesia and gave a slight nod.

Lirome had better be in place.

<Kesia, now!>

"And so, I call upon you to vote for the Curious Intrigue. For your lives. For your betterment. For your future."

Kesia leaped out of her seat in an explosion of green smoke and rage. "No! These are lies! She's a manipulator and a murderer. You can't listen to her!"

As she spoke, green smoke poured from her mouth. Flowing around the crowd, and causing some of them to blink in confusion.

Lurien shot a warning glance at Shance, clearly demanding he push the green smoke out of the way. The winds shifted the smoke away from the audience, nestling around both platforms, including where Lurien's faithful crouched.

Her hate-filled eyes turned toward Kesia, but her voice stayed calm. "My dear girl—for you are barely a woman, yes?—you are sadly mistaken. And seem to be much afflicted. The Curious Intrigue has wonderful treatments for those who, like yourself, have uncontrolled Talents."

"The Curious Intrigue made me like this! That's what they do. They capture you, and create monsters." Her voice shook, and Maira could feel the reality of the sorrow Kesia let loose with her words. "Then they come after you. Just as Lurien came after my husband. She killed him!"

The crowd stirred more. Maira smirked. Mention of death had a way of doing that.

Meritas Ovin glared at Kesia. "Junior elocution acolyte, you are making a mockery of this debate. Please control yourself—"

"Everyone's against me," Kesia shouted into the audiceptor. "Now, you've turned my friend against me." Her expression suddenly turned to deep despair, and she backed away from the audiceptor. Dangerously close to the edge of the platform. Clutching the voicelator pendant. "Everyone's turned against me."

Then she stepped back—and fell off the edge with an ear-piercing scream.

Chapter Thirty-Two

It was an odd thing, falling to one's death.

Almost relaxing. Peaceful, after the trauma of the past three months. Kesia leaned into the winds pressing at her.

No more pain or stress.

Nearby, there were crowds staring up in shock and horror. Some might never have seen a death up close before.

What a curious possibility to imagine. To live a life surrounded by happiness and peace.

Lirome's frantic voice broke through her thoughts. <Kesia, shift now! You're almost at the ground. Shift. NOW!>

In the final remaining seconds, she compressed into the shape of a tiny retriever ant, landing lightly as only the insect could and scurrying away amidst the shouting and fear.

None would be the wiser. It wasn't quite bright enough for them to see the transformation. All they knew was that a woman had jumped from a building and killed herself. Only she had disappeared instead, leaving only clothes and the remains of a voicelator pendant.

A small twinge of sadness filled her. Zephryn had created it for a reason and a purpose, and even if that reason didn't matter anymore, it was still a pretty object. Guilt joined the sadness. People would be concerned that she had died. It would alarm them. She knew the pain of losing someone. On the other hand, the fear and concern for her would break through Lurien's soul-enslavement. Better a hard situation that breaks than walking through life in a meaningless daze.

<Kesia?>

Lirome knew she lived. He would have felt it otherwise. But she still heard fear in his voice. More guilt clutched her. She reached out to him, into the depths of the soul that Maira had united to her heartflame a day ago. <I'm here, my Shadow. I'm alive.>

<Fire-breather, I'm near the edge of the crowd. Time is short.> Warmth and deep, intense love surrounded her. She let it fill her, sharing her emotions with her mate. Coming to a place of peace once more.

<I understand.> She shifted into a hopclaw, skipping along faster until she was near him, then growing up and out. Kesia blinked eyes that couldn't see as well in the night. At least her arms could reach around and embrace her husband tightly. Briefly.

She quickly slipped into the clothes he provided and turned to face the three Keymark monuments where Lurien's joy potion still issued. As one, they ran to the first monument. Lurien had dismissed all guards for the night, trusting the crowd to adore her and her generous gift.

All the more convenient for Kesia. She turned to Lirome. "Where did you say the opening was?"

"From the construction, the load-bearing sections are every six inches." Lirome placed his hands over hers. "Press in here, and here to access the central valve."

She did so, shifting the matter around her hands like water until a large square was clear. Inside was a simple valve and tube system. Kesia sighed.

"It seemed Lurien didn't account for us after all."

Lirome nodded. "Shut it off."

She did so.

One down, two to go.

The crowd was in an uproar. There was something shocking about a suicide happening before one's eyes that even the mind-numbing joy potion couldn't cover. Meritas Ovin shouted over his audiceptor, pleading with them to come to order.

Kesia's act certainly jolted Shance, even though he knew she could shift into a flying creature. The jump was a bold move. He shouldn't be surprised by the dragon and yet, she continued to push limits.

In the midst of it all, Maira sneaked off the stage with Ademis in tow. Lurien might have weakened the mother-child bond, but Shance was willing to bet there was enough left for Maira to find Brennar.

All Shance had to do was keep Lurien distracted.

Lurien turned to him, her face twisted into a scowl, hands on her hips. "Very clever, Windkeeper."

He only stared at her. "Read my emotions, Lurien. I'm as surprised as you are."

"I know you are. How did you become a warlord in the city of the gods when you are so utterly useless?" She sneered and pulled a small vial of clear liquid from a pouch on her chair. "Fortunately, I always have backup. All the important dignitaries are on this platform, and the stupid sheep below have already inhaled more than enough of my potion." Lurien smashed the vial on the ground. The liquid quickly transformed into puffs of white cloud that immediately vanished into the air. "Disperse that around the platform. Keep the wind currents flowing consistently."

Shance tilted his head. "Why would I help you?"

Lurien sniffed. "I still hold your son captive. You try anything with your winds outside of my command, and he's dead."

Damn the woman. If Kesia wasn't already assigned to execute her, Shance would have gladly volunteered to do so. And he hated killing people.

"I'm waiting, Captain Windkeeper. Don't forget to push a little to the airships."

He breathed out through clenched teeth and shifted the winds to disperse the smoke throughout the crowd. The joy potion must have been at a high potency, because they immediately quieted. With another reluctant flick of his wrist, the airships also received a share of the chemical.

Shance's only small consolation was that, in her focus on the crowds, Lurien didn't notice that he'd shielded the servants behind her—the ones on his side. Out of the corner of his eye, he saw Cortin give him a small signal. They were ready.

But nothing could happen until Brennar was safe.

Lurien flashed the crowd a smile. "In these extraordinary circumstances, I think it is fair to assume that the debate is over, yes? Just terrible, how that poor woman killed herself. The Curious Intrigue will ensure nothing bad like that ever happens again."

The crowd murmured and nodded their agreements.

Meritas Ovin's brow wrinkled. "Yes, the debate is certainly over, Lurien Alistil. It will have to be rescheduled, and investigations will need to be made into the young woman's words."

"Investigations? Such a silly thought." Lurien's tone was smooth and authoritative. "There is no need for investigations. Why, Meritas, I never thought of you as a foolish man, but now?"

The crowd hummed and nodded again. Bile rose in Shance's throat.

Maira had to find Brennar, and Kesia had to make her move before Lurien managed to coax the crowd into a revolution.

Maira raced down the staircase that ran through the center of the Celestis Tower, searching for her connection to Brennar.

<Brennar! Bren, where are you? Brennar!>

Her sweet Brennar. The lost one. She and Shance had done their best during the ambush, placing Brennar in a large pot outside a peddler's doorway and ordering him to stay there while they dealt with the threat.

She'd meant to come back. He had to know. She'd never meant to abandon him. But her capture had taken away her choice in the matter. <Brennar, I was going to return! They locked me away, but I never forgot about you.>

She poured every lost hope, every shred of love and caring into what was left of her connection with her son, praying it would be enough.

<Brennar!>

Faintness overcame her, and she leaned heavily on Ademis. <Maira, you need to slow down. You haven't slept, fool girl. You'll pass out, and then where will we be?>

She had to find him. That was her mission. Shance was trapped. Kesia and Lirome were disarming the monuments. Nula and Tiers were monitoring the crowd from various ships, and Zilpath was on *The Silver Streak* to stay out of trouble. And likely trying to match Tegan with someone now that Lirome the Eternal Bachelor had settled down.

A faint smile curved Maira's lips, even as tears trickled down her cheeks. <Brennar. Brennar, I know there is better for you than this. Better than Lurien. Please, Brennar. I'm here.>

<Mother?>

The mental voice was nearly imperceptible, but it was there. She latched on to it, offering every bit of soul magic she had left in return. <I'm here. We're here to rescue you, me and Ademis. Where are you?>

<I … don't know. Bag … over my head … On … floor. I think.>

<Well, stay there.> She giggled a little hysterically. What a silly thing to say. <We're coming for you.>

Protest weighed his words. <Dangerous. Guards…>

<We'll manage.>

She mentally reached for him through the thread, trying to discover his location. Two floors down. She raced down the steps, nearly tripping on the last one, and faced a hallway lined with doors. Too many to check. And what if he was behind a hidden one?

Maira sought the inner thread tying her to her son. But it gave out. This was the floor, yet she didn't know where.

"Try every door, Ademis," she snapped. "Every one!"

The cat-dragon began yanking the doorknobs, responding to her wild emotions with hissing. "We don't have time for this!"

"What other choice do we have?"

A rather disgruntled presence emerged behind them. "I can help you."

Maira spun around. "Flamemaster? I thought you had abandoned us after Kesia rebuked you."

"My duty lies here, whether I like it or not. While I believe the crown princess to be in grave error…" He paused. "Lurien is the true enemy. So before I regret it, use your soul magic to give me some sense of your son, and I'll find him."

Maira gripped his hand, their touch flowing with every thought, every memory she had of Brennar.

Arthurim gasped and yanked his hand away. "Enough! I'll have a headache for weeks from that influx. Follow me."

He led them to a door and kicked it down easily. Dragon strength. At times, enviable. Within, she heard the sounds of screaming and thudding. Alarm flared through Maira. "If they see you, they'll kill him!"

Humor flickered from Arthurim as he looked inside the door. "That would require them to be alive. I believe your son has dispatched his guards. A valiant young man, all things considered. Go in. He needs his mother."

Maira rushed through the door, past the overturned tables and dragon-burned, bloodied bodies, and fell to her knees beside the broken young man collapsed in a corner, his body curled up from abuse. Her heart blanched—then decades of experience took over.

"Come now, Bren." She smoothed his disheveled hair. "Let's get you sorted out."

As she pressed her hands into his wounds, feeling her healing Talent at work, she glanced at Ademis. Or where the cat-dragon had been.

"He has left to alert Shance Windkeeper."

"Good." Her head felt light. So light. "Arthurim, I forgot to mention something."

"What's that?"

She leaned over her son as weakness overtook her. "You might have to carry us out."

One final valve.

Lirome identified the location, then pressed his hands over Kesia's to guide her to it. One more opening. One more valve, twisted into the off position.

One last Keymark. Disarmed.

She grinned, staring out into the crowd. Unease filled her. Her faked death hadn't done enough. Most of them still laughed giddily, as if drunk, and listened raptly to Lurien's voice on the nearest speaker. She currently was in the process of declaring Meritas Ovin unfit for office and calling for a summary impeachment vote.

Completely against all established procedures in the Scepter of Knowledge. The rogue death unicorn was getting desperate.

Still, the mindless agreement of the bystanders disturbed Kesia. How dare Lurien twist these people! She breathed out a large plume of green smoke and starting walking toward the group, inhaling for another.

Then a hand grabbed her arm and stopped her. "Don't think small, Kesia. We need to return to the platform."

She stared up into Lirome's eyes and sighed. "I know. I just hate seeing them like this."

His sober face showed his agreement. "So let's assist Shance in clearing out the whole city and gain the opportunity for you to kill Lurien."

"I knew there was a reason I married you."

He shook his head and gave a short laugh. "Oh, was that the reason? My bloodthirsty side?"

Kesia shrugged. "Now you know."

"Ah, how I was deceived." He nodded. "Let's return. I might need some assistance returning to the platform, since I have no wings."

"Really? I think unicorns should have wings. That would be a useful addition." Kesia backed up and allowed her wings to emerge, bursting through the back of her crimson tunic. She wrapped her arms around him, pulling strength from her larger, scale-form wings that rested in the Nether, the place between dimensions.

"Careful, fire-breather. You're starting to sound like the Curious Intrigue."

She leaned forward, nudging the tip of his nose with her own. "Someone convinced me that not all experimentation is inherently evil. But it always comes at a cost. Now hold still, my Shadow."

Kesia began to flap her wings, lifting them both off the ground to face Lurien's final reckoning.

By now, the crowd was cheering at practically every word Lurien spoke. If Shance Windkeeper had to hear one more joyful agreement, he was going to vomit.

To his credit, Meritas Ovin still looked bewildered and angry. The man certainly had an indomitable will. But it hadn't helped him against the mesmerized dignitaries. He now stood on the dais on the far side of the platform, studying the crowd in fear.

"Lurien Alistil, I insist you cease your horrific actions at once!" he demanded.

She clucked. "Oh, my dear Meritas. If you cannot handle the disagreement of your own people, maybe you are unfit for the position. After twenty years, it must weigh so heavily on your shoulders."

"The only weight on my shoulders is a strong conviction that you are a dangerous threat to this city!"

<Shance! Your son is safe.> Ademis's voice was urgent. <Let's finish this so everything can go back to normal, and I can finally get a proper nap!>

Cat-dragons and their priorities.

Shance leaped from his chair, flinging his arms into the air. Pain spasmed and arced all over his body, but it meant nothing. Not compared to freeing these people.

Thunder cracked in the suddenly heavy sky, and lightning flashed down his arms, drawing cries and shouts from the crowd. He funneled the winds around him, using them to amplify his voice.

"I agree, Meritas Ovin. Dignitaries and honored guests, may I have your attention please!"

The booming sound silenced the crowd at last. It felt familiar. Powerful. Shance had been a speaker as well as a singer. He remembered commanding awe and fear at a glance, even as he did now. He also remembered hating it back then, as he hated it now. No one should be able to command the attention of others so easily. That was reserved for a real deity.

But occasionally, using wind magic as an audiceptor was useful.

He thought back to when he had first met Kesia and heard her voice in the air. Had that been his true magic as well, emerging at a point of weakness?

Something to consider later. Right now, he needed to stop a madwoman.

"The woman you know as Lurien Alistil is no ordinary woman, but a traitor."

Lurien's eyes widened. She started to run, but Shance cocooned her in a funnel of wind, sparking with electricity. "She has been amassing power in your city for years, blackmailing your citizens into her service and enslaving them to her … Talent."

This wasn't the right time to explain the intricacies of death unicorn soul magic.

The crowd shouted their disapproval of Shance, raising their fists. A few of them drew the dulled ceremonial swords they wore and aimed them at him.

Kesia was welcome to arrive at any time.

Meritas Ovin frowned and finally managed to grasp the far audiceptor. "This has been a most frightfully unusual night, but even so, your claims are outrageous. Do you have proof? Witnesses?"

Cortin stepped to the forefront of the crowd. Shance gestured toward Lurien's abandoned audiceptor, and the elderly man made his way to the dais. His creaky voice echoed over the crowd and through all the speakers in the city. "I am a witness to this claim. I am Ezra Cortin. When I first applied to work for the Lady Lurien, she seemed most gracious and kind. But after I signed the contracts, she threatened to murder my family if I ever left. The things I've seen…" He paused and shook his head. "You can't unsee, not in a lifetime."

"I, too, faced her abuse." A middle-aged woman stepped up,

her double chins set in a firm scowl. "When she hired me, I was grateful. Having no husband and three children, I saw it as a mercy. But she took one of my sons … as her lover. Did something to his mind." The woman shook her head. "I've never seen the like. And I couldn't leave, neither. Such fear as she could give you!"

The crowd murmured and rumbled at this. Shance spoke up. "As you see, she has afflicted many. I have more servants willing to testify against her. My own son was taken by her to entrap me for her own ends." Then he caught sight of Kesia in the crowd, with Lirome close beside her. "And there are others she has wronged."

Shance gestured to Kesia. After a moment's hesitation, she stepped toward the dais, holding a pistol in her hand, her emerald green wings and scales causing whispers to race through the crowd. When she spoke, her voice was clear and certain. "I'm sorry for the ruse, Meritas Ovin. It was necessary as part of my plan."

"Your plan?" The Meritas's face was turning dark red with confusion and anger. "Explain yourself, young lady!"

"Lurien Alistil murdered my husband in front of me. As terrible of a crime as that is, it runs deeper than many of you realize. I am Crown Princess Kesia Ironfire, the last of the ruling line of dragons and a member of the Lawless. My husband and I came to this city seeking peace and open discussion through the proper government channels. But Lurien Alistil ambushed us and attempted to kill us both. My husband," her voice shook only slightly, "Crown Prince Zephryn Nightstalker, sacrificed himself so I could live. And so, I stand before you now, demanding justice on his behalf, as his widow and as the leader of the Scepter of Justice."

The crowd erupted in a cacophony of questions and exclamations, most of them hate-filled. After all this, still loyal to Lurien.

Meritas Ovin remained silent, his eyes never leaving Kesia's.

Shance's gut tightened. Were their claims too much?

Finally, the Meritas spoke. "I have my own informants in the city. They have not seen everything, but neither are they blind to the disruptions and disputes caused by the Curious Intrigue and the Lawless. They reported on some of the meetings, including the one led by Zephryn Nightstalker. Apparently he was quite well spoken."

Kesia swallowed hard. "Yes, he was. Thank you."

"Can you end her hold on the city?"

"I can, with the assistance of Captain Windkeeper. But first," Kesia lifted her chin, "I must insist on my right to dispense judgement as the sovereign of the Scepter of Justice. In this case, justice means the execution of a terrible criminal whose very existence has harmed and will harm many others."

Meritas Ovin leveled a stare at her. "I do know the old place of the Scepter of Justice royalty. So I have one question to ask of you, Princess Ironfire. If you execute the justice you claim to represent, do you take all responsibility on your hands and on your head? Absolving myself and all others of any guilt should the criminal prove innocent?" He glanced at the raving crowd. "Admittedly, unlikely in this case."

"Yes. I take full responsibility." Quiet and clear.

He stared hard at her a moment more. At last he nodded. "There's truth in you. Execute justice as you see fit, remembering that even as you are free to do so, you are accountable to this Scepter, as well as to the others."

Kesia nodded.

"Captain Windkeeper, if I may?"

"Absolutely."

He lowered the wind funnel enough to expose Lurien's head

and torso. Kesia inhaled. "Lurien Alistil, you have committed crimes both grievous and heinous to many and have in all ways proved unrepentant. Your continued existence is a threat to the public and civil good. Upon my authority as crown princess of the Scepter of Justice, I hereby sentence you to death. Effective immediately."

Lurien opened her mouth to speak.

Kesia aimed the pistol. Cocked it.

Fired.

The death unicorn fell to the ground, a bloody hole in her head. The crowd froze, stunned. Their beloved leader, the woman who had warped their souls, lay motionless on the ground.

Shance swallowed. He'd wanted Lurien dead too. But now, her corpse only reminded him that he hadn't escaped the bloodshed. The war still went on.

The wounds in his body suddenly throbbed and ached all the more.

Then he met Kesia's amber eyes. Relief and sorrow mingled in them. She held out her hand. "It worked."

"Yes, it did." He took her hand. His dragon friend, after all of this. "We should probably clear out Lurien's affects before this crowd comes to."

"Agreed."

Kesia inhaled deeply, and breathed out plume after plume of green smoke. They covered the dignitaries on the platform, evoking shrieks and shouts. Using a few gentle gusts of wind, Shance settled the smoke around the crowd.

Meritas Ovin frowned. "Is that the green smoke that cancels Talents?"

"Trust me, Meritas. What other choice—" Kesia's words caught as Shance jabbed her in the ribs. She shot him an aggrieved look. "Please, trust me. It will free them."

After a few inhales, some of the crowd started blinking in confusion, as if coming out of a deep sleep. Kesia breathed out more smoke, and Shance dispersed it around the nearby airships.

Meritas Ovin shook his head in disbelief. "You have a lot to explain, Princess."

"And I will." She turned to Shance, her face pale. "Many more to go. I never knew breathing could be so exhausting. I'm not sure how we're going to free the entire city."

His mind raced. "Lurien's joy potion will wear off, yes?"

Kesia nodded. "Yes. Sometimes the withdrawal is difficult, but the effects will fade. Yet the gas still lingers in the air."

"A good storm will clear it away. Stay with the Meritas. I'll finish this."

"What about the airships?"

Shance winked at her. "Do I look worried?"

"No. That's what makes me nervous."

Shance turned away before Kesia could see his expression. Before she could sense the anxiety flickering through him. Calling a full-fledged thunderstorm? He knew he could. He remembered doing so. But it had been ten years. That knowledge ate at his confidence. The agony that shot through his body at every movement didn't help either. Still, he had to try.

Everyone depended on him.

He summoned more winds and rose into the air, stretching out his arms on either side of his body. He felt the humming of each wind current, heavy with mist. The potential for storms flickered around him, waiting for the music to start. For it wasn't a matter of science, of finding the perfect ratio and analyzing every step.

It was music that beckoned him to join in.

Music that called up water from the nearby sea and mist from the city air. Music that pushed it high into the sky, forming clouds like layers of crystal notes, piling atop each other. Loosening, freeing, funneling the wind currents, allowing them to whip through the Scepter of Knowledge. Mingling the winds, the distant cold high above him.

Rattling the clouds, the storm awoke.

He breathed in. Time for the main theme.

Shance brought his hands down, and with them, the rain. Gentle at first, then growing heavier as he worked to call up more water. Form more clouds. Waving the wind around with the flair of a conductor.

Thunder crashed in the sky. Lightning slashed at the ground. All of it, a glorious, musical cacophony. His blood rushed.

It was his to command, if only for a moment, and to respect as it beat down on his mortal body. He was resistant to the weather, but not impervious. For he only manipulated it.

Shance turned toward the airships, which were struggling to fly to the suspended dock. He reached out and cocooned each one in soft currents that brought them safely to a dock tower.

At last, it was only him in the sky. His body still echoed the energy of the storm but was exhausted from the work, screaming pain from the wounds Lurien's torture had inflicted. The music was demanding. It asked everything from him. And he wouldn't give it.

With his last magic, he soared through the storm to *The Silver Streak* and landed on the deck. He fell to his knees, releasing the storm to dissipate as it wished.

Rest. He needed to sleep.

No.

He had to see Brennar.

Shance pushed himself to his feet and stumbled below decks, his soaked boots slipping on the wood. The glass shards slicing deeper into his feet. Tegan found him, but her words were mere noise after the music of the storm.

Finally, he turned a corner and saw Maira standing next to a bed, tending the wounds of their son.

His wife. His son. On his airship.

His family was safe.

Shance closed his eyes and slumped to the floor.

Chapter Thirty-Three

Lirome waited in the safe house for Kesia's return.

There were Lawless agents who had fallen prey to Lurien's attack and were now enduring withdrawal. There were the soldiers who were healing from wartime injuries.

But he didn't belong there, tending their wounds or calming withdrawal symptoms with gentle touches of soul empathy.

He belonged at Kesia's side, as she endured questioning by the Meritas. As she completed form after form with documentation and testimonials. As she negotiated agreements with the Meritas.

But the first thing the Meritas had done upon arriving at his office was contact the Lawless. The dragon council had been quite clear that there had been no civil marriage between Kesia Ironfire and Lirome Ukerys, only some kind of private religious ritual that the council refused to acknowledge. There was no formal alliance. He had no place in representing the Scepter of Justice. So Meritas Ovin had politely dismissed Lirome from the proceedings. After all, the Meritas had said, if the Scepter of Knowledge was going to formally ally with the Scepter of Justice, he needed to speak only with those who were deemed officially in charge. It was purely a matter of politics.

Lirome glared at the sink as he washed his hands. Damn politics to the void depths of Ucurit, that held all the fell creatures who refused the grace of Bonilus. The depths that now held Lurien Alistil.

He sighed. The rogue death unicorn had been defeated. Zephryn Nightstalker had been avenged. Maira was reunited with her family. And Kesia was on her way to the safe house.

At least that much was right with the world.

He needed tea.

Lirome walked into the main room and made himself a cup from the kettle that had been heating all night. Was this his fifth cup? Sixth?

It didn't matter

He stared at the leaves floating in the hot liquid.

"You know, I've heard that some human cultures believe they see the future in tea leaves." Warmth and happiness filled him at Kesia's voice. He looked up to see her walking across the room, soaked from the rain, her amber eyes weary.

"Indeed? That sounds quite foolish." The tea could steep itself. He strode across the room and wrapped his arms around his wife, breathing in her scent. He had just enough dragon blood to detect it. Dark honey and iron. Kesia said Zephryn had smelled a different scent. But people changed. And she smelled perfect. Unexpected. A gift he would never deserve.

At last, they broke apart enough for her speak. "Sacrificing the perfect cup for me? I'm flattered."

He placed a gentle kiss on her head. "You're loved."

"I know." Her affection flowed over their link. "And I know you wanted to be there."

They walked back to the table. Lirome made another cup of tea for her, strewsberry leaves only, and they sat next to each other on the bench.

"The Meritas wants me to stay here for a little while. Apparently there are a few more crooked areas that could use some officially-sanctioned vigilantism—backed up with the proper paperwork, of course. Too much paperwork."

Another thing he could help her with. Lirome sipped his tea and winced. Definitely over-steeped.

"What do you want?"

"Answers." She traced her finger around the edge of the cup. "Answers about myself. About how you and I connected. About what I was made for—what I can do. I'm guessing you haven't had a chance to decode the journal, with that slight ruckus we had at the festival?"

"I have been a little preoccupied." He rubbed her back. She sighed and leaned against him. "But even so, we weren't wrong in calling Garishton a mad scientist. His journal has information, some of which I can understand. He was manipulating you to be used by him, somehow. We already know that you do contain blood from all the shifter races. I think being around death unicorns, even in the general vicinity, brought those traits to life.

"So if I'm around seals in the Scepter of Pleasure, then those traits will manifest?"

"Yes, potentially. If the seals are even there. They're vagrants who live most of their lives on the ocean." Lirome pushed his teacup away. "But Garishton's methods, his thought processes, are beyond me. He's a madman."

She nodded. "I spoke with the dragon council. They will not acknowledge you or our marriage even now. But they admitted that I succeeded in my mission and told me that Garishton has been spotted in the Scepter of Pleasure, running Pinnacle operations

JANEEN IPPOLITO

while posing as a human." Despair and disbelief streamed from her. "Apparently he is very well thought of."

He sent strength back to her. "I see."

"They strongly recommend I travel there with Arthurim Flamemaster and bring Garishton to justice."

He sensed her disgust as she mentioned Flamemaster's name. "And they expect you to spontaneously develop feelings for the dragon in the process?"

"They're misguided. In denial." She shrugged, leaning her head on his shoulder. "But … they have a point."

"Oh?"

"I need to deal with my uncle. I don't want to. But I need to." Kesia pulled her head up and shifted on the bench until she faced him, her expression revealing the fear and helplessness that filled her. "I can't do this—I can't face him again, in this place—without you."

"You won't have to." He closed his hands around hers. "I will be there. We are married, even if the dragon council doesn't acknowledge it. And they won't acknowledge it until they see us working together."

Resignation showed in her eyes. "They might not, even then. Dragons can be remarkably stubborn."

"Be that as it may, I am your husband. Even though I did much good here this evening, this will be the last night I am away from your side due to council wishes. We are mates. We are going to lead together."

She studied him skeptically. "I know you prefer the shadows. That's why I gave you the nickname."

"Yes, but I am *your* shadow. Where you go, I go." He squeezed her hands. "If that means facing the whole world together, as one, it is a duty I will bear with gratitude."

Kesia chuckled. "Or try to. I don't bear it with gratitude all the time."

"Nevertheless, this is the path the All-Maker has set." He stood up, pulling her up with him. "We will face it together."

She studied him with open appreciation. "I don't deserve you."

"Likewise."

Kesia wrinkled her nose. "Also, I might find water alluring, but my wet clothes are not."

"Perhaps not to you." He chuckled. "I think we can do something about that as well. As long as you don't mind sharing the shower with the death unicorn who so wickedly enthralled you away from your people."

Humor and fatigue danced in her eyes as they walked toward the room they now shared. "I thought you'd never ask."

"Technically, I didn't."

"I'll overlook that. This time."

They shared a quiet laugh, trust and respect flowing between them, with desire flickering on the edges.

But not tonight was not for desire. That would come in due time.

Tonight was about nearness and comfort in the midst of turmoil and sorrows, old and new. Caring for each other, sharing emotions and moments. Growing a little closer, a little more comfortable. Falling asleep together. Secure.

As Kesia rested in his arms, Lirome studied her. Still amazed she was here, with him. After all the tragedy that had occurred.

Then she breathed out a stream of green smoke across his chest—and his skin absorbed it, as though it had been her flames.

He raised his eyebrows.

Well, that's an interesting development.

CHAPTER THIRTY-FOUR

The Greenbow Tavern was the same as when Shance had left it over three months ago. The same pinwood walls and polished floor. The same square tables. The same scent of salt and seafood, melted butter and damp air blowing through the entryway into the dining area. A band played on the stage at the end, and three or four couples squeezed in their dances on the small section of empty floor.

But everything was different.

He was no longer simply Shance Windkeeper, a hopeless romantic seeking a woman for the night. He carried the weight and memories of Tyrius Stormsong, a magically enhanced god from a fallen kingdom. A kingdom he had helped to destroy. He had an incredible death unicorn wife whose time, though not her bed, had to be shared with her political mates to maintain the stability of their herd. He had a son, and herd-sons and herd-daughters. Even grandsons and granddaughters, all of whom wanted to reconnect with him.

He had a tenuous belief in a deity who had, for some reason, permitted him to be entrapped for a decade.

Part of him desperately wanted to jump back into that life. Mediator at the right hand of the death unicorn queen. Trusted guide and patriarch. Father to a son who still needed so much guidance. Seeker of answers in a religion with mysterious aspects that frankly baffled him at times.

Another part of him wanted to jump into the Cresida Inlet and swim until his arms gave out.

Which left him here, sitting in the tavern while Maira continued her healing treatments. While Brennar slept long hours as his body recovered from a trauma his mind still struggled with. Even the cat-dragon had run off somewhere.

Shance belonged in that life. He knew he did. But he also belonged in the tavern, drinking his second beer and enjoying the stringed instruments and pipes.

"Can I join you?"

Kesia sat down in the booth and ordered a strewsberry juice, a glass of ashberry grape wine, and an empty water glass. Shance mock-glared at her.

"You know you're supposed to wait for me to say 'yes' before sitting down? That's the custom."

"It's a stupid custom." She winked at him. "At least when it comes to a friend."

"My, how the student has become the teacher." Shance rolled his eyes. "Are you thirsty?

Kesia pressed her lips together. "Maybe."

A few moments later, the waitress returned with the drinks. Kesia sipped the juice and then set the empty glass at the place next to her with a sigh. "I know Zephryn is gone. I know there is no possible way he is here. But still…"

"It feels right. To have something there."

"Yes."

An easy silence fell between them. Kesia kicked up her boots on the booth next to him and shut her eyes.

Shance had never seen her shut her eyes in public. The dragon had never trusted anyone else, or herself, enough. She really had changed. He nudged her boot with his elbow. "So, how is life as the Princess of Justice, as the papers call you?"

"I'm only glad I avoided any pictures. It's hard to be a vigilante when all of Sekastra knows what you look like." Kesia opened her eyes. "The work is a lot of meetings now. Discussing things. Updating old policies. At least the Scepter of Knowledge is now on the side of the Lawless."

Shance snorted. "So they get to be attacked as well."

"Apparently this city has quite a good standing arsenal hidden away. But the Lawless are sending reinforcements too. Meritas Ovin has even been voted in for another term. His wife talks too much about nothing and his children are spoiled, but overall, I can work with him."

"Well, if you ever need advice about dealing with children, I now have a lifetime of experience." Shance shook his head, running his fingers through his hair. "I can't believe I said that."

Kesia laughed, loud and hearty. "But you did. I'm sure they're eager to see you."

"Yes. Maira and I need to return to the Lost Refuge and meet everyone again. Reconnect. She needs time with her mates. All of that." Shance waved his hand vaguely. "The Lawless have officially released me from my service as an airship captain, out of respect for my role as mediator on behalf of the death unicorns. And I'm keeping the ship out of appreciation for my work. Maira and I hinted at some kind of political hubbub if they said otherwise." He smirked. "I spoke with the crew of *The Silver Streak*. A few of them are local and want to stay here, but most of them want to stay on.

They're ready for a longer voyage, and many are curious about the far eastern part of Sekastra, where the Lost Refuge is. While I'm at the Refuge, Tegan will command them on a few side missions and practice runs."

She nodded. "That sounds busy and useful."

"Yes to both." He took a long drink of beer. "I'm looking forward to it."

"Yet you're here."

"So are you. Why is that?"

Kesia paused to give her order to the waiter that approached their booth. Three full meals featuring everything from fish eggs to raw oysters to a half dozen fried potatoes. Plus two appetizers.

Once, he would have cared about her drawing attention. Now, the idea seemed stupid. She was a dragon, and she should eat what she needed to survive.

At last, she turned to him, her usual optimism dimmed. "The dragon council is unsure about my case."

"How so? You brought Lurien to justice and executed her lawfully."

"Dragons aren't so easily won over."

Shance scoffed. "What do they want?"

"For me to have a dragon embermate and to be expecting an heir at this very moment," she said flatly. "It's better than it was. The council is split. Lord Direclaw and Lady Brightstriker are deeply disturbed by my choice of mate and what it means for the future of the dragon kingdom. Lord Sunscaler and Lady Dayflier are more willing to speak with Maira and Lirome to discuss our marriage as an official alliance. Since they are at an impasse," Kesia winced, "In civil terms I am an unwed crown princess and official seeker of and executor of justice who must cope with an unwanted dragon suitor."

Shance thunked his beer stein on the table. "Do they really think that's going to work?"

"I don't know. But Lirome and I are together regardless. We're married. Flamemaster will have to deal with that."

In the meantime, perhaps Shance could see about resurrecting the human-dragon council. Something to push things in Kesia's favor and stop the impasse. After all, he was a Windkeeper, the last remaining Windkeeper. It was his authority, his mantle to take up now.

He sat up. "So what will you do?"

The shadows on Kesia's face turned tense. "My Uncle Garishton. Reports of him have surfaced in the Scepter of Pleasure. I knew he and the remaining members of the Pinnacle went to ground after I destroyed their tower. But they are still operating and probably doing terrible things. Besides," Kesia hesitated and looked down at her hands, "the more I use the green smoke, the more it changes me. Lirome doesn't mention it much, but he's concerned." She paused, as though she wanted to say something else. Then she took a sip of wine instead. "Even with all his intelligence Talent and Garishton's notes, Lirome can't pinpoint precisely what my uncle did to me."

"So you're going after him."

"It seems like the next logical move." She sighed. "Besides, there's a human word—a honey month? Something like that. It takes place after a marriage, and it's a tradition of the Scepter of Pleasure in particular. I would like to explore that concept with Lirome as well, at our leisure. The Scepter of Pleasure probably has a lot of honey, since there are so many flowers growing in the warm weather."

Shance grinned. "I don't think it literally means 'honey' any-more, Kesia. If it ever did."

Her amber eyes twinkled. "Maybe not. But it amuses me to think so."

"Well, the Scepter of Pleasure does have places to relax and enjoy yourself as well."

She raised her eyebrows. "What kinds of enjoyment?"

Shance huffed. "Not just sex!"

"Look who's being uncouth now."

He sighed. "They have some of the best museums, concerts, food, sailing, and other amusing ways to escape. Officially, they support the war, but unofficially, as long as you don't reveal yourself as a dragon and don't stir up trouble, they'll let you in to experience their pleasures and take your money. It's their main income, after all."

"Only I can't stir up trouble?" Kesia laughed. "I'm doomed. I think stirring up trouble is part of my job description now."

The waiter set down many platters of food in front of Kesia, and then brought another beer for Shance. Kesia sat up, her expression curious as she studied the food.

At least that hadn't changed.

He glanced at the empty glass. "Still can't believe he's gone."

"I can," she said quietly. When she looked up at him, grief showed in her features. "He spoke more to Tiers, and he could be an ass to you sometimes. Still, he respected and valued you. He struggled sometimes with life outside the prison. Could never seem to get himself out of that mindset of protecting me."

"Well, at least he's free now. Somewhere."

"Yes. Somewhere." Kesia nodded, her expression pensive. Probably fretting over something metaphysical about the Four

Corners religion versus dragon beliefs about death and where everyone ended up. Shance knew all too well how easy it was to dwell on stuff like that until the thoughts turned to bilge. Which was why he couldn't let her spend the whole meal brooding. It would likely be their last evening together for some time.

"Well, let's give him a toast, then have at this food." Shance raised his beer. "To Zephryn."

She nodded and raised her strewsberry juice. "To Zephryn."

They clinked with the empty water glass.

Sign up for Janeen Ippolito's newsletter and get exclusive bonus content from The Ironfire Legacy series, plus monthly giveaways, book recommendations, and excerpts:

Thank you for reading!

The Ironfire Legacy Series:
Outlaw of Smoke
Scion of Scales
Captain of Storms

About the Author

Janeen Ippolito believes you should own your unique words—and make them awesome! She's a multi-published author of bestselling fiction, nonfiction, and poetry. She's also an experienced book editor and marketing strategist. In her spare time, she helps her missionary husband with his youth swordfighting ministry, indulges her foodie ambitions, reads whatever books she feels like, and explores a slew of random hobbies. Her life goals include traveling to Antarctica and riding a camel while wearing a party hat. This extrovert loves to connect, so join her on social media or at janeenippolito.com.

ACKNOWLEDGEMENTS

First and always, thanks to the One who always shines light in the darkness and gives hope for the hurting.

Second, another huge thank you to my husband, Stephen Ippolito, who always supports (and endures) my writing!

Major thanks to alpha readers Bethany Jennings, Sarah Delena White, and Hannah Keeler. This one had a lot of drafting ups and downs, and you saw me through them all.

Shout-out to beta readers Rachel Harbour, Heidi Lyn Burke, Anne Jones, and Sophia Hoxie. Your pickiness and honest feedback led to a much better story.

Also, a huge shout-out to my editor, Sarah McConahy, who never seems surprised about any of my craziness, even when I tell her a character has to die. Of course, this only means I'll have to keep leveling up the crazy! And thanks for the insight into Lirome Ukerys. Carry on.

Endless gratitude to Christian Bentulan another gorgeous book cover!

Special acknowledgement to A.C. Williams and Tosca Lee, who let me vent about the travails of character deaths and sad feels.

And all the joyful appreciation for my reader group, The Marvelous Misfits. You are all truly amazing, superpowered readers of awesome, and I'm blessed by your cheerleading.